A Hooker in The Choir

by
Joseph T. McFadden

© 2009 Joseph T. McFadden

All rights reserved. No part of this book may be reproduced in any form or by any electronic or mechanical means, including information storage and retrieval systems, without permission in writing from the publisher, except by a reviewer who may quote brief passages in a review.

First Edition, 2009

The characters and events in this book are fictitious. Any similarity to real persons, living or dead is coincidental and not intended by the author.

Library of Congress Cataloging-in-Publication Data

McFadden, Joseph T.
    A Hooker in the Choir: a novel / by Joseph T. McFadden

ISBN: 1-4392-2248-7
EAN: 9781439222485

1. Fiction 2. Mystery 3. Gambling 4. Money laundering 5. HMO and Nursing Home Abuses 6. Bribery

Printed in the United States of America

Printed by BookSurge Publishing

1

Facing the row of books on gambling, those about God behind her, she looked up as the librarian sidled down the aisle wearing an anxious expression and towing a tall, good-looking guy by the hand, her other arm outstretched, bringing them together.

"Celeste Howard, I want you to meet an old high school classmate, John Colburn," but she said nothing about physics or the famous physicist. After the introduction she left them alone among the shelves.

Celeste received him graciously. She gazed up at his intense blue eyes and curly black hair. She heard history of physics in his explaining his presence there, answering her questions, then about where he worked, and the space center in Huntsville. She left, hugging an armful from the religion shelves and thinking of his graceful and angular leanness.

He returned to his search among the reference collection there in the state university catacombs at Cambridge, Mississippi, his whole being awake to possibilities, a glowing feeling of hope, this on the Friday afternoon before Easter.

Thus, his second encounter with Cambridge women began, although he still felt leery and discouraged from the first. While searching for a misplaced old document he had first seen Celeste standing between distant stacks, gazing down into an open book in hand, slim and all golden blonde, the long, tangled curly hair, the dress intimate to skin of a hue made darker from leisurely tanning. In an intimation of early maturity, he guessed her to be thirty-six, thirty-eight, maybe, just right for his fifty, his hopes soaring again.

"Who is she?" he asked the librarian.

"Well, damn your lonesome soul, come on, I'll introduce you," said the librarian, as she impulsively took his hand and led him over to the browsing woman. This had happened so quickly, the new turn in his life so strong he could hardly believe it.

As he returned to work an air of emptiness settled in the reading room and the librarian came to his table. He looked up from the dusty open book into her gaze of grave concern and guessed she was ready to tell him things.

She asked, "So?"

"Dinner tonight," he said, dropping his pen and leaning back, getting ready to give her time.

"Then I have to tell you, a good woman, a grieving widow, everybody loved him. The funeral was mobbed; they were all the way out into the street. A real gentleman, the best of family lawyers, Jake Howard was, very kind and caring, really compassionate, and still she spends her time grieving, can't get over it, for four years now, all alone, lost, and very religious. She's in here often to get books, mostly on religion, a great comfort to her." The librarian, his age or less, appeared older, wizened, wrinkling too fast, seething a low energy of moral indignation. The keeper of the moral gates, he guessed, self-appointed in her own mind, the way things are. Life had passed her by. A spinster, bereft, she would be the first to rise and object to duplicity. He emotionally associated this bareness with absolute uprightness and reliable opinions, his hopes way up, becoming quietly eager with this reassurance.

"Well how's your *History of Physics* coming along?" she asked. "You've been in here scratching around in dusty books now for how long, about five years?"

"Yes, at least, but only on weekends, and I finished the research part this afternoon, the basics in everyday language from the earliest times to the present."

"I'm sure it will be a hit with the common man."

"It should help people to understand."

"Now I have something to say on another subject – your mother, Rachel, out at Golden Age nursing home. It's none of my business, but …"

"Okay."

"I have to tell you I don't like the rumors coming out of there. I hear too many old people are dying, maybe with a little help from somebody besides God."

"Really?"

"Oh yes, and what's more, injuries in the night, battered patients, cut faces, broken bones."

"Now that would need to be stopped."

"I should think so, and if you get into it, some other unexplained deaths and injuries need to be investigated."

"I'll talk to the people running the place, but we have no other choice with Rachel here in Cambridge where she wants to be. She has a daytime nurse and sitters at night."

"But others there are not so lucky or so safe. It's all due to greed, stockholders, or at least one of them, wanting to get rich."

"Who?"

"Peter Mallory, the sneaky devil, owner of the biggest bank and just about everything else in town."

"I've heard talk of him."

"Yeah, but the street chatter does not get to the heart of the thing. I think he's just hiding behind the small-time stuff."

"Well, now you've piqued my interest. What's going on?"

"Okay, I guess I'm telling you this because of your position with NASA and with the government of this country, especially your involvement in advanced warfare technology, and your being accustomed to secrecy. Something bigger than anyone would expect seems to be brewing in our lovely little town with its glittery literary façade, something I'm really frightened to talk about."

"I guess you do know something or you wouldn't be saying such things."

"Yes. They, that is to say, certain students, come in here and slip down deep in the lower levels. They stand facing each other through the stacks, one in each aisle, and whisper back and forth, the pall of Persia hanging in the air even the next day, redolent like a stack of rugs preserved in perfume, Patchouli or something similar. Occasionally, they're in the company of obvious outsiders, bringing the silent movement of robes, some wearing the turban, the frequent black beard, then after an elusive day or two never to be seen again. The students don't really think anyone could be listening. But I know where to hide."

"What do they say?"

"Most of it is in a language foreign to me, but some of our words can't be translated to theirs, like Peter Mallory, and certain other American words as well as unfamiliar names, among them Thornton Webb, Diamond Till, Tunica, and Dr. Kadsh. Sometimes five or six of them will slowly gather down here and get a book each, then come to the same table in an obscure corner. While pretending to read, they talk quietly to each other."

"So, what do you make of it?"

"Well, obviously, they are into something besides getting an education. They are very secretive, and they could not know the name Peter Mallory unless he is in some way connected to their secretiveness. They use his name too often."

"Would he be so corrupt?"

"Yes, but probably more through naivety than intent."

"Have you told anyone else?"

"Yes, but only the chancellor, Bruce Madison, personally. You know him?"

"Of course, a great friend."

"He has cautioned me to not reveal myself and asked me to continue listening."

"Which means he will take measures when appropriate."

"It means he knows something is taking place, and he knows the Muslims have an organization on this campus. As usual, he will be very careful and effective."

"Knowing him, yes. In the meantime, I'm over here every weekend, and we will be vigilant."

"Oh my, every weekend, all the way from Huntsville across Alabama to Cambridge, Mississippi. How many miles is that, John?"

"And back, about four hundred."

"And during the week days what are you working on now, or can you tell me?"

"Very real and realistic robots, and a new development in laser light, and some things I'm not allowed to talk about."

"Man, you are dedicated, and you sure fooled everybody in our high school class, the drowsing genius, the only one of us to become world-famous, and now you have something not so old and moldy as the books."

"Yes, possibly, thanks to you," he said, while rising to stand. "I appreciate all your help, and I'll send you a copy of the book, if you like."

"Please do," she replied, reaching to shake his hand.

He left her smiling.

Arriving home in late afternoon, Celeste Howard rushed to her computer, pulled up Google and typed the word *physics*, then the name *John Colburn*, and clicked search, and there, a page full about him, famous, no doubt about it. She dialed her closest friend and confidant, Mary Ann Dickey, hoping to find her at home. She would very likely know more and juicier facts. They had been bunnies at the same time for Playboy and still ran together. She answered on the first ring.

"Back safe?"

"Yeah, what's up?"

"Something heavy, maybe. Ever heard of John Colburn?"

"Yeah, why?"

"We've just met."

"I'm surprised it hasn't happened sooner."

"Never heard of him before today."

"Born and raised here in Cambridge, late blooming genius like Einstein, expert in rocketry, robots, exotic new materials, advanced weaponry, Washington's darling."

"He said nothing about all that. He just said physicist at Huntsville."

"Modest and known for it, and a tender catch. He's straight as an arrow, lonesome soul, his wife dead five years of cancer. He can't get Cambridge, Mississippi, out of his blood, tools over here every weekend tending to his farm out Yocona way, and a hundred-year-old mother in the Golden Age nursing home with that hell-raising woman, you know her, Clara Bartley, hired to ride herd."

"Well, I'll give her plenty of room. And how do you know so much?"

"Talk of the town."

"And he's into something else, also."

"What?"

"Cruising the underground stacks out at the university library, writing a history of physics, he said."

"Published a bunch of 'em already ... that where you met?"

"Yeah, the librarian, bubbling do-good and matchmaking, brought him down an aisle for the introduction. And she left us alone to talk."

"*You* talked."

"Mostly."

"And he invited you to dinner."

"Let's put it this way, I invited him to invite me to dinner."

"Well, I hope this works, but everybody knows he's looking for the right woman and a couple of years ago he found one. It lasted less than two weeks."

"Oh, really."

"Yeah, you know her. She's now a widow, but not then, old Floyd Beazlie's wife, Sarah, when he was terminal with Alzheimer's."

"He went for that little bitch?"

"Believed everything she told him, and she betrayed his every word until Clara Bartley wised him up and he cut it off clean. He still suffers the gossip Sarah started."

"I can imagine."

"Yeah, he's a type all right, a woman's face more important than her fanny, like it's her soul he's got to see, a bit of the errant knight."

"How romantic."

"Whatever that means, but watch yourself, there's a tang of danger, like the treachery of ideals."

"Gives me room to maneuver."

"Well, so what were you doing in the library?"

"Searching the books on gambling until they headed my way and I turned to religion."

"And he never knew the difference."

"Didn't seem to notice. How was your day?"

"Oh, the usual, University-Cambridge airport at ten for Toy Boy's jet to Memphis this time, then the routine frolic, then lunch, then back to Cambridge by four thirty. I walked in the door as the phone was ringing."

"Fast."

"The jet age, twice a week now, day after tomorrow to New Orleans with him aboard, and back the same time. And by the way, his new secret apartment in downtown Memphis is gorgeous, with views of the river."

"Secret?"

"His wife won't know."

"Wonderful."

"Could be with the right man."

"Does Horace suspect?"

"Not a clue, too busy, thinks his little innocent wife is as helpless as his dumb patients, scared shitless, letting him get away with his act, Dr. Important sticking his tubes up this or that, including his smug little nurse, I'm sure. Let him sleep."

"Good luck."

"Don't worry. Leaves home every morning before daylight; I'm sleeping or supposed to be, and never home before ten p.m. We don't see each other in the same house for days at a time, which suits me just fine."

"Hey, I got to rush, shampoo and the whole thing yet, meeting him at seven."

"I'll call you. We've got another foursome coming up soon to Las Vegas."

"Okay, but this time, you keep Toy Boy for yourself, no playing wife swapping with him again. I got enough toy men already."

"Don't blame you; I would like to have the coach for myself."

"Better than average, compared."

"To what, Peter Mallory?"

"You got it."

"What's he doing now?"

"Tunica mostly. He goes off and leaves me in one gambling area or another while he disappears upstairs for hours doing his thing with the powers that be without an inkling of what I really do."

"Making progress?"

"Yeah, but I'm not ready to talk about it yet."

"What about the Golden Age?"

"On hold until Monday. I'm not risking anything while John Colburn is in town. But I will find out who is doing the dirty stuff."

"You think so?"

"Somebody is killing people out there and I intend to get to the bottom of it."

"Why?"

"I want to know just where Peter Mallory stands in all this."
"Right. You wouldn't want to be a tainted Mrs. Mallory."
"Way to go on that yet."
"Besides his wife?"
"Right. In over his head, I've begun to suspect, and that could be fatal."
"Be careful."
"I shall."
"See you, babe."

As evening darkness deepened John Colburn sat in a quiet booth of a downtown restaurant, Celeste beside him. He thought she was a good woman, an honest woman, a reliable woman, and saw her as pretty and maturing. She already has told him her age, thirty nine, while describing the purity of the life she leads. At last, my God, at long last, what a find, what a treasure. She had arrived breathless, excited, animated in a wispy aura, the bright blonde hair richly resplendent down the front of her shoulders draping the tanned face, tantalizing over her chest. She appeared dream-like in sheeny, flimsy, delicate, almost see-through clothes. In her presence he felt transported to surreal awareness. She seemed magical and out of focus, as she turned her face to him, and he caught a glimpse of something different, the face of a girl with opaque putty eyes, a beguiling little girl. He refuted the fleeting insight, and saw Celeste as beautiful.

Listening through the meal until the restaurant emptied, he heard about her life and about her husband Jake, who had been the center of her universe and still was. She has not been with another man since, and Jake had been the first and only one, and she wanted to die but God just refused to take her and she still sits at home and grieves and does not want to do anything. Stretched out on the sofa she cries herself to sleep every evening and awakens near midnight and pours herself a little glass of wine, just one, and goes upstairs to bed. But nobody has been able to break through to her and she can tell you about being been hit on by some real pros. So many friends and other people have introduced all sorts of men, but with no luck for them. They have assumed and they have tried and they one and all have been bitterly disappointed, but she is just not interested, not after having had a man like her husband. And there can never be another one, not of his caliber. She had rather cry herself to sleep every night, alone and grieving, than to be with the wrong person.

While sitting beside her and listening he grew still with respect for, even envy of, the dead husband. He suffered a fleeting awareness of his own inferiority; he would never be able to meet her standards or expectations, he feared. He felt a loss of hope. He could never be the perfect man she lost, and he had not lived the purity she described.

She laid a hand on his arm, the long, elegant fingers gripping gently. "Do you go to church?" she asked.

"Mostly to weddings and funerals. And you?"

"Oh, yes. I'm a devout Anglican. I must have my church. It's my great strength, and I sing in the choir. So I'm there for the services and for choir practice."

"You sing?"

"That was my major in college, music."

"Well, indeed, how nice."

"And where do you stand on Genesis?" she asked.

"As contrasted to Darwin?"

"Yes."

"The language in Genesis, of course, is poetic and couched in far-reaching metaphor, and in mythology dating back thousands of pre-biblical years, and written by several authors. I certainly don't take it literally."

"Oh. That's a safe answer."

"Where do you stand?"

She turned to him and fastened her eyes toward the tip of his nose and a little bemused smile settled on her face as she said, "You know something, I've heard all the arguments, and frankly, I don't give a damn who's right and who's wrong. It serves my purpose ever so fine just like it is."

He laughed, and for a fleeting second recognized the calculating detachment of this new woman's intelligence, but chose to ignore the possibilities of its reach. He said, "And that's the frankest, most sensible comment I've heard yet on the argument, from either side."

She leaned closer and squeezed firmer on his arm, "*Won't you come and hear me sing on Easter morning?*"

And after a hesitation, her eyes level in his gaze, she raised him above all others at the moment with a teasing promise: "*You just might prove to be my resurrection."*

"I've never been in an Anglican church."

"You'll like it, John Colburn. Besides beautiful music we have lots of pageantry and ceremony."

And the evening ended.

Outside the restaurant he walked Celeste to her parked car and told her good-night. He went to his hotel in a state of euphoria, with the feeling of having taken a major step in the flow of his life.

Two days later he came to hear Celeste Howard sing in the choir of the old church he had seen at a distance since boyhood but had never entered. Radiant in the morning light, she sang with joyous ease, her voice soaring into the vaulted heights of old St. Paul's. He watched her profile in the distant choir, facing the lectern, the hair shiny with highlights, the amber half-glasses down her nose, the songbook open in her hands. She appeared serenely devout, and brainy, and poised. He thought of angels and he thought of women. If only he could prove worthy of her, poor lonesome widow, defending herself against evil encroaching from every direction upon her purity and grief. She had described her life to him, how wariness and care and precious memories made it so easy to hold all the eager men at bay.

This was it. Safe and secure in the hushed sanctity of holy cloister, he without doubt at last had found his woman. But a little tug of caution nagged at his new happiness. Had he been sent a warning in the very church itself, he wondered vaguely, distantly? His spine still tingled from the dark surprise, the sobering incident just moments ago as he stepped out of the Easter morning sunshine into the hushed shadows of St. Paul's vestibule, glimpsing the sextant's hands as they released the dangling rope, the tolling bell still calling, and at the very pinnacle of this serene and tranquil moment an explosive and nasty eruption blew the ambience apart like splattered glass. From high in the belfry a rattling violence slithered down the tunnel, whipping the tubular walls, and flopped out of the ceiling.

Dust and fibers of age and rot billowing into the still air revealed the old frayed and broken rope collapsed on the worn stone floor. His ankles tingled as he walked around the sinister coil. The bell's reverent clamoring quieted in diminishing reverberations as the choir stood to sing. He chose to ignore the supernatural possibilities, but the emotion remained. While he felt adrift in the negative wash of ethereal warning, the librarian's words came back as a bother and he wondered if he was unwittingly being pulled into the current of something maybe overwhelmingly powerful.

He watched the ceremony from the back pew. Shafts of iridescent sunlight slanted through the windows and cast down across the cavernous reaches of the nave to reflect on the heads of hair and the backs of pews. People appeared so small beneath the architectural arms striving upward for the reach of heaven.

The icons, the white head-covers, the white gowns, the medieval weaponry of black iron, the candles, the fire flaming atop torches carried down the aisle with pomp and ceremony, altogether created a pagan flavor, archaic and heraldic, reminiscent of clansman-ship, and an astonishing contrast to his life of physics. He had found her in a world so far removed from his way of thinking, a world he had never taken seriously. Now his awareness hovered over the brink at the edge of eternal darkness and doubt where the church professed to understand the greatest of all questions. Perhaps he had missed a mystery and a beauty hidden by arid icons and empty gesticulations. He drifted in sentiment and permissiveness, the noise of the plunging rope still uneasy in memory, gravid with the inert finality of a sprung trap. Then he thought *Have I been wrong to refute all this for so long? Maybe there is some good if it can harbor and nurture a Celeste, a very gracious gift at last.* Perhaps he should look more carefully and get closer. From appearances it soon would become a part of his life.

She joined him in the lobby, and they went first to lunch then for a ride through the springtime countryside. In his elation, as the landscape rolled by, he looked beyond the roadside litter of the pick-up truck culture. Budding dogwoods blurred in a haze, the pink blossoms of the redbud bushes and the wild plum, and the yellow-greens of baby leaves streaked through his preoccupied awareness. In controlled excitement he talked tentatively, being the careful gentleman in the presence of an elegant, refined lady, a lady so injured by the world, so devout, so devoted to memories, a lady to be rescued and saved from smoldering grief.

"Do you come to Cambridge every weekend?" she asked as John turned back toward her car parked in the church yard.

"Most of the time, but not every one."

"For your latest book and your mother."

"And the farm, yes."

"Well, I do hope you will include me."

"Yes," he said, not really believing his good luck, "I have another reason now."

She placed a hand on his as he drove on.

Now his trust in a woman did not rest on a foundation of treachery. Of this he could be sure with Celeste and he could put his worries aside. Yet, strangely, they were there, the far-away, quiet little cautions tugging for attention. But such doubts were not necessary. This one was right; he had discovered her himself in the hushed shadows studying the shelf of books. From first sight he had thought of her in terms of wife. But he would have to wait nearly another week before seeing her again, and she had seemed so delighted with his returning on weekends.

2

When alone on the week nights she usually went somewhere with a purpose, and the nursing home problems nagged for attention. The answers had to be found. She had gone there in the night more and more often to look, and on this Monday after Easter and a few minutes past midnight Celeste Howard, almost as if sleepwalking, stepped inside the shadowy cul-de-sac at the far end of a sprawling wing of the Golden Age nursing home and closed the door. Dark areas filled the spaces between baseboard lights serried down the long hallway. She moved against the wall into deeper shadows and waited. Tonight she deserved a special treat; she had promised herself. She had tolerated the tepid passions and the inept, amorous probings of Peter Mallory and the other guilt-ridden little middle-aged adulterous boys in the banks and gambling joints of the affluent world. Her heart raced with excitement and anticipation. This would be something else, something beyond her imagination, a man who truly excited her and took her beyond herself, beyond all control. In the silence and emptiness, in the semi-darkness outlining torpid shadows down the distant walls, nothing moved in protracted time. She waited. Fear, too, charged the excitement. He would appear in complete silence, materialize out of nothing, startling her, making her heart stop with fright, as he did the first night she came looking in these dark wards.

On her first night time visit, months ago now, she had watched the shadowy movements of a pillow being used on a mindless old patient who had been hanging on for years, running up the bills. Peter Mallory had complained about this one in particular, but he had not asked her to do anything herself, nor had he suggested it. But someone was doing it to hurry on the events promising to make her the next Mrs. Peter Mallory, the richest woman in Cambridge. A gaunt figure had hesitated near the hulking bulk mounded under the covers, within sound of the sonorous breathing, then moved to the bedside and placed the pillow. Within an eternity of five minutes, the old thing had just died, without raising a hand in defense, or moving, or uttering a sound, as though predestined to this violent end without violence.

The light was too dim and she feared exposure. She wanted to find more evidence. Her fright faded and a callow and fleeting guilt engulfed her in the surrounding darkness, her awareness filled with a surge of remorse for betraying the defenseless. A menacing silence hung in the room. The attacker rearranged the bed, turned the old thing on its side again, and vanished. Nothing appeared to have been disturbed in the silent emptiness. The amputated rhythm of a life left not a whisper, not a squeak, not a flutter. And nothing moved.

Nor did she hear the man when he stood at her side, just standing against her as if he had sprung straight up out of the floor, and whispered, "Skillfully done."

She whirled to face him. He stood a head taller, her nose almost touched his white coat, and she smelled the faint musk of his excitement and a whiff of arid cologne. Her heart raced, her mouth went dry, and she almost crumpled. He knew, and placed a palm flat against her mons, grasped a wrist, and led her through the shadows into an empty room, then stooped and lifted the hem of her chemise and carried it above her naked breasts. The opening belt buckle tinkled, the zipper zipped as he turned her onto the foot of an empty bed. Light from the courtyard streaked dimly around the drawn window blind.

When he released her and she stood, the dress falling into place, he said, "So, you come here in the interest of murder?" inflecting the statement with question. He backed into a shadow against a wall. She tried but she could not see his eyes or his true coloring. The light dimly outlined the masculine profile, the hooked nose, the springy hair, the lanky strength.

"Who are you?" she asked.

"I work here, Miss Howard."

"How do you know me?"

"Mallory's woman ... everybody knows you."

"Well ...?"

"So, you are here to look after his interests, too?"

"I follow no one's instructions," she said.

"I know ... no instructions from him, just ideas and hints and wishes, his way of commanding."

"So who are you?"

"You don't need to know, at least not now ... maybe if I learn to trust you."

"Meaning what?"

"You will be coming back for more."

"You think so?"

"Yes, now that you have more reason than on previous visits or missions might be more like the truth."

"You have proof."

"More questions than proof."

"Like what?"

"Like what happened to a couple of guys who were always very busy around here?"

Her heart raced for another reason now. Could he possibly know the frightful thing she had come to suspect? Possible? Yes. The way he moved he could be anywhere anytime, silent, invisible, watching, seeing things she had never witnessed. Perhaps Mallory had a hand in it, and if so, how far had he gone? Perhaps she had found a source of answers to her annoying questions about the deaths and injuries. She wanted to know the answers.

"Like who?" she asked.

"Like David Beckette for one, the great Dr. Beckette who didn't believe in letting people just die." He whispered in the dark, a smooth accusation, almost a caress, establishing control with emotional blackmail.

At once she knew she could be used. But the excitement gripped at a pitch beyond all caution. She still tingled down to her toes. No one had ever reached her like this man. The new pinnacle justified any risk, even the risk of enslavement, and the exhilarating fear of being caught. She said nothing.

He continued, "I guess you know about the other way the death of dear Dr. Beckette works for Mr. Peter Mallory?"

"Maybe I don't."

"Well, you wouldn't have a way of knowing. What's he promised you anyway ... the next Mrs. Peter Mallory, maybe?"

"That's none of your ..."

"Ahhh, I thought so. Fooling you too, or thinks he is. So let me tell you. It's the widow, the lovely Helen Beckette. He's determined to have her to sport into the glamorous world of his new riches. And he will dump all his other women then, including his sad little wife."

"On what do you base such ideas?"

"I will trust you with that when I know you better."

"I doubt you anyway."

"Oh, don't worry. Helen Beckette turns him down cold every time he calls. She wouldn't have him on a bet."

"Then he can look elsewhere."

"I think you don't know your man. Peter Mallory sooner or later destroys any woman who turns him down, especially if she gets in the way of his money."

"He would harm her?"

"Already they are plotting to frighten her into surrender."

"Surrender what?"

"She guards the patients here, and spends too much money for better care. He not only wants her for himself, he wants her out of the way, out of administration here in the nursing home business."

"Who is *they*?"

"You name it, and he's into it, one way or another, always hidden. The most dangerous people are the outsiders brought here to do his dirt, or the dirt of maybe somebody higher up using Mallory while he uses."

"Meaning what?" she asked.

"Never mind."

"Are you bluffing or are you really up to something yourself?"

"It's a wicked world, and only the wide awake survive. You best be looking out for yourself."

"Whatever that means."

"It means more than you can guess and many questions, like what happened to another victim, poor old harmless Jack Williams, now rotting in the Veterans Nursing Home? Why don't you finish him off and free his poor trapped wife? How did you do it anyway?"

"Trapped?"

"She feeds him twice a day and spends every evening by his bedside, watching him breathe his way through a now senseless life. That enslaving task and having to work make up her entire life."

"So, I've heard."

"And she works for Mallory as his secretary. He abuses and uses her. He takes her on the desktop, like he has all of his secretaries in the past."

"I don't believe you."

"Then let me inform you. Even the cleaning people in his building know. They hide to watch what he does and overhear his talk on the phone, and then gossip. And he ain't so well equipped either, the way they tell it."

"How do you know all this stuff?"

"Five of my cousins push the mops and brooms and dust cloths in Mallory's bank, and in the offices above in the same building."

Her eyes had adjusted there in the night and his silhouette took on a deeper substance. He remained in the darkest spaces while easing out of the room into the shadows of the hallway.

She followed, trying desperately for a look, but he kept to the darkness. Damn, everything he said had been dead-on right, but how in hell did he know?

He gave her a moment, then continued, "How was it done? Both of them?"

"I don't know what you're talking about."

"Oh, I think you might, but it will out sooner or later anyway, whether you know or don't."

"You've no right ..."

"We'll see. But since we are in this together we need to understand some things."

"Like what?"

"You do charity work?"

"Yeah, I do pink lady at the hospital and here too, but what are you getting at?"

"The animals."

"What animals?"

"You have dogs at home."

"Yes, two little white terriers."

"And they can read your mind; they know when you are worried; they sit at your feet and try to look you in the eye when you got troubles."

She gasped and said, "Damn, you are right, and just how did you know?"

"You got all that about you, and Miss Howard. I can smell things."

"Tell me."

"Well, first I smell you, the perfume. Just right, it teases a man's soul. Then there is the whiff of the dogs in your house, and every time I get near you, the taint of Mallory, too."

"I am just astounded."

"Yes'm, but to get on with the animals, you carry another trail, Miss Howard, and it's got a wild natural whiff, and I've seen you there."

She hesitated, drew in her breath and said, "The pound, the animal shelter. What do you do there?"

"Well, you might say I'm God's official kidnapper. Some of the folks working down there got real heart, and when they get a customer they think ought to be back in nature, like a captured squirrel, they call me. I take him back in the woods 'til I see his kind, then I let him loose. That's one thing comes close to making me happy."

"I go there. But I can't do much except cry about it. If I followed my impulses I would have a house full of dogs and cats."

"Yeah, two places where folks get rid of things they don't want no more, for their own kind, this awful place where we are right now, and out there in the stinking cages for the animals."

"I stand by the cages and cry."

"I've seen you."

"I can't take them all home with me, and they are waiting to be put to death."

"Those here are put to death."

"But out there, one that far gone never gets beyond the merciful veterinarian needle. There are no terminals living by respirators and tubes, only to rot in their own filth."

"You have no regrets here?"

"I don't approve of anything about it, and I'm here to find out who is doing what to whom."

"Don't you have an idea?"

"Yes, but I want to see for myself. Do you know?"

"Afraid so," he said.

"Then why don't you do something like stopping it?"

"Time's wrong, too early in the game," he said.

"Mercy killing."

"The law would call it something else."

"Oh yes, especially when done for other reasons."

"Why don't you put a stop to it?" he asked.

"Maybe the same reasons as yours, and how would I?"

"It doesn't bother you, ever?"

"Yes, it does, for more reasons than one, but only when I find something worse than God himself invented on this earth will I have reason for regrets."

The pitch and the energy in his voice changed. "What do you know about God?" His whisper, now harsh, echoed down the corridor: God God God God God.

Startled, she hesitated, a chill in her back, a shudder, then she said, like a child in defense, "I go to church every Sunday."

"No church in this world reaches for the sky like a tree. You belong in the woods," his whisper quiet now.

"Then take me there when you go to release a precious little animal."

"Maybe one day, but you got to earn it first," he whispered. Then he vanished without a sound.

Since beginning her night prowling she had watched three pillow jobs, then on the last visit, the man. Such excitement, she could not get enough; she had become his willing slave. He would appear without sound, without warning, out of empty darkness and silence. Eerily, she had no sixth sense of his presence: no hair prickling up her neck, no tingling from being watched, nothing to warn her, none of the protective perceptions to betray the approach of danger. Only the smell, his cologne, as if he moved in and retreated. Then it grew stronger and he would have stood and watched her soundlessly, she imagined, bemused and grinning in the darkness for God knew how long before he frightened her with a sly peremptory whisper, his lips almost in her ear.

Tonight, just one day beyond Easter, she watched the moving shadow of someone slipping into a room, dim light outlining an inert form on the lone bed. The person snapped on a table light. Clearly now a skinny woman, she pulled the sheet down, revealing the still form of a female patient, thin and worn out and unresponsive. The intruder rolled the patient up on her right side, grasped the slack left breast with one hand, pulled it sharply up and to the right side, stretching skin over the prominent ribs. She reached with the other hand to retrieve something like a hat pen out of her own hair in the darkness and from the hand motions appeared to push its tip deep into the chest toward the heart. Then a hand went into a dress pocket and a snapping metallic pop followed, like nipping off a big round hat pin head, caught it in her fingers, and used it to press hard against the amputated shaft, sinking it below the skin. She released the skin, and skin and breast slid back to normal slack position far around the chest wall as the body went slack and supine. Stabbed with a hatpin, Celeste guessed. The puncture wound would, of course, disappear under the fallen breast. The intruder vanished after putting the patient back in place, straightening the bed linens, and turning out the light.

Celeste smelled the aroma coming closer, her heart fluttered, her mouth went dry, and a strange excitement stirred in her belly as he materialized at her side. He ignored her and took a stethoscope from his pocket, placed it over the patient's heart and listened, then handed the earpieces to her. The wild flopping heart struggled in its death throes. He turned to her. She was trembling. He laughed, took a wrist and led her into a storage room and turned her on an empty gurney, lifting the chemise, exposing her nakedness. He took her again and again, orgasm after orgasm, until she flung her hand away from her mouth and he stifled the scream with his palm as he finished.

They left the room. Celeste expected him to hide himself in the darkness and talk. In the hallway she reached for his arm and grasped emptiness, nothing. He had vanished into the shadows and the solemn relentless silence of the progressing night. She waited and listened for the sound of receding steps. His odor faded. She was furious. She wanted him in the daylight, she wanted to know who he was; she wanted to be alone with him where she could scream out her passion, a passion she didn't know existed before he took her the first time. Tonight he had not uttered a single word. Now she could only leave and go home.

Back in her living room she turned off the television, poured another glass full from the wine bottle, and sipped while sitting alone to worry and wonder. Jake's beatific smile gleamed in the portrait spotlight over the mantel, as if he had owned the world and left it to her. The room and the two dirty old terriers at her feet smelled of dog. But she could not afford another vet bill, or the cost of having them bathed, or new puppies to replace these when the time came. A beautiful and elegant lady deserved riches and grandeur and no limit on the money necessary to comfort and style.

The night had passed, nearly to daylight. Damned porch, damned rotting-down house, the whole scene a squalid mess. Why did he have to leave her, Celeste Howard of all people, so destitute, the insurance money each month a mere dole, just penny ante? She needed a better man and she would get one, Peter Mallory. Yes, but more money than man.

Peter had complained to her on their gambling trips about the overzealous care of the living dead in Golden Age nursing home until she had come to have a clear idea of whom he blamed. The health-care professionals who were just a bit too health-caring and a bit too professional, helping those clinging to already finished lives, and wasting the resources, namely money. She got his message the first time he talked, the hidden promise of great wealth, and life together sharing it. And she would continue to do everything possible to find out what he was doing to make his plans work.

But who was the man in the darkness of the Golden Age home? She suspected he knew more than he let on. Was he playing dumb by informing her of the events she herself perhaps had unwittingly helped plot and plant? She drank another glass, the bottle now almost empty. The dogs had settled down again.

She mused; Peter Mallory about to come into big money, truly big time. She would take him, then do as she pleased. Or could she take him? She could, as soon as he got rid of a wife; a resentful, tolerant, placid woman who put up with anything to keep her status, including his poor little natural endowment and his pitiful performance in bed. His sour marriage ought to be easy to break up once she got control. But Peter was hanging by his teeth. The Golden Age nursing home might defeat him yet. If it did not start turning a greater profit he could lose the sale of his entire chain to the HMO conglomerate now dickering to buy it. Then he would be just what he was already: a small-time, small-town banker, stuck with a dumb, boring, tedious wife, only a little fish in a little bowl, and she was sick and tired of smallness.

Why couldn't Jake have been big? No. He stayed too busy taking care of the downtrodden, giving his time and talents to any and all riffraff who wandered into his office in trouble through their own stupidity.

And money should go to greater causes. She giggled at this from Peter. Greater causes ... Peter's coffers, and hers, too, eventually ... give her time. She would continue to go gambling with him, just another chance they were taking together, and she always won when she gambled with him, always came home flush with cash. But she did do secret things in the daytime at Tunica after Peter disappeared officiously into the guts of the casino for business with the owners. When he returned to the gaming area hours later, she ignored his superior bearing and they usually stayed up most of the night in one casino or another. She couldn't sleep anyway until dawn approached. Dawn would begin its slow glow as she drowsed, the image of John Colburn vague in her reminiscence of last Sunday. Now, with him, she had another possibility, but his old mother Rachel was a great impediment to Peter's intentions, and John Colburn was here many weekends to see about her.

She sipped more wine and gazed up at Jake's picture again. Oh, Jake. Thank you for sending John to me. You are my savior. Now I can forget the likes of Peter Mallory. As the new Mrs. John Colburn she wouldn't be as rich but she would have security and respectability, and a beautiful home in Huntsville. Once old Rachel was gone, she would never have to face Cambridge again. How refreshing to have a real man who was straightforward and earnest and honest. Yes, and he would give her the one thing money could never buy, real fame, real respectability, real importance based on real talent. Such recognition was sweeter than all the money in this world. What a coup it would be to tell Peter Mallory nothing, just suddenly announce her engagement to John. Of course, she would invite Peter to the wedding, and the crew over at Tunica, too. And she would be dressed like an angel there in the church, sweeping down the aisle, all innocence and so precious, hovering under the protection of her man, her renowned and brilliant physicist.

Oh, Jake, you have saved me from some terrible people. She cried with happiness, the tears rolling down, so glad she had saved herself for someone like John, getting her just reward at last. With fleeting whimsy she thought, but what of all the others, and dismissed them at once. Oh, they were nothing. And nice, dear, old John was too innocent and inexperienced to know such things existed. He wouldn't believe it anyway. Just taking life as it came, nothing to worry about; she would forget them as though they hadn't happened; it was all in the mind anyway. Oh, how nice, how comforting. What a triumph! And in less than a week she would get to see him again and take him further into this world he dreamed of and wanted so eagerly. She got up from the couch, staggered to the stair rail, and ascended to the bedroom to sleep until noon.

3

The next Sunday she stood on the front row of the choir facing across the nave, a little taller than the other women, the amber spectacles down the bridge of her nose, distinct and angelic, beautiful and scholarly, mature and gifted, singing audibly above the choir, in a clear fine voice. Earthy, woman, angel, chaste, lusty, lithe, and delicate: The images swirled in his head. John stayed through the ceremonies again and after the recession they met in the vestibule and went to lunch, then for a ride in the country.

Down on his farm, the old family place, they walked the hills and fields and talked. On a knoll overlooking the river valley he showed her a site he had picked for the house he planned to build eventually. Oh, how wonderful, what a splendid view, and she would love it, but she would have to keep her place in town. She had to be in town. Town meant her whole life.

"But, oh my, this is so beautiful and expansive," she continued. "It just goes on and on. Was this your old home place?"

"Yes, my great grandmother bought it from the Pontotoc Land Bank in 1843. It had belonged to the Chickasaws. So we were the first, and so far the last. I have been adding to it piece by piece over the years to its three thousand acres more or less, twelve hundred in cultivation crops, the rest in forest and cultivated trees. It now borders on the university campus, on the incorporated limits of town, straddles two rivers, and has four spring-fed lakes, stocked."

"What will you ever do with all of this?"

"I will have to decide someday, and I have several ideas."

"Does it extend to the boundaries of the Cambridge Animal Shelter?"

John thought for a moment, then said, "Why yes, I guess it does. Why?"

"I have a special interest in the poor little animals."

"The Humane Society," said John, "Death within a few days unless somebody turns up to claim you with love."

"Oh John, you do understand the ironic cruelty of the place."

"Indeed."

"Have you ever thought about the similarity of the places where mankind gets rid of the two things he professes to love most, the nursing homes for his own people, and the animal shelter for his discarded pets?"

She felt a twinge of guilt for presenting as her own the thoughts of the man in the shadows. But this was hardly the place to offer references.

John regarded her calmly. These exact thoughts and sentiments dwelled on his mind at moments when he paused at work and at reading.

He said, "You have keen insight." She seemed to be more and more like the woman he wanted and needed.

She reached and grasped his right forearm in both her hands, looked up toward his face, and said, "I hope to God we can do something about both someday."

She gazed down at the ground as they walked and continued the conversation. She could not just live with someone, she explained. It had to be honorable; it had to be a marriage.

Of course, marriage could be arranged, he thought. He felt sure of his emotions this time with this ideal woman for whom he had been looking all these years: truthful, beautiful, reliable, capable. But caution overrode his emotions, and he said no more at the moment.

They talked about traveling. Their first trip would be to his home in Huntsville, two hundred miles east. And here on the seventh day since Easter Sunday, she was telling him ... you have rescued me. You have been my resurrection. It was Easter in more than one way. You have come into my life and into my church and lifted me up. I love Jesus; I believe in him just as I believe there is a heaven. I will be there some day, and Jake, the man of my life, will be there waiting for me. He is smiling down on me now, I can feel it, I know it, and he is giving me directions. And I want to ride where he used to ride with me on Sundays. Then she looked up and said, "Come on, let's go down toward Taylor."

They drove through the countryside, talking, their casual pace blurring the roadside garbage trail of discarded bottles, cups, papers, wrappers, beer cans, and other trash thrown from passing traffic. They passed through miles of sorry trailer homes trashy on cinder blocks, and old rusty cars abandoned, and mobile homes listing on the crumbling and lopsided impermanence of ugly concrete block pillars unfinished, and roadside junk, and all the signs of poverty and indolence. In the midst of this appeared a Spartan white plank fence around an emerald green field as manicured as a city lawn surrounding a restored home shiny white with an open porch. She told him about the woman who inherited money and bought the place and restored its present pristine elegance amidst the dilapidate neighborhood. He admired the fence, but it protected nothing, not a cow or horse in sight, and no closed gates secured the house. Anybody or anything could crawl behind the planks.

Then before he could stop it, before he even thought, an old country saying escaped with revealing overtones, betraying a hidden insight into her true inclinations, an insight he had not yet admitted to himself. He said, "About as useful as tits on a boar," and she sucked in breath and flipped her face toward him with this astounded expression set by its muscles, yet the eyes were opaque and empty; still, he ignored this and sped right on past its meaning.

Uneasy, he said, "What?" thinking he had used language too crude for this fine lady. He was just feeling his way along and maybe he had blundered and ruined it all. He didn't know where the statement came from or why he said it, and she said, "He said that; it was one of his favorites."

"Who?"

"Jake," she said, "My husband, very practical man, you know. I believe he is sending me signs from up in heaven. He is watching us; he approves of you. God has sent you to me. Jake has sent you to me."

John drove on, saying nothing. Their rapid progress across vast wastelands of the unknown separating two people created a shifting sands sensation, and he sensed a closing net. But faintly wary, he was not sure he disliked the developments. In the heart of Taylor, they went past a country store, and the odor of parching peanuts filled the car. He sniffed and said, "Peanuts. Boy, I love peanuts."

"Peanuts!" she said. "You love peanuts. Why, Jake loved peanuts, too.

He could never get enough. The two of you are so alike. And that's the other sign. He just keeps sending them, and now I know this is right. He approves of you. He wants me to have someone and he has chosen you. What else do you like, native to this part of the world?"

"Blackberry jam, with the seeds in it."

And she almost shouted, "That's the other sign. He loved blackberry jam with the seeds in it. This is just too much. It is positively inspired – all this sent down to me from Jake up in heaven."

The little warning voice had begun to think and caution. In the last few moments he had crossed even vaster stretches between the two, and not much space could be left. But he would try to be more careful and reserved. He must not let his guard down again and risk saying the wrong thing off-color.

He left her in the early evening at her car in the church parking lot, to return to his hotel, where he would spend Sunday evening and night alone, out of respect for her struggle against the evils of her world. So he reasoned to himself. He later wondered what would have happened had he been aggressive. And he could console himself with at least one certainty. He would never know.

On Monday morning John Colburn went to the Golden Age nursing home to speak to his mother again before returning to Huntsville. In the fetid hallways he moved among the ruins of once normal, healthy people who had lost the joy and the freedom of good health. At such moments he almost held his breath, fighting the emotions of pity and disgust and shame and fear, his distant awareness trying to ignore the warnings of fate as he wended among the haphazard wheelchairs with their slack senseless burdens slumped in apathy.

When he entered the room, Clara Bartley, the private nurse, hovered over Rachel Colburn, finishing her usual morning ministrations. Only her devoted attention had kept Rachel alive all these years. Clara straightened up, petite and alert, and said, "Well, good morning. And how was your weekend?"

"Oh, great, but a bit unusual, and how is Mama?"

"Perky this morning and she has had a good breakfast. I'm taking her for a ride in the country at ten."

Rachel said, "We've going in the van, John, the wheelchair lift works perfectly. I certainly do appreciate it. Otherwise, I would never be able to get out of this place."

"My pleasure, Mama," he answered while studying her idle, old hands gone soft with wrinkles, and he thought of the places the hands had been in days long past for the sake of her family and everyone who came to her in need – those hands had milked cows, killed and dressed chickens from the yard flock, had been covered in flour and dough, caked with dirt from setting out plants and gardening, had grown raw from washing clothes, worn from scrubbing and cleaning floors, graced from cleaning the sick … the list was endless. He could never do enough for her. Then he turned to Clara and asked, "Has her doctor seen her recently?"

Clara gave him a studied look, picked up her purse and said, "The floor nurse is waiting to talk to me about supplies." She started toward the door. "Meet you at the front door in five minutes. We'll talk on the way to your car."

John talked to Rachel a few minutes then told her goodbye, and followed Clara. Out on the grounds, she stopped in the shade of a tree and said, "Actually, I have to go back to her room. I'm not quite finished yet with her morning stuff. But I wanted to tell you, where she can't hear it, there has been no consistent medical attention since her real doctor, David Beckette, died. That sorry devil, Isaac Dodson, took his place, and I have to raise a stink every time a doctor is needed. And I question his wisdom when he does get here."

"Well, he *is* a board-certified internist."

"Oh yes, hell yes, but he's into money and real estate and if rumor has it right, some unsavory things also. Anyway he can't be bothered with the elderly. As far as he is concerned they have already lived their lives and it makes no difference if they do die. He is responsible for her having to be here, his errors and his negligence. I'm damned sick and tired of the attitude."

"My God, do you want to get another doctor?"

"Well, who? Dodson's group has the only internists in town, and she needs the expertise. No, let's wait awhile. I'll handle him."

John studied her aggressive stance. No one crossed this fiery, red-headed little woman. No one got away with dishonesty, incompetence, laziness, cover-ups, neglect, lying, or other sorriness. Anyone who tried would be held accountable sooner or later. His mother was in good hands. He said, "And how are you fixed for supplies?"

"A constant struggle and I'm having to buy more and more. The latest economy pinch is a switch to cheaper absorbent diapers. All fluids run right through, soaking clothes and the beds. I would never leave Rachel in one overnight. She would get bed sores for certain. And that's just one example. Too many people have been laid off and there are not enough to take care of the patients."

"False economy."

"No question, but Peter Mallory would practice any cruelty to make a dollar as long as he avoids jail. This place and every one I know like it is not for the patient. It's to make money for the stock holders, mainly Mallory himself."

"And what else is there to Mallory?"

"Nothing to smile about. Besides being small, greedy, and puffed up, I hear he is into gambling with an interest in the casinos at Tunica."

"Anything else?"

"He's tainted, but I don't think anyone knows for sure exactly why or its depth."

"Frankly, I'm uneasy, but I'll leave it to you."

She said, "You can depend on it." Then after another hesitation she asked, "And how was your weekend unusual?"

"Do you know Celeste Howard?"

"Celeste Howard? Celeste? Oh, yes, Jake Howard's widow. Not personally. But I know who she is. He was highly respected, one of the few honest lawyers, died a tragic death of a heart attack, worked himself to death. I understand she is still grieving. Why do you ask?"

"I've met her."

"Now, that might be a match for you. I've heard nothing bad about her. But actually, I've really not heard anything at all, one way or another."

"Great."

"Are you going out with her?"

"Have been," he said.

"Man, you don't waste any time."

"Well, I'm very encouraged about this one."

"Be careful now, and don't get yourself in a mess with another Cambridge woman."

"I will look to you for guidance, but I'm sure about this one."

"Okay."

4

In the main office on the square, Martha Williams, secretary to Mr. Peter Mallory, president and CEO of Peoples National Bank, overheard enough of his midmorning conversation on the phone with Helen Beckette to predict his next actions. The elegant and beautifully self-controlled Helen once again had just turned him down, politely, firmly, and charmingly. She had consistently refused to go anywhere with him, especially out of town to business luncheons. He tended to forget caution and discretion in the pursuit, and his voice carried clearly through the open door. He had to control himself and remember to replace the receiver gently when he really wanted to slam it down. Then angry and frustrated, he called Celeste Howard and arranged to pick her up for the trip.

Patient, serene, matronly Martha would be next, to prove himself and vent his anger before leaving for Memphis, or Tunica. She might as well get ready so the encounter would be briefer, and the briefer the better and less the danger of getting caught. She dreaded it, but did feel a tinge of excitement. He paced around his office, small man, removed his coat, and hung it over the back of a chair. In a moment he would be calling her in. She went to the lady's room, stripped out of her underpants, placed them in her purse, and returned to her computer. She waited while he talked on the phone again, always brief and rude unless he needed another woman or money bigger than his.

Oh God, if only her husband could know. He would just finish dying, curled up in his bed in the Veterans Nursing Home. But her life had come to this. All day in Mallory's office, then to the nursing home in the late afternoon and evening to feed Jack Williams, a motionless form, responding only with dim recognition in his eyes. For two years now, the routine had not varied, and she was trapped. Mallory knew this from the beginning of her employment with him, and calculatingly broke down her resistance.

The buzzer sounded, Martha picked up her steno pad and pencil and entered Mallory's office. He stood in the door waiting with his hand on the knob. He threw the lock and followed. She turned as he came forward and took her in his arms. He smelled of cologne and cigarettes with a whiff of fetid, carnivorous, carrion-breath before lip contact, his tongue bitter. Her nose rebelled but a baser impulse surged through her belly.

He pushed until she sat on the edge of his desk, his belt buckle tinkled open, and memory rushed with images of boys and men – the sounds of belt buckles and zippers, the male sound of dominance, some of it cruel like her own father removing his belt to whip one of her brothers, and her on too many occasions. She remembered zippers zipping open on the front seats and back seats of automobiles in the heat and passion of necking struggles. Mallory's hand grasped for the hem of her skirt. She pushed him away. "Now Martha," he said.

"You know the terms."

"But there is too much danger this time of day and I've got to leave in a few minutes. Besides ... God knows who might be coming in here."

"Then forget it." She began straightening her clothes.

"Oh, Goddamn it, Martha, come on ... "

"Take 'em off, Mr. Mallory, every stitch, or I'm going back to my desk."

"Oh, damn!" He rushed the door and double-checked the lock, then stripped off his clothes and returned, wearing only his shoes and socks, with the air and appearance of a cocky bantam, his penis erect.

"The shoes and socks, too."

"Martha, for God's sake."

"Everything, or you get nothing. I won't be taken like a strumpet in an archway."

"Strumpet? Archway?"

"Fornication, Mr. Mallory."

He slipped out of his shoes and socks and turned toward her, but his passion had deserted him, his penis shrunken almost out of sight in a scrubby thatch of tame graying pubic hair. She lifted her dress, turned, and lay amply supine upon his leather couch, naked from navel to shoes, and opened her legs.

"Come on, big boy." She laughed, tantalizing.

He fell on her, but he had gone, and no amount of trying aroused his challenged and frightened dominance.

She let him struggle a few minutes, then reached down and grasped his shrunken penis and massaged it until it grew half erect, about the size of a stubby and malnourished finger. What a contrast to Jack Williams' vigorous and well-endowed manhood before his ruinous injuries. This time Mallory hurried, ill at ease, and not in control. After about five strokes he lost it, spurting off in weak little pulsations. Cursing and mumbling, and with no endearment, he jumped up and ran into his private lavatory, and without closing the door, in plain sight, began washing his genitalia with the wet end of a bath towel.

She watched. How vulnerable and ludicrous is man when naked. His little belly pouted out, his arms already shrinking from disuse and advancing middle age, his head and neck and hands of a darker hue than his pink-white and pimple-blotched body, a red-neck in an air-conditioned shade, a small man early old.

He strode angrily back into the office and began dressing as he gathered his discarded clothes off the floor. She still lay on the sofa, her dress hiked, her legs spread in the couched attitude of a slattern, wide open, waiting, her expansive and exuberant and wild black escutcheon wet and lusty with the fluid invitation of love and arousal unrequited.

She gazed at him behind a bemused smile, silent and tolerant. But he missed the fellow human in the room with him for the moment, the sweet tolerance readable in the quiet gray green eyes. The head of curly graying hair cushioned on the pillow, the hardy, mature, safe woman who has learned to tolerate the finicky and treacherous male apparatus and its befuddled owner, waited for him to prove himself. He could do nothing with his unfueled instrument at the moment, and he had neither the love nor compassion in his heart to give her relief otherwise. He turned his bare back while slipping into his sad little white jockeys, and refused to look again. She had taken him down to his real size.

She did not stir as he went back to his desk. She lay still, listening while he phoned Celeste Howard and he did not try to modulate his voice. He stormed out the door, and his Mercedes burned rubber, the tires squealing as he left the square.

Across town, at home, Celeste Howard had endured the morning ennui too long before Peter called. Anything would be better than nothing, and she would get to see somebody interesting at the casino. If he had not called by noon, he would not. The afternoons do wear on, and she dreads them. She needed to get him under her control, so she could begin to live her own life in a better way, not to be at his beck and call. Marriage, yes, but they would have to be rid of his wife, precious little Sugar Mallory, first.

She watched the dogs and sniffed. She should bathe them herself, but the very idea of a lady stooping to such menial messes! Revolting! She looked up at Jake's picture, the lamp shinning on his face in bright daylight. Poor Jake. She loved him so much, the only man ever. Tears welled up. How pure their love had been, how careful he had been, taking her the first time, so tender with her innocence. How he had loved knowing she had saved herself for him. She sobbed. The older dog awakened and came to her. He sat at her feet and watched her face, turning his whiskers side to side, searching with his gaze. The dog odor swelled, and the phone rang. At last!

"Oh Peter! I'm so happy you called ... nothing, sweetheart. I was just getting ready to bathe my precious darling puppies, but it can wait. Sure. Call back when you are ready."

Zelma Taylor phoned Martha at eleven o'clock and wanted to have lunch. Lunch meant at least two hours discussing Peter Mallory and his behavior, and always she added new information to the growing collection of his abuses. Zelma Taylor, who preceded Martha in the job, left the bank in tears because her able-bodied boyfriend had become suspicious. None of Mallory's promises had been fulfilled to this rawboned, skinny, buck-toothed country woman from out at Yocona, a very bright and good secretary, hot as a cat and willing. She had had no life except farm work and a country high school, then a short secretarial course before she landed in the citified and glamorous atmosphere of a big bank, naive and blind to danger. She waded murky water without thinking of snakes or alligators. She never had a chance. Mallory used her from the first week. Helpless in his clutches, she layback on the desk top, legs spread wide open, and he took great glee in tickling her exposed clitoris with his little naked hardness, making her have tantalizing surface orgasms until exhausted, all the time promising her the world, her deeper yearning, waiting, expectant. But he did not have much for the depths.

Others had preceded Zelma. Martha knew them all and had heard their tales directly or through rumor. And the strange thing, Mallory didn't have a friend left among the lot of them. They were all seething for revenge. They had been had, fooled, used, and discarded. So many enemies for one man meant certain trouble.

At first Martha had discounted Zelma's talk, attributing it to anger alone. But the evidence had become too convincing. Zelma's case against him continued to mount, and Martha became wary and uneasy. Daring, reckless Zelma would blow the whistle at the right time. She came from wild, tough country people who ignored the consequences and died in duels and shootouts and ambushes in the name of revenge and righteousness, death and the penitentiary be damned. Revenge she wanted, and she would have it or die trying.

At the restaurant, the moment they were seated, before the waitress appeared, Zelma's anger erupted.

"Where is that conniving sonofabitch today?"

"Gone to Memphis or Tunica or both to make another sales pitch. He's meeting the owner of the world's biggest HMO conglomerate, a Zeebeckystanian named Bin Kadsh."

"And Celeste Howard with him."

"Every time, after he gets turned down by Helen Beckette. He can't do any better."

"Does he take her into the meetings?"

"No. Under some pretext, which she buys obediently, he sends her shopping and gambling."

"She's too smart and too cunning for that."

"Yeah, but he won't know it until too late."

"Memphis and Tunica again, huh. Man, he is determined to pull it off."

"Do you think he can?" asked Martha.

"Well on his way when I was there. If he could just get the profit margins up high enough on the Golden Age in Cambridge, then he could sell the whole chain. The others, Pontotoc, Sardis, Batesville, Holly Springs, Water Valley, were all showing the profits he needs, but Cambridge is a different story. It costs too much to maintain the quality care demanded of it, and he has done his best to break the holdup. Two in Tupelo, he has bought, and they are showing a nice profit already."

"Well, that's just the ones in north Mississippi," said Martha.

"Yeah, what about all the others?"

"Since you left he has sewed up over ninety percent of everything in north Mississippi, west Tennessee, east Arkansas, north Alabama, east Louisiana, west Kentucky, south Illinois, east Missouri, more than a hundred of them altogether and all making handsome profits, with no threats hanging over his head. Cambridge is his big headache, and all because of one or two people who really care."

"And mark my words, they are in danger."

"Yes. I worry most about Clara Bartley. Almost every day she is down in the nurses' station or the administrator's office raising hell about the lousy care being given to patients in the Golden Age, so I hear."

"She's the nurse taking car of old Rachel Colburn?"

"Not just her. The employees ignore the advanced Alzheimer's and others who can't feed themselves, and they just starve. Clara lets administration know it, and she feeds as many as she can at noon on her own time, but she can be there only sporadically. The nurses and their helpers fear her and they don't like her, and sooner or later someone is going to shut her up."

"Speaking of that, Martha, what do you think happened to Dr. Beckette?"

"Somebody got him, poor, sweet man. The death rate was too low in Golden Age. He made rounds there nearly every night, sometimes into early morning hours, after the rest of his day had been finished. He saw to it that the starving were fed, the neglected and unrecognized pneumonias treated, the heart failures rescued ... you name it, he found it and treated."

"While Helen worked overtime in the office."

"Oh, yes. The two of them were determined to show what could be done with nursing homes. And they were well on their way to accomplishing this dream. She had become the assistant administrator."

"Who did it?" asked Zelma.

"Nobody could break his arrangement with Medicare and Medicaid, so he had to go. A contract, I'll wager. And you know what I think ... I think Mallory is so full of himself that he really doesn't understand the dragon he's messing with. I get this idea from the phone conversations and the correspondence that Kadsh really wants the nursing home chain and will have it, profit or no profit, and is just stringing Mallory along, tantalizing him with the impossible, for some reason not clear to me yet."

"So what happened? Dr. Beckette's death looked like an accident of nature."

"So did Jack Williams' damage."

Zelma gasped and stared at Martha. "Oh, My God! You mean you think they got your Jack, too? That never occurred to me."

"I'll bet you Kadsh or somebody just as big or bigger sent an outsider to do the dirty work. Maybe Mallory provoked it, not really believing such viciousness. He's just a little, ambitious, self-important prig, in over his head and blind to the danger."

"So, why the killings and injuries?"

"Not truly identified as such yet, but a way of keeping control."

"But why in hell would anyone want a hundred damned nursing homes?"

"Think about who this Kadsh really is, and think about what is going on in this world now, of how much money could be laundered on a hundred homes, especially if they were not making a big enough profit."

"Good Lord, Martha."

"And you know where laundered money goes?"

"Lots of places, no doubt."

"And no doubt a lot of it to finance the terrorists. In fact, laundered money from illicit drug sales is their lifeblood."

"Then Kadsh might be one of them?"

"Yeah, maybe. Something big is happening and I'm biding my time."

Zelma thought for a moment then asked, "So what's happening with Helen Beckette ... Mallory still after her? "

"As late as this morning."

"With no luck, as usual."

"He wanted her to ride up to Memphis with him to meet Kadsh. She turned him down, as usual. She sees right through him. Damn! He's dying to nail her. One more notch on his gun."

"Shit! Some gun. I've seen bigger ones on twelve-year-olds."

Martha laughed. "And when she turns him down, he's fit to be tied."

"Yeah, how well I know. Every time, he took it out on me and I got fucked spread eagle on his desk ... we broke a lot of bric-a-brac in two years. Wasn't too bad, either ... he knew how to play a tune on my clitoris with that little thing of his. And goddamn, I would get so excited, just the idea ... me nothing but an old country gal in a big air-conditioned office with all that money and all that power, and him so beside himself with my little tits and big butt, my black-haired thing open for him ... spreading my legs wider and wider and I'm coming like a freight train ... Jesus, how exciting. I bought his cologne and put it on my Fred, but it wasn't the same, smelled different, and Fred ain't got no money and no power, up to the hilt splaying me like a middle-buster wasn't as exciting. Poor Fred, he ain't got the slightest idea what a clitoris is for, one reason I never married him. What about you? Don't Mallory come onto you too?"

"Don't worry, I know how to handle him."

"Well, you're the first one then, including his wife."

"I know him. He won't be back before midnight, maybe even tomorrow morning."

"Never did get back the same working day. Returned by way of Tunica every time, and usually came back carrying a wad he had won at one of the gaming tables. And when he had been especially nasty to me he would come in sheepishly, stashing a wad of the stuff on me ... five thousand dollars, ten thousand. Like nothing for him to be carrying forty or fifty thousand in his inside coat pocket, like he had grown a big tit. Then the little bastard would stand there waiting for praise or a reward of some kind, the rest of him almost as gray as his changing hair, his expensive clothes always tired, looking like he might have slept in them."

Martha waited in silence. Mallory had done the same to her, numerous times, and she had put all of the money in a safety deposit box, more than fifty thousand by now. Out of her concern for Zelma she asked, "So, what have you done with it?"

"You'd be surprised. I've never touched a shred of it with my own flesh. He comes in, see, throws it on the desk, and says it's a gift; he wants to share his good luck, and leaves. God! How he tries to make himself look big. And soon as he's out of sight I count the bills by turning the edges with my eyebrow tweezers, and pick up the bundle with a napkin, take it to my lockbox back in the vaults, and it's all there, still, every penny of it. I expect it to backfire on me some day ... like income taxes, or like maybe he really didn't win it, like maybe it could be the bank's money. Each batch is labeled and dated. Like seventy-five thousand and more by the time I left my job there."

"So what do you think?"

"About that? I think if the bank inspectors knew about his gambling habits there would be a thorough inventory of the whole operation with the front doors locked for however many days it took."

"Yes, but what do you really think?"

"You mean the guys in the casino."

"Yes."

"They are letting him win just enough to get real cocky."

"No doubt."

"So what's to be done next?

"Everybody he's insulted, every woman who's ever worked for him, all of them are just watching and waiting. Every waitress in town has heard about his nastiness, or has had her behind felt up while taking orders, both hands busy with pencil and pad, and they eavesdrop on him when he has lunch with one or another of his cronies. We get together, us women, and we've formed what we call The Mallory Club. We meet, never the same place twice, and never by a schedule. We want you to join," said Zelma.

"About his town cronies – who do you think's in cahoots with him?"

"Nobody local in cahoots. He's too secretive and too greedy for that. But I think he does a lot of small-time buying and controlling."

"Who?"

"Somebody in the sheriff's office, maybe the sheriff himself, or that meathead deputy of his, Wyndham Jones. That's at the town level."

"My God, Zelma, do you really think Mallory would do bodily harm to anyone for such small stakes?"

"Have it done, and the stakes are not small, not by any means. Over a hundred nursing homes under his control. Once he proves himself a business shark and sells to the conglomerate he will make millions, to stay on as a partner with a seven-figure salary. When he is about to accomplish that, he won't let anybody or anything get in his way."

"Okay, I agree with all you say. We both know what he is. We've both heard him bragging. But there is still the question. What's to be done?"

"Martha, you are in a better position than anyone else to know what he's up to."

"And in just the right position to get myself killed, too."

"You got to be careful, honey. Give him what he wants, keep your eyes open and your mouth shut."

"Tough assignment."

"Yes, but who's to stop him if we don't, not his next victim, not the helpless patients, not his next woman?"

"Well, maybe you are right. Who's likely to be his next victim?" asked Martha.

"Whoever carries the greatest risk to his endeavors, like Helen Beckette. If he can't seduce her then he will control her another way, or try to. And I'll bet if he can't fuck her he would just as soon kill her. Now, he wouldn't try any foolishness with Clara Bartley. She would break his nose, and if her husband, Tom, found out he would walk right over to the bank and make hash out of Mallory. But Clara's too dangerous to ignore. I'm afraid somebody will get her without warning."

"And the danger will not make her cautious."

"Oh, hell no. She don't know the meaning of the word," said Zelma.

"She stirs up superficial trouble all right, but I don't think she's much more than a nuisance."

"Well, let me tell you something maybe you don't know. She carries a loaded snub-nosed .38 in that little black purse of hers."

"No kidding," Martha said. Then after a moment, "Can she shoot it?"

"Not only that, but she's a crack rifle shot, hunts deer every season, too, and keeps her freezer full."

"Well, well."

"Yeah, Tom built her a hidden tree house, the fanciest hunting blind in the county, up among the limbs of a huge oak down on the back side of John Colburn's land, and she goes out there in season, climbs up and waits, and it don't take her long to bag one. And she shoots wild turkey gobblers through the head at a hundred yards or more with a little scoped .22 rifle she carries along, just for the sport of it. She never buys a turkey in the grocery store at Thanksgiving or Christmas."

"You know this for sure?"

"Yeah, I know it for sure ... my brothers are all hunters. They belong to the hunt club that leases the Colburn hunting rights and they make room for her," said Zelma.

"Yeah, I guess I had heard something about this. Wasn't Tom a game warden at one time?"

"Yeah, after he came back from Vietnam. In fact, she was one of his deputies ... that's how they met, and they would track poachers together."

"I'm glad to hear she can defend herself, but I don't think that will help with this situation. She may bring down a state inspection on the heads of the nursing homes, but not a major upset as a quieter, more deadly person might do."

"Like who?"

"I'm betting on Helen Beckette. She's not going to let David's death go quietly into memory," said Martha.

"I hope not, and we need you in The Mallory Club."

"Zelma, I'm keeping out of sight, no public appearances because I know not to trust such meetings to remain secret."

"But you are with us?"

"I'm with justice, so let's keep in touch."

5

When alone on mid-week nights Celeste became restless and bored. To relieve the tedium she assumed another role, searching for her own depths. She dressed for these occasions, her hair in twin braids down her back, separated by the bill of a baseball cap turned backwards, eyes an intense blue from contact lenses, and she wore a denim unisex suit and blue shirt with the collar rims opened up her neck and folded to obscure her ears and hide her throat. Several layers of pancake makeup and other colorings transformed her face to new youth and character. Incognito, she went to join the Acid House students. In the darkness of secret places she could pass for a late teenager, roughed and weather-beaten by fast living.

She entered the *Inner Sanctum*, just off campus, into a techno-synthesized and synchronized world of noise and smoke where whirling psychedelic lights strobe the room in vertiginous rotation. The music, pulsing in relentless tom-tom insistence, led a steady and growing beat of background bass, the drums going on and on, never pausing, never breaking for a free breath. She took a tiny table in a far dark corner, faced the room, and paid seven dollars for a bottle of water. She watched the crowd. Pill purveyors passed among the tables, and twenty- and fifty-dollar bills changed hands. No alcohol crossed the bar. The puckering mouths, the swelling tongues, the growing thirst of Ecstasy demanded more water. She told the pill purveyor, no thank you, I have my own, and she swallowed an antacid wafer and sipped more water.

As she thought she would, she spotted the deputy sheriff, Wyndham

Jones, standing at the far end of the bar leaning on an elbow, his bulky back turned to the room, talking to someone almost hidden by his protruding sidearm. A recognizable silhouette stood beyond him, a familiar and particular body posture, dressed in a trampy slouch get-up and wearing an old sloppy cap, none other than the eminent Dr. Isaac Dodson, the town's most prominent internist. Busy, he concentrated on something, his face turned toward the bar top. By the shoulder movements, she guessed he must be writing.

She did not have to wait long. Her looks appealed to a student, who had visited her before on her trips to *Inner Sanctum* and other bars. He came to the table, burly Ray Haaps, star fullback on the varsity.

"Where have you been? I never see you on campus or in classes. What's your major anyway?"

"I'm a student of sociology," she said, smiling.

He pulled back a chair and sat down. "Yeah," he said. "And this is the place to study it all right. You want a lesson in sociology, just look around."

"Well. I see plenty going on but to what do you refer specifically?"

"Not the intimacy, not the touchy feely, not the emotional openness," he had moved closer, leaning across the table, his face almost against hers. "It's the vicious greed." She waited. "You see that meatball with his back turned at the bar?"

"Yes."

"Know who he is?"

She didn't plan to admit anything. "Who?"

"No less than the infamous deputy sheriff, Wyndham Jones."

"So..."

"So, the guy he's talking to. The one who thinks he's disguised in the trampy clothes?"

"Yes?"

"The sneakiest sonofabitch in town, the prominent internist, Dr. Isaac Dodson. You know what he's doing?"

"What?"

"Signing prescription pads for Jones. The shame of it, Dodson giving the law the means for getting students hooked to help feed the illicit trade in drugs."

"What has you so upset? You on a crusade?"

"They got my girlfriend hooked, and she's lost and she's ruined. She has never been the same since she got into a certain batch of Ecstasy and almost died."

"He didn't prescribe Ecstasy?"

"No, but they got her on codeine, the worst, one dose and she was off, hooked and quickly addicted,"

"I don't understand such almost instant addiction, with so mild a drug."

"Some people are predisposed to it, a well known fact. And she is super intelligent, exuberantly passionate, burning and intense, and very vulnerable to the delectables of being alive … and now ruined." He almost whimpered.

"What have you taken tonight?"

"When I saw you come in forty-five minutes ago, three Viagras."

"Ohhh, you think so, huh?"

He had shifted his chair to her side; his fingertips touched down on her hand and moved up her arm, the lightest touch, the lightest feel, caressing with mere touch. He loomed beside her, a mountain of strength contained, and vulnerable tonight with a burden of grief. Then he reached up to her face and ran the fingertips down her neck beneath the upturned collar.

"Yes," he said, "yes."

She met his gaze and said, "Yes."

He stood and she followed him out the door.

She had experienced in the past, so many times, the capriciousness of the male mechanism. The sensitivity ended too often in quick termination of the act. Sometimes the tricky business emptied before it started, leaving its owner devastated in impotent embarrassment. But Viagra in the young had eliminated all the difficulties. Now, in the real and sublime present, she experienced the early emptying; but the motion continued, the rigid readiness continued, and the flow seemed endless. She thought, *My God, how much of this stuff can one male body manufacture and store* and tonight Ray Haaps was still rigid when he exhausted himself and rolled over on his back.

"My, that was simply commendable, Ray."

"Well, thank you," and he chuckled and became silent. Troubled, she knew he was troubled.

Then he said, "You are a blessing, a relief for the moment of almost unbearable frustration and regret. It's my fault for not stopping her. She would do anything I said. But I failed to say the right thing at the right time."

"And you confide in me. Am I to wonder why?"

"In your wisdom and maturity, you've been places and done things."

"Yes, I have seen it all."

"Then you don't mind my presumptions?"

"I guess we both sense that you are, for the moment, my little boy."

He grasped her in his arms and snuggled. "I promise you, I promise the world, I will deal with that damned doctor when the time comes."

He spent the night in this position, sleeping in her bed with her naked buttocks nestled in his crotch.

6

On Sunday night a week later, John and Celeste sat on her couch, the framed countenance of Jake over the mantel beaming down on the room, a full gleam of benevolent well-being. She had served a splendid dinner by candlelight, amidst sparkling crystal and shining silverware, good wines, delicious food she had worked over most of the afternoon. He had admired her from across the table, the look of serene maturity, the woman so gracious, so graceful, so healthy and normal and uncomplicated, so competent, his great find. Now she seemed to be waiting for something; no sounds broke the silence. Pungent perfume permeated the ambience, palled by the distraction of dog. After awhile, she took a deep breath, a two-stage gasp, and began to talk.

"I have fought with this alone all week and I stayed awake all night last night, thinking and struggling with myself, and Jake was there with me upstairs in the bedroom, and I have come to a decision. Jake, down out of heaven, helped me make it. I prayed with him long and hard. He at long last gave his permission. Without a doubt I know it's time to end the marriage to him."

She held up her long hands, now naked of the big diamond, the simple silver-colored broad filigree wedding band still on the marriage finger.

"End the marriage for me now."

He said, "What?"

Looking at him she said, "Take off the ring. End this marriage so I can begin my life with you," and she handed her left hand to him. He took the hand and held it and looked to her face for guidance, and the gaze gave no clue. She said, in a strained whisper, "Take it off."

A strange vicarious and powerful emotion kicked him in the belly and his soul stirred, and his cock stirred, and regrets and grief stirred. He grasped the ring gingerly between thumb and fingertips, but it clung too tightly to flesh. It would not budge. He looked up. She was watching with the steady, gleamless eyes. The hand moved. With almost reptilian deliberateness the pointed finger slid on his lips, into his mouth and crawled onto his tongue, the ring crossing his teeth, his jaws and tongue enveloping. She took out the wet finger and held the hand toward him again. He pinched onto the ring lightly, carefully, respectfully, with gentle fingertips and it slipped off into his palm and he handed it to her, and his belly lurched with a strange thrill.

She whispered, "Thank you," and looked at him steadily. "And please, please, please, I want you to live to be a hundred-and-ten."

Then she took him into her arms.

Her lips were sweet and warm and moist, her tongue pointed and tentative, flicking just inside his mouth. With deft, secret movements she took off her bra, releasing the breasts, big as coconuts, and long, tugging down on her thin chest, the wrinkles of maturity, marginally over the bone above. The nipples didn't erect, not to his fingertips nor his lips nor his tongue, nor his teeth so gently nibbling, but she made the right sounds of ecstasy: sucking in breath, sighing and saying, "Oh John, it's been so long. I can't stand it. When he ran his mouth and lips up along her long neck, she gasped and exclaimed, "Oh, John! Oh, God!" When he put his tongue into the notch above her breast bone she gasped and nearly fainted. With a hand on each breast, a warm, soft abundance overfilled his palms. But it stopped here.

She has not had a sex life since Jake died and she stopped her birth control pills the day he died; she didn't think she would ever need them again, and has not taken one since. There has been no need for it. She had been doing nothing and never would. Now, she will start as soon as possible. But not right away, her period is due in three days and will last about five more, then she will have to wait five days before beginning the pills, and then it will take a couple of weeks of the pills before she will be safe. The intimacy vanished and her mystical mathematics of female physiology confused him. She talked on. He interrupted, "But a child would be a blessing – Oh, I would love that."

"No! No! Never! Children would ruin my life."

"Well, as you wish. But it would be beautiful."

"By the time I am safe we will be on the road to Huntsville, and we will have to have separate rooms if we stop en route because I don't want to be tempted."

"Three weeks off, yet?"

"I want to wait. I want you to make love to me the first time in your bed, in your home, our home."

But the birth control pills will be a problem. Her regular gynecologist won't give them to her because women of her age should not take them – too risky for cancer. And she wouldn't ask him anyway. He knows her too well. He would know something is up, and she does not want to start gossip. She wants Jake's memory honored. The doctor and Jake were very close and he knows she has been in mourning all this time since Jake's death, and there would be no need for pills. Maybe she will just drive down to Jackson and find a gynecologist in the yellow pages, or maybe to Tupelo. Then, she does know someone in New Orleans, an old friend. Anyway, don't worry. Don't worry; she will take care of it. Confused again by her rambling mathematics and circuitous logic, John retreated to neutrality, and the visit to her home ended.

Talking to him on his Huntsville phone every night of the week, she said, "I love you John, I love you, I love you, I love you, I love you, I love you, I love you. Please hurry back."

He believed it. He believed her. She couldn't wait for him to get back to Cambridge, but the following weekend presented a problem. She would have to be in Biloxi from Friday morning until Monday afternoon visiting Jake's mother and his children by his first wife. They are so dear to her, and their ties so close. She was so sorry, but she could not change the arrangements she had made before she met him. She just couldn't, under the circumstances, disappoint them.

She went. She called every night, just couldn't wait to get back. She said so on every call. On the second night she gave him a number where he could reach her. For some innate reason he knew better than to use it. He put this aside when she returned, telling him about the wonderful weekend she had had with Jake's children and his dear old mother, who had grown so attached and so dependent on her.

And two weekends later they went to Huntsville. There she gasped when she saw his beautiful home furnished with antiques, and she took over immediately. She polished the silverware, tarnished from neglect, and stored it in bags with camphor, a new bit of knowledge to him. She rearranged the furniture, fluffed up the draperies and cushions, gave the place a woman's touch. Knowledgeable, gifted, industrious, capable, she set a beautiful table and took over the kitchen and cooked delicious meals. She preferred not to go out. My God, was he lucky to have found her. He offered her a guest room that first night. "I've been on the pill a week," she answered.

Contrived, he won't admit to himself, but will remember in future moments of greater emotional sobriety. His whispered endearments, his gently sustained foreplay, were met with bemused detachment. Her orgasms were voiced, but her face never changed, the putty eyes remained opaque, the carotids calm, the veins in face and neck flat, her body receptive without reflex response. He exhausted himself with long bouts of pitching and plunging, holding himself back, trying for an emotional upheaval, trying to master her, but it never happened. Her pulses and breathing remained calm, and she vented only in words, the right ones but without emotional color. Many days into this he reached slyly toward her wrist pulse while she proclaimed orgasm, and she drew violently away, protective. The little voice of wisdom whispered repeatedly far back in the brain where listening is so difficult, *she's faking*. Her skin sheened and moved like latex. Her agile and extreme positioning provoked primitive instincts. On her knees she could aim the vagina almost toward the ceiling. Experienced, whispered the little far-away voice.

In Cambridge, the elegant table at her home: the pristine cloth, the tall candelabra, the gorgeous flower arrangements, the shining silver, the beautiful china, the dripless candles, the delicious food – with these she became the real thing. He ignored the voices of caution, those asking where had she been in the past to accumulate this array of elegance and the polish of her experience? He dismissed this reality. He dismissed the odor of dogs. They discussed the generalities of marriage.

"I would have to be married in my church, by my bishop," she said.

"And the church will have to be a part of my life."

"I would expect so."

"Would you make it a part of yours, too?"

"Well, yes."

He assumed discretion. Nothing would be said until the announcements. They still had to understand each other about some things. They still had talking to do. He thought of a ring.

Back in Huntsville he looked at diamonds and talked to a jeweler. Sixty thousand dollars would buy a fairly decent one. He had not proposed. He had not made a formal commitment. But he dreamed an old dream; he had found her at last. He felt the eyes of the town upon him, the man with qualifications to make a real conquest, to fulfill her unique needs, to take the place of her late beloved husband, to take charge of the waiting treasure. The men in particular would be aware of his good luck. He would create a certain envy, and so he would be especially cordial and careful. He would be congratulated and envied. But he still was positioning himself for the momentous decision.

His days at work went this way, in hazy far-off musings, working things out in his own mind, the way he would come to see them as the reality unfolded. A slow and mounting elation took over, and he became more productive than he had been in recent years. But a persistent tug never let him soar with happiness. And he now returned faithfully each weekend to Cambridge.

7

Clara Bartley stopped just inside the back kitchen door of his mother's vacant house where he sat doing paper work at the counter on a Sunday just five weeks after Easter, and stood with her back against the screen. Without preliminaries, she asked, "How are things going?"

He looked up from his computer. In the petite body stance he read reticence and determination and on her face a bemused concern, the red hair cut short and fluffed an airy sharpness about her head, the green eyes focused on his face.

"Great. I'm really happy."

"You and Celeste?"

"Yes."

"Well, I hear you are getting married."

"We've talked about marriage in general, yes, but nothing official yet. Where did you hear?"

"From a member of her own church, and it didn't come as glad tidings."

"Oh ... meaning what?"

"A member of her own church now, mind you, who has known her for years, and knows her whole history, is very concerned about what is happening to you."

"So, what is happening to me?"

"Oh God, I feel I'm partly responsible for this, so I have to tell you, I'm hearing some things I don't like. Not just from a church member, but from other people, too. In fact, they are coming out of the woodwork to talk to me ... all saying the same thing. And I am so astonished by the talk, and so furious with myself for being so damned gullible in the past."

"But I have been very discreet. I've not mentioned her to a soul except you, and I have not proposed."

"But she has talked."

"Oh, God, not another one!"

"I'm afraid so, and the gossip is rife."

"And that?"

"My God, she's got one hell of a reputation. Now let me tell you something ... you remember when she had to go to Biloxi to see poor dead husband's children and his mother?"

"Sure, I remember."

"You know where she was?"

"Well, as of now I'm beginning to suspect I don't."

"In Biloxi with one of this town's big shots, gambling. She loves to gamble. And they say she will crawl in the car with just any man and go off on a gambling jaunt, for a night, a weekend, a month, whatever, as long as he has the money to afford it. And as I hear it, she sits by the phone every morning waiting for one of them to call with an invitation to go."

"Do you have names?"

"Yes, I have names."

"I want names, dates, times, proof. I won't lose this one by rumor."

"I won't tell you myself. I want a man to tell you, someone who knows the facts, someone who has no ax to grind in telling you, someone concerned for you and your family."

"And who could that be?"

"Would one of the town's most prominent lawyers do, one who shared offices with her now dead husband, Jake Howard?"

"All right."

"Ten o'clock this morning in his offices."

"But it's Sunday."

"He's expecting you and will be waiting. But he's sticking his neck out only because I asked for his help and advice. Let me tell you a little bit about him. He's not only a lawyer, he's a philosopher and a psychologist as well. He teaches classes in both and also in law out on the campus."

"Hmm. Unusual man."

"In every way."

An hour later, John climbed the stairs to old established law offices familiar to him in his boyhood, the area above Henry's Grocery. He went down a long, narrow, dark hallway and entered through tall, heavy oak doors into rooms with twelve-foot ceilings. Sam Sheffield, behind an immense old desk, resembled the movie star Gene Hackman, the same benign but keen intelligence and well controlled sensitivity, the look of forthrightness and integrity, and a steely alertness. John gazed through the window behind the desk down upon the town square as Sam stood, came around to shake hands, and took a chair facing him.

Then Sam began talking. John listened, incredulous at the unfolding story. Jake Howard dumped his first wife after he caught her cheating with the town's most flagrant rake. On the rebound he married Celeste, an exchange like jumping out of a campfire frying pan into the cauldrons of Hell.

She immediately squandered his small fortune, and he began moonlighting to try to pay the mounting debts. All the while, she ran around with other men, numerous men. He couldn't make enough to keep up with her, but he tried harder and harder. Jake finally dropped dead in a mid-morning rush after working all night at a second job. People blame her. Through avarice and unbridled misconduct, she had killed him, albeit indirectly. When Sam paused, John wanted names.

"This has to be held in the utmost confidence."

"You can rest assured," said John.

"The first on the list is well known to the entire town. He's very prominent, and I won't say what else. And this is dynamite. Do you know Peter Mallory?"

"No."

"He owns the Golden Age Nursing Home, the majority of County Hospital stock, and most of Peoples Bank."

"Oh."

"The weekend that she supposedly visited her late husband's children and mother in Biloxi?"

"Yes."

"Peter Mallory and Celeste Howard were together at the gaming tables on the gulf coast, and stayed in one of the posh new hotels."

"So Clara told me. I had suspected something, but I didn't want to admit it."

"You were right."

"Are you absolutely sure about this?"

"Impeccable source. We have pictures if you want to see them."

"At the moment I'll take your word for it. And who else?"

"On other occasions, a very renowned member of the university faculty, Billy Walker, in the athletic department, one of the football coaches."

"And."

"A wealthy manufacturer of toys, Ralph Tyler, in Memphis, frequently. He switches back and forth from Celeste to her pal in outrageous fun, Mary Ann Dickey, and in jest they all call it wife swapping."

"Are these men married?"

"All three. And there are others, among them several members of the university football team."

"I must ask how you know all of this with certainty."

"And I have to trust you implicitly in this." He leaned forward almost whispering, "The information has come to light as part of an undercover operation of much greater importance than who is dallying with whom. A leak would blow the cover."

"Well, now curiosity is aroused,"

"I am sworn to secrecy, but your position in the scientific community allows me some leeway."

"Thank you."

"We are onto something, a trail leading from our little banker, Peter Mallory, up and up to huge quantities of illicit money, drug money laundering, and as you would guess, to suspected terrorist funding."

"Oh, hell."

"Right you are."

"How should I handle this?"

"Walk man, without a word. I know this woman well. She has done what she has done to you and she will repeat it on and on if allowed. She's done it before to other men, like she is looking but has never found the right one. And she has a new risk now. She is working her way up in the world where Peter Mallory has taken her, dealing with dangerous people who would get rid of anyone suspected of knowing too much. So cut it off clean."

John Colburn had turned pale.

Sam continued, "On the other hand, you could go on and marry her. She is clever, she is attractive, she is a great hostess. She's quite entertaining; in fact, she's a blast. But she is also an actress in her everyday existence, and the truth is whatever she wants it to be. You would need a very strong stomach, and several fortunes to survive her profligates."

"I suppose one should love the real person, not the imaginary one created by romance."

"My friend, mankind steadfastly refuses to learn that lesson."

"To his detriment, I know."

"Through seeing it happen so many times I am convinced that love is too often a temporary state of madness leading to a permanent state of misery. Perhaps an arranged marriage is not such a bad idea."

"Well, I want you to know I appreciate your concern and your confidence and trust in me."

"Only for a man of your reputation would I take the risk of this exposure."

"I won't disappoint you."

"Not even Clara is to know what I have told you."

"Indeed."

They both laughed.

"By the way, how is your mother?"

"Remarkably alert and manipulative for her age, thanks for asking."

"Surviving the nursing home okay?"

"There are problems."

"I would imagine."

"Why?"

"The management is being forced by Peter Mallory to economize. He has bought a controlling interest in more than one hundred such homes and hopes to sell them to a conglomerate. But they all will have to show a substantial profit to make this possible."

"I've witnessed some of the effects. People are suffering deprivations. So would my mother had I not hired Clara to check on her every day, and we have to supplement the supplies," said John.

"What a shame."

"Certainly so for families who can't afford it." John stood, shook hands, and said goodbye. "I'm over here every weekend. I'll let you know when I'm in the clear."

"Come to see me in two weeks, same time of day."

"I'll be here."

"Call sooner if you need to."

Clara Bartley sat at the kitchen counter, wiping tears when John returned to his mother's house. "I'm so damned sorry about this. You don't deserve it, and I'm at fault for giving you the wrong impression in the very beginning. My God, I had no idea. I'd heard nothing but good things about Jake Howard. I can't believe she pretends to be one thing and is in reality the exact opposite. In my ignorance of what she really is I misled you. Jesus! The stuff I've heard in the last week! Out of respect for her dead husband I guess everybody's been just kind of holding back until now. But boy, they have sure come to your rescue."

"I wonder why."

"Your mother, for one thing. Everybody respects her and your family name. Then, they just don't want to see Celeste do to you what she did to Jake Howard."

"I've been told not to call her, not even to say goodbye."

"You could get killed telling that woman goodbye."

"Well. Here I go again, back to limbo, I guess," said John, talking on to Clara while he shut down his computer and began gathering his belongings for the trip back to Huntsville.

"And let me tell you one other thing," Clara continued. "And this certainly is not hearsay; in fact, it's a most remarkable coincidence. I'm at lunch, see, just two days ago, in the Kitchen Counter over on the square. I'm more or less out of sight in a booth when the waiter seats someone behind me in the next booth, my back turned so they can't see me. Right away as they settle down I recognize the voices, Celeste and that tramp Mary Ann Dickey lunching together and talking. The first thing out of their mouths is about you, John Colburn, Dickey saying in a conspiratorial, almost whisper, what about that friend of his, Clara Bartley.

"Celeste answers, 'Ohhhh, you just wait till after the wedding. I will get rid of her. Just leave it to me to shut her up once and for all, but right now I'm being all sugar and spice to her face'.

"Then they go on to discuss two of their boyfriends, Ralph Tyler, known as Toy Boy, the toy maker from Memphis, and Billy Walker, a coach at the university. They laugh gleefully about their trips to various places in Toy Boy's jet and their shenanigans in Las Vegas and on the gulf and elsewhere.

"Next, sweet little Mary Ann gets started on her husband, the great Dr. Horace Dickey, and you should have heard the bile, saying the worst things about him. All the while she has been robbing him blind while he has his head up his ass with a horde of patients who need him.

"I sat still as mouse, taking it all in. I wanted to jump up and attack her in their booth, but I wanted to hear it all, and believe me, I did. I stayed right in my booth, prolonging lunch to watch them leave. No doubt about who they were."

"Well, that removes all doubt if there was any."

"Indeed it does."

"So, I think I will just go on back to Huntsville this afternoon. I've done enough damage here for one weekend."

"Will you be back next Friday?"

"No, I think I'll skip one."

Celeste Howard, navigating the Monday morning wreckage of her kitchen, suddenly realized something was not right. John Colburn had not called all day Sunday, and the night had vanished and he still had not called. She had entertained him royally on Saturday evening with one of her very best meals, but to her surprise he had left early without so much as touching her. Had something happened to him? She would bet not ... more likely something had begun happening to her, again. Only one person would know, Clara Bartley. She phoned his hotel first. He had checked out the day before, Sunday afternoon. Peculiar! Then she dialed Clara. "My dear," she said into the phone, "John didn't call yesterday or this morning, and I was wondering if he's all right ... do you know where he is?"

"Yeah, I know where he is. He's back in Huntsville."

"That's peculiar, a day early. I wonder why didn't he call me as he promised?"

"Well you are bound to know he would find out the truth about you sooner or later."

"Why, what on earth do you mean?"

"You know who you are and what you are, and it's time you realized just about everybody else in this little town knows, too. I'm just amazed that I didn't myself until you started hoodwinking naïve John Colburn, and the town caught on. I've been hearing from no less than dozens of people for the past ten days."

"I demand to know who told him anything bad about me."

"Members of your own church, for starters."

"This is all false, a pack of bloody lies. You call him and tell him I want an apology now."

"No. I won't call him. And I know this man. He will never call you again, let alone apologize. So you can forget it."

"It all lies!"

"No."

"What do you mean? Are you calling me a liar?"

"For instance, your recent weekend in Biloxi with the mother-in-law and stepchildren who love you so much. Bullshit! You were at the The Lucky Diamond with our infamous Mr. Peter Mallory. And if the truth were known, the stepchildren can't stand you, and the mother-in-law has never spoken directly to you, even when her son was alive. You didn't go near them."

"Not true."

"Oh, yes. It's true. I have it from her closest friends, and I called her myself to confirm it. I nursed her when she was sick two years ago, remember, and we've been friends ever since. What's more, you were seen, photographed, and reported. Do you want to see the pictures of you dry-fucking old Mallory on the dance floor? The digital camera automatically records the time and date."

"No."

"Yes. One of your friends didn't want to believe all this garbage about you, so he had you followed. And the detectives confirmed some things, all right. You are even worse than the rumors."

"Who had me followed?"

"You'll never find out from me."

"This is unfair."

"Well, you've certainly been that, and do you want to hear what the stepchildren think of you?"

"No."

"I didn't think you would. Then there are the trips with your girlfriend, the prominent Mary Ann Dickey, the great Dr. Dickey's sweet and innocent little wife, to Memphis on double dates with the toy manufacturer and the golf pro, or the assistant coach of football, the four of you to Las Vegas in Toy-Boy's private jet, doing your little so-called wife swapping, and not even married to each other. Visiting his sick mother! Such slime! And little MaryAnn talks, you know, while her dumb husband is too busy being important and fucking his tacky and officious little physician's assistant. The whole town knows the details."

"Well. I am just shocked."

"Well, I'll just bet you aren't really."

"You can't talk to me that way."

"I just did. And something else: you told your precious little Mary Ann about John Colburn's lovemaking, and she blabbed that in the beauty parlor, just as she blabs everything else."

"Well, since we are being so frank, I can tell you he enjoyed it a lot more than I did."

"And from what I hear about you, that's got to be the absolute truth, rare as truth is from your mouth, since you have no feelings outside of play-acting. As people tell it, every emotion in your being is completely false, unless you've lucked up on something a thousand times worse than the lowest, filthiest truck driver, like maybe you found an alligator with a hard on."

"Damn you!"

"You've damned yourself."

Celeste's rage mounted until she called Mary Ann Dickey a week later and told her how John Colburn has broken her heart, how he left without a word of explanation. She has received no more phone calls from Huntsville in the nights, no more flowers, and she has seen him on no more weekends. Everything abruptly stopped without reason, he just deserted her, got what he wanted then dropped her, threw her away. She never thought he would turn out to be such a cad, and after she had broken her marriage vows to Jake, after Jake had sent his signs of approval down from heaven. She had given her innocence to John Colburn and he had flaunted it. God will surely punish him for that. But MaryAnn Dickey, she knew, would go to the beauty parlor and start talking. The word about the wickedness of John Colburn would get around. Oh hell, she had more interesting things to do anyway. She hungered for the man in the nighttime shadows of the nursing home, and she wanted to go to him, but he did not work on Thursdays. He had told her, but he had told her nothing else about himself. She wondered in a state of frustration, who is he?

8

Sam Sheffield, in his office, talked to John briefly when he returned from Huntsville again, then said, "Come on," moving toward the door. John followed. They descended to the town square. Sam hesitated on the sidewalk, then asked, "Where's your car?"

"Right here at the curb."

"Let's go for a ride."

Sam remained silent in the front seat until they were out of town. Then he spoke. "Your farm is in this direction?"

"Yes."

"I would like to see it."

"We're already halfway there; in fact, we're already passing part of it."

"Good."

They parked behind the barn and walked downhill onto the levee of a catfish lake. There, Sam turned to talk. "I promised you the facts."

John interrupted. "Well, first, what's going on here? Do we have to isolate ourselves to talk confidently?"

"I don't actually know. But I'm cautious." He gazed out across the river valley as a flock of wild turkeys landed in freshly plowed fields. After another moment, Sam said, "With the facts you will enter another level of responsibility and danger. You should understand the situation up front. Since we first talked I've had to get clearance before revealing anything more to you, and in doing so, I came across your true identity. I might have suspected you of belonging to Pegasus."

"Only the members of Pegasus can come to know the names of other members."

"Thus it was revealed to me. You belong because of your expertise in the most powerful of all forces, quantum mechanics, the scientific side of Pegasus."

"And you?"

"My Pegasus is the legal world. I belong to and represent the CIA, the FBI, the DEA, and the National Security Agency, the NSA. I have access to information from all four. Only a Pegasus can cross these boundaries. Even the president himself would have difficulties because they trust nothing politically motivated."

"How did you come to be chosen?"

"Pegasus is an outgrowth of NSA. Through NSA I've done legal work for the CIA for years, right here in our own community and on so-called vacations in Europe and South America, among other places. Only the most trusted people on the frontiers of investigative work are invited to join the legal side of Pegasus. And, of course, all the sciences are represented there by their own forerunners, you in physics, for instance."

"Yes."

"Here is my identification." Sam reached between the buttons of his shirt and presented a tiny gold horse, with wings folded flat into its body, attached to a gold chain around his neck. Hunching over and stretching the chain to its limit, he pressed the muzzle, and the body opened, revealing a two-carat diamond embedded in gold, the initials SS engraved below the stone. He snapped the horse shut.

"And here is mine," said John.

Sam inspected John's icon, then said, "I assume you are aware of the realities. We were, in fact, created to cap off and control State Department and CIA arrogance and cavalier behavior, and to put an end to wasteful competition and undercutting by the various federal agencies. Our duty is to supersede the spying of one agency of the government on another, or others. We are above all deception."

"Yes."

"All right, to get down to the basics, Peter Mallory, the little banker, the grasping little man, is using without the wisdom to know he is being used, and I predict, eventually he will be used up. In his arrogance and his avarice he has trod on the wrong toes. Also a second danger to himself, in what I think could prove to be a fatal flaw, he abuses women while using them. One of his most recent secretaries reported Mallory, a country gal named Zelma Taylor, from a family known for a hot and hair-trigger temperament and a thirst for vengeance along with a disregard for consequences. Laundering money she said, drug money she added, connected with Haiti, she claimed, and gambling trips to the coast and to Tunica, even to South Africa and Las Vegas, she elaborated, and all the while she remained anonymous but just as effective. This brought down the feds: the CIA and the DEA. Hospital murder, she accused, in an institution supported largely by federal funds, and the FBI began looking. These federal agents, and eventually a fourth, the FDA, snooping around, called for supervision to avoid infighting. So, politically, NSA got involved."

"How does Celeste Howard fit into this scenario?"

"Mallory uses her, too. She's a good front when he goes to the casinos, wherever. At least he thinks so. She's pliable, discreet, never meddlesome, always available, and always seems to be satisfied as long as she wins something. She's addicted to it by now."

"Does she win?"

"She always comes away with cash."

"How does she come to win every time?"

"When she's with Mallory, the casino manager gives her ten little packages with $9,999 in each. She uses one package at a time to purchase chips as the evening progresses. She gambles under one rule. She has to spend the entire amount before she quits. In other words she loses it all back to the house. She may go through three bags in one night. Sometimes management gives her a million dollars in ten-thousand-dollar chips to gamble away. But she always comes away with money, from five to fifty thousand dollars. Management sees to it."

"Money laundering?"

"The chips convert to clean money simply through the transaction. Winning, Mallory thinks, is a house arrangement to keep her from knowing Mallory's real reason for being there. After he finishes upstairs with the bosses, Mallory gambles the same way. Together they may each launder a million dollars or more on a weekend, but, of course, they wash nothing like the amount moveable by an electronic-transfer scam."

"The source of the dirty money?"

"Drugs directly."

"Oh. And she gambles with other men?"

"In our surveillance we have seen her with numerous others. As to the whole picture, we've hardly more than begun our investigation. But we do know Mallory is stupidly playing with very deadly people."

"Does this place Celeste in danger?"

"Of course it does, as well as anyone involved with her in any way."

"Does she know?"

"Yes, she knows. She disappears from the gambling area while Mallory is in meetings upstairs, moving, we suspect, behind his back, as she does with all men, and he does not have a clue. But still, she's a moth brushing the flames."

"Where is Mallory's head?"

"He thinks he is about to pull off a brilliant investment coup by selling his nursing home chain to an HMO conglomerate, if he can just get the profit margins higher at Golden Age. We think there is something a bit too naïve about this. He's into other stuff as well, and in all of it, he is too arrogant and cocksure to see the danger of taking orders from a casino boss who takes his orders from hidden powers higher up, with involvement of labor union money, all of it further tainted by an element of the Mafia. And they are in cahoots with an HMO tycoon, Bin Kadsh, who is a native of an Arabian country. From the accumulating evidence, he seems to be into laundering money for political use in his native country if not for the entire terrorist movement. It was Mallory, actually, who got the casinos involved with Kadsh. He went looking for places to lend money. We suspect he has placed himself in a trap."

"Sounds as though you have reason to suspect something really big sort of hidden behind smaller agendas."

"Exactly, and with great importance to the country and great danger to every person caught up in this evolving web."

"Well, what can I do?"

"A great deal, in two ways."

"Okay."

"First, use your enormous influence to bring serious action from NSA;

and second, help with the surveillance."

"All right, but I will have to go to Washington."

"I can arrange for your expenses."

"Not necessary. NASA will send a plane to Huntsville or Cambridge for me."

"There is some urgency."

"Yes?"

"The FBI, without the most sensitive equipment, has uncovered local corruption. But their listening techniques require the placement of sizeable bugs. And this is a bit too clumsy when we need to listen to the sheriff, among others."

"Why him? Killing sparrows with cannon."

"The fin of the shark."

"Good God! You don't mean it."

"I wish I didn't. He's in their pockets, and a red herring without knowing it.

"Red herring?"

"Yes. We suspect the sheriff is being deluded by minor payoffs in a small drug-running operation, which deliberately or otherwise serves to hide a second and much bigger operation. We especially need to know what the HMO mogul is up to, and I think we can do so by following the path of Celeste first, and Mallory in her shadow. We think she is working her way up the power structure."

John took a satellite phone from his pocket and punched in a code. He held the instrument to his ear for a moment, said nothing, then folded the flap shut and replaced it in his pocket. He said, "A NASA plane will be at the Cambridge airport waiting before we can get back to town and I check out of the motel. I will be at work on this in Washington less than three hours from now."

"How did you get such quick results without saying a word?"

"I simply code instructions to a certain target, and I get what I want."

"This, I think, will turn things around," said Sam.

As they ascended the hill toward the car, John said, "Evidently, you are nervous yourself about being spied upon."

"Yes. No talking on sensitive subjects in offices or automobiles or cell phones. The whole scene, I suspect, is bigger and has more ramifications than anyone would expect in a small town like Cambridge. That may be one of the reasons for the place having been chosen."

"Little Cambridge."

"Yes," said Sam. "You know our chancellor at the university, Bruce Madison?"

"Yes, I do know him."

"He is in with us, too, because a militant Islamic club of students meets on the campus, and it seems to be part of a network. And he wants to keep ahead of any such movement."

"You know about the librarian?" asked John.

"She has been a great source of information; in fact, she put us onto them months ago."

"Is she in danger?"

"Possibly. We have started protection but she does not know. She never leaves home or the library without one of our men following."

"That serious?"

"Yes."

"Then we do have work to do."

9

Sitting on her living room couch near midnight Celeste Howard studied Jake's picture and mused about her circumstances. She had loved him truly, poor man, so torn with concern for others, the only man ever in her life, and so good to her. He had tried to give her everything she needed. It's not true, what people say. They are so jealous of the lovely Celeste. She *didn't* work him to death. She misses him so ... and wants him back ... but he is gone forever, up there in heaven at God's right hand where she will be with him someday. Until then he will continue to look down and guide her. She knows. Dear, dear Jake, the only man who has ever touched her. She will remain true to his memory. And if some man, the right one, should come along some day, Jake will give her a sign, and she will know he approves of the only person who could take his place. But poor Jake had none of the excitement of real money and power. It's a funny thing about money and power though, so full with promise, so empty of fulfillment, too often. Almost all her men were that way: moneyed, affluent, prominent, but with a wilting streak of weakness. Guilt, she thought. Guilt weakens their manhood. Not a one of them has the detachment of a real male free of inhibitions – powerful appeal, vapid performance, sneaking around, cheating with money, cheating with sex. All are mere pawns, except the man in the shadows of nighttime Golden Age.

The deputy sheriff, Wyndham Jones, had just left after eating another of her home-cooked dinners. What a rutting stupid brute, but he serves other purposes, too, so he is to be tolerated. And there is a certain excitement. He loves to play leapfrog naked. He is so big and strong. He hardly teeters when she takes a running start naked and leaps at his face and lands astride his shoulders, her legs clasping around his neck, her hot desire right in his mouth, her hands clasping and tousling his hair. And he knows what to do, carrying her light as a feather, his hands holding her up by the naked buttocks, lapping into the middle of her as if drinking from an endless cornucopia, her spread legs reaching and reaching.

He went early tonight because he had a favor to do for Mr. Peter Mallory. Jones talks too much, bragging, ignorant of who knows whom. If it sounds big he says it without thinking of consequences. He is up to something dirty, carrying out Mallory's or somebody's directions. But Mallory himself, she now is pretty sure, obeys higher powers, and she has come to think for him while he talks on. She slips the words in and he never realizes the ideas are not really his. But he uses them, dropping hints in the casino meetings, and someone tells the sheriff what to do. The sheriff sends Jones, she supposes. But Jones, she knows, does only part of the harassing. No, there is not enough to him for the scene. Something more powerful, something out of sight up there somewhere pulls the strings.

She wondered if Jones actually knows who. And the more astonishing thought – did Peter Mallory himself really know? She would bet not. Perhaps she should have followed Jones to see what he was up to tonight.

Poor lonesome, heart-broken Celeste felt vulnerable and weak and exposed, then she wept, tears rolling down. John Colburn be damned. He had done her so wrong. The older dog sat up on his haunches and looked at her face. He cocked one ear and watched, rolling his little whiskered face side to side, waiting. Precious little animals, so faithful, never treacherous like people. Oh, she would do anything to deliver them from the cruelties of this world. Then a wave of anger gripped her. Damnation to this wickedness! She would get to the bottom of it all, and she had an idea of just how to do it through working her way up the hierarchy at the casinos.

Helen Beckette awoke to midnight darkness, through a storm of arousal, her heart beating too fast, the dream too real. The bedside light had been out only half an hour, her instant deep sleep filled with memory ... Old Paul died at daybreak, his face visible in the dream. A black eye already had turned yellow and green along the margins of his cheek in the three weeks since the nurses on 7 a.m. rounds found him sitting up in bed staring in bewilderment across the room into morning light, his right eyelids black and swollen shut, seeping the clear tears of irritation along closed margins. Knots under his scalp oozed clear fluid at the bruised tops. If he knew what had happened he wouldn't admit it. So, no cause could be recorded. Fell out of bed, maybe? No, nobody falls out of bed and gets a black eye and bumps under the scalp on the opposite side and no other marks. What had happened to Old Paul? No one could imagine, such a good guy, such a placid, pliable patient. But every person knew in his own heart and nobody cared to admit it. No witnesses, so nothing could be proven and no one wanted to dare the evil stalking these wards after midnight. Old Paul had been hit with a fist or worse, a hard blow in the face, in the darkness of his cubicle where nobody else could see who did evil and cowardly things to defenseless old people, hit because he had peed on himself, an annoyance to somebody on the midnight shift. And Old Paul had slowly sunk deeper and deeper into somnolence until he quit talking and quit eating and just gave up. The internist covering the wards paid scant attention. Old, old Paul, old and worn out, had lived up his life. Nobody called for a neurological consultation, or for a brain scan, or bothered to investigate his injuries. David Beckette would have ordered brain scans and a neurosurgical consultation.

Visions of his face haunt Helen. Old Paul won't go away. He's often back in her dreams and ruminations. She tried to persuade the family to allow an autopsy. Old Paul died from a clot on the brain, she was sure – age ninety-five, a tough old sharecropper, a Medicaid patient, a benign and loveable little man, always smiling, always pliable and obedient, but helpless when his prostate disease gripped him with sudden bouts of urgency and incontinence. He couldn't help wetting himself in the middle of the night. He often said, "I was dreaming I had gone to the toilet, but woke up doing it on myself ... I can't help it ... I don't even know I'm doing it until I wake up wet. Lord I'm so ashamed."

The family refused autopsy, supplying their own platitudes: he's suffered enough; he's lived a long, long life; it's God's will; when your time has come it has come; God works in his own mysterious ways; God has called him home; and other self-deluding and irresponsible statements. Relieved of the burden maybe, worn down by twice and three-time daily trips to the nursing home to help feed and care for him, they seemed in a hurry to be rid of the interference with their lives.

But as she knew with a direct sureness, somebody murdered him indirectly with a blow to the face and blows to the head delivered out of pure hatred. David had explained such things to her. An old brain, shrunken with age, slides about easily on the slick, coated cavity inside living skulls, tearing the friable bridging veins stretched across space once occupied by the full volume of normal brain. These old veins break easily, sometimes at the slightest blow, and bleed until this space fills with an enlarging blood clot big enough to slowly compress the brain, squeezing out its life. She would bet a big clot rests on Old Paul's brain, now in the grave, still well enough preserved to be proven.

The family also refused embalming and buried him the same afternoon. So, there would be a chance to look even yet if she could gather enough evidence to convince the right people. Patients had begun falling victim to something with a deliberate intent, she suspected, something more than simple negligence, something to take the place of nature's old remedy, like pneumonia and other infections people used to call *the old man's friend*, in these modern times where antibiotic therapy has filled the nursing homes with the lingering, who in the old days would have been dead long ago. No longer could such events be due simply to carelessness. Helen thought, we are dealing with a phenomenon of social abuse now put to calculated use, and her suspicions had grown to puzzlement then astonishment, then disbelief and anger, then fear and now determination. She watched, checking everything and keeping voluminous notes, but keeping them at home hidden and locked up, being very careful, very circumspect, but her fear had been growing again.

Now she lay wide awake, panting, sweating, flat on her back in bed, staring through darkness toward the ceiling, listening to the silence out in the night beyond her bedroom walls. She shivered ... someone creeping up on her house, someone breaking in, what had awakened her? She could remember nothing from deep sleep but the dream and reality mingling beyond the depths of REM arousal, with the vision of Paul's pitiful old face. She heard no sounds in the deep stillness other than those any silent house makes of its own existence, the popping, cracking, settling noises. But something extraneous had awakened her, she knew. She listened for footsteps, and heard nothing rhythmical or repetitive, for the sound of a lock being picked, for the sound of breaking glass, and she grew very still in the waiting, her body tensed, almost rigid, almost holding her breath ... and the phone rang.

No voice responded to her answer: hello ... hello ... hello, the silence while she waited filled only with the void, the unknown beyond the receiver. Then a breath, a strong exhalation puffed into her ear, then another, and another, measured, rhythmical, menacing, a wordless, calculated threat. She hung up, snapped on the lights, and got out of bed.

Caller ID listed no number and displayed the words, *anonymous call*. She made decaf and thought of calling someone, but who? No one could do anything about this scary threat. The phone company would be useless, and she feared and distrusted the sheriff and his deputies. She was into something and alone. Did this have anything to do with the nursing home? Was someone stalking her for sex, for blood, for craziness, for another murder? She drank the coffee and read for an hour, then returned to bed, turned out the lights and crawled under the comforter ... and the phone rang. This time after a long pause, a voice, muted, deliberate, disguised, unknown to her, said, "Good girl, Helen. Now that your lights are out, go to sleep and don't worry. Just be careful to do your job and mind your own business, and nothing will happen to you. Follow doctor's orders, Helen darling, to the letter, and don't overstep your bounds. We think you already have, Helen my sweet ... what were you doing up so late tonight ... making notes? You don't keep a record do you, my precious? We'll find it if you do. You would make such a lovely vegetable lingering there in your own wards, what a shame and what a waste that would be, and believe me, we know how to do it. We're going home now ... Goooood night, Helen, precious."

Closed blinds, drawn draperies, locked windows and doors gave her no real sense of security there alone and vulnerable in the house isolated atop a wooded hill three miles out of town, someone out there, probably parked below the hill, watching. A motor started up, and remote rumbling receded into the distance. She lay rigid in bed, not daring to risk peeking under a lifted slat in the window blinds. Anyway, the car surely turned back toward the highway, running invisible in the night without lights until beyond the copse a half-mile away around a bend.

Who would sit in the after-midnight darkness watching her house? The night orderly, Ruble? If so, it would have to be his night off duty. She could find out. A perusal of the duty schedule when she arrived at work in the early morning would reveal whether he had the duty tonight or not. But no, he's too small-fry to be harassing her alone. Something bigger must surely be behind all this. The person out there tonight takes orders from someone in control, someone who knows she lives alone in grief since the loss of her husband. And surely the person knows, too, the circumstances of his death have left her suspicious and frightened. David Beckette, the most respected internist on County Hospital staff, healthy and handsome and very smart, alive and busy one day and gone the next; David and Helen Beckette, the most devoted couple in town, separated by death. She still reaches across to the other side of the bed in twilight sleep and finds the empty space and his unused pillow. A year has passed and the memory and the disbelief have not diminished, her head full to bursting with bad emotions: Grief, and anger at injustice, and suspicion, and a growing disgust with the negligent treatment of nursing home occupants. Nursing home! Ridiculous! Not a home for anybody – a place of business, for profit only. Ruble. Would Ruble, the orderly, abuse patients if they inconvenienced his girlfriend on duty? But she had no real reason to be suspicious of him other than his surliness and unfriendly demeanor, and some of the nurses wondering if he is the culprit.

Now someone brings this threat in the night to frighten her into silence and paralysis of purpose. David is gone forever; she might as well go, too. She might as well die for the cause. Nothing on earth holds any promise for happiness, anyway; the grief is interminable. Greed will continue to feed on the old and the helpless. She will not let this frighten her away; she will not lie still in the pretended disinterest of a coward. She dozed, then drifted in and out of light sleep until daylight.

In her office before 7:30 Helen, with the phone off the hook and the door closed, perused the records. Ruble Crouch had worked the midnight shift, so he was innocent of the events last night. She turned to the daily statistics. Deaths balanced against the total inventory and the patient admissions, plotted on the graph she worked over each night at home, continued to be a climbing line.

A secretary tapped on the door and entered without being asked. She said nervously, "The president of the board, Mr. Peter Mallory, insists on talking to you at once."

"No problem," she said, to dismiss the girl. She picked up the phone. Mallory had asked her to lunch while David still lived, and he had not waited very long after the funeral to become insistent. She always refused politely, offering him no encouragement. As the major stockholder in Golden Age, and president and practically the owner of the biggest bank in town, he usually got what he wanted, and his pursuit had become relentless. He made her nervous, his friendliness a threat, and her job at stake, she suspected, when she refused his overtures.

"Helen," he crooned when she answered, "How are you, my dear?"

"I'm fine thank you." She seethed with resentment. Did he know about last night? Did he know something about David's death? Did he expect to find her shivering with fright, ready to cry for help from a strong man waiting to rescue her? Did he recognize the harm done to patients by economic strictures on supplies and manpower? But she curbed her tongue.

"Great opportunity to talk business ... I'm driving up to Memphis this morning for lunch with the owner of the biggest HMO empire in the country, the world, in fact, Bin Kadsh himself, no less. As I'm sure you know by now, he's looking to buy our nursing home chain. I want you along, as an administrator, to listen in. It might prove very profitable to us in the future."

Us! God, the assumption infuriated her. Take your own nursing home administrator, take your stockholders, take your wife, but she simply said, "Oh, no. I would be out of place in such an important meeting. Though I do appreciate the offer, I think it would be more appropriate if you invited my boss, your administrator, Dan Rattner."

"Rattner! Why would one of the financial wizards of this world of ours want to gaze at Rattner across a lunch table rather than a face that could launch a thousand ships?"

Helen of Troy, the pretentious fake, probably the limit of his indoctrination into mythology, trying to kill her with his debonair erudition, fooling no one but himself. She wouldn't be seen at the zoo with this middle-aged sophomore. "Yes, but the face of Helen launched more than ships, and more than the Trojan War. Ultimately, she paid a terrible price."

"Helen? Who? Oh, yes. And what price was that?"

"Strangled in revenge for her debaucheries."

"Oh, really. But we are not talking anything like that here."

"Appearances are as condemning as circumstances."

"This is business, all business."

"Oh, Mr. Mallory, you do flatter me, but I won't go because I would be most uncomfortable. Thank you, anyway. I'm not a big-business person, and you need an expert for this one."

"Now Helen, there comes a time when everyone needs to take advantage of opportunities."

"I do agree with you on that."

"So change your mind, meet me at the front entrance of the hospital at ten, and we will be off. If you are worried about appearances, no one will know the difference."

The rash fool, the whole town talks about his escapades already: his used-up secretaries deluded into believing him to be serious, his gambling junkets with one or another available woman, his lecherous taste for much younger and not very bright women. She would not be added to his list. "I suppose that includes my boss, Rattner."

"He takes orders from me."

"No, thank you."

"Okay. I won't hound you anymore now. But Helen, we must have dinner one evening soon. I can set you straight on how to live a life of much greater fun and productivity. We must talk."

"I'm doing perfectly all right for my abilities and my circumstances."

"Oh, no. You are uselessly and endlessly grieving, and I intend to remedy that."

Yes, and what had he to do with the cause of her grief? The very idea of being seen alone in an automobile with the great lover, Mr. Peter Mallory, headed out of town! Revolting, and the word would spread through town on the winds of gossip, sullying the memory of David. Nor did she need the enmity of this dangerous man. She would be as diplomatic as possible. "Kind of you to think of that; maybe time will heal my loss of David, but I doubt it."

"I can wait if I have to. I'll be calling you."

At ten o'clock Helen worked at her desk, more at ease with Mallory gone, her door standing open. The administrator, Dan Rattner, appeared. So, he had not been invited to the Memphis meeting, and probably did not know about it. This she expected. Always secretive, Mallory tried to keep administration in the dark, and Rattner under constant stress to do the impossible financially and at the same time stay out of trouble for not being able to deliver quality care. She glanced up from her desk just as Rattner said, "May I help you?" to someone standing in the foyer. The person stepped forward, a tall thin man with graying streaks through a head of thick black curly hair.

"Yes, are you Mr. Rattner?"

"Yes."

"I'm John Colburn."

As they shook hands and exchanged the usual amenities, Rattner led the way down to his own office and the sound of their voices diminished behind closed doors. Colburn? Oh, yes the old, old lady Colburn down in Wing C, a hundred years old, but fully alert, cognizant of her surroundings, and a handful to manage. John Colburn?

He must be a relative. But she had never heard of him. And a startling change happened. What on earth? What is this? She blushed, a thrill down the middle of her belly, her solar plexus suddenly turbulent, the vibrations of John Colburn's deep mellifluous voice resonant down the hallway.

Across the desk, David studied her with a level gaze from his photographed face. Dear David's benign and trusting eyes, his slow, benevolent steadiness, the comfortable security and trust – his kind of love protected but did not consume, and the love she felt for him, love without fire, without uncontrolled passion. Now with this brief glimpse of the sensitive face and angular figure of a total stranger, an entirely new and intense emotion gripped her. God! She had heard about this, unbelievingly, and now it had happened without warning. She had hardly seen him, just a glance at the passing figure beyond her door: his erect, alert bearing, moving effortlessly, the air between them charged with a power transcending physical appearance, a message had emanated into her very being. Not possible; she would not let it. Who is he? What is he? Is he married? Is he taken? Is he straight? Forget it; she had too much strength and good sense to fall victim to irresistible desire. She sat perfectly still, hardly breathing, waiting, listening for sounds to begin in the hallway again, resisting the urge to rush out to meet him. The turmoil slowly subsided, her attention came back to reality and she moved to reach for the next waiting document, and gasped. She sat in a pool of warm fluid, the lubricant anointment of love.

In the lavatory, underpants down, she cleaned herself, stunned to disbelief – the controlled, super intelligent Helen instantly out of control, racing heart, grief colored with hope, grief beginning to fade in the midst of a new awareness. Who is he? What an astounding find! Would her luck turn to a blank wall, an obstruction? She rushed back to her office, closed the door, and turned to the work waiting to be done. As she began typing at the computer, the murmur of voices grew out in the vestibule. Rattner told his visitor goodbye; then she stopped typing and listened to silence, waiting, quelling the impulse to go out and introduce herself, or to accost Rattner for all the facts. To her relief, Rattner tapped on her door, entered without waiting, and announced, "We now have a heavyweight interested in the happenings here in paradise."

She laughed, "Oh?"

"Do you have any idea who that was?"

"The walk-in?"

"Yes."

"I heard him tell you, John Colburn?"

"Does that ring a bell?"

"A relative, I suppose, of old lady Colburn down on C Wing."

"His mother, and when he told me where he lives and what he does I knew then who he really is."

"I'm lost on that one."

"I knew from what I have read about him, the world-famous physicist, now employed at Huntsville, Alabama. He's the boy genius who helped perfect later improvements in the hydrogen bomb, the missile system, and the whole defense network and space program of this country. Already a rocket expert, guided missile authority, master of the electromagnetic realm, he now directs the development of advanced robotics and laser Intense Light. He's renowned, Washington's darling, politically powerful, and he can get what he wants out of the government bureaucracies. He could bring ruin down on the heads of deterrents."

"God, I hope so."

"He came to see me out a growing concern for the well-being of patients in this facility."

"Especially his mother?"

"Not selfishly so. His concern seems to be for those whose families will not, or financially cannot, hire extra help as he has done for his own mother."

"So he's the Colburn who pays Clara Bartley."

"Yes, and she not only rides herd on the care Rachel Colburn gets here, but I'm sure she fills his ear on what's happening to our system."

"Dan, do you suppose we have lucked up on a man who can deliver us and all places like us from this living hell?"

"Don't even say the words."

"Only a hope."

Then he came close, and almost whispering, said, "The walls in this place have ears like none other."

"Sorry, I will be vigilant."

"If you so much as think it, the gossip and the rumors thicken the air."

"I know."

On impulse she thought of telling him about the threats last night, but she controlled herself. Who could she really trust? So long as she said nothing, no one would know of her fright and her determination. Whoever is paying the stalker could also bring Dan Rattner to his knees financially and force him to cooperate. Even now, could Rattner be testing her, spying for the hidden hand? She would keep quiet and calm and wait, already having said too much. She wanted to know everything Rattner knew about John Colburn, but stopped the impulse and simply asked, "So, what does he have to offer?"

"Just his concern at the moment. He has observed the lack of personal attention some people suffer."

"God, is he ever right. And we don't have the personnel and we are not likely to in the near future, barring radical and unexpected changes."

"I fully expect help through his influence in Washington."

"Do you really think so?"

"I have spent only a few minutes with him, but as a result I know his benevolence is calm, his purpose undeviating, his charisma as electrifying as that of a zealot."

"What's to be done?"

"Make every effort we can to take care of the aged."

"Well, speaking of care, it's time for me to check on the wards again."

Down a hallway, she stopped at the sight of a familiar slender figure bent over a motionless form in a wheelchair within the far corner of a semi-private room. She turned through the door and approached. Clara Bartley looked up, tears running down her cheeks, but she never stopped the motions of feeding the slumped old man.

"What on earth, Clara?"

"I want you to see this, Helen. As sure as God, this man is starving to death. He can't feed himself, and no family member comes to help, and the aides simple put the tray down and leave. When they return later, they scold him for not eating; then take away the tray, food and all, that is, what the flies have left. It's a damned shame. Mr. Beazlie weighed a hundred and sixty pounds when he took sick, I've known him for twenty years, now he's down to ninety."

She brought another spoonful of an amorphous mass of soft diet and Beazlie opened his mouth like a voracious nestling and gobbled down the food.

"My God, look at that ... starving, hungry as hell, and helpless ... Helen, do me a favor. If I ever get Alzheimer's just shoot me will you? Jesus!"

"Why are you feeding him?" Helen asked, wondering if someone had hired her.

"Because he's sitting over here starving to death."

"Are you doing this out of the goodness of your heart?"

"I'm doing this because he's so damned pitiful and helpless."

"Is this the first time?"

"Hell, no. It's every time I come in this damned place, and not the only one."

"Where is his wife ... at work?"

"You know damned well where she is and what she's doing. At least you should, the whole town seems to."

"Well, we don't have enough manpower to feed such patients. And there is nothing I can do about it. We have just enough people to carry the trays back and forth."

"Then hire more."

"It's not within our budget."

"That means somebody's making too big a profit."

Helen thought, absolutely dead-on right, and loud about it, as usual, but she said, "Well, I will bring up the matter at the next board meeting, and in the meantime present it again to Dan Rattner."

"Okay, I believe you, but Rattner can't do a thing about it. He's not even a cog on the big wheel that turns this place."

Right again. Clara Bartley knows what goes on, a caring concerned person, incensed by the callousness of the system, but she talks too much and too loud. Helen wondered about her safety. Sooner or later someone would move to shut her up. And more than likely it would happen with no warning. But at the moment Helen wanted to change the subject.

"How is Mrs. Colburn?"

"The same. Every morning I find her in a mess, lying in wet clothes, with the buzzer in her hand, swearing she's been calling for help for hours. I go down to the front desk and confront them, and get the same excuses every time, always doing their best, can't stop her from playing with the buzzer button, tired of running down to the room for false alarms. This morning she had smeared excrement everywhere ... in her hair, under her nails, on the bedclothes, on her wheelchair, on the walls. She's got so much pride she wants to do for herself, always making things much, much worse."

"We would have a tough time without you."

"Oh, hell, she would have been dead long ago, but for me and for that son of hers, John Colburn."

Helen's pulse raced. "I've not met him."

"Wonderful man, absolutely devoted to her welfare. She still gives him hell, like he was a little boy again, and he just stands there by her bedside, smiling. You would never know he is world-famous, one of the powers in the scientific world, but not all that lucky. He lost a beautiful and devoted wife to cancer years ago and has had no luck finding another."

"How do you know that?"

"Oh, he confides in me. He's looked. But he says it just has to happen. It can't be forced. You either stumble upon the right one, or you never find her."

"Like roulette."

"Yeah, I suppose."

Helen wanted to ask questions, but she dared not. To ask what he looked like would be false, or coy to say the least. She would not let this be spoiled by a rumor. After a moment Clara started talking again.

"Anyway, I feel like I'm nursing two people, both mother and son. I think he's getting desperate, casting about for the right woman, and a bit reckless at it. I think he's so in love with love that he will have a hard time filling the empty place with a woman, a real woman, or more to reality he's likely to fill it with the wrong one. And he would be a tender and helpless morsel in the matrimonial clutches of a grasping female."

"Clara, what are you saying?"

"Well! He tools over here almost every weekend from Huntsville where he lives and works. It's not all that far, you know, and he's had to do with two of the local women, in particular. I think he's going soft, thinking of coming home, hoping to find here in this little town a good woman he cannot find in the wide-open world in which he lives. Maybe he thinks we still live in a simpler age of innocence in this small town. Little does he know."

"What?"

"Oh, those two especially have handed him a bunch of crap about their purity, just what he wants to hear, and not a word of truth in it."

She wanted ask who, but stopped herself and said "My God. Poor man."

"Yeah, right," spooning more food into Beazlie. "I've got to finish this and get back to Mrs. Colburn. She insists on feeding herself."

"And I've work to do." Helen turned back to the hallway and to the cafeteria. Good news and bad news – free all right, but what had he done to himself in the company of other women? Already she wanted to rescue him

10

John Colburn suffered the embarrassment and regrets of two disasters with Cambridge women, a double dose of frustration and lost hope within two years. The first he knew innately from the beginning to be just a surface event, surprisingly lifting him ever so briefly out of his loneliness for the right person, tinged as it was with only the remotest possibility for permanence. The second had undertow, still tugging, diverting and pulling more and more people into a stream of events and human strife fired by greed and money, or greed for money. The first happened little more than a year before he met Celeste, when he unwittingly walked into a trap baited by his own loneliness. He didn't plot it, or go looking for it. It just happened within minutes after he entered the Golden Age nursing home on a Saturday afternoon at the beginning of a weekend visit. Going directly to Rachel's room he found her sitting up in her chair beside the bed.

The sight of her always wrenched his sentiments and his regrets for the hard life she had lived, always at these moments the visions from his childhood rose to haunt him, memories of Rachel at the wash-pot doing the weekly wash regardless of weather. The big, waist-high cast-iron pot in the yard stood on brick-bats, the fire smoking and slow burning and not as hot as it should be from the green wood sizzling beneath it, the pine slabs she has chopped into manageable lengths herself. Her stooped body, bundled against the cold, she poked the clothes from time to time with a long stick in the water boiling and steaming and of foul gray color and bubbling with yellow lye soap she made herself from grease and ashes or grease and lye.

He remembers the bleeding fingers. Lye soap burns away flesh, leaving raw and red bleeding nail beds. She never folded under endless hard work, in the cold, suffering from the cold, the fatigue, the poverty, her determination relentless. And in those scenes, out in the open wind-blown yard, the boiled clothes had to be rinsed twice, through two baths, and this water did not come from a hydrant. She drew it from the well, bucket by bucket, and placed in the tubs. Wet clothes in the washing had to be wrung by hand, then dried on the line where they froze temporarily with sudden winter weather changes. She ironed every morning until 2 a.m., never sent a child to school in soiled or wrinkled clothes – at an age when he was still too small to lift the ax himself.

As he entered the room he spoke. She looked up and said, "Who's that? I can't see you."

"John, Momma."

She held up her arms, and he bent to kiss her cheek.

"My goodness, I'm so glad to see you."

"Why Momma, I'm here every weekend."

"I know it. I wish you could stay all the time."

"I have a job, you know."

"Oh, I realize that, but you know how it is. And this time before you leave, I want to have a talk with you."

"Okay. Let's talk now."

A nurse bustled in, shaking a thermometer.

"Time for your temp, Mrs. Colburn."

John stepped toward the open door.

"Be a few minutes," the nurse said. "Time to change her bed."

In the room directly across the hallway, a tall slender woman in a deep black dress, her back turned, bent over the side of a wheelchair. She shifted position, revealing the slumped form of Beazlie – Alzheimer's: advanced. With a few careful strokes she finished shaving him, then gently wiped the foam off his face with a cloth towel, picked up a pan of water, and disappeared into the lavatory.

In sentiments awash, inner turmoil verging toward tears, John sauntered down the hallway to the end of the wing and stopped at a picture window. He gazed over the landscape beyond, toward the new construction under way in every direction, steel skeletons taking form, brick walls rising, another wing near completion on County Hospital next door, a wing going up on the rear of Golden Age, and a huge parking ramp rising across the street. New ditches gutted the grounds, pipe partially laid, cable strewn across raw red clay mounds awaiting burial, heavy equipment creating an uproar in the Saturday afternoon quiet. Yellow hard-hats bobbed up and down among the piles of dirt. Progress! He would never have believed this little town had such growth potential. These grounds on which the hospital and nursing home were spreading topsy-turvy had been the site of Tidwell's barn and cow pasture, and a small airport where World War I pilots kept their planes during the thirties. Here they took off on clear days to stunt fly over the town square and the campus, doing spins, simulating aerial combat, to the astonishment of gawking students and farmers.

Wheels rolled toward his back; he turned. From directly behind the slumped form of Floyd Beazlie, the woman in black gazed steadily into John's eyes, her long slender fingers grasping the chair-back as she pushed it forward until the extended foot rests touched the wall beneath the windowsill. Beazlie's pasty face, sagging in gravid inertia, showed no emotion, no recognition. He never raised his eyes toward the window, his destroyed mind in the grasp of a horrid visitation, a wretched, plethoric stupidity. A great weight of dullness bent him down into a humped curve, the back of his head wrenched over to the right, his face perpetually twisted to the left, his gaze aimed off at something in the distance, but focused on nothing.

A full head of tight bronze curls, light blue eyes clear as ice, a long slender neck, a very slim waist, and tiny breasts barely mounding beneath a thin covering of clothes – her appearance already told him volumes before she spoke. No cultivated rose, this wild flower in all its tough, natural beauty, he thought. A hint of feline rapacity animated the pretty face.

"Hello, I'm Sarah Beazlie," she said as she set the brake on the chair with a pointed shoe toe.

"John Colburn."

"Yes, I know. I visit your mother every day when I come out to see Floyd. She's such a wonderful woman."

"Thank you for saying so, and thank you for visiting her. She gets very lonesome."

"Oh, I would do anything in the world for her. She lets Clara Bartley come across the hall and feed Floyd at noon when I can't be here."

"Clara does that on her own, but of course we support her in it."

"I can't be here all the time because I have to work."

John already knew from Clara. No one showed up to feed Floyd Beazlie at night either, not on a regular basis, just sporadically, but not often, Sarah's real whereabouts and activities a source of gossip. But he rationalized: what could Sarah's life be like in this trap? How much of this grind can a normal human mind tolerate without breaking? How much denial of normal and human appetites and biological needs can be tolerated without disrupting social barriers in this living hell? There in the warm, sunshiny end of the hallway, by the bright window, her floral perfume evoked memories of church women, fanning in the heat of Sunday sermons, an aura and benign aroma of goodness. The sight of her tenderly shaving her husband's face had filled him with a rush of sentiment. Excited by goodness, he discounted all the hinted rumors, and never thought her emotionally capable of any deception.

"Well, we will be glad to help anyway possible."

"I do appreciate that. But what I need most is somebody to talk to. I go for weeks at a time from work to here, without seeing another soul, and it gets me down, nobody on my level, nobody who understands." She looked directly into his face, sincere and defeated.

John recognized the overture as an overture. But beneath their gazes, a distraction, a subliminal sound, a subtle change caught his attention. Floyd's complexion had darkened, and he seemed to be straining against the twisted head posture and the restraints across his belly. His speechless existence could produce no word, not even a grunt, but his body posture and reaction expressed an angry helplessness, an objection, an impotent outrage. He actually seemed to swell, to reach a larger size. Awareness! God yes! In all his static bewilderment he had caught the meaning of the overture, too, in a helpless, speechless, soundless rage.

"Okay, I'm back here every weekend, and I will step across the hall and talk to you and Floyd. At the moment I had better get back to Miss Rachel."

"Time for me and Floyd to finish our walk." She bent forward over the chair back, unlocked the wheels with the pointed toe, and said, "Come on, sweetheart, let's go out in the sunshine." Floyd's face had resumed its grayish pallor, his body diminished and collapsed again against the restraining cloth around his waist, tethering him in a duel hell.

John returned to Rachel's room, sat in a chair at the foot of her bed and read the paper while she slept soundly, sitting in her own bedside chair. Half an hour later she awoke.

"John, I want to talk to you."

"Okay, Momma."

"I want us to sell the house in town and go back out on the farm and finish the house your daddy started, then live out there so I can have a garden and some chickens and turkeys and a nice healthy milk cow."

"Who's going to milk her?"

"Why I am, of course."

"Who's going to weed the garden?"

"I am. If I can just get someone to plow it up every spring."

"All right. I'll do even better than that. I'll buy you a mule, and we'll get an old farm plow at a flea market, and you can do the plowing yourself."

She cocked her head back and strained to see him.

"I wish I could see you, I'm nearly blind, but I bet you've got a smirk on your face, you devil you, just teasing me. You know good and well I never hooked up a mule in my entire lifetime. Did everything else in the way of work, but not that."

He chuckled. "And you are teasing me."

"Well, I got a right to live in the past if I want to. God knows I can't do much living in the present, not in my shape."

"Look around you, Mamma. You have an alert mind, your hearing is sharp, you are aware of being alive, you have your memories — these are all blessings."

"I know it. I know I've still got a lot to be thankful for."

"And we are thankful to have you around."

"Oh, while we are on the subject of transient states, have you decided to give the farm to the university?"

"Now?"

"No, in your will. You were talking about it."

"Well, what do you think of the idea?"

"A great honor to your ancestral name, which the gift would preserve, and the land could never pass on to other hands. Could they put it to good use?"

"They have assured me they can, and they liked my idea of creating a huge pharmaceutical farm for the study of drugs produced by plants. And I liked their idea for using it also as a training ground for survival tactics, utilizing the woods, the rivers, the lakes."

"Have you discussed this with the chancellor, what's his name? I've known every one of them since I was in high school, let me see, Oh yes, Bruce Madison."

"Right. We are friends and I have talked about it at length with him. He's enthusiastic. Three thousand acres added to the existing campus would triple its size, geographically. I have a letter of intention from him, committing the university to accepting the gift in perpetuity. It would always be a part of the school."

"Well, you have my blessings."

"Thank you, Mama; I will tell Bruce."

She stopped talking and dozed again. When she began snoring, he slipped out of the room, intending to go to the farm. He would return later.

In the distance, as he approached the exit, Sarah Beazlie arose from a chair in the lobby and went out the door. She appeared at his side when he reached the sidewalk

"I hope you don't mind. I was waiting, hoping you would be coming out soon. I want to talk."

Her frankness increased his trust. "Oh, not at all," he said as they sauntered side by side. "Let's talk. Shall we go somewhere for coffee, tea? It's too early in the day for cocktails."

"Where are you staying?"

"At the Uptowner."

"Under the circumstances, that won't do. I'm surprised you're not at your mother's little house in town."

"I'm spooked there alone."

"Well it's not all that far to my home, so let's go there."

"Where?"

"Close to Abbeville. Why don't you follow me? I'm in a red Honda. Meet you at the gate."

"I'll walk you."

"No. That only increases your exposure. This town gossips, you know."

"Okay."

"When I enter my garage, park beside me."

"Right."

The garage door came down, hiding both cars. Sarah led the way through an attached walkway into a kitchen open to a house with few walls. On the opposite side of a large open space a gigantic sofa awaited with open arms beneath a large picture window framing a vista of woods.

"Tea?" she asked.

"Tea would be fine."

While she worked rapidly with kettle and teapot, he sat on a bar stool and watched. The immaculate house, with modest furnishings and walls of grooved, veneered plywood panels, smelled of gas heaters.

"I live here by myself since Floyd had to be confined, and man, does it get lonesome."

"It's certainly quiet and peaceful."

"Not a sound of highway or neighbor. The nearest one is half a mile away."

"And, I notice you have a pretty vegetable and flower garden alongside the driveway." It had reminded him of Rachel's gardens when he was growing up, the exuberant growth of vegetables and flowers above the loamy soil.

"Oh, yes. I love to garden."

Her delicate and clean hands on the kitchen utensils, the nails perfectly manicured and perfectly detailed, the skin of her face and neck and hands smooth, silky, and nowhere tanned or sun-burned – probably wears a sun bonnet and gloves and a scarf, he thought.

"I do too," he said. "By nature I'm a food gatherer, but had to break myself of the habit. It took up too much time."

"I understand. You need all your time to write your books."

"Exactly." How did she know? She didn't look the part of reading physics for the masses.

"And there's the one thing I want to talk about." She finished loading the tea tray and picked it up. "Come on. Let's go to the living room."

From a sitting position on the couch, she poured and served while talking. "Clara has been telling me about your writing. I want to write a book on my experience with Alzheimer's, and I thought you might help me get started."

"Well, indeed, but nobody can tell you how to write."

"Just help getting started."

"All right, anytime."

"I'm not quite ready yet."

"I can imagine it's been rough."

"From the first day, and I'll never forget the way it started."

"Not all at once?"

"Yes, just right out of the blue. Oh, maybe there had been a little forgetting, bills not paid here and there, dates mixed up, but nothing to prepare me for the unexpected."

"I would have thought the beginning subtle and the disease slowly progressive."

"No. It started this way. In pretty weather we always had our last cup of coffee after breakfast, right out there on the porch swing, before he went to work. On that particular morning he finished his coffee, then just sat there, looking off down the hill like he was in deep thought. After a few minutes he asked me what day it was. I told him, but he just sat. Then he asked ... he looks at me with a strange expression on his face and says, 'Where are we?' In a few minutes I realized he was completely confused."

"He never improved?"

"Never. After a few minutes, on that morning, he got up and went to his car and drove off. But he didn't go to work. Several hours later the sheriff called me at my job. Somebody had found him parked on a side street staring off into space. He didn't know who or where he was. I went and got him and took him home and it's been awful ever since."

"My God."

"My God is right. At first he was unmanageable, trying to use his car, and wandering off in the woods. We would have to go find him, the neighbors helping. And he was mean, strong as an ox, and he bruised and battered me. He got worse until there was no way I could handle him at home. He finally had to be committed down at Jackson where he stayed until he got in the condition he's in now, so bad off he can't harm anyone, or run away."

She put her teacup down on the coffee table and reached for a tissue.

Tears trickled down her cheeks. "I want the world to know how bad this is, what it does to families, what it does to the poor person who gets it. Oh, he was such a hard-working man, so fun-loving. We laughed and talked, made love sometimes three times a day, and went camping and fishing and took trips in the camper, and just enjoyed life and each other. Now look at him, reduced to a helpless, speechless, mindless ... Oh! Dammit, worse than an infant! At least a baby can cry, and coo, and look at you with twinkling eyes, but this ... this is a living death."

She had moved against his side. Half turned, she laid an open palm on his thigh while she wiped tears with the other hand. Her face came close to his, her lips parted, her eyes hungry and searching, an unhappy woman looking for sympathy and love. Heat from her face radiated against his cheek.

He would try to remember afterward what happened and how it started, but the rapid movements would never be clear, his mouth inside her lips, the tip of her tongue searching, exploring, her hand moving up his thigh, his hands on the buttons of her dress front.

Afterwards they lay in the shadows and talked. She had closed the blinds while he undressed. She needed and wanted a buddy, somebody to take her on short trips, to get her out of town for brief respites, someone to talk to, an intelligent person who could understand her predicament and not condemn her for being normal, someone who could be discrete and not start gossip. And she would love to go fishing and camping again. But it had to be with someone who could be trusted completely. She couldn't divorce poor Floyd just because of his illness. So she needed a life to live until the end came. She didn't want John, the first man she could trust, to think she was bad. She had to be so careful about gossip, and she had been deprived for so long she just couldn't help herself. Thank God she had found him, a real man, a completely honest and trustworthy man.

Deferent and understanding, flattered by her trust in him, he knew a satisfaction, though tainted by the circumstances. This called for largesse of spirit exceeding restrictive and cruel moralities. He needed and had been hoping for a buddy, too.

They talked until the day began to fade. They would make the most of these quiet, secretive hours together, short drives to see the countryside, even trips lasting only a day or two. She could get her sister to feed and shave Floyd in her absence. And John would help her get started on her book. And the book would be a success because she would write from the heart, and the heart is always honest. At twilight she said, "I've got to get back over to Golden Age and feed Floyd his dinner."

"Yes, and I best pay my respects tonight. I have to be in Huntsville by two o'clock tomorrow, which means an early start."

"I know a wonderful little hidden place out at College Hill for a late dinner."

"Great."

"We can go from the parking lot at the nursing home ... I'll drive," she said.

"What time?"

"Let's meet at my car at eight o'clock."

Cooper's Barbeque occupied an old clapboard store behind a rusty abandoned gasoline hand-pump out of use for forty years. John and Sarah followed the owner across the main dining room with its three tables covered in oilcloth, down a passageway to a tiny stall with one small table and two chairs, lit by a single candle three inches in diameter and a foot tall. A drawn curtain covered the entrance. The waiter served the only entree, barbequed spare ribs with blazed vegetables, and red wine. The privacy lent an air of old-world intrigue, a separate and private dining booth for a secret assignation lasting all evening, in a public place, guarded and sheltered. Rough planking covered the walls, the raw wood reminiscent of a stable, the food delicious, the wine ordinary. They talked of the future, of their trips and time together. Forgetting their nursing home burdens and sadness, they said nothing of the past or the present. Well into the meal, she asked, "When are you coming back?"

"Next weekend."

"Do you dance?"

"Yes."

"Why don't we go to Memphis Saturday evening, and dance, and spend the night?"

"All right, I'll come over on Friday and get the preliminaries out of the way. Do you know where to go?"

"Yes. Well ... that is, I know where Floyd and I used to go. I guess they are still open."

The time passed quickly. The lights went out in the main dining room. "I think we have been given a hint," John said. Only the proprietor remained in the restaurant when they left after eleven o'clock.

Back at the parking lot, she said, "Follow me home and spend the night."

He had more fun Saturday night a week later at Buffalo Bill's out on Poplar Avenue than he had had in many years. Sarah Beazlie could follow his leads easily and naturally. The country western band played for an hour, and she melded into every move of the Cotton Eye Jo, the Texas Two-step, the waltz, the western swing. Dressed in a little red shift, as slender as a reed, as agile as a gazelle, laughing all the while, she lifted his spirits, and stirred his heart. The western band left the room, still playing, and the big band came in the opposite door playing, and took their seats. The music never stopped – shades of New York in other days, the foxtrot, the swing, the waltz. They ate lamb chops ravenously, drank red wine, and talked of their plans for little short trips here and there. In the deafening noise they had to speak directly into each other's ears. She stuck the tip of her little sharp tongue into his concha and tickled, tantalizing his lonesome soul. The band played a cha cha, then a rumba, and a tango, as well as big bands can play such music, and she followed these steps, too. This surprised and pleased him; he had found a real buddy. What a hell of a lot of fun. When they left at 1 a.m. another would-be cowboy rode the bucking mechanical bull in the lobby to the noisy hooting and cheering of cowboy imitators around the rink in big western hats.

On a king-sized bed in the Peabody she took him as she had six days earlier, eager, her passion high-pitched. They talked. God, it had been tough, doing without all these long years, but she had saved herself for something special like this, and now she had no regrets. But she had to be so careful. You can't trust many people not to talk; in fact, she had trusted no one until she met him. He lay with her encircled in an arm, listening, feeling a deep empathy for her and a regret for her sick husband, no longer the cognizant human being she had married, but he felt no remorse. Cruel abstinence made no sense in these circumstances. How lucky to have found her; now he had a friend to go places with him, someone to talk to, someone who had experienced his same grief, someone who understands and can be trusted to be discreet. How lucky indeed. They fell asleep talking and awoke at 8 o'clock, and moved together again.

After a leisurely breakfast they drove back to Cambridge, and parted in mid afternoon. She had to be at the Golden Age to feed her husband at five, and he would go to visit with Miss Rachel. He would call next morning before returning to Huntsville.

At six o'clock Monday morning Clara phoned him at the Uptowner Motel. She woke him up. "Are you going by your mother's house on your way out of town?"

"Yes, for breakfast."

"Good, I'll meet you there at eight o'clock. I got to talk to you."

"Anything wrong?"

"I'll tell you when I get there."

At Rachel's home he fixed himself a breakfast and had just finished eating when Clara stormed in the back door. Without preliminaries she said, "Well, so you've got a little brown mole on your pecker."

John blushed, his mouth dropped open, he stammered. "What ... what ... what do you mean?" Right, he did have a brown mole.

"And it's about an inch out along the shaft on the right side, like at three o'clock."

He said nothing. How would she know?

"And you had a great time in Memphis, you can dance like a pro, and you know how to satisfy a girl in bed, and you are polite to the help and over-tip, and you made love Saturday night until she was completely whipped, and again when you woke Sunday morning, and you had hickory smoked sausage and scrambled eggs for breakfast, and you had lamb chops and red wine at dinner Saturday night at Buffalo Bill's."

"Right on all counts, Clara. What's up?"

"What's up? Man, the bird is up, and singing, too, singing loud and clear."

"What?"

"That mealy-mouthed, two-timing, lying bitch you were with is telling everything you said and did from Saturday a week ago to the minute you got back from Memphis yesterday afternoon, including all your phone calls from Huntsville during the week. She hadn't been in the door two minutes before she was phoning the glad tidings to her dearest friend, who happens to be the biggest gossip in town. Now everybody knows you have a brown mole on your pecker. And they know every word you said in confidence to her. They can't wait to see where you are taking her next, and what you are going to do with all the fish you two intend to catch."

"Good God."

"Do you want to hear more?"

"No."

"Well there's plenty more you need to hear."

"But she is so brave and deprived, all this time without love while her husband has been totally incapacitated."

"Bullshit! There's a guy at her house every day, a carpenter. Repairs things and works her garden."

"She does her own gardening."

"The hell she does. She hasn't set foot in it, not even to pick what he raises. He complains to the winds about that. It's a known fact all through the countryside. And he spends the nights with her and some weekends and they go on trips, leaving his wife at home, and I feed poor old starving Beazlie."

John remained silent. No wonder she had no calluses on her hands, no broken nails, no sunburn. Then he said, "There's more, I take it."

"Oh, yes."

"Damn!"

"Damn is right. And I'll bet she told you she hadn't been dancing in Memphis since her husband got sick."

"That she did."

"A big lie, the biggest! She burns the road from here to there with every Tom, Dick, and Harry who can sneak off from his wife on weekends. Oh yes, more of everything, including men. You don't have to worry your head about her. She's been taken care of more than if she was married to a healthy man. Lots of guys like to trot out to her house when the carpenter is not there."

"We had to hurry back yesterday afternoon so she could go feed Beazlie."

"That's another big lie. She fed him twice recently, last night and last Sunday, all for your benefit, just putting on a show."

"You don't mean it."

"Oh, how I wish I didn't. For his sake."

"What now?"

"Drop it, man."

"I promised to call her this morning."

"You are a damned fool if you do. What are you going to say to her? Whatever it is will be broadcast like all the rest. But if you don't call and you don't say anything to her she will have nothing more to betray."

"You are right. I simply walk away?"

"And keep walking."

"Damn. And I trusted her."

"You are too big and too important to be kept a secret. She had to let the world know what she had found."

"I don't feel that way about myself."

"I know, but she does, and so do most of the people who have heard about you. And everybody either knows or knows about the Colburns."

"You think I should not try to explain to her?"

"Leave it alone right where it is. Anything else you do will lead to more of the same. She does not have the ability to keep her mouth shut. Conquest is her idea of love."

"So be it."

"And by the way."

"What?"

"Congratulations."

"What does that mean?"

"She says you are really hung."

"Ohhh."

On the next Saturday morning, Clara, bent over the bed when he entered the room, straightened up with soiled bedclothes in her hand, her nose turned up, and said, "You better wait outside until I get this cleaned up."

Without a word he turned back and caught a glimpse, across the hallway, of Beazlie slumped over in a wheelchair by his bedside, in the room alone, his mouth hanging open, his face slack and wrenched to the left. On the bedside table, the breakfast tray stood untouched, a pile of scrambled eggs and bacon now the sumptuous banquet for three busy flies. The coffee cup stood full nearly to the brim, brown rings forming above the fluid level. John squelched an impulse to enter the room and feed Beazlie. No! Neither the contaminated food nor the specious gesture, and under the circumstances he could be accused of poisoning him, or choking him. An aide entered the room. "Oh, mah goodness, Mistah Beazlie, yew outa' be 'shamed yo' self, yew ain't ate a bite o' yo' food," she said as she picked up the tray and left, the flies following, flying in circles. Beazlie didn't move, nor did his facial expression change as a string of saliva drooled down onto his lap.

John hurried down the hallway to wait by the picture window and to watch the construction site. Clara joined him in a few minutes, her face sweaty, hair down in strings. She brushed both temples with the backs of her hands. "Wheee. Boy, was that another mess."

"What's going on?"

"Same old thing. I come in here and find her in another pile of her own filth. God knows how long she's been lying in it."

"She'll get bed sores that way."

"Damn right she would if I didn't ride herd on this sorry bunch every damned day."

"What's to be done?"

"Nothing. This is the way it is. I'll just have to watch her."

"I want you to know the family appreciates this."

"I know it, and that helps me to keep going. But I'm concerned about you. Are you doing all right?"

"Yes, I'm okay."

"I'm really sorry about Sarah Beazlie."

"Yeah. Me too, and I see no one fed him his breakfast."

"Of course not. I don't think she's been here since last Sunday night."

"God."

"Oh yes, she's got other fish to fry. And man is she mad. You hadn't been out of town an hour when she called me looking for you. When she found out you had left without calling, she blew up. And I just told her that her talking had got back to you and that was it."

"I should have told her myself."

"No, no ... uhhhh, uh. You say nothing and she's got no ammunition. Right now she's spouting off in the beauty parlor where everybody can hear it, high and low alike."

"Well, I meant well."

"I know you did. Nobody knows you like I do; I know you are a good man and you have a soft heart. But next time, don't stoop to conquer."

"I didn't. It just happened."

"Like with everything else, you got to pick and choose."

"Happenstance. That's all we've got in this world, happenstance – for life, for death, for romance, for love, for health, for wealth, you name it."

"Man, you got that right."

He never saw Sarah Beazlie again, but he saw Floyd Beazlie alone, slumped in his wheelchair beside the tray of drying, flyblown, untouched food. John had gone back into limbo for the many months until this Easter week. The episode with Celeste had ended just as abruptly, but he knew he would see her again and in an entirely different light. Through her he had entered into a world of war and unknown dangers.

11

When she arrived at Tunica with Mallory, Celeste Howard went to a gaming table and played at playing, secretively watching and waiting for him to disappear, his short posture slumped and diminishing toward distant shadows deeper into the caverns, his walk a slouch as if carrying guilt, the coattail wrinkled. He thought she didn't know where he really went, pretending urgent business with someone in a remote office. While he presented himself to a receptionist, quaking and posing his importance, all bluster, Celeste left the gaming table and went to secret doors, and entered informally into rooms hidden to him. There, Thornton Webb, the black-haired, black-eyed giant who ran the place, gave her his ferocious attention for a good forty-five minutes while Mallory, waiting, fidgeting, just beyond the walls, idly fingered the glossy pages of almost-pornographic magazines, cooling his heels in tepid and jittery insignificance among those he knew to be above him.

The after-love confidences with Thornton had grown to be more revealing. He described the structure of the organization, telling her about Fritz Kramer, the go-between and messenger and enforcer, more or less, for the many casinos in Tunica and Las Vegas and on the Gulf Coast among other gambling towns. He told her about Lapkin Lewis, the silent lawyer pulling strings behind the scenes, and about Kadsh himself, the recent outsider investing big money from HMO and nursing home profits, an unseemly amount, possibly most of it from other sources.

"Drugs?" she asked too quickly, without pause for caution, Thornton just looked at her steadily, saying nothing, while she sat naked across his belly looking down at his dark-haired intensity. Then she knew she had struck a spark at the truth, and she knew better than to breathe a word of it outside his office.

She informed Thornton Webb again about conditions in Cambridge. He used this information when he greeted Mallory later in an adjacent office, and his decisions and actions were based on this information and not on what Mallory had to say. As usual, Mallory never knew the difference. He joined her at a gaming table hours later, smug and cocksure about keeping her in the dark. She let him get away with his air of superiority.

When they drove home the next morning, Celeste appeared to be asleep in the sharply reclined front seat, with her eyes closed, thinking of other men, of John Colburn among them, and once again imagined being Mrs. John Colburn, new wife of the renowned physicist. Too tame for her, she decided.

At home Celeste Howard wiled another afternoon away, the imagery of decay haunting her reverie. Two of the four posts on the back porch had rotted across at floor level and hung loose, squeaking in the wind. One more and the roof would collapse. Her world might go with it, and the shadow grew longer. Dear Jake, such precious memories, her only real love ever in this world. She glanced at his face on the wall over the fireplace; tears welled up and ran down her cheeks as she wept again. The older dog reared up and cocked his head to one side, his ears alert upward, and made eye contact. Oh, Jake! My Jake! Died and left me nearly destitute. Dammit! This was too much. But she had hope. It's time for something to happen; she sensed it and she needed to know. Damn Mallory!

She got off the couch, phoned Deputy Sheriff Wyndham Jones and invited him to dinner. After the love making, maybe she could find out something, maybe persuade him to reveal plans, if he actually knows. Then she went out on the balcony for her usual sunbath, when she had the time and the weather was right. She wore nothing. A worn ragged quilt draped over an awry rail shielded her nakedness from the neighbors' eyes.

After Jones arrived, he did not know or would not tell any details. He proceeded gloomily to drink too much wine before dinner, and snored in bed immediately after finishing his performance too quickly and rolling off her insatiate belly onto his back. He slept soundly for two hours. "Give 'em time," was the most she could wheedle out of him. He left before eleven o'clock, and she knew he did not head home.

Near midnight Helen Beckette opened the built-in safe hidden behind the foldout shelf doors on the back wall of her kitchen pantry, removed a briefcase, and took it to her bedside. With all blinds closed, the doors carefully locked, all lights out except the bedside lamp, she crawled under the covers, opened the briefcase, and began to study her notes again. The only leads becoming obvious didn't add up, so far. Perhaps seemingly insignificant and unrelated bits of information woven together would reveal a pattern sooner or later. One glaring fact had become obvious – the death rate in Golden Age had slowly climbed since David disappeared from the scene. True enough, but surely there had to be another reason for premeditated murder.

Could the name Isaac Dodson be connected? She turned the ledger pages to the D's, and studied her notes on Dr. Dodson, the town's busiest internist since David Beckette died. He neglects his duty to inpatients of the Golden Age. His attendance has become more and more erratic and infrequent. More and more patients die while waiting for medical attention. He shows no concern for the old and the helpless. David had said years ago he thought money motivated Dodson, not the pursuit of excellence.

Helen has made private and careful inquiries over a period of months. Dodson is on the lay boards of County Hospital, the Golden Age nursing home, and the People's Bank, and a holder of stock in all three. So he has a vested interest in the profits. The bank is heavily invested in both the hospital and the nursing home. The more money spent to maintain the daily existence of patients in the nursing home, the less the profits from the flat rate for health care. A patient death causes no financial loss, but a life prolonged with life support and antibiotics and other expensive medications and equipment lowers the profits. Under the circumstances, Dodson makes money whether they live or die, but more when they die. From the relentless supply of waiting patients, each empty bed fills immediately. And with these new admissions the sudden despondent atmosphere of nursing home incarceration has a profound psychological effect, and many die within a few days or a month or so. These are the profitable ones, in and out with no expensive treatment. So years ago, when David Beckette on his daily rounds started a spate of special treatment every afternoon, transferring many of those in trouble over to County Hospital for treatment, the profits took a dive. David's death has made a difference in the profits, saving hundreds, even thousands of dollars per patient for the investors. David did his work in an air of kindness and benevolence, with no motivation except compassion. To restore the benefits and protection the patients lost with his death would require authority, someone to step in and order better medical attention. This had to be done, one way or another, but such a person might be exposed to the same fate David suffered. Who would do it? She will have to, herself. She will need to find and hire the person as soon as she has the evidence she is looking for.

She flipped the pages to the C's. Ruble Crouch had been hired over her objections five years ago. Peter Mallory wanted him hired to work off his debts. Mallory had brought him out of the state penitentiary, Parchment. Now Ruble routinely works the night shift, doing orderly duties, carrying bedpans, pushing loaded wheelchairs and stretchers in the halls. When Helen enters one wing or another of the home before 7 a.m. she often encounters Ruble Crouch with a mop and a mop bucket, on the tail end of the midnight shift. Ruble doesn't speak, busy as he is mopping the floor, nor does he move aside when she reaches for a handful of records. His stance exudes silent and sullen indifference, if not hostility and arrogance, with his peers and superiors; he does not give a damn for politeness. He couldn't be fired without a long string of citations, and no one has anything on him in writing, not yet, and not likely.

For the past three years, according to hearsay, he has lived with a licensed practical nurse, Sybil Snyder, who supervises Wing B on the graveyard shift. Administration honors their request for the same schedule now, midnight to 7 a.m. Ruble covers the entire institution in the quiet hours of the morning and returns as frequently as possible from the darkened and lonely caverns of the hallways to loiter and banter with Sybil at the nurse's station until called to another errand. Other nurses have described this scene and reported this behavior numerous times. Sybil's short cropped blonde hair, showing black roots and revealing large flap-like ears, accentuates a long nose and face; her tall skinny frame and long legs move with calculated indolence, her stark white skin almost ghostlike in the pools of nighttime light. Ruble's dark bronze coloring, his curly, close-cropped, copper hair blends in the shadows where he is almost invisible near her in the dead of the night. They hover together and giggle. She suffers an attitude: "I don't take no damn shit off no damn patient."

Violence happens in the night. Too many old, defenseless people have been found on morning rounds with unexplained black eyes, and face and arm bruises. But proof of Ruble's connection to the physical violence has not been found. Rattner has no reason to fire Ruble. Administration has no progressively documented proof of wrongdoing, and Ruble has been given no warnings. They would have a discrimination suit on their hands. They need proof, but his work in the wards at night is valuable. He knows how to use catheters for the obstructed, how to take temperatures, how to check pulses, and how to help the nurses with many other duties.

From appearances Ruble does not get adequate sleep in his hours off duty. He dozes on the job, hidden in dark corners near Wing B. This Helen knows. And she has heard the talk about him. In the daytime, when he is supposed to be sleeping, he has been seen often on the Sardis Reservoir, traveling at high speed in a long, sleek powerboat. The same rig frequents the roads on a red trailer, towed by a spanking new three-quarter-ton pickup with dual rear wheels. The equipage, the boat and trailer and truck, altogether cost at least ninety if not a hundred grand. Ruble and Sybil together don't make enough to afford the truck, the boat, or the house they live in six miles south of town, a real home, a real house, no mobile-home, trailer-court junk for them. Money comes from another source. Someone is paying him or her or both for another service, people say, and he is losing sleep in the endeavor. And where does money come from, huge wads of cash, in a place like this? Drugs, a distinct possibility, or hidden nasty work like egging on the fringes of death, Helen wonders. Could such evil really be going on under their very noses? Ruble fits both bills, and he has the upper hand. Everybody is afraid to touch him.

Is a plan being used deliberately to eliminate the tenacious patients who are costing the most, those who require frequent antibiotic therapy and other expensive drugs and treatment to fight off infection, heart failure, and other recurrent assaults on their survival? Ruble moves through the long dark hallways after dark without anyone knowing exactly what he is doing. He has startled her more than once with his chilling ability to appear silently out of nowhere. And the ledger further reveals the facts. Many old people die in their sleep in the long stretch from midnight to daybreak, and most of those who go this way are high maintenance. This evidence cannot be ignored. But where can she turn? She cannot trust Rattner's passive, indecisive manner in the crisis of a showdown. He probably would naively turn to Mallory for advice. She and Rattner have not discussed Mallory.

What about John Colburn? Maybe his genius would spill over into other disciplines, or is he just a nerd, or an ineffectual sophist? Most likely, the practical genius, but he has trouble enough of his own without knowing it, according to Clara. She felt sleepy and glanced at the clock. Time has disappeared, twelve-thirty already. She closed the folder around her notes and replaced it in the briefcase, removed a handful of loose papers for perusal, and the phone rang. She jumped, reached for the receiver, and answered. The voice came this time without hesitation.

"Hello, darling. Guess what, we can almost hear you thinking. You would be surprised at the sophisticated equipment we have for surveillance. It helps us to know what's going on. And we want to tell you that you shouldn't be staying up like this worrying yourself over things you can do nothing about."

The menacing tone surprised her and she gasped.

After a brief hesitation and a snide sound, almost a snicker, the voice continued, "Now don't be frightened, dear. We won't do anything to you, not tonight anyway. But we do want to discuss death with you, Helen darling. Death is one of God's most sacred instruments. He uses it every day in this world, millions and millions of times. For every life, no matter how insignificant, there is a death just as significant for the lowliest as for the highest. It evens out in the end to zero. Therefore, you must realize that death is just as important as life to God. This finality is for everyone, sooner or later. It's a matter of when, my sweet. The very best any of us can do is to delay this inevitable event for our fellow man. That's so noble when it's right. But, don't you think it just too cruel to interfere when nature should be allowed to take its course? Why prolong the misery of the miserable? Be careful, darling. Don't meddle when you should look the other way. Don't forget, we know how to take you out so no one would ever suspect. Imagine them saying, 'Don't she look so natural ... why, it's just like she's asleep.' Be careful not to hasten your own zero, my sweet. And Helen, you would never guess how close we are right this minute. We don't have to be, but we are. Now be real quiet my dear and listen."

The voice stopped, several breaths transmitted into her ear, then silence, and a sharp metal point rasped across a pane of the window behind the drawn drape by her bedside. The voice came back on the phone laughing, "Goood night, sweetheart."

She sat very still in the bed and left the light on. She would not let them know they had frightened her. She recovered, replaced all papers in the case, took it to the kitchen, and by the light of a flashlight, put it in the safe and replaced the panels of the cabinetry. She returned to bed and lay awake, thinking. She needed help, but she did not know where to turn, nor whom to trust – not the police, not the sheriff, not the people she worked for, not the doctors who had been friends with her husband. Who was in cahoots with the people threatening her? The doctors? No, probably not overtly or intentionally, but they were likely to be so open and incautious as to talk in the wrong place about her trouble, and to take it to Peter Mallory.

Her thoughts returned again to John Colburn. Her hunches told her he could be trusted. But how could she approach him? She fell asleep remembering the one brief glimpse, his angular grace and fluid movement, as he entered Rattner's office the first time she saw him.

12

Jones, standing in the middle of Celeste's living room and dressing after a short visit, waved his arms while laughing and bragging about scaring the hell out of Helen Beckette the previous night; then he left. She wondered. If fright was to do the trick it would take a long time. Too long! Jones' description, even mimicking the panic in Helen's voice on the phone, was too loud with too much laughter. Celeste suspected Jones himself did not really believe such tactics would work. She glanced at Jake's picture from time to time as the evening progressed, and the level in the wine bottle receded. She already had showered, and applied the faintest traces of a dry, subtle perfume in anticipation of the hours after midnight, and wore nothing except a thin gown the color of night, her long blonde hair now swept up in a stack atop her head. Always when the hour arrived, she found the stealth so easy as she made the after-midnight visitations into the shadows of lingering death, to witness the mischief of the over-zealous. She had a talent for stealth, an unbelievable natural ability. She did not really need the television noise to drown the whisper of her movements as she rose from the couch, inhaling her lungs full, holding her breath while crossing the room in sock feet, and went out the door, making no sounds. The dogs didn't stir. In the shadows of the yard she slipped on her yard shoes. A front wheel of her car parked on the hillside street abutted the curb. She wrenched the steering wheel, shifted to neutral and the car rolled silently downhill. At the upgrade she started the engine and turned on the lights.

She parked a block from the hospital compound, sidled through the shrubs, and crossed the grounds in darkness. A sprawling one-story wing of Golden Age extended into the shadows beyond the last floodlight, its rear entrance hidden in the night. The lock yielded easily to her key, and she entered the darkened hallway. Maybe tonight she would identify the person attacking another target, another costly burden annoying Peter Mallory.

Ruble Crouch in the after-midnight hours followed the path of a woman on a rampage. Sybil Snyder had disappeared in the shadows of the wards, mumbling curses as she went. He had been blamed and held suspect of abusing patients: the black eyes, the bruised faces, the sobbing stories of being slapped during the night hours, the hurt feelings from rough talk. He had seen her do it, but he would see more. She had given Old Paul the black eye and whacked him over the head. He just folded up, kind of shrunk into himself, and died within three weeks. Helen Beckette still wanted some answers, he knew, and she very likely would get them. Sybil stomped down the hallway, entered a room where a buzzer buzzed continuously, snatched the cord out of feeble old hands, slung it in a loop above her head and whipped the button end down on the patient's face.

"Damn you, you old shit, stop holdin' down that goddam buzzer!"

"I wet myself because nobody answered to hep' me."

"Damn you, I'll teach you to sass me, you old coot."

Sybil's bony, knotted hands flashed. She grabbed the cord and whipped the control end against his face again. Bone cracked. The old man screamed. Her blonde hair scraggled in wild and stiff disarray, her face turned fiery red, her visage narrow and alive with hate. She grasped a handful of his nightgown at the collar, dragged him off the bed, and dropped him onto the floor, where she left him. Ruble stayed in the shadows and waited until she returned to her desk. Then she paged him on her two-way radio. Her story would be the same.

"That old fool in 23A has done went and fell outa' bed again. I think he has really hurt hisself this time."

"What do you want me to do?"

"Get a stretcher, stupid, and get him off the goddam floor. I'm calling the rescue squad to take him to the emergency room."

Ruble walked down the hallway and disappeared into the shadows. He would not dare touch the patient she had battered. The rescue squad could get old Samson off the floor.

Ruble would continue to live by the rule of silence, as he did in the woods and in the streets. He seldom spoke unless asked a question. He had tolerated Sybil's abuse, her assumptions of superiority, her racial slights, her unruly temperament. Silent dangers were meaningless to her. But he had reached the limits of his tolerance, and he would settle things in their own home at the first opportunity.

At this moment the other scent, faint but unmistakable, tainted by excitement, reached him in the malodors of the hallways, but he would not dare touch Celeste in his state of anger. He followed the trail of familiar perfume and quickly found her hidden in shadow and trembling in a state of fright.

"Oh, I'm glad you are here. I've never been so frightened."

"You saw her in action again, but on a rampage this time."

"God yes! Who is she? Do you know?"

"Oh, yes."

"Then do something."

"You don't understand. Report her and you get killed for knowing too much, and she might be killed to shut her up."

"So what's to be done?"

"Nothing now, just wait, the time will come."

"I almost walked right up on her."

"Best you leave here now. Things are really getting rough."

"When will the time come?"

"Soon."

"I do hope so."

13

At seven-thirty on a Monday morning Peter Mallory parked a battered old pickup truck in the lot at French Quarter landing and restaurant overlooking the Sardis Lake near the mouth of Hurricane Creek. Dressed in camouflaged hunting clothes, and carrying a rod and reel and a small tackle box, he went through woods toward the creek. Within moments, Ruble Crouch's rig backed down the launching ramp alongside the restaurant. Mallory, hidden in the undergrowth, watched the boat float off the trailer into the lake; then he walked on to the creek bank. The boat skimmed along the lakeshore. Ruble steered it into the creek, throttled down, and drifted along the bank. The bow slid onto the sand bar. Mallory stepped aboard, Crouch backed out of the creek, and they sped across open water. At the northeast end of the Sardis Reservoir, they proceeded upriver past Wyatt's Crossing. There, Ruble ran the trotlines he had set out the previous afternoon. He placed several large catfish in the cooler and threw the smaller ones back. Ruble let the boat drift downstream with hand lines out. As they entered the lake waters, they began catching crappie as fast as they could re-bait hooks. Then Ruble stopped fishing, took a long oar, and glided the boat into the mouth of a large, rapid creek. He poled around a curve into view of an old weathered crib, its walls lap strake, resting on a sand-rock and mortar foundation holding it two feet off the ground. This building and several smaller ones, an outhouse, and a barn, all had new tin roofs of a gray color as dull as the aged wood of the old walls. A small pristine white church nestled among tall pines and oaks. An idle helicopter stood in another clearing. Mallory never stopped fishing. "Is this it?"

"Yes."

"Which building?"

"The old corn crib."

"Why?"

"Rats. It's the only building with a solid rock foundation, built to keep rats out of the corn, common practice in the old days, sets three feet off the ground ... lots of storage room under there."

Mallory, busy removing another fish from his hook, did not look up. "The floor?"

"Never touched it."

"Access?"

"Thru the old storm cellar. A tunnel."

"They dug one?"

"Yes."

"The fresh dirt?"

"In the river."

"And the old storm cellar?"

"Hidden in overgrowth. It's roofed with sod anyway, and invisible unless you know it's there. They never touched a weed or a bush."

"Crib looks pretty small to me. So did they finish a basement under the church?"

"The basement beneath the church is three times bigger than the church area, lined with cemented sand-rock. It has a concrete ceiling poured on steel mesh supported by steel beams, its entrance hidden by a secret panel in the back wall of a small storage bin beneath the rear steps. A very safe storm cellar, just in case anybody asks. It would hold the entire congregation and more."

Ruble waited. He would answer Mallory's questions without supplying any additional information. Mallory said nothing more about the church. Did he possibly not know about the second underground room, bigger than the basement level, deeper into the hill, and the bank of computers there? A virtual army of men and machines had appeared unannounced before the sermons started and had gashed into the hill. In less than a week they completed the concrete-and-steel room two floors below the church, and hauled the fresh dirt away in dump trucks. The computers had been installed at night when no one was around.

Mallory, hunched in the boat, fished busily, too casual in the questions, and Ruble knew Mallory was either hiding something from him, or he was being duped himself. Why was Mallory fooling with him, just Ruble, if he was such a big shot? Ruble sensed something way beyond Mallory, an unknown, all-powerful, bigger than any of the local players, menacing and waiting. This called for alertness to a greater evil. Standing in the stern, long oar in hand, he looked down on rumpled Mallory crouched on the middle seat and felt an irrational impulse to violence, to smash this weak evil being and lose him in the water forever. The sensation passed instantly, Ruble aware in his native way of absurdities.

"Be damned sure all visitors to the lodge always catch fish, and the place lives up to a reputation of fishing lodge," said Mallory, giving directions.

"We always get something, one way or another."

"Nobody leaves without a cooler of fish."

"Right."

"Action?"

"Roaring. The congregations can't get enough of the preacher, Grantham, shouting, screaming about hellfire and damnation, foot stomping, dancing and waving his arms. He gets the people in his grip and they ask no questions about the stuff being unloaded from the buses during the sermons, and they don't even pay any attention to the helicopters coming and going. Stuff from the buses goes into the church basement. Stuff from the helicopters to the crib."

"God, how do they not notice?"

"Oh, I think they do, but they think it's food and more free supplies for the buffets and wine they serve several times a week, free."

"Greed blinds them?"

"That's the idea."

"Any of the stuff moving?"

"After midnight, after all the fishermen are asleep and the congregation has departed, the boats move it according to plan."

"Are you keeping an eye on things?"

"On my night off duty at the Golden Age, but it's a handful. Either job is enough without the other."

"Well, you can't quit the Golden Age. Too many important things have to be done there yet."

"I know."

"Soon as it's sold."

"I can hold out."

"Okay," said Mallory, while looking at the water as he brought another fish to the surface.

Ruble poled the boat back down the creek and entered the lake again. He gunned the motor and they planed across to the south side and anchored in Mallory's favorite trout hole. In the calm quiet of the morning Mallory began to talk, giving his instructions and making his wishes known in the form of manly concern and man-to-man talk, the first words after a long silence, as though he had been struggling with a bothersome problem.

"You know, Ruble, it's a shame the way old people are treated. The way they are made to hang on is actually cruel. We think we are doing them a favor, keeping them alive at all costs. The Lord used to take them gently with infections in their aged weakness. Pneumonia, the old man's friend, they used to call it, relieved a lot of problems. Now we revive them, to start another downward cycle, and we do it over and over until they finally go down for good – cruelty at its worst, and a terrible drain on the resources of this society."

"Yes sir, I know what you mean."

"Hell, I remember the old days. Now you take old Dr. Lawson. He would just pull the plug or shut off the oxygen, without asking anybody. And if they quit eating, he let 'em. Took care of a lot of problems that way. They yip with pain, the dying, and he would keep edging up the morphine until they were comfortable and sleeping. Enough of it stops the breathing, you know."

"Yes, sir."

"I am most anxious to see the place make a profit. There will be some nice Christmas bonuses when it does ... Whooooo! ... boy! ... got a big one!"

He snapped his rod up, stood to reel in the fish and after a ten-minute struggle landed a prize.

"That's a beauty, at least seven pounds. Want to keep it?" asked Ruble.

"Yeah. Got to have something to show my wife."

Mallory threw his line out again. He looked off across the stillness of flat water and said, "So, how do you like your job?" He was fishing for something else now, hoping to uncover some unpleasantness, some dirt.

"Work for some good people. Dan Rattner has been good to me, and Helen Beckette a real lady. Too bad she's still so broke up over her husband, Dr. Beckette."

"Yeah, so I've heard."

"You know, I will always wonder what really happened to him."

"Yep, the detectives never found a clue."

Mallory kept his back turned as he stared out over the water. He heard no hint of prying in Ruble's inflection, but eye contact would not do. Ruble had too much native intelligence and intuition. Never let him suspect anything.

"And the autopsy didn't help," said Ruble.

"Nope, and that just goes to show you, nothing is perfect."

"If somebody got him, it was done very clever."

"Oh, I think he just had one of those peculiar cardiac arrests, arrhythmia they call it, right?" said Mallory.

"I've heard the term."

Mallory began to reel in.

"Let's call it a day. I'll take the trout home; you may have the rest."

"Thanks a lot, Mr. Mallory."

"Oh you're welcome. And by the way, Ruble, you finished your payments on the boat and trailer this month, so you don't have that worry anymore."

Ruble had never made the first payment, but he went along with the pretense.

"You mean I don't owe any money on it?"

"Not on the boat rig, not a dime."

"I'm glad to hear that. I never kept up with the payments."

"The bank did. Is the boat all right for the purpose?"

"Yeah, it does the job."

"Good. Then you help us and we will help you."

Ruble guided the boat back into Hurricane Creek. Mallory stepped onto the sandy bank and walked to his truck carrying tackle and a big trout. If anyone in the landing area or restaurant had been watching, he had simply gone fishing where the creek empties into the lake.

While driving home Mallory mulled over the situation. Did Ruble think he knew something about the death of David Beckette? He didn't think so. And actually, he didn't know himself, although he did possibly have something to do with it. All he had to do was drop the name of a person who threatened the success of the operation, and something would happen as though they understood more than he was telling them behind the scenes over in Tunica; or maybe they really knew more than he had intended telling. Could someone else be supplying information? No. Who could possibly?

He hoped the method would bring Helen Beckette around, and rougher tactics would not be needed. He had great plans for her future. She is just what he wants and will need when he comes into the really big money. He can then be rid of his wife, who is a drag socially, even if he has to pay her a million dollars, and she's just the type of dummy who would think a million dollars is a lot of money. A million dollars would be nothing in his new and enormous wealth. Helen would be such a gracious hostess. But more important, he really loves her. Imagine entering a banquet room, or a supper club, with the gorgeous Helen on his arm, introducing her to other couples and to important people, "I'd like you to meet my new wife, Helen. … " the looks of astonishment, and envy, and the looks of approval as she gazes at him adoringly across the dining table, and on the dance floor. He would adorn her in diamonds as big as pigeon eggs and drape her in ermine and the most exquisite gowns. And sleep with her, just imagine, every night. He would give up other women then, he could promise himself, although he would, of course, have to hurt some feelings, turning them down, fighting them off. Helen has been very standoffish and pretends to be grieving, but grief will end when she finally realizes how wealthy he has become, and what a good man he really is. He fully expects not to have to resort to other tactics. She would respond to his charm, his erudition, his vast knowledge of things. Quite a scholar he would be if he were not so occupied in his financial wizardry. Celeste never entered his thoughts.

Ruble put his boat on the trailer and started toward home. Now he had time to get plenty of sleep before going on duty after midnight. While driving along, he wondered, with annoyance, why his mind clung to the image of David Beckette. The memory still puzzling and bothersome, the really weird scene, the way he found Beckette there in a dark corner of an alcove, just sitting up in the lifting shadows of dawn like he had stopped for a little rest, leaning back against the wall, dead for hours, dried vomit on his face and clothes – something very strange about it all. And he had to give the alarm himself, and he feared he had aroused some suspicion. Who else had been down those dark corridors during the night except him and Beckette? Poor Beckette, nearly every night over there in the Golden Age after hours puttering around, prolonging the lives of the miserable, perfectly healthy one day and gone the next. Touched him only to feel the coldness and withdrew as if struck, nor had he seen anything unusual during the long hours from eleven o'clock to dawn. Beckette had to have been in the corner dead all night hidden in the darkness, must have passed by him many times in the shadows, and only by a fluke did he happen to see Beckette at all. Ruble remembers it over and over, bending as he did at the moment to pick up a pen he had dropped while rushing down the hallway, the something odd in the corner catching his eye, and he went to look.

And he still feels a gorge at the way the police questioned him again and again, but he stuck to his story without changing a word and they had no choice eventually but to leave him alone. The autopsy showed no definite cause of death. Beckette had vomited, possibly strangled, some stuff in his trachea, some signs of asphyxiation ... such fence-walking bullshit ... he wondered about doctors. But through his sense of things he knew Beckette to be native to goodness in his own heart.

14

Throughout the day Celeste again languished in boredom, her sunbath finished, the wine tempting, her unhappiness mounting. Her phone had not rung. She waited, expectant, anxious to get to Tunica again. Thornton Webb, the big black-haired giant, had given her a tiny beeper, now hidden in her purse, She presses its control button as she and Mallory approach the casino. Alerted, the big man will be just inside the secret and momentarily unlocked door to his personal quarters when she slips in. Not as exciting as the man in the dark shadows of the Golden Age, but a lot bigger and better man than Peter Mallory, with the excitement of money and real power, and the wonderful feeling of strength and protection.

But nothing has happened today, the great silence surrounding her. She listened to the phone and found the dial tone alive, nearly three o'clock. Then it rang, and Wyndham Jones invited her for a ride in an unmarked patrol car.

"Come on, let's have some fun. You need to learn more of the tricks."

"Well, Jonesey, it's about time you called. Where are we going this time? You promised me the Goonsbys, remember. And I'm just dying to hear more about Dynamite Don. And I want to see where they live."

"Shhhh ... don't talk so loud and give way our secrets. Tell you when we're on the way."

"Okay."

"Half hour."

The back roads of the county confused her, so she gave up, relaxed, and reached back to pet the German Shepherd on the back seat. Somewhere in the hills south of Yocona River they turned into a narrow blacktop road, *towards Tula*, as Jones said. Ten minutes from the last house, Jones pulled over and pointed to the entry of a narrow, rutted dirt road winding quickly out of sight beneath overhanging undergrowth. "A mile of that and worse to the house" he said. He then drove to the side of the next hill and pulled off the road into an open space covered in a growth of weeds.

"Where are we?"

"Out in the county. We just crossed over the line from John Colburn's spread. Isom's Knoll, they call this place, a good lookout spot." He handed her a pair of binoculars. "Now just aim 'em out your window over the trees out there," he said while pointing across a wide valley below. He gave her a minute or so before he said, "See anything?"

"Nothing but trees and a faint trail of smoke coming out of something looks like a small cabin."

"Well, that's all you will ever see of a Goonsby, until a Goonsby is ready to be seen."

"This all you can show me?"

"Right."

"That's where they all live?"

"Including Dynamite Don."

"How do you get in touch?"

"Why do you want to know?"

"Just curious, I suppose. Is everything they say true about them?"

"You get a new meaning of the word *lowdown* in a Goonsby. And there ain't a worse stink in this world. You want to meet them?"

"Dynamite Don might be of help someday if we came to need him."

Jones looked at her funny and said, "Let me know when you are ready." He started the car and drove back into the road. "Right now we got to hurry or we will be late."

Continuing on southwest, they took winding narrow roads at high speed, and returned to Highway 7 South toward Grenada, below Water Valley. He came to a crossroad, turned around, and parked, partially hidden in bushes and half off the road, headed toward Cambridge, and cut off the engine.

"Why are we here, Wyndham?"

"To stop returning students."

"For what reason?"

"You watch."

"How do you know a student?"

"The look, the way the sorry things drive, the front seat passenger asleep – ragged after a long weekend hauling down I-55 to I-10 across Texas. Then by one route or another they go to Laredo and across into Mexico, a total of some 900 miles, for just an hour or two, then return, one driving, one asleep, turn about, stopping only for gas and takeouts. Empty paper cups and scattered drinking straws litter the floorboard dirt, the car smelling of sweat and greasy wrappings, always the same."

"My goodness, what for?"

"Just watch." He started the engine.

Ten minutes later, a battered Honda whizzed by, going ten miles over the limit, the front passenger asleep, his head thrown back, mouth hanging open, baseball cap on backwards. Wyndham scratched onto the highway, wheels spinning, throwing dust and gravel, and dashed precariously at the rear bumper of the speeding Honda. He let go with the siren and flashers hidden behind the radiator grill, so they jumped with fright and made a panic stop. He got out with the dog on leash and walked toward them. The dog strained toward the trunk lid immediately, sniffing. The driver lowered his window and handed a package through before Wyndham said a word. Neither spoke. Wyndham waved him on.

Wyndham returned to the car and put the package in Celeste's lap, and the dog in the back seat. He got in and drove toward Cambridge.

"Did you give them a ticket?"

"Naw. They gave me a package."

"Why?"

"They know I will be waiting for my pay since I'm their source of some of the prescriptions they get filled in Mexico, two or three hundred pills on each, for very few dollars there across the border, each pill worth twenty dollars or more back on campus and in the bars."

"Prescriptions for what?"

"Date-rape pills from the Mexican merchants, the sedatives, Xanax, Valium, and others, a different name typed in the blank for the patient's name, all old out-of-use names."

"Signed by whom?"

"Your friend, the one and only Isaac Dodson, the world's greatest internist. The package in your lap is the payoff, cocaine from Mexican dealers. Students in the bars clamor for it, already hooked on codeine and other drugs handed out free by pill-pimps like Littlebox who cruises Tank Hall and Inner Sanctum and other bars giving out free samples. Dealers pay handsomely for the coke."

"Perverted little creep!"

"Know him do you?"

"Yeah, who doesn't? Who pays him?"

"All concerned pitch in."

"Where do you get the codeine?"

"Dodson, of course."

"Oh my God, Wyndham, I'm not sure I want to know this."

"Yeah, you ought to know what goes on in this town."

"Well, then I take it you bring the prescriptions from Dodson to the dealers, enough to create addicts for the trade."

"Right."

"And also the prescriptions for students to use in Mexico?"

"Right. To some extent, but down there just across the border, doctors' offices and pharmacies are lined up like casinos in Tunica, and runners are waiting to escort buyers through the system."

"How?"

"The student names a symptom and receives an appropriate prescription, one to fit the need, enough to treat an army for the same condition."

"And Dodson?"

"Oh he gets a cut, and he don't come cheap. He gets a hundred fifty dollars for each prescription and a ten percent cut of the sales. Three hundred pills at twenty dollars is six thousand dollars. So on one little slip of paper like that, he rakes in a total of seven hundred fifty dollars, cash, no records, no taxes."

"Wyndham aren't you afraid of getting caught?"

"Who's to catch me? I'm the law."

"Well, take me home. I'm a nervous wreck."

15

Peter Mallory ended a 7:30 a.m. board meeting in the bank's conference room at 10 a.m. and returned to his office. He attended to the stack of waiting papers on his desk, ignoring Martha Williams, who tiptoed in bringing more work. While perusing the last document, he realized he would have to pay another visit to Tunica. And he would never go alone, letting himself appear too vulnerable. His total disappearance might be a temptation when the stakes got high enough. For company he could always rely on Celeste Howard to be ready at a moment's notice, for any period of time.

Once they arrived, she would lose herself quickly at a gaming table. He could then go about his business, in his estimation without her ever knowing his real reason for being there. Just give her enough money to play with and there would be no problem. And she always won, never really big, but enough to keep her interested. Of course, it went to her head; she won just because he had taught her how to be a good gambler. There would never be a reason to let her know otherwise, and he thought she would never have a clue. But he could rely on her; she never talked out of school; she kept her eyes open, always discreet. And she never asked where he had been when he disappeared hours at a time after their arrival. She made things easy for him by not asking questions or getting nosy. Too bad she wasn't something more: a Helen Beckette, a keeper, a lady, someone he would be proud to show off in the best society. But she would do for the purpose, for the time being, while he made his big money. Yet, she too is looking for security and more, and he would have to be wary. She's gifted, talented, a very capable hostess, sets a beautiful table, prepares delicious meals, knows all the ins and outs, knows all the things a man needs and wants and supplies them, but among those who know her, she is notorious. He couldn't live with her reputation; he has to be able to hold his head up, to be proud of his woman. Imagine the snickers behind his back if he turned up married to her. Right now she is a lot of laughs, a lot of fun, and reckless, thrillingly so, but he could never parade her before presidents once he moves up to an ambassadorship, a post he would surely get someday in recognition of his capabilities and the large contributions he expects to make to political campaigns.

He dialed her number on his private line. When she answered he asked, "Are you busy today?"

"Oh, Peter, I was hoping that would be you. I'm bored stiff."

"So am I. Can you be ready to go in an hour?"

"Would love to. "

"Airport."

"Be there."

An hour later he drove past her convertible, parked five spaces down, and waited with the motor running. After a few minutes she left her car, walked to the right side of his, entered and sat low in the passenger seat. He drove out of the airport parking lot, through back roads and streets to Highway 6 West. Thirty miles away, he turned north on Interstate 55 toward Memphis for another thirty miles and then cut across state Highway 304 toward Tunica. On the secondary road, he expected no patrolmen and set his speed up to 100 as they zipped through the flat delta landscape of cotton fields and catfish ponds. The skyline of the Tunica gambling town came into view: sparkling, high buildings rising out of the rustic surroundings of farmland and squalid dilapidated hovels. He paid no attention when Celeste, with head bent down, searched in her purse, then applied a touchup of lipstick, returned the tube and closed her purse.

At The Royal Nugget, Mallory pulled ahead of the stretch limousines jammed around the entrance and went under the porte-cochere. A valet took the car. Neither he nor Celeste carried more than a small overnight bag disguised as briefcase and purse.

A croupier appeared at the reception desk and escorted them to roulette. Mallory played a few turns by her side. He lost. She won three out of five. He slipped away, went down a hallway marked Private. A guard in uniform, blocking the passage where it ended at heavy wooden doors spoke politely, "Good morning, Mr. Mallory." He wore a .45 revolver on one hip.

"Morning."

Mallory meekly raised his arms and was frisked quickly and thoroughly. This really annoyed him. He had been coming there long enough to be one of the boys. The guard escorted him through the doors to a waiting room.

"Have a seat, Mr. Mallory. Mr. Webb will be with you shortly."

The guard left. A trim blonde secretary never looked up from her computer. Mallory picked up a month-old copy of Penthouse and sat down. He would wait at least an hour. Heads would roll for this once he became an insider with power.

Celeste stayed for two more spins of the roulette then went to the back of the lobby, through a door into a narrow hallway and negotiated a maze of turns to the rear entrance of Webb's office suite. Webb would be waiting for her. On the outskirts of Tunica, she had beeped him when she reached for her lipstick.

He crossed the room and she sighed, "Oh, Thornton, it's been too long."

Behind Webb's private office the suite contained a fully equipped kitchen and a bedroom with a king-sized bed. She suited him. He liked the blondness, the litheness, the passion, the eagerness. Besides the physical excitement and gratification she brought, she had a very sharp brain and a fascinating deviousness.

After a thirty-minute bout of vigorous sex, they lay naked on the pink sheets and talked. She was such a relief to him from Mallory's tediousness.

"Well. What's the situation?" he asked.

"Mallory wants Helen Beckette, but she won't give him the time of day, and obsession interferes with his judgment."

"Yeah, we know. And he would drop you if he could get her."

"Without a second thought. But she will never let him near her. More important, she is determined to solve the mystery of her husband's death."

"You should know we believe in the very strict rule of reserving capital punishment for capital crimes in our own league, those of us in the gambling and money business."

"I am more comfortable with that."

"You can count on it. Now it's time for you to dress and let me welcome Mallory." He handed her a big fat brown shopping bag with handles. "This is a million dollars in ten-thousand-dollar chips; gamble it all away tonight."

When Mallory entered the office, Thornton Webb put down his phone, came around his desk, and extended a hand. "Hello, Peter."

"Hello, Thornton."

"Nice drive over this morning?"

"Oh yes, it's a beautiful day. Celeste, came along as usual."

"Blackjack?"

"No, I left her at roulette."

"Great. We'll see to it that she has a good time."

"Thank you."

Mallory shifted uneasily. Thornton Webb resembled a big tomcat playing with a mouse, too big, too powerful, in fact, all powerful with a discomforting smoothness, and his too perfect control smacked of danger, of sinister reserve. The organization had proved to be far more serious and intense than expected. He had merely mentioned, in a board meeting with Thornton Webb, Kramer, and Kadsh, the name of a man impeding the goals at the Golden Age home, and before his next visit to The Royal Nugget, Jack Williams was comatose and ruined, permanently out of the way. He expressed his satisfaction on his next visit, but Thornton reacted with surprise and a certain resentment of the assumption. He seemed to know nothing of Williams. Mallory stopped himself from mentioning the death of Dr. David Beckette.

After the sale of his nursing home chain to Bin Kadsh, owner of the world's biggest HMO conglomerate, Total Health Care, Inc., Mallory expected to be repaid at a rich interest rate and a generous share of the stock. In the case of failure, attempts to collect might prove deadly, and Mallory had begun to suspect the price might be more than mere money.

Thornton controlled his distaste for the next subject to be discussed and asked, "Have you news about the fishing lodge?"

"Yes. I saw it a few days ago."

"Storage?"

"More then adequate and well hidden, conveniently surrounded by woods, on a high bank at the mouth of a big creek emptying into the Tallahatchie. It's rustic, no electricity, no running water, a single outhouse, a helicopter pad hidden in weeds and bushes safely clear of the trees, graveled road access."

"The church?"

"Blackwater Congregational, in the nearby woods, restored with a new roof, a cleared and freshly graded and graveled parking lot. The major vault is in the church basement."

"No plumbing?"

"Nope. This was to be a place for old-fashioned revivals, which calls for sweat on hot August nights, and the bushes for privacy."

Thornton chuckled. "You know your revivals."

"I should, I've lived through enough of them."

"And the nights and days in cold weather?"

"A big wood-burning heater in the middle of the nave."

"Old-fashioned revivals. I've never been to one," said Thornton.

"They have a huge following down here in our part of the country."

"Brilliant idea, Peter."

"The Reverend Grantham already has a big following locally. He naively and enthusiastically accepted the job, and doesn't have a clue and never will. Television advertisement starts tomorrow. Word of mouth has already spread, and all available spots have been taken for the next three weekends. There will be a constant coming and going in the air and on the road."

"Okay. Now, there's the matter of the sheriff."

"He's amenable, but I'm sure he's to be trusted for penny ante only. If he knew something big was afoot without his getting a cut, he might resort to heroic tactics, for the glory of it," said Mallory.

"He needs that?"

"He would love to be a hero. I've heard him talk. He imagines himself on CNN or FOX Evening News giving a local report to the nation, wearing his big dude cowboy hat, splendid in uniform, his gut bulging a tailored shirt like a slick German sausage, butchering the King's English, himself responsible for the arrests."

"He could pull that off?"

"Oh, he would have the FBI, or the state troopers, or the National Guard with the governor's help, or all of them."

"So what do you think?"

"Use him, but keep him in the dark."

Thornton said, "We don't need him for anything else. As the operation is going it will bring in millions; in fact, your share will be that big."

"You mean my share of ownership in the HMO conglomerate buying the nursing homes?"

"Kadsh has promised to work something out to your satisfaction."

"Good."

"For tonight you have the Emperor's Suite on the top floor." He leaned forward and handed Mallory two door cards and a bulging manila envelope, sealed.

"Delightful."

"I suggest you blackjack tonight. Robert's at the table. Empty the envelope before you quit."

"Thank you."

Thornton grimly waited. Mallory hesitated, then tiptoed out the door into the hallway, the envelope tucked under an arm. Why did he tiptoe? Damned little sneak. Thornton did not like any of the recent developments, Kadsh leveraging them into drugs, Mallory involved with his slippery personality. The syndicate had plenty to do and plenty of wealth without having to taint itself with the likes of these two amateurs.

Mallory went past the same guard and down the hallway. He found Celeste at roulette, still winning, and too busy to notice him. He pressed one of the door cards into her hand, whispered the Emperor's Suite, and went to a blackjack table. They had had the same accommodations on previous trips, and she loved it.

Robert simply raised one heavy black eyebrow when Mallory approached his table, and gave no other sign of recognition. Mallory lost the first hand and the second, down five hundred dollars. After still another losing hand he started winning, sporadically, then a run emptied the brown envelope. He left the cashier's cage at three thirty in the morning, with a hundred thousand dollars in his inside coat pocket. As he walked toward the elevators, his footsteps echoed in the emptiness. He showered and came to bed. Celeste lay wide awake in the semidarkness, waiting.

16

Helen Beckette entered her office at 7:30 a.m. and began poring over the stack of paper work. The night had left her sleepy, tired, and discouraged. She had no idea what to do next about the frightening threats, but she would not go home alone again, not to another sinister night without protection. Where could she find safety? A hotel? A motel? Oh, God no. Living in Cambridge is like living in a fish bowl; every move is seen and talked about. And people are just waiting for the widow Helen to go astray.

She sensed someone in the entrance to the office suite and looked up. Clara Bartley stood in her doorway, trim, green eyes alert with anger, red hair fluffed.

"I hate to interrupt, but I need to talk for a minute."

"Sure. Come on in, have a seat."

Clara walked silently and swiftly across the office and sat down. "Dan Rattner is not here. I already looked in his office. It's empty. I would dump this on him, if he was here to hear it."

"You'll have to do with me. Dan's out of town on business for the next three days."

"Oh, you'll do just fine. In fact, I trust you more than I trust him. Not that I think anything bad. It's just that he's too namby pamby. I want somebody who will do something."

"What's happened?"

"Rachel Colburn. Once again, she would be dead if I hadn't been here last night."

"What happened?"

"I come over here at five o'clock to see that she eats her dinner and find her slumped in bed gasping. I had to prod her awake, and she looks up at me, her eyes all watery and out of focus and says 'Oh, Clara, I'm, so sick! Can't get my breath.' Poor old thing, a hundred years old and lying there suffering and helpless with no one paying attention to how sick she's become. So, I pull her up in bed, and make her cough and she brings up this green sputum. I listen with my stethoscope and I hear rattling over both lungs. I ring the bell and after fifteen minutes here comes one of those damned sorry aides skulking in the room, and I hand her the scope and tell her to listen and show her where to put the bell. She goes through the motions and says, 'I don't hear nothing,' 'sides that, she's always ringing that buzzer.' So I get the real nurse down there and she can't hear anything either. I get the supervisor, and by that time I'm madder than hell, and point to the place to put the scope. She listens and hears the rales and the soupy noises. She looks at the greenish yellow sputum and goes out, breaks the rules to call that damned lazy Isaac Dodson and he prescribes the pneumonia package over the phone. You think he got his sorry ass over there to see that sick old lady? Hell no, he just shotguns the medication whether it's right or wrong, and at that it took them a solid hour to get the first dose in her. I've had it up to here with this situation," she said, raking a finger beneath her chin. "I stayed all night with her. I'm afraid to leave her alone. Now I want to know this, and I'm sorry Dan Rattner's not here to bear the brunt of my frustration ... I want to know this, why do I have to do the work your nurses are being paid to do? They don't look. They don't care. They just sit up there at their desks doing paper work and let these old people die of neglect."

Helen watched her while she talked. God, what a woman, the most respected medical person in the whole town and the most feared. Clara stopped for breath, and Helen said, "Clara, thank God you were here. We would have lost her long ago had you not been so vigilant. I wish we had one of you on every wing of the building."

"Helen what's gone wrong? It's always been bad, but now it just keeps getting worse and worse."

"We simply don't have the personnel to give private attention to each and every patient. In fact, with the cutbacks, we have fewer than ever for a given number of patients, and lower wages bring lesser skills."

"Why?"

Helen scribbled rapidly on a note pad and handed the paper to Clara. She read it, paled, and held out her hand for Helen's pen. She wrote a brief reply and handed the paper back.

Helen had written, "Wrong place to talk."

And Clara wrote, "Come to dinner at my house tonight, 6 p.m."

Helen nodded. Clara stood, and without another word, went out the door.

Tom Bartley, soaked in sweat and caked in dirt from work, walked along the porch past the open door of the kitchen where Clara and Helen were preparing dinner. Clara said, "Oh, here's Tom ... let's put the steak on."

He disappeared into the house and the shower came on. "Oh, does he work," said Clara. "He's building a new post office for the government. They have to meet deadlines and he's got a sorry bunch he has to ride herd on all the time. Turns his back and they goof off and steal anything that can be moved. He's the contractor; he's the boss, but he gets down in the dirt with the rest of them and works like a dog."

"I've always heard great things about him."

"Solid, reliable, so honest it hurts, and very concerned. God, am I lucky."

"So was I until mine was taken from me."

"Oh, Helen, I know. And I think about your David every day, what a fine person he was, what a dedicated doctor. He was good, so good, and his patients loved him."

"I grieve as much every day as I did the night I lost him. And I guess that's because I think he was killed by someone for some reason I can't fathom."

Clara had stopped moving. She stood with a dishtowel in one hand, her face gone pale, her mouth open. "Helen ... I've wondered myself. What do you suppose?"

"I wish I knew. But I'm afraid to talk to anybody."

"So. I had asked you a question today in the office."

"I don't know who's listening, and who belongs to whom in that place. But the answer to your question is simple. The nursing home has become a business, not a home. People don't come there to live; they come there to die. And the sooner they do just that, with the least cost and trouble to the owners, the better they like it."

"So they economize on manpower and supplies."

"The cheapest of everything, regardless of what it is."

The shower went off. After a moment, Clara said, "Tom will be in here in a minute, and I want you to know you can trust both of us. We have already talked about everything you and I have said tonight. He's as solid as a rock, calm and controlled, and afraid of nothing. What I'm saying is, you don't have to be alone in this world. So feel free to talk. Tom won't repeat it, and he will come to your defense."

"This would be exposing both of you to danger."

"He came back from the Vietnam war no longer a boy, mature like middle-aged, with a purple heart and a medal of honor, but he has never told anyone what happened there."

"Ohhhh."

"Valor in nighttime surveillance, he now meets regularly with the reserves."

Tom stooped to enter the kitchen door, a big man, but all muscle, his pale blue eyes alert, his face shiny clean, a full head of brown wavy hair freshly scrubbed and still damp. Helen immediately relaxed. Clara crossed the room and hugged him and kissed his cheek.

"Welcome home, sweetheart. How was your day?"

"We got the foundations poured, but we all had to stay until it was done. Mixed concrete won't wait."

"Well, we are about ready to eat." Half turning she added, "... you know Helen? She's having dinner with us tonight, so we can talk privately."

Tom advanced, his hand extended. "Of course, how are you, Helen?"

"Fine, Tom."

His enormous hand felt firm and dry, his grip careful and respectful. He didn't talk much, politely carrying his end of a conversation, but remaining silent most of the time.

Tom, careful of his manners, kept his ravenous appetite in check. Clara waited a few minutes, then said, "While waiting for you, we were discussing some of the nursing home problems."

"Still going on, are they?"

"Not Helen's fault; I know she has tried to improve things, but the trouble is higher up, at the business level, the level above management, the level that tells management what to do. Am I right, Helen?"

"Yes ... I think so."

"Yeah, I know the problem only too well in my business," said Tom.

Helen had stopped eating and sat straight up staring across the room. Tom and Clara, both sensed something and looked at her. She was fighting for self-control, her face distorted in a whimper. Clara reached a hand to her arm and said, "Oh my God, Helen, I didn't mean to hurt you."

The tears began to stream down Helen's cheeks and she said, "Oh no, it's not that. You meant no harm. What you say is right and for the best, but it's far worse than you can imagine. What bothers you, Clara, is just superficial, while in truth there is something sinister seething beneath the surface."

"Oh, Helen, what is going on?"

"God, I don't know who to trust. But I've got to trust somebody. I can't handle this alone anymore."

Tom said, "Helen, out of respect for David, let Clara and me help."

"I've been suspicious and dissatisfied about the circumstances of his death, and about the turn patient care has taken at Golden Age. There is an undercurrent I can't identify, and recently I've been receiving anonymous and threatening phone calls in the middle of the night."

Tom placed his knife and fork across his plate and waited. "Do you have any idea who might be calling?"

"Not the vaguest. At first there was only the breathing, then the threat to render me into a vegetable like the saddest cases we have to care for, those just waiting to die, those who have reached a fate that makes us all shudder in revulsion."

"The coward, at a safe distance on the phone," said Clara.

"No. The caller has been close enough to know when I turn out my reading light, and knowledgeable enough about my habits to accuse me of keeping a record of the happenings inside Golden Age and working on it there in my bed. It's as if they can see into my house to know what I am doing."

"Oh Lord! This puts a different face on things," said Clara.

"Perhaps more the face I've suspected for some time now," said Helen.

"I've got cold chills running down my spine!" said Clara. Tom remained still, his head up, alert, his nostrils flared, his jaw muscles working.

Helen said, "And even closer," then described the scratching of her bedroom windowpane. "I got very little sleep after that."

"Okay," said Tom. "Let's finish the meal. We all need food. Then we will deal with this."

He picked up his knife and fork, and returned to his slow and deliberate way of eating. He remained silent, thoughtful, obviously not so much angry as set on a determined course of action. Over his coffee and dessert, he asked, "Helen, do you think anyone knows you are here?"

"I don't think so. Would you believe it, I have taken to watching traffic out my rearview mirrors. I saw no one."

"Good. You have an attached garage?"

"Yes."

"Then we can get into the house without being seen?"

"Yes. The blinds are still drawn, and my bedside light is still on. For all anyone might see from the outside I could be quietly there right now."

Tom left the table and went into his storage attic. He reappeared carrying in one hand a large green duffel bag, U.S. Marine Corps insignia in black letters fading in the worn cloth, and an army blanket over the other arm. "Okay, here's the plan," he said, setting the bag on the floor. He opened it and began examining its contents while talking. "We go to Helen's house. If no one is in sight, we enter without changing the lights. While I'm getting set up, no one will speak a word, not even a whisper, and only one person at a time will walk anywhere inside."

"Why, Tom?" asked Clara.

"Because the people watching the house can pick up every voice, and every motion. They can hear what you say, as well as the sound of feet crossing the floor, a safe opening, the turning of pages, writing, computer keys, the opening and closing of drawers, a closing book, and even know the directions taken by two or more people walking. So we must not betray the presence of more than one person in the house."

"Oh, my God!" said Helen. "That's how they knew I was working on my notes."

"Yes," said Tom.

"Such equipment must cost a lot of money."

"Yes. The FBI, CIA, and military intelligence use it."

"Who besides the government can afford it, organized crime?" asked Helen.

Tom stopped his motions in the bag, and looked at her. "You know, I'm beginning to wonder if we aren't dealing with something much bigger than just a nursing home problem."

"Damn, this is getting to be scary," said Clara.

"Helen, is there a door in the back of your house?" Tom asked.

"Yes, in the kitchen beside the refrigerator."

"I will need a key."

"Hanging on a large ring on a keyboard by the door."

"You girls stay on Helen's bed without a word to each other after we arrive. Helen, after the call comes in, and after I then go out of the house, and with Clara still on the bed and quiet, you turn on the shower and pack a bag with all the things you will need for the next few days. You can't go back there again, except during the day and never alone. We will return here after you receive your phone call. Where's your car?"

"Tom, it's in the garage," said Clara. "I had her put it there when she arrived, just in case anybody got nosy."

"Perfect."

The phone rang at midnight. Tom snapped on headphones and Helen picked up the bedside receiver and answered, "Hello."

A brief period of silence, then several deep exhalations, and a voice said, "Ahhh, Helen, your behavior has been better tonight. No writing, no worrying. Perhaps you've come around to our side. We are real close again."

Tom removed his ear phones, and went out, silent as a cat. With night-vision goggles he surveyed the landscape, gray and dark beneath a solid cloud cover. In the distance stood the shadow shape of a van parked in a cul-de-sac at the foot of the hill. He spotted a form coming up the edge of the driveway ascending the hill. It moved to the edge of the front lawn and stopped. A second person, from behind the first, slunk through the shadows toward the window of Helen's bedroom.

In the house, Helen replaced the phone receiver after the caller hung up, then she went in the bathroom and turned on the shower. She packed a large bag with cosmetics and clothes. She showered and redressed and returned to bed. The phone rang again. "Ahh Helen we want to show you again how close we really are to you.

Tom eased forward. Amazing what he could see with night-vision goggles in almost total darkness. He recognized the form and the gait of the first man, now dressed in work clothes. The second man seemed more a part of the night, indistinct from his own clothing. Then the odor pervaded the surroundings and Tom knew with hair prickling clarity the malignancy of the threat, the odor unmistakable, the fetid stench of the totally unwashed white man, the stink of a Goonsby. This second man went to the window and waited. Tom knew the gait, Dynamite Don, game leg and stiff ankle movement. Tom controlled an impulse to attack. But premature action would bring down only underlings. These men, or someone in their place, would eventually lead to the people who sent them. The sound of a beeper emitted a signal, from the area of the first man a brief flicker of a penlight swiped the air like the path of a firefly, and the second man scratched the window pane, one strong screeching stroke of metal on glass, then he slunk away. The first man instantly turned a pen light on a beeper, and punched a key. Then he, too, slunk back toward the driveway. Tom took a shortcut through the woods down the hill and crouched behind the van. The figures approached the passenger side and got in. Tom photographed the rear end repeatedly as the motor started up, the lights came on, and the van moved off. He would remember the tag number, and it surely would be obvious in the pictures. He waited. The vehicle left and turned toward town. The sound of it diminished and disappeared.

At the Bartley home Tom said, "Well, Helen, I guess you will be staying with us for the time being. We are dealing with something big and dangerous."

"Tom!" said Clara. "The suspense is killing me. Who was out there?"

"A van with at least three men. The one responsible for scratching the window was none other than our beloved deputy sheriff, Wyndham Jones. The man who actually scratched the window was a Goonsby."

"Oh my God," said Clara. "Was it Dynamite Don?"

"Yes."

"What did you do?"

"Nothing. I want to find out who sent them."

"Jones," said Clara. "That lowdown scum."

"He's insignificant in himself. But this does mean that somebody has bought our honorable sheriff. Now it's every man for himself," said Tom.

"Well what next?" asked Clara. "We need an ally."

"At the moment, I wouldn't know who to trust in this atmosphere," said Tom.

Helen said, "Maybe I do."

"Who?"

"Besides you and Clara?"

"Yes."

"Do you know John Colburn?"

"Why, yes, of course," said Clara.

"Dan Rattner tells me he has powerful connections in Washington."

"Then we need to talk to him," said Tom.

"I can arrange it," said Clara. "When he comes back next weekend, I will talk to him."

17

Thornton Webb, chairing a business meeting at his Royal Nugget conference table, listened to the proceedings, watching each speaker. Kadsh, at the other end of the table, addressed his own business manager in the presence of Fritz Kramer, who was there representing Lapkin Lewis, the syndicate attorney.

"Buy Mallory's nursing homes, but buy them right." Fritz Kramer, regarded him silently, too poker-faced for anyone to read the disdain he hid so well every day of his life behind a mask of neutrality and dignity. And today Kramer was controlling himself, holding his power in check. Kadsh bulged aggressively and belligerently. Jowly, bald with a black-haired rim, black eyed, vigorously scrubbed, closely shaven, and overfed, he resembled a hog in mufti, and had no idea of the power he so ignorantly flaunted. He turned Webb's stomach. But let him make the most of his arrogance and disregard for powerless people. Certainly, he had put together the most financially successful HMO conglomerate in existence. He had cowed into submission to his principles doctors on the most prestigious medical school faculties, and in the most renowned clinics, and those in open practice alike. He had proven to be cunning and ruthlessly clever. He gave shares and an interest in his HMO system, Total Health Care, Inc., to the carefully chosen doctors on his staff. This method tied their pay to stock options and turned them from concern with treatment to concern with profits. He had bought dozens of HMOs and brought them into the system.

Now he gobbled up nursing homes in the same aggressive way, adding them to the system, and he wanted Mallory's southern collection, The Magnolia Homes. And he would succeed in his way unless something unexpected blocked him. Give him his rein and he would continue to make fortunes for all investors. But Kadsh skirted the outer fringes. He was getting more powerful by the day and impatiently created the aura of command even in the presence of Kramer and others around the table, as he did with his own underlings.

Fritz Kramer, despite his impulses to retaliate, remained quiet and neutral, his sharp profile keen with attention. Kadsh should have known better than to overstep the bounds. He had come too close this morning. Kramer moved before he went too far, and rescued him with a single remark.

"You have to give this a little more time."

Thornton sighed as Kadsh backed off, but still on the brink, and this left Fritz with his hands full. Out of necessity, this problem now would go back to the great arbitrator, Lapkin Lewis, the undercover lawyer, the go-between among the casino owners, the controllers of the union funds, the owners of unwashed money, the labor unions of many sorts, the building contractors. Had Kadsh known such a person existed, his arrogance would have lost its edge. Thornton would not tell him. Sooner or later now Lapkin Lewis would enter Kadsh's realm one way or another. Lapkin Lewis, smooth and elegant, never touched anything, never claimed any credit for acquisitions or accomplishments. He merely acted as a fixer. Nobody owned him. Nobody could buy him. He moved silently, deftly, and stayed out of the limelight. But through a long career he had grown more and more powerful, and had outlived the rash and the incautious. It would sober Kadsh to know the realities. Bullet wounds in the head, slashed throats, sunken dismembered torsos, and penitentiary cells had taken many out of circulation, while Lewis remained untouched. Most of his contacts knew him only as a voice at the other end of a phone line, the voice of deadly finality.

Kadsh no doubt had proven to be an unusually successful business manager for a medical doctor, but he had the unyielding and naive arrogance of the medical mentality. Such characters would incautiously finger the trigger of doom and inadvertently blow everybody to hell unless silenced or controlled.

Listening, without adding a word to the exchange, Thornton Webb suspected Kadsh would resort to deceptive and unilateral methods to make the nursing home industry largely his. He had revealed himself in negotiations. In his cynical and ruthless arrogance and avarice, Kadsh considered making money off of nursing homes almost laughably easy, simply because nobody goes there to live. They all go there to die and relieve their families of odious burdens, and the sooner they complete this one-way journey the better for everyone else. There could be no clingers. They were too expensive, and Kadsh would not tolerate them very long. Webb regretted, more and more, the intrusion of Kadsh into the syndicate's business.

After Kadsh had finished giving orders, excused himself, and left the room with his business manager, Thornton Webb turned to Kramer and said, "I want to know how a patient's insurance dollar, one of the scanty and inadequate few, not only comes to no effect in his treatment, but instead ends up in the coffers of somebody like Kadsh, who progresses in two or three years from the ordinary income of a practitioner to the rarified atmosphere of owning more and more HMOs and nursing homes. And among other private homes, acquires an eighteen million dollar mansion atop one of the most elegant buildings in Manhattan, and a palace in Las Vegas?"

"From the HMO profits."

"Oh, for God's sake, I know that. But how is it possible?"

"Management."

"Yeah, well, does the money come from anyplace except the insurance companies?"

"No."

"And where do the insurance companies get their funds for the HMOs?" asked Thornton.

"Insurance premiums. The patients pay it, one way or another."

"Then it's the patients' money in the pockets of the HMO owners and executives."

"Right."

"And how do they do it?"

"Economize."

"Meaning?"

"The word means only one thing ... do without."

"Who does without, and without what?"

"Patients do without, and do without everything from unnecessary studies and unnecessary treatment on the one hand, to life-saving procedures and drugs on the other," said Kramer.

"Who decides?"

"The wrong people, too often."

"Like who?"

"For instance, a nurse, otherwise unemployed, with a desk and telephone, intercepting the treatment route, often a frantic call from a qualified specialist seeking authorization to perform a life-saving emergency procedure."

"How can such a person make a negative decision?"

"However they can, they do. Often they have a score of resentment to settle. Smart-assed and not too bright, for the first time in their lives they reach a status above the smarter and more qualified person, with a chance to control, to make trouble, to be authoritative, to get even in the pecking order ... gleefully, maliciously, and profitably. Actually, the stupidity and the rigidity of the rules they must go by may make an intelligent decision difficult or impossible. At other times the stupidity of the referee creates the impasse."

"At the risk of the patient?"

"Oh, yes. The truly sick get sicker, and some die, some who could have been saved."

"This is inexcusable in the American system," said Thornton.

"Speaking of that, my doctor friends tell me that the referral system has been thrown into reverse. Before the HMO era, the generalist referred patients to the specialist to obtain higher skilled treatment for difficult and dangerous problems. In a way, the generalist thus protected his own reputation. Now, the generalist is paid indirectly not to make a referral. He is rewarded financially for not practicing the wisest and safest management of his patients' problems and is punished financially for referring to a specialist. So the driving force behind the new system is profit for the system and for the owners of the system, not for excellence in treatment."

"But the enormous profits to the few."

"An anomaly of an out-of-control insurance industry. No doubt, some day public resentment will close these loopholes. And pray to God the medical profession can eventually unload the burden of insurance, which is a bigger cost to treatment than is the treatment."

"What would take its place?"

"Everyone, including government itself, fears it would prove to be something resembling the hostile and rejectionist atmosphere of the post office or the waiting room of the Social Security office."

"A nightmare of inefficiency and second-rate service."

"You got it ... or worse."

"So?"

"That is precisely why the insurance industry is getting away with it. No one has come up with a better idea guaranteed to work."

"Pity."

"Yes, a better way needs to be found."

Thornton shifted about uneasily. He had more to say, more concerns to express, and he did not know how far to trust Kramer. But a flag needed to be raised. He knew any word he uttered would go to Lapkin Lewis. He said, "Something is wrong with this scenario. We are accustomed to easy money in amounts most people only dream about, but this Kadsh has made more money faster than seems possible. In fact, in amounts astonishing even to us, and I wonder ... for laundering money, you know it would be hard to beat a hundred nursing homes, all of them unprofitable, or not very profitable, especially if they served as a front to hide a bigger operation, like electronic transfer of sums not moveable otherwise. I'm suspicious. Is Kadsh laundering money and contributing to the terrorist movement? It's the only thing that makes sense. If so, this man could get us into serious trouble with the feds."

Kramer said, "I will pass on your concerns, and I suppose you know he's trying to get us entirely out of the drug business."

"I did not, but I'm encouraged to hear it. But we have other concerns like Peter Mallory's little nursing home situation at Cambridge."

"We think the real problem lies elsewhere."

"I've considered the possibility. Are you alluding to Bin Kadsh?"

"Yes. Kadsh appears to be giving him help he probably does not really recognize or want."

"Like what?"

"Like the death of Dr. David Beckette, and the ruination of Jack Williams."

"I'm sure we are suspect in that."

"We had nothing to do with it. And Lapkin Lewis is furious. Now they are working on Helen Beckette, trying to scare her into quitting her job," said Kramer.

"Why her?"

"They accuse her of spending too much money taking care of patients. Actually, she is doing her duty and spending no more than is needed. But she does try to avoid harmful strictures. I think this is simply another of Kadsh's by now renowned and inhuman cruelties to the common patient. And Mallory has a fixation on Helen Beckette like crazy."

"But he consorts with Celeste Howard," said Thornton.

"Because he can't do any better on short notice, I'm sure. And you know she's a piece of work."

Thornton did know indeed, but he played another role. "Meaning what?"

"Mallory is just one of many."

"That, and what else?"

"We are sure she is not involved in the killings."

"What killings?"

"Terminal patients, and possibly others, with more to come, people like Helen Beckette probably in grave danger."

"So where does Celeste stand in all this?"

"Our surveillance is limited to line tap at her house and we've listened to her nighttime phone conversations. Quite an actress, histrionics from joy to tears, instantly, sounds drunk by midnight if she is alone, which is getting to be more and more frequent. From her conversations with numerous men, we know she can slip from one role to another, even convincing herself."

"Stable?"

"Yes and no. Over the long run, she has goals and she will try to attain them. Unstable? Yes, but only in being emotionally labile."

"You think Mallory is taking a risk with her?" asked Thornton.

"Mallory takes risks with everything. And his worst gamble is himself because he thinks he's so clever," said Fritz.

"Will he keep her in the dark about what he really is doing?"

"Try to, unless he gets too intoxicated on whiskey or his own importance. He is prone to brag, to be careless when he starts talking, trying to make himself look great."

"That is dangerous."

"We will continue to check her out."

"Okay," said Webb, "Speaking of danger, have you looked at Wyatt's Crossing?"

"Yes. We've monitored the operation and we went in at night to double check. It's more or less as described by Crouch to Mallory and by Mallory to you, perfect for housing fishermen out for a rustic good time."

"Okay."

"That's the small stuff, even a red herring if necessary. The real operation is the church. The underground vault there, ostensibly a storm cellar to protect an entire congregation, is actually three times the floor space of the church itself, well hidden and tight as Fort Knox, with a recent hidden enlargement, at least 300 percent, the space filled with a bank of computers."

"Will the setup work?"

"Oh, yes, initially. The entire operation will be behind the facade of two big F's: fundamentalism and fishing, as well as a third screen, the traffic in relief supplies for disaster areas in other parts of the world, only token amounts, however. What could be better than a religious revival, totally free to the worshipers, in a beautiful rustic setting by the river with free helicopter flights and bus trips in and out, free flowers to decorate the church, free food after the services, hellfire and damnation sermons, baptisms every Saturday? This attracts the crowds."

"The stuff is moved only after dark, I suppose."

"Only after midnight ... people will be coming and going day and night, the fishermen not so much as the church goers."

"Women at the lodge?"

"No mixed company, no indoor plumbing, and only bunk beds in an open dormitory with no privacy."

"Not a foolproof setup, you think?"

"No. Of course not," said Fritz.

"Well?"

"Suddenly one day the whole world will know."

"So."

"So, take your choice. Are these the doings of a fool, or is something truly stupendous being planned, so profitable as to need the setup only once for its real purpose?" said Fritz.

"Yeah."

Thornton waited. Fritz Kramer never came to these meetings without instructions and plans from the confraternity of owners, and in a moment he would transmit the edge of the controlling power in all its menacing reality. All decisions about disagreements came from Lapkin Lewis. And without doubt Kramer had reported yesterday's meeting to him in detail, and the reaction had been strong, otherwise Kramer would not be back so soon.

Thornton asked, "You have news from Lewis, I suppose?"

"Yes, your banker, Peter Mallory has about used up his time. An ultimatum has come down. Mallory has one more month to settle matters with Bin Kadsh."

"I'll pass the word on to him."

"Of course, he is not the real problem, and this brings us back to Bin Kadsh who seems to have another agenda, and the feds are inching too close for comfort, putting us all in danger of interference with our business. September 11 has changed everything, you know," said Kramer

"Yes, but think of the possible continuity."

"What do you mean?"

"I've been wondering why Bin Kadsh would need our money, and since he has it, why the delay in completing his transactions? And that brings up another possibility. Is he using this entire Golden Age problem, which I think is blown out of all proportion, as an excuse to delay payback until he can accomplish something else he is up to? However you look at it, there is no way for Peter Mallory to remove the highly respected obstacles down in Cambridge. Every imaginable law enforcement agency would be down on his head and ours if harm came to them."

"Yeah," said Fritz.

"It was a mistake to have dealt with Kadsh in the first place. He and Mallory hid from us the entire drug operation, which we should not be tolerating. It's time to be done with this man, who I think is proving to be more and more a monster, and if we don't get rid of the drug business it will mean our downfall. Once the federal government decides to put an end to us they will do it one way or another."

"You are getting close, but not making yourself quite clear yet."

"Fritz, money laundering, the soul of the drug business, and the life blood of terrorism ... and Kadsh is from Zeebeckystan, and he is a zealot at everything he does."

"Yeah," said Fritz. "You're beginning to sound like Lapkin Lewis."

"What else would it take? This foreigner, this total newcomer, has screwed the American patients royally while our bungling government sits back and does nothing. What's to stop him from going all the way?"

"Maybe nobody but us."

"I would not want to be accused of not sympathizing with the Arabian cause."

"Nor would I, but terrorism is not their official arm, and the United States is at war with terrorists worldwide. Therefore, we cannot allow any activities that would cast suspicion on us."

"I agree. Now another possible risk, what do we know about Ruble Crouch?"

"We've been looking and his affluence is showing."

"Tell me."

"Nice house, nice rig worth at least a hundred thou ... boat and trailer and truck together, and he is living with a white woman, a divorced licensed practical nurse with an alcohol problem and an old drug problem, too. But we have seen neither of them on the street."

"Is Crouch to be trusted?"

"He is a wily survivor, and he has a record, you know."

"For what?"

"Drugs. Two years at Parchment."

"Where's he getting his money now?"

"Peter Mallory."

"Any other source?"

"We're not sure."

"You are watching him?"

"Sort of."

"Meaning?"

"We can't follow him on the water without being obvious. He reveals nothing in phone conversations from his home, but there is a certain traffic coming and going in the daytime when he's there. He and his live-in girlfriend both work the shift from 11 p.m. to 7 a.m. When he gets home he sleeps until early afternoon, then the visitors begin to arrive. At about three on some days, he goes to the water with the boat rig. We have seen airdrops at dusk over into the trees. He fishes in the cypress swamps along the edge of the lake obscured by trees and vines, and we really can't see whether he makes a pick-up or not. He sells fish and we suspect distributes drugs from his home. Chicken feed, penny ante anyway."

"Well, if he's doing that he will be caught."

"He's protected locally. The sheriff is in Mallory's pocket.""What's his future?"

"There for a purpose. Mallory will sacrifice him to hide the bigger operation."

"We must get out of drugs," said Webb.

"Lewis' orders."

18

Celeste Howard rolled onto her belly across the bed and studied Wyndam Jones as he dressed hurriedly and said, "Wyndam, my darling."

"Yes."

"Come here."

Wyndam approached. She reached in his unzipped pants. Wyndam, standing with his knees against the bed, surrendered to her ministrations. Minutes later as he approached another zenith, she freed her mouth but not her hand, and rolled her eyes up toward his face, and said, "Wyndam, darling, do you like what I'm doing to you?"

"Oh, goddamn, yes! Don't stop!"

"But you've got to do something for me." She slid the tip of her tongue up the length of the shaft, popped the turgid head in her mouth, popped it out again, and looked up.

"What? For God's sake, what?"

"Are you going to do it for me?"

"Yes, of course, you know damned well I will."

"Promise?"

"Celeste, dammit, yes! But what? Christ, don't stop!"

She raised her body up, lifted her head and looked him in the eye, "Wyndam, darling, little ole Helen Beckette is in our way, and somebody's got to do something."

"Oh, Christ, Celeste. I'll get that goody two-shoes out of town."

"How?"

"Scare the hell out of her?"
"How?"
"I got lots of tricks up my sleeve."
"When?"
"Tonight, dammit!" He shoved himself at her mouth.

As Helen Beckette prepared to leave for work, Clara said, "The notes concern me. I wish you had brought them out when we were there."

"I wanted to, but we were committed to silence, so I let it go. I'll try to go back at noon today."

"No, not alone."

"I'm not afraid."

"I'll be at the front entrance of the main hospital, noon sharp, in one of Tom's pickups, a red one." Clara was gazing at her severely and soberly, with a no-foolishness expression.

"Okay. But don't you think that's overdoing it a bit?"

"Face it. You are being stalked and watched. And those two endeavors always whiff of potential violence. We are going to stick with you until this is ended. But you have to let us help."

"You are right, I know."

At the Golden Age, Helen parked in her assigned spot and walked across the lot. At a side entrance for carts and wheelchairs, a black Mercedes 600 in all its dynamic threat stood front bumper against a blue sign with a schematic wheelchair embossed in white, a similar sign on the pavement almost out of sight beneath the car's massive body. This would be Peter Mallory, parking without respect for the disabled, flagrantly exploiting his own self-importance.

His presence at the home this early morning hour meant trouble. He came at such times to put more pressure on management to cut costs. Her throat constricted in a knot of dread. His $125, 000 automobile, parked amidst the squalor of hundreds of discarded cigarette butts, scattered trash and litter, overflowing garbage cans, overgrown grass, untrimmed hedges, bespoke his avarice and profligate ways with money acquired at others people's deprivation.

She walked around to another side of the building and entered her office through a rear door. The front entrance to the office remained locked as she went to work on a stack of papers. The sounds of early morning activities – rattling wheels, murmuring voices, banging pans – beginnings of the day, muted down the wings of the home. Birds stirred in the limbs outside her window; a lone mockingbird exulted a dawn rapture, ignorant of the sadness within these walls. Helen worked to subdue rising anger and dread, and a dreary oppression expanding inside body, head, and mind to the point of erupting. She braced for the inevitable intrusion of Mallory when he finished whatever he was doing, snooping around somewhere, most likely. She again puzzled over the two deaths reported yesterday morning. Both people had been very old, both totally unaware of their surroundings, and both constant medical problems. But no warning change had occurred in the vital signs prior to death. Each had been found dead in bed on morning rounds. These two deaths would save the home significant cost in care and medications.

An hour passed, and at seven o'clock, tentative tapping sounded on her door. She ignored the interruption and continued work, Mallory no doubt. It would not be the cleaning people; they did their work at night. And just how far would he carry his intrusion? A louder knock, then silence, keys rattled, the bolt turned, and the door cracked open. Helen slid down in her chair out of immediate sight behind the desk lamp. God, he wouldn't have the nerve to do this! Or would he? What could he want in her office? The record she was keeping? The nose first appeared at the jamb, then the whole profile, the head, and the rest of Mallory eased inside. He turned, threw the inside latch, and locked the deadbolt. Helen remained still as Mallory moved swiftly across the room. He braced himself on extended fingers of one hand atop her desk as he rounded the end on tiptoes sneaking toward her chair and the filing drawers. Then she suddenly stood straight up. He started and gasped, but recovered quickly.

"Oh, Helen, darling, I was hoping I would find you here. You didn't answer my knock, so I was just going to leave you a very private note."

His appearance – his medium stature diminishing, his sandy hair scraggly and stunted, his presence a weakness, his demeanor slinky – made her think: Cur. Despite the expensive tweed coat and gray flannels, he appeared seedy, rumpled, his limber button-down collar stale. He grabbed her hand clumsily and as she snatched it back he managed to brush her knuckles with his lips, bowing ungainly at the waist. She quelled the impulse to strike his face. He pulled up a chair and sat almost against her.

"I've great news for you ... for us," he said in a conspiratorial whisper.

She remained stolid and silent, still standing rigidly. He hitched his chair closer, looking up.

"We are going to become a member of a great chain of nursing homes."

He paused and waited for the effect. Helen, trapped and waiting, said nothing.

"You realize what this means?" his voice rising, growing impatient with what he took to be her incomprehension. She still made no reply. "Helen, my dear, this means a great promotion for you, we will all move up, for that matter, and I will need you by my side in the new responsibilities in a big city. I will be vice president in charge of operations, not only of the nursing homes, but of the hospitals in the HMO conglomerate buying us. You will be my executive secretary, my right-hand person. We will be together all the time."

"Mr. Mallory, I ... "

"No Helen, don't shotgun me a negative answer now. I want you to think about it. I want us to go out to dinner where we can sit down and talk it over."

His manner made her angrier. What were his real intentions in her office? Would he have searched for something in her absence? Did he have a key to her desk drawers and filing cabinets also? His locking the door on entry removed any doubt about his deviousness. Should she play along with his game? God no. Not with this revolting creep. She would just keep her dignity and privacy and her silence. He would trap himself sooner or later.

"Mr. Mallory, I cannot be what you want. Find someone else to do the job, because I will not be taking it."

"Now Helen ... "

He stood, leaned closer, and lifted a hand. But as he reached toward her shoulder, she already had moved out of range. She rushed to the door, snapped the lock, and opened it. Dan Rattner at that moment strode into the office vestibule. Mallory spoke first from behind her back. "Good morning, Dan. Helen and I were just finishing a conference about conditions here. And now the three of us can have breakfast and continue the talk."

Helen turned as she strode across the lobby and said, "If you gentlemen will excuse me, I've my morning rounds to make." She walked rapidly down the hallway. Lying devil, yet she had to give him credit for being quick on his feet. But Dan Rattner is not stupid. He would know they had been behind closed doors and he probably heard the locks as he entered the office area. Damned little snit – Mallory would taint her reputation despite all of her efforts to avoid him.

At the first nurse's station, she received news of two more deaths during the night. Each person had been there more than two years, costing the nursing home increasing amounts of money in extra care and medical treatment. She took the charts and retreated to a workstation. One patient had been running an increasing temperature rise for forty-eight hours prior to death. The pulse rate had slowly risen, the respirations increasingly rapid. Pneumonia, she would bet on it. In the nurses' notes she found thirty-six hours past, *Dr. Dodson's office notified of changes.* And twenty-four hours later, *Dr. Dodson's office notified again by fax.* Then an hour ago, *pronounced dead by intern from County.* The other chart revealed a low temperature, ninety-seven, two days ago; then ninety-six a day ago. She found a note indicating this change being reported to Dodson's office. She supposed this to be an infection of some kind, the old body unable to respond with the usual defense mechanisms. She questioned the head nurse. Isaac Dodson had not responded to the calls. And he had not made his rounds in six weeks.

She left the nurses' station alone and proceeded to inspect patients' rooms for telltale signs of neglect and abuse. The odors were enough, the rank insult of old dried urine, the oppressive musk of fecal traces, and she followed this trail to an inert form bulging under stale bed clothes. Rings and wavelets of dried brown stain reached up to shoulder level. She drew back the covers and felt the clothes on the silent body, soaking wet. A fiercer fecal stench reeked from beneath the lifted covers. Neglect at its worst, and sooner or later, each of these helpless people would develop bedsores in the flesh compressed for hours under the inert body in this filth. Then nothing would cure these rotting undermining ulcers, not even the most extensive plastic surgery, the body too old, too debilitated to fight back, the cost of treatment rising out of control, the neglect becoming worse, and death sooner. False economy: There simply were not enough employees to give the proper care needed for these hopeless people.

Helen continued down the hallway. As she passed an open door, a voice called her, "Helen." She stopped and looked in. Rachel Colburn, sitting up in bed, alone for the moment, said, "Come in here, Helen, I want to talk to you." As Helen approached the bed old Rachel held out both hands and took Helen's. "I want to thank you for your concern for all of us out here. You are so kind and considerate, and I share your grief for David Beckette."

Surprise, Rachel actually knew her by sight.

"But that's not what I want to talk about, something I want to ask you do you know my John, my son?"

"I know who he is."

"You've not met him?"

"No."

"Oh, what a shame."

"Why, Mrs. Colburn, I would love to meet him."

"Well, that's not exactly the way I meant it. You see I have this feeling about you, and about John. God knows he needs someone like you, and you are the only one like you in this whole world. I think you two were meant for each other. I feel it through my old being, in my bones as they say …" She still held Helen's hands gently, the silky old skin warm and caressing. Helen felt it coming, beginning down in her belly and rolling up, and the tears suddenly erupted and began pouring down her cheeks, and Rachel's eyes brimmed too. The bathroom door opened Abruptly, and the attendant came back in the room with a bedpan. Rachel released Helen's hands and said, "You know it, too."

Helen said, "Yes, I've seen him once, but only at a glance, and I know."

"God love you," said Rachel.

Helen left the room and went from wing to wing for the next two hours, finding the same signs of neglect on every ward. The operator paged her three times over the speaker system, but she ignored the calls. Mallory, she guessed, was trying to corner her again. At noon she went through the back entrance to the adjacent hospital, through its underground tunnels, and found Clara waiting at the curb.

Helen and Clara entered through the kitchen into a wrecked house and a fetid stench. They sniffed and looked at each other. The door to the pantry stood open and contents of the storage cabinets had been emptied onto the floor, glass containers of jams and jellies and condiments smashed, dishes broken, flour, salt and sugar and other staples dumped onto the counters and the floor. Clara held an arm at full length in front of Helen.

"Don't go another step until I get Tom out here."

She removed a cell phone from her pocket. Wrecked furniture and broken bric-a-brac littered the floor of the living room and hallway. Slashed upholstery, books ripped apart and stripped of pages, and other papers littered from wall to wall. Helen craned toward the pantry, straining to see in, her face gone stark white. Clara held her by an elbow.

"You can bet they got to the whole house ... Tom! ... Yes, Helen and I are at her house ... somebody has trashed it ... no ... we are standing in the back doorway ... no, not a step forward ... Okay!" She snapped off the phone. "Tom says to wait in the truck, aimed toward the road, and to run down anybody who appears and tries to stop us. He'll be here in five minutes."

On the front seat with the motor running, Clara watched the terrain downhill toward the highway. "Well, I suppose they were after your notes, or journal, whatever, but I hate to think what would have happened had you been here during the night."

Helen stared straight ahead, rigid, sober, tearless. "Somebody really means business."

"Oh, no doubt. But I want Tom to see the evidence, untouched by us. Do you think they found it?"

"No. I could see in the pantry just now. The secret panel has not been opened."

"What else could they have been after?"

"Nothing, unless to frighten or kill me."

"When do you suppose?"

"Last night, I imagine."

"Man, I don't like this at all ... "

"Sorry."

"Oh, don't be. Neither Tom nor I would want to miss the action."

Tom took two steps into the kitchen and stopped to survey the damage. He sniffed and turned to Clara. "Goonsby," he said. "Don't move, either of you, until I have a look."

He reached for a broom in the pantry and tiptoed through the rubble and the mass of scattered paper and gutted cushions in the adjacent rooms. Raking a clear path ahead of his feet, he worked his way into Helen's bedroom. A moment later he said, "Well, I'll just be damned."

He returned to the kitchen holding the broom by the end of its handle. A big gray rat lay stiff, caked in melting ice, on the straw platform.

"Where did you find that?" asked Helen.

"In your bed under the covers. I will keep this gentleman in alcohol at home while we gather other evidence."

He went out the door, pitched the rat into the bed of his pickup truck, and returned to the kitchen. Clara and Helen waited.

"Do you suppose there are others in there?" asked Clara. "Most likely, and God knows what else, but I'm not about to go poking around under furniture and beds and among all that debris on the floors."

Then he turned to face them both and asked, "Why did you two come out here?"

His face was pale, his jaws clinched, obviously angry and trying to contain it.

"To get Helen's notes."

"Okay. I guess it's my fault for not warning you. But this leaves no doubt. We are dealing with diabolical people, and very nasty ones at that. Come on, Helen, let's find your notes."

He turned and entered the pantry, and with the broom swept trash out of the path, then stood aside while Helen found the secret panel, opened the safe, and removed the briefcase.

"Take everything of any value. You can count on them coming back."

She opened the briefcase and found the journal safe inside. She dumped in her jewelry and bundles of cash and stock certificates, and bonds and other savings. She closed the safe and the secret panel. Grim and silent, she picked up the briefcase and walked into the yard. Tom and Clara followed. At the truck door she turned to Tom. "Now what?"

"Gas to kill snakes and insects, then a dog to sniff out any explosives, such as land mines hidden among the scattered paper on the floor and under the furniture."

"Who?"

"I'll see to it if you want. It will take several days."

"Thank God for you and Clara."

"You two stay away from this place."

19

In the warm weather of mid May, Ruble Crouch drifted his boat to the next cypress tree, dropped anchor, and started the engine on an air compressor attached to a small paint sprayer mounted at the end of a twenty-foot pole. He extended the pole up the east side of the tree, pulled a dangling string attached to a trigger, and sprayed two squirts of a liquid fluorescent paint on the tree trunk. The fluid trickled down the bark. He then moved downstream to the next tree and repeated the operation. Five trees a hundred feet or more apart should be enough, he thought.

Further downstream, he dropped anchor again and began reeling in a trotline. The bigger fish, the real keepers, the big yellow channel cats, were on the far end of the line where its sinker had pulled it down into the main stream of the inflowing river. He worked casually, throwing each fish onto ice in the cooler. The sun went down, and darkness deepened as he worked two more lines, taking his time, waiting for something. By eight o'clock his anxiety had begun to mount. Then the plane drifted in low, a moving shadow among shadows, its engine idling in surges. Light beams flashed on and knifed down into the trees. Fluorescent reflections answered the searching beacon, one, two, three, four, five in a row. The lights disappeared, the plane swooped, then the engine overhead roared full throttle and lifted the plane out of its slow dive. It went on west out of sight and out of sound toward Batesville and Sardis. After a moment of receding sound, a shower of missiles plunged through the dark foliage, splashing. Several balls, reflecting the dim light, drifted within dip-net range of the boat. Ruble retrieved these quickly. Then he snapped on a headlight and followed the reflections until he had gathered all fifty packages, each perfectly round, each covered in a shiny surface, and each too slick to get tangled in a tree. He dumped half in a cooler, threw a layer of fish on top, then poured ice over the fish. The remainder went in the second cooler under fish and ice.

At the mouth of Hurricane Creek he trailered the boat, placed one cooler on the floor in front of the passenger seat of the pickup, left the other in the boat, and headed toward Cambridge, driving slowly, warily, on the lookout for trouble. After several miles of gentle curves, nothing had appeared. As he approached Abbeville, he had begun to think he had slipped by this time, but flashers suddenly burst out of the following darkness almost atop his rear bumper. He started, recovered quickly, and pulled off the road into a field behind a thicket of bushes. The cruiser followed, the gold letters COUNTY SHERIFF visible on the door panels in the revolving light. Ruble remained behind the wheel. The deputy approached his window.

"Howdy, Ruble."

Ruble looked cautiously at the man hunkering down to peek through the open window, and controlled an impulse to shove the door open and smash this stupid coward, then knife his pot gut, but he calmly said, "Howdy, Wyndham."

Wyndham Jones. Why the hell couldn't the sheriff send someone respectable?

"Catch any?" asked Wyndham.

"Yeah. Got me a nice mess of channel-cats."

"Well, I'd like to buy some offen' you. Mah favorite fish."

"Just help your self to the cooler in the boat."

"I don't know as I can use that many."

"Oh, go on take 'em. More than I'll ever use, and I don't like 'em froze."

"Okay, but you gonna' have to let me pay you."

"Naw, just hep' yourself."

Wyndham reached in his pocket and handed Ruble a folded bill.

"Can't let you give me fish for nothing."

Then he turned, walked back to the boat, lifted the cooler over the gunwale, and carried it to the trunk of the patrol car. He backed into the road and waited for Ruble with his flashers off.

Ruble maneuvered into the road and drove through Abbeville and on toward home. The sheriff's patrol car followed at a distance. Ruble drove slowly, musing to himself. God, how he would love to take the air out of that strutting bully! When all of this is finished, and Mr. Mallory has his money and is in complete control, then he will deal with Wyndham Jones. Not fair – half of all he hauled out of the river went to the sheriff, who shared none of the expenses and did none of the work. Bastards! Ruble unfolded the bill still in the palm of his hand and held it up toward the windshield. A dollar bill! Damn!

Cheapskates! But he had no choice, buying protection. Without it he would not dare drive down the highway with more than fifty thousand dollars worth of heroin hidden under only a layer of dying catfish and a skim of melting ice cubes. He would love to speed up and race home, but no. He must do nothing to draw attention. He would just take his time, clean the boat, wash it down, then dress the fish, wash the fluorescein off the balls and hide them until tomorrow afternoon when they would be picked up by another of the sheriff's men for delivery down the line. And he had to make a show of selling dressed catfish from his house to disguise the real activities there, damned tiresome this danger, all of it for Mallory. He didn't trust Mallory, not an inch out of sight. Chicken feed, this dipping of balls of dope from the river, compared to the size the operation would take on as soon as the church and the fishing lodge became really busy at Wyatt's Crossing. Did Mallory think him stupid, that he would not get the big picture? So why the exposure, why the penny ante now? Ruble had grown suspicious. The big shots from big government could easily be watching him, and they were likely to, in view of his record. Had Mallory been setting him up? Would they use him as a foil and get him back to the pen for dealing, just to hide their own big-time operation? This routine made him tired and sleepy; before he could get all this done, it would be time to go to work at the Golden Age home for the rest of the night. He would be able to catch some naps there in dark corners of the far reaches of the wards if Sybil Snyder didn't cause too much trouble prowling and watching him and bruising patients. His dread of going into the place and his awareness of the dangers had grown steadily. But maybe Miss Howard would slip in and light up his night.

20

Helen Beckette's door eased open and her secretary peeked in and said, "Mr. Mallory's on line three, insisting."

Helen suppressed an impulse to refuse the call one way or another. This could not be good at seven o'clock on Monday morning. He had to be up to something again. She picked up the phone and answered with a simple and soft, "Hello."

"Helen, darling, was yours a good weekend?"

Her anger flared. His simplest statement betrayed his insincerity. She withheld an answer as the silence grew, he obviously waiting for her surrender to his charm. Finally she said, "Fine, thank you," and waited.

He recovered, and stumbled on with his attempt at casual familiarity, "Oh Helen, I hate to bother you, I know how busy you are, but this is of the utmost importance, and I'm counting on you for your inimitable support."

Inimitable! Where did he come up with such an overwrought word? She held her breath as he continued. "Great news, I've just been called to conference about the sale of our nursing homes to the great HMO chain, Total Health Care. The buyer is ready to close the deal, and Helen, my dear, I hope you realize what this means for both of us. I will need your help. I will need you by my side with your charming way of handling people and your very smart business acumen."

She waited. He continued, "I have to run over to Tunica this morning for the meeting, and I need you to be with me. It would be such an honor to have you there at the moment of finalizing the deal. Beginning today, after the deal is clinched, I want you to be my chief executive officer."

Helen, trying to control her impatience, replied, "Oh, Mr. Mallory, this is so kind of you, but I must refuse. I would be in over my head."

"Now Helen, I would be right there with you on every decision, guiding your hand, and before you knew it, you would be fully oriented and doing a great job."

"No. You need a man with an MBA. In fact, I'm considering a less stressful job, away from the health business entirely."

"Oh, no. What would you be doing?"

She detected a note of alarm. Would he be feeling a surge of disappointment at the possibility of losing his hold on her through her job, or had he sensed a more sinister threat? This insight released an impulse and she took a shot in the dark.

"To be perfectly frank with you, I'm thinking of devoting full time to finding out what happened to my dearly beloved husband, David Beckette, Mr. Mallory. There aren't many real men in this world, but he was one of them, and I think it would be appropriate to honor his memory by finding out what actually did happen. I do revere his memory, so, and still love him, even in death, Mr. Mallory. Perhaps a little successful detective work would help assuage my grief."

No immediate sound came from the other end of the line. Helen sensed a moment of triumph, a surge of satisfaction at having delivered a sadistic blow to a vulnerable and cowardly solar plexus. He recovered quickly.

"Oh, Helen. I had so hoped I would be able to help you overcome your great loss. And I want you to know I am always here for you. And I will have to let you go now ... got to hurry."

Martha Williams braced herself and waited, listening while she typed away at her computer. Helen Beckette had just turned him down again, but this time something had gone haywire. His face blanched and he slid the receiver down, then immediately phoned Celeste Howard and did not talk very nice to her. It came through more like an order, like he had control, like he owned her and could call the shots anyway he wanted. Meet him at once, throw on anything, grab a bag, hurry. He sounded conspiratorial, like they were in trouble together. He slammed the receiver down this time, without explanation, and without taking his frustration out on her again, he strode past Martha's desk and out the door. The car tires screeched on the pavement as he turned toward the interstate.

She felt a surge of relief and of curiosity. What had Helen said to him? Did she finally tell him to get lost, to leave her alone, or had she threatened him in some really alarming way? The phone rang. Zelma Taylor said, "Martha, are you alone?"

"Yes, I am."

"Is he out of town this morning?"

"Just left, and I don't expect him back before tomorrow."

"We need to talk."

"Where are you?"

"Home. I work the evening shift today. Could I come by now?"

"Sure."

"Be there in ten minutes or so."

This would be interesting, as always with Zelma. You could count on honesty and openness, and a burning sense of what's right and what's wrong. Zelma would tell it like it is, damn the consequences. Anybody who misused her would pay back sooner or later and pay dearly. And something had made her hot this morning.

Zelma entered the bank in a rush, drew up a chair, and came right to the point. "You know after leaving the job here with Mallory, I took a job in the sheriff's office, part secretary and part receptionist."

"No, I didn't know."

"I did, six weeks ago."

"You like it?"

"Well, it ain't no bank, baby. Pretty rough the first few days until I got used to it."

"Should be interesting."

"That ain't hardly the word for it. Anyway, I got me a desk right out there in the open where I can see what's coming and going, and listen to most of it."

"Yeah, like what?"

"Plenty, let me tell you."

"Something I need to know?"

"I'll bet on it, in the long run."

"Zelma! What? Anything to do with my Jack?"

"I'll bet on that, too."

"For God's sake, what?"

"You know, I take all incoming calls. From where I sit I can hear just snatches of the talking. But I heard enough to get me curious, and I went out and did something really sneaky and illegal. But sneaky is justified if the evil deserves it."

"Zelma, what have you done?"

"Well on my day off I drove up to Memphis and bought me the fanciest little recording machine you could imagine, the latest thing, all digital they called it, so small I can hide it in my purse, hardly bigger than my thumb and so sensitive it can record conversation in a room from inside a closed purse, and it starts recording when anyone starts speaking. Cost me three hundred fifty dollars. And to record the phone conversations, when I'm there, all I got to do is plug into one side of a double phone jack, which you can buy for two dollars. I have be careful to unplug it and take it with me when I go. I would love to leave it during the nights, but I'm afraid it would be found."

"You are taking a big chance."

"You know me. Piss me off and I take chances."

"Who, Zelma?"

"You know that dumb prick, Wyndham Jones? Deputy dog-face, the blacks call him?"

"Yes."

"Well, I ain't been there half a day 'till he's comin' onto me like a pig in heat. I wouldn't let that ham-hands touch me if he was the only man left on the face of this earth. But he don't take no for an answer, and begins struttin' and showin' off, talking too loud, and I get onto him. That's when I start taking notes and then go buy my little machine. Then I got him when he lowered his voice."

"So, what did you hear?"

Zelma inched her chair closer and lowered her voice to a whisper, "Martha, this fuckin' little town is rotten to the core. They are taking payoffs down there, and drugs are coming in with the sheriff's protection, and dirty money, but my God that's not the worst."

"What is worse?"

"Physical stuff. Bad stuff."

"Have they harmed people?"

"I'm pretty sure, but I don't know who nor when, just yet. But I do know Jones is working with an out-of-town bunch. They've been here before, that I did catch. As hard as I listen I can't quite be sure exactly what they did but I think they killed somebody, maybe more than one. And somebody has been sent here to scare Helen Beckette into giving up. Stupid Jones brags about it."

"Giving up what?" asked Martha.

"She's keeping too many old people from dying out at the Golden Age, running the costs up too high, and the profits down too low ... gettin' in the way of Mallory's sale to a big-time HMO outfit. Then there is the rumor that she's gettin' more and more nosy about what happened to her husband, Dr. David Beckette."

"Would they harm her if she does not give in?"

"Martha, after scaring the hell out of her with nighttime threatening phone calls, and scratching on her window panes at the midnight hour, they broke into her house, trashed it, and put a dead rat in her bed."

"Oh my God! How do you know?"

"They were laughing about it on the phone."

"So what happened?"

"They don't know. She's stopped spending the nights at home."

"What do you think this means?" asked Martha.

"I think she would already be dead if Peter Mallory did not have his mind set on seducing her. And when he realizes he won't ever, then that's the end of her."

"How awful."

"And something else ... they seem to think she's nosing around too much, keeping some type of record or diary of the happenings that shouldn't be happening."

"Why?"

"I think it means she's determined to find out what happened to her husband, and to establish a permanent record of the harm management is doing by depriving patients."

"I hope she does."

"Also it means they are worried and more determined to stop her."

"Zelma, this is much worse than we suspected. You realize we are talking about nothing more than the local sheriff and a cheap little small-time banker, and I can tell you that little banker has stirred up things on a much bigger scale. Now there are outside interests behind the scenes, among them the most ruthless of HMO moguls, and at least one gambling syndicate. That means big-time union money, money tainted by mob interests."

"How do you know?" asked Zelma.

"I've picked up enough in his correspondence and his phone conversations, which I hear whether I want to or not, to know, just from his careless way off blowing off his big mouth. He's got to brag, you know."

"I know, little man puffin' up."

"But the mob ...Would they move into this little town?"

"No government or boundary has stopped them yet. But I think it's more complicated. The mob concept is too simplistic," said Zelma.

"Well, as you've heard me say, I fear some possibilities worse than the Mafia ever dreamed up."

"Yeah, and this Kadsh is from Zeebeckystan, and if he is laundering money and belongs to the Middle East ... think about it. This could really take on serious international ramifications. And Peter Mallory ain't that big."

"This is bad."

"Yeah. Since the nursing home profit is thin, even marginal all too often, why would Kadsh want a hundred of them?"

"Greed."

"Worse, much worse, I'm willing to bet, greed with a purpose, like the money laundering, and on a pretty big scale at that," said Zelma.

"The purpose of a second, if not hidden, agenda."

"Yes, politics and religion, one and the same, leading to terrorism and other war activities. Somebody's got to stop this."

"And there is some more local stuff going on I really don't like."

"What, Zelma?"

"Jones is thick with the Goonsby clan, one of them in the office nearly every week, walk in like they own the place, spending time behind closed doors with Jones or the sheriff or both, being paid off to do dirty work of some kind, I'll bet. You can smell one of them when he comes in the door and the stink don't leave the same day."

Martha laughed. "They make ordinary white trash look like royalty."

"I know, and they don't come any meaner and lowdown or any more sneaky. That's probably where Jones got the rat, and they are probably using Goonsbys to scare Helen."

"Zelma, you really got to be careful. Don't get yourself killed."

"It could happen, and I'm wondering, should we call Clara again?"

"I'll call her now. She's buzzing around town with her cell phone on, I'll bet," Martha said as she picked up the phone.

Ten minutes later Clara Bartley walked through the door and joined Martha and Zelma. Martha did the talking. When she had finished, Clara let out a breath and said, "Mallory! Why that dirty little bastard." Her face had blanched and turned grim, her jaws tight. "So he's the one behind that fool Jones. Well, well, well, this do make a difference. Helen is safe in our hands for the moment. We have started seeing her to Golden Age every morning, and one of us brings her back after work, and we don't let her go anywhere alone outside the house. We will keep her until this matter is settled. I can't wait to give Tom the news. And I can tell you one thing, girls. I would hate to be in Mallory's shoes for what's coming down."

"And Clara you ought to know that Jones is messing with the Goonsby clan. They are up to something together."

"Yeah," said Clara. She would not tell them yet about Tom seeing them in action at Helen's home.

"So, what next?" asked Zelma.

"Everybody just hold to your course like nothing is happening. I'll talk to Tom and maybe some of my other buddies and get back in touch. Don't breathe a word of this, and Zelma, don't get caught listenin' with that recorder. Come to think of it, you ought to give the damned thing to me right now."

"Can't. It's at home,"

"Well. Don't take it to work with you again until you hear from me."

"Okay, I'll leave it home, I promise."

"And watch out for Jones, he's dangerous. Don't get caught alone with him anywhere, not even at the water cooler," Clara said, as she went out the door.

21

Peter Mallory sped up to 110 mph on Highway 304 across the delta. Celeste stared at the cotton fields zooming toward them like blurring terrain beneath a full-throttle lift-off. Finally she broke the silence. "Peter, what's your hurry?"

"Most important day of my life."

"Well, tell me about it."

"Got a call at five o'clock this morning from Thornton Webb, wanting me to be in his office by ten thirty. That can mean only one thing. They are ready to close the deal, and I wanted you to be with me. This is our big moment."

"Oh, Peter. And you've worked so hard for this."

"Yes, I have. And it's only the beginning. I'm ready to move on up."

"And I'm ready to go with you."

"Well, I hope everything is all right. And it is if they've decided to ignore the little problem at the Golden Age."

"Oh God, Peter, I'm damned impatient with it."

"So am I. But what can we do?"

She turned to him and fixed her eyes on his face.

He knew the look but could not divert his attention from the speeding car, even for the briefest glimpse.

She said coldly, icily, "Anything it takes, Peter, anything it takes."

She reached in her purse, fumbled as though searching for something, and by touch entered Thornton Webb's code and pressed the send button.

After Peter left her in the lobby, she went directly to Thornton's private door and found it unlocked. She crossed to the bedroom. He had already undressed.

In the after-love pillow talk, Thornton became stern. "Celeste, your earnings at the table tonight will be small, as you report them to Peter on your way home. We plan to put the pressure on him; he has wasted too much time."

"What can I do?"

"Marry him and take charge."

"There is the small impediment of his wife."

Thornton studied her soberly with a black-eyed gaze and quietly said, "Don't let little things stop you. Get him out of our way and we will take care of matters."

"How much time do I have?"

"Two months, and I can't change it."

"Whose decision? What's his name?"

"I hope you never need to know."

"Well, I'll do what I can, but I don't really see the need for such urgency."

"We are dealing with an uncontrollable factor here, something bigger than we are accustomed to, and exceedingly dangerous. We have come to fear an end run, so to speak, a move around us with consequences we cannot predict. Loss of control we do not want."

"Why so dangerous?"

"Growing evidence of terrorist support has the feds nosing about. We don't want their attention. Peter has placed us in an untenable position by creating a standoff with Kadsh. We need to be finished with the whole problem and move on."

"Thornton, I'm not following you entirely, nor do I understand the insistence on this one little nursing home becoming profitable, more so than it is already. It's not losing money, you know."

"I know, but it gives Kadsh an excuse not to complete his deal. In other words he continues to control the money, and Peter, whether right or wrong, may end up broke, or dead, or both. It's time for you to move in. You're a smart woman; just do it. Now you get dressed and go. We've kept Peter waiting long enough.

Thornton Webb, sober and unsmiling, remained seated when Peter Mallory entered the office. A second man sat at the end of the desk. The guard stopped two steps short of the desk and stood at attention. Thornton swiveled his chair to face Mallory, and said, "Peter, you know Fritz Kramer here, business manager for the organization. He brings us the news that Bin Kadsh is ready to play hardball. His offer for the Golden Age home chain will remain valid for only one more month. And that is entirely legal since your formal contract expired four months ago and he already has given you a two-month extension twice, gratis, so that you might get things in order. If the Cambridge unit has not reached the projected profit margin by that date, the offer will be withdrawn, leaving you with the entire debt to pay yourself, some $250,000,000. As to the money owed your bank by the same organization, you would have to use your own strong arm to collect it, if you have one."

"Well, I will certainly do my best with the problem ..."

"Peter, we would never stoop to deprive the aged by failing to deliver proper care, and to be perfectly frank with you, we wish we had never become involved. We intend to be out as soon as some debts are paid. But you created this problem with your promises to Kadsh, and you have to solve it. Within one month, forces beyond our immediate control will take over, take the homes, and you will say nothing while you slowly pay off your debts as the years go by, simply a matter of business, Peter. If you remain obedient, we will say nothing to the IRS about your unreported winnings at our gaming tables, which by now have mounted to a tidy sum, and we will say nothing about your secret drug operations. We do know about the plane drops in the lake at night, Peter. Shame on you for risking all the big stuff to play penny ante, and using the sheriff's plane, Peter. How dumb can that guy be?"

"Oh, no. That was set up deliberately as a foil just in case..."

"Bullshit and shame on you again. You would try to put the blame for something as big as the hidden operation on one insignificant little ex-convict with no money, no wherewithal, no power, who does your nefarious bidding only because he is your financial slave. No serious investigation would buy that. Your patsy will break one day, Peter, and watch your back when he does."

"What do you mean?"

"Oh, Peter. Look at the man. He's equipped with the ultimate native gift."

"What?"

"The blood of Africa, the blood of the Indian, the blood of the white devil, all mixed, seething, intelligent, wily, fearless, waiting for his chance, Peter. He knows none of the white man's tepid conscience, or crippling fears."

"How?"

"We make it a point to know what our people do, Peter."

"I have nothing to hide."

"From us you can't. So, I am passing down orders to you. Be rid of all your problems within the month, then you have another month to up the profit. And that's it."

"But how?"

"You made the promises to Kadsh, we didn't. Live up to them and we will support you.

"Thank you." Mallory took a step backward, ready to turn and leave.

"And Peter."

Mallory turned to face Thornton Webb. "You and Celeste wash these before you leave."

Webb handed over two large overstuffed manila envelopes.

As the cotton fields blurred by in the opposite direction, Celeste said, "Peter, I didn't win but ten thousand on nine hundred and ninety-nine thousand worth of chips, I was having to make such huge bets to get rid of so much money."

"Hell, I got only five."

"They are angry with us."

"Worse than that. We are in deep trouble, baby, if we don't get rid of the people who are standing in our way."

"Did they say who?"

"They did indeed."

"Who?"

"Old expensive Rachel Colburn, hell-raising Clara Bartley, pussyfoot Dan Rattner."

"Peter, that's too much. They are pushing you to impossible limits."

"I can't get rid of the employees. They are staying now on limited salaries only because they are trapped. I would have to pay twice as much to replace them, and I would have to start a war to remove Clara Bartley from the premises. And damn it, you know something else? Our friend, the good doctor Isaac Dodson, created this Rachel Colburn problem himself. I can't do a damned thing about her, not legally, that is."

Celeste already knew the details from John Colburn in intimate and impassioned fury, but she pretended ignorance and surprise.

"Oh, really!"

"Yeah. He's become lazy and careless."

"What did he do?" she asked. She would let Mallory know nothing of John Colburn's story or her familiarity with Dodson's behavior gleaned from his frequent visits to her bedroom in the past. Someday she might get the chance to confront Isaac Dodson with a few of his cruelties.

"Really messed her up so she had to become a nursing home patient. Otherwise, she very likely would still be living in the cottage her son bought for her."

"That's really too bad."

"Oh, indeed. And that leaves us stuck with her and her overzealous nurse."

Celeste despised Clara Bartley and her unrestrained confrontations. She would be tough to get rid of. But it could be done. Shutting her up would be more fun than total elimination. Maybe Jones would have an idea, something natural or appearing to be, or maybe an accident, a one-man accident, unavoidable ... she seemed to remember something about Clara, what was it? Oh yes, something unusual for a woman in this part of the world. Yes. She hunts. Yes, she does, and alone, deer she has heard, and wild turkeys and in the summer months, squirrels and rabbits. Keeps her table supplied with wild game. Hmmm. She would speak to Jones.

She said, "Okay Peter, we will get these people out of our way."

"Are you hungry?" he asked when they were halfway to Cambridge.

"Yes, but there is no time to eat now."

"Why?"

"I have to be at church in an hour. We have choir practice, and the church is my whole life. I couldn't live without it."

She reclined her seat sharply, lay back and closed her eyes and thought of herself facing the pulpit and singing *Gloria in Excelsis Deo*, peering over her glasses across the apse. The words and the music come automatically, her bemused attention on the smooth profile of Bishop Gregory Peterson. Celeste Peterson? No. Would never do. He would be excommunicated, and wouldn't divorce his precious little Susan, the proud clergyman's insipid wife, under any circumstances. Too weak anyway, a church mouse pittance would not be enough. But Gregory *was* such fun with his chasuble lifted, and he would be there alone waiting for her an hour before time for choir practice. She dozed until Peter stopped beside her car in Cambridge.

22

Before sunrise on the first day of the June squirrel season, Clara Bartley parked her jeep behind a copse of bushes just off a field road, took her .22 rifle from the gun rack, and went toward the tree house on the Colburn property. Ideal time, and Tom did love squirrel stew. The big red fox squirrels had been stripping the pecan trees every fall and it was time to thin them out anyway. Besides, she loved practicing shooting them through the eye. A correctly placed shot saved the jaw muscles, which were especially tasty. Everything else was out of season.

She wouldn't be long at this, back by mid-morning to relieve the sub she had hired to watch Rachel Colburn, and Tom would be so surprised by the steaming dish of fresh squirrel this evening. At the front ladder, ascending straight up the oak trunk, she slung the gun strap over a shoulder and reached up for a rung, and froze in the motion. One short note in an upper register of a dog whistle, the single solitary sound like the lonesome peep of a tiny bird, stopped her. Could this be a bird? Or was it a warning? She held her breath and waited, a blank stillness in the summer heat, and waited, and it peeped again, this time just a preemptory pip, the briefest note, but unmistakable, the sounds she and Tom had used to signal each other while stalking poachers and while hunting and fishing and hiking through dense woods and undergrowth and along river banks in years gone by. Something has gone wrong, somebody is in danger, or she would never have been given the signal.

She went into the mode they used when working together on a job as game wardens years before. Always crouch and go toward the sound without moving weeds or bushes. Twenty-five or so yards away and ten minutes later she crawled around the trunk of another big oak and found Tom crouched stone still in the bushes. She knew never to speak under such circumstances.

He held his .30 .30 rifle ready and wore a holstered .45 magnum. What was happening? He was supposed to be at work. She rolled over and sat near his feet. He kept still, listening. They waited. Tom removed a whistle from his pocket, placed it to his lips and the whistle emitted perfect sounds of a crow cawing, then without the whistle, Tom blew through his front teeth the sound of the bobwhite call. He was signaling someone else; what on earth was going on? But she knew she had placed herself in danger, and Tom had come with backup. Silence settled on the scene. They waited again in the heat-radiant summer silence. Ten minutes later, the coo of a nearby mourning dove fell into the space around them, and then a brief mocking bird trill overhead.

Tom whispered, "Walk to the front ladder, get in the blind and stay there, shoot up into the limbs toward the open field just like you are killing squirrels, then wait, don't move, don't try to come down until I signal you. And don't get where anyone can see you, and don't shoot anybody regardless of who they are or what you think."

In the tree-house blind, Clara sat on a shooting bench and poked her rifle barrel through a port. As she brought her eye to the scope, a big red squirrel and two fat gray ones scurried up a limb far overhead. She shot the red one and it fell into the bushes below with a resounding plop. She dropped the other two as they scurried to the ends of the limbs, the last one as it leapt into space toward another tree. Her limit, she didn't need anymore. She waited.

She wanted to get to her kill in the heat but she controlled the impulse. Silence settled in once again. Then she sensed something, and felt the faintest vibration. Someone was sneaking up the rear ladder to the giant limb supporting the back of the blind. She peeked out a rear port and stifled a gasp. The barefooted thing in ragged overalls and loose filthy shirt already walking down the limb and within arms reach of the wall horrified and frightened and revolted all in the same impulse.

She recognized a man from the Goonsby clan, the scariest, filthiest, stinkingest people in existence, scavengers, poachers, thieves, wife beaters, child molesters, totally amoral deadbeats, murderers. Some had never bathed in a long lifetime. This one, the oldest boy, Clink they called him, miraculously surviving so far to his mid twenties, in and out of jail for bootlegging, stealing, fighting, burglary, and once shot by a game warden in self defense, she knew to be the most corrupt of the lot. The depraved stupid face, the milky crossed eye, the rotten tooth stubs, the vicious laugh, the rough skin green blotched from never bathing, overwhelmed her with a profound sense of discouragement. And in this moment of psychic inertia, insight suddenly overwhelmed her ... Wyndham Jones is behind this and already she would have shot Clink a half dozen times if Tom had not warned her. She held her breath; she held her fire.

A copper-colored hand behind Clink reached down from the limbs overhead, grasped the slouched shirt collar, pulled it up the nape, and another hand came down and funneled a big fat snake tail first down inside the shirt and released it, all done swiftly and deftly. Clint screamed and began tearing at his clothes with both hands, teetering on the limb. Then a hand reached down again, grabbed Clink by the hair of the head, and flipped him off the limb. He crashed into the undergrowth twenty feet below. The two hands came down again, this time holding a long white sack by a drawstring. One hand reached further down, caught the sack carefully by the bottom seam, upended and emptied it down on Clink. By a second and different fetid stink, Clara already knew they were cottonmouths, four now altogether. The last three landing atop Clink got him on the face and neck and hands while he fought with the shoulder straps of his overalls. No one moved; no one came from hiding. In total panic, Clink leapt up and began running, one overall strap flapping. He went down the edge of an open soybean field, and skirted the riverbank until nearly out of sight. He had begun to lurch and stagger before he disappeared over the riverbank at the Colburn property line.

Tom stood and approached the tree beneath the blind. Ruble Crouch lowered himself down out of the foliage overhead to the big limb then descended the back ladder. Clara came down the front ladder and crashed through the bushes. She returned, holding the three squirrels in a bundle by the tails. She turned to face Tom as Ruble quietly watched.

She said, "You don't have to tell me. This was some more Wyndham

Jones crap. It's got all the earmarks, and I know he badgered and threatened that monster into something very stupid. What the hell was he trying to do to me?"

"Kill you with your own gun and make it look like an accident."

"How do you know?"

"I got old Wyndham on the bug I planted in his cruiser the day after I saw him scratching Helen Beckette's bedroom window. It's been fun listening to him while I worked."

"How did you know the day and time?"

"Everybody knows you go on opening day of the season and everybody hunts squirrels in the early morning. Besides, I heard his instructions to Clink."

"Where and when?"

"Yesterday while they're riding around in Jones patrol car."

"Yeah, well why the snakes?"

"You mean the moccasins? Because they don't kill as quick as the rattlers. That gives him time to run far enough toward home to be off the Colburn property before he drops and dies, which he has done already by now. And nobody can be accused of killing him and getting that crazy Goonsby clan burning for revenge ... a clean job, untouched by human hands, no gunshot wounds, no stabs, no strangulation, just nice clean moccasin bites. And ole Clink was just stupid enough to get a snake down his pants."

"Yeah, but this is only Clink. That maniac Dynamite Don will come looking for trouble now."

"We won't give him much to go on."

"How can you be sure that Clink won't get home and talk?"

"Ruble's truck is parked over in that general direction. He will trail him to be sure. But nobody survives that many bites on the body, especially when he gets scared and runs. The panicked heart pumps the poison home in short order. Then there are the ones on the head and neck. And the snakes will all be gone by the time someone finds him."

"Why me?" she asked.

"For rocking the boat out at Golden Age, I guess."

"Well, I guess they'll leave me alone now."

"It would be more like them to strike again quickly, thinking your guard is down."

"So how will we handle this?"

"Keep absolutely quiet about it. We don't know a thing. And I'll be listening to see what Jones tries next."

"Well, thanks for the rescue, guys. Ruble, would you like one of these squirrels? Two's enough for us."

"That would be mighty nice."

She handed him the red fox, by the tail. "Here, you take this one, the two grays are all we can eat." She turned and walked toward her jeep.

On a sunny and quiet midweek morning, Clara Bartley, after delivering Helen Beckette to her office and doing the morning care of Rachel Colburn, turned into the highway from Hospital Road and headed home. Before she reached the first stoplight, the sudden blare of a siren made her jump. She looked in the rearview mirror to see a car on her rear bumper flashing its roof lights. She pulled over. Somehow, as she watched the heavy figure strut and waddle to her window, she knew she had been expecting this. The sheriff himself, and she wondered what she might have done while thinking about something besides her driving. Within a minute or two she knew ... failure to yield the right of way, and ten miles over the limit. She knew better on both charges or thought she did, but she could not swear to it. Stopping at the highway entry and looking both ways came naturally, as routine to her driving habits as breathing. Going over the limit? No. She always went under the limit. But she and Tom both had thought they might be caught with trumped up charges sooner or later. Curly Watts, his gut hanging like a stuffed sausage over his belt, trooper's hat cocked forward, his fat face malicious ... she had known him all his stupid life, and she had never known a sorrier human being. He inspected her driver's license and wrote a ticket with the same surly formality he would show a total stranger caught speeding through town. He said, as he handed her a copy of the ticket, "We no longer are going to tolerate chronic law breakers in this town. Second offense you lose your license, third you go to jail." As he turned and walked back toward his patrol car, guns heavy at his side, he added flippantly, "Have a good day." She never said a word during the process. She and Tom had agreed they would use this approach if trouble appeared. Now she knew they would be pursued and hounded. She seethed with rage, the crooked, lying devil. The insolent *have a good day* as far as she was concerned could be his epitaph, and at the moment she was mad enough to chisel it on his tombstone. She knew she had done no wrong, but she would have to be extremely careful in the future. She would get herself under control, maybe even wait a day or two before telling Tom.

23

John Colburn, in the kitchen of his barn lodge and sitting across the table from Sam Sheffield on Tuesday morning, said, "Luckily, I covered a lot of territory in Washington yesterday."

"I'm surprised you're back so soon."

"We can get all the political backing we need, and access to the latest technology."

"Great news."

"Okay. So what do we need to find out?"

"All we can about the important little banker, Peter Mallory, everything he says in the office, his correspondence, what he says and hears on the phone, who calls him, where he goes, what he does when he gets there, who his local cohorts are, who he is dealing with outside Cambridge ... everything."

"Okay."

"You have a plan?"

"Yes, with the help of NSA. It took some string-pulling at the highest level, and not a hint must ever leak out. This is the heavy stuff."

"I know," said Sam.

"A suspect's name or code spoken into a telephone or typed into a computer online anywhere on earth or its vicinity can activate the most sensitive of listening devices."

"How is it done?"

"Electronically, with satellites."

"How do we get ready?"

"We don't. Give them the go-ahead and NSA will do it without leaving any evidence or ever going near the place. The information they gather would be fed into your office also, unless you want to set up a center elsewhere."

Sam said, "No. The office is okay."

"I will need names and phone numbers to pass on."

"Easy enough."

"And, Sam, we need a pickpocket."

"Be serious."

"I'm most serious."

"Then why?"

"So we can get our hands on Peter Mallory's wallet, specifically, his credit card carrier for just a minute. Then it should be returned to his pocket."

"You've lost me."

"We need to track him when he leaves the office, when he is not on a phone or at a computer. Bugs now can be as small as a grain of rice. Hidden in his credit card carrier several would go with him everywhere for later distribution to the people he sees."

"I don't imagine there's a really skilled pickpocket in the north part of this state, maybe not even in Memphis. We'll have to resort to another method," said Sam.

"However you do it, we need to get to his wallet, or something personal he carries with him where ever he goes. And his watch won't do."

"Okay. I'll bet Clara Bartley would have an idea."

"And we will need a full-time employee who can be completely trusted to monitor these activities."

"Maybe a NASA person, your people?" asked Sam.

"No. It would raise too many questions in this little goldfish bowl we live in."

"I'll look around."

"What's our next move?"

"You proceed with the technology and I will recruit the personnel," said Sam.

"One phone call will start my part. And why don't I return here at two o'clock with Clara Bartley?"

Clara Bartley remained silent while Sam talked about the facts and the plans. Then she said, "I know some of this through people already involved."

She mentioned Martha Williams and Zelma Taylor, and what they knew, describing Zelma's dangerous recording device in the sheriff's office.

She added, "And I'm sure I have the right person to monitor the operation in your office. I think we all ought to meet here after dark tomorrow evening, say eight o'clock, if that's okay with you, John."

"It is indeed."

"I'll bring Zelma and Martha along with Helen Beckette and my Tom. And don't eat dinner. It'll be here waiting. I know what everybody likes," said Clara.

John Colburn arrived at his barn lodge with Sam Sheffield. The women came with Clara and Tom Bartley. Clara introduced them as they got out of the car. Zelma Taylor preceded the others, tall and thin, with black close-cropped hair, shiny clean, black eyebrows, black eyes, a flat chest and a pelvic curvature slightly overwrought. She emanated rustic sexy wickedness, and the aura of a good-hearted soul. He thought, willing, even eager, and probably swept up by it. Her vibes titillated his virility, but he didn't need more trouble and she had a jealous boyfriend already watching her. Anyway, he awaited with keen anticipation the introduction to Helen Beckette. Martha Williams next came forward to shake hands, a solid matronly woman, the coloring of a brown mouse, in control of herself, conscientious, school marmish, and little plump. He knew her to be grieving, but making the most of life while hoping for justice.

Helen Beckette turned to help Tom unload the trunk of the car, and came forward with her arms full of packages. She stopped at the words, "... and meet John Colburn." From behind the armload, she looked into his gaze with the most alluring gray-green eyes beneath an exuberant head of auburn hair, a slender, graceful, alert woman.

John took the bags from her hands. And he knew at once. A surge of emotion rushed, of regret for not having waited to find her, for his misguided errors with Sarah Beazlie and Celeste Howard. But the uneasiness passed. They lingered a second, gauging each other. John caught the little motion, the shadow crossing the iris, the emotional revelation of acceptance, a biological tremble of approval in the brooding gaze, the closure on a decision. The moment passed, and he carried the bags into the kitchen.

After fried catfish, Clara served pecan pie and coffee, and the talk turned to the serious business at hand. Sam started the conversation. "To begin, Helen has a chart she has been putting together for many months, and it seems to verify the problem we all now suspect or recognize. Would you show us, Helen?"

Helen unrolled a large graph, and pointed to the red line between abscissa and ordinate, running up to the top right-hand corner of the page. She said, "This represents the death rate compared to the daily census. It has climbed steadily since the death of David Beckette and the ruin of Jack Williams. The blue line is the profit margin, running almost parallel. This leaves no doubt."

John said, "Good work, Helen, and the results do indeed leave no doubt." Then he said, "Sam, let's talk about what you will need."

"Okay. In addition to the equipment about ready to go, we need a trusted person to sit in an isolated and locked room in my office and monitor the information coming in by the various techniques. This, of course, has to be extremely confidential. I don't want my regular office staff to know any of the details. We need an intelligent and quick person, computer-literate, and fired up for the challenge of this job." He hesitated and turned to Clara. "Clara, I believe you had someone in mind."

"Yes, I did say so, but I've not had a chance to ask her yet. I was thinking of Zelma, here."

"Oh, I've got a new job in the sheriff's office already. And it's important. I'm listening in on their shenanigans."

Sam said, "We have better ways to do the same thing without exposing you to the danger in which you have placed yourself already. Whatever you do, don't go near that place again in possession of a sound recorder."

"Why?"

"Because it's illegal there. You could be prosecuted and jailed if caught, and you are dealing with treacherous people."

Zelma paled in the candlelight, and after a moment she said, "And you're not illegal?"

"Zelma, and everyone here, this must remain a secret. We are protected. We have the blessing and the approval of more than one federal agency."

Then Zelma asked. "Well, what should I do? I can't up and quit. I just started."

"I have an idea," said Clara.

"What?" asked Zelma.

"Let's see now. You told me Wyndham Jones was coming onto you like gangbusters, right?"

"Yeah, right."

"So, you give him a little more rope, then hang him for sexual harassment, and quit cold."

Sam said, "I have just the young lawyer in my office to bring suit in your behalf, at no cost to you."

"Hey, I like you guys. I think I'm going to enjoy playing your game," said Zelma, beaming a lusty avarice for revenge. "But I don't need the miserable little glory of outdoing the likes of Jones. I'll tell them something and just quit."

John said, "Great idea. But would you plant a supply of bugs in strategic places before leaving?"

"Okay. You've sold me on it. I get to sit there in Mr. Sheffield's office, by myself in a room, and listen to everything comin' in from both Mallory and the sheriff?"

"Right," said Sam. "And a great deal more from several monitoring devices and methods".

"God, I can't wait.

"And you'll get paid for it, too."

"Hadn't thought of that."

"Before you leave tonight, I'll give you a supply of bugs and show you how to plant them."

"Okay."

John continued, "Now, we will need to get to Mallory's credit cards, however he carries them."

"In his wallet," said Martha Williams, but she caught herself and stopped. John saw her blushing and averted his eyes.

"Then we need a pickpocket."

"Why do we want his wallet?" asked Clara.

"To plant another type bug."

"Won't he know it ... won't it bulge?"

"No bigger than a grain of rice,"

Zelma couldn't contain herself any longer. "I'm going to like this. Boy, the Mallory Club would love to be in on it."

"What's the Mallory Club?" asked Sam.

"Every woman he's shafted, those with the guts to admit it ... every secretary, every waitress, every employee, every somebody else's wife, every poor struggling fool promised something she never got ... lying little creep. We meet once a month for lunch and listen to the latest reports on his tricks, every one of us stewing to get even."

"Wow!" said Sam.

"Martha, we don't need a pickpocket. This is a job for us. You get his pants off, and I'll plant the bug," said Zelma.

Martha blushed. "You get his pants off and I'll plant the bug."

"All right."

"When?"

"Tomorrow, ten o'clock. I've got the evening shift." She turned to John, "Show me your little bugs."

John opened his briefcase atop the table. He placed a tiny brownish-black rectangle, about half the size of a grain of corn, on the table. "Now Zelma, you place one on an electric cord, say to a lamp. Current makes it stick. The surfaces are non-conductive, so they won't shock you. They are not likely to be found for years, if then. Best place is on a surge protector cord. Nobody ever looks there. Be sure to get one in the sheriff's office, and another in Wyndham Jones' cubicle, and several in other strategic areas. Stay away from computer cords."

"What about the phones?"

"Don't worry. We can get to them without bugs or a wire taps."

"My God! How?"

"Digital technology and satellites."

"Well, I guess nobody's private anymore."

"Not if the snooping is serious."

"How about the bug for Mallory?"

John opened a tiny jewelry case, revealing little dirt-colored bug-shaped objects sulking in the candlelight, each half as big as her little fingernail and not much thicker. He turned to Martha, "You take this, case and all. Open it when ready and dump all of these bugs into the main compartment of his wallet. Don't worry about them falling out. They won't."

"All right. It will be done tomorrow with Zelma's help."

John turned to Tom and said, "Tom, we need a tracking bug on the van you spotted at Helen's house, so we can find it. If you could ..."

"Well, just hold on and let me spare you the trouble. I already found it, parked and partially hidden inside the Sheriff's carpool. Jones has a rookie driving for their mischief. I already bugged it. Follow it anywhere you want."

"How?"

"On the underside of the battery cable. Gets plenty of juice full time."

"Good. How does it work?"

Tom said, "Same as yours, digital and satellite."

"Well, this is a big help."

"Glad to do it, but I don't have any tolerance for these devils. They ought to be stopped before they do more damage."

"I agree," said Sam. "And we will move as quickly as possible. But we need to know the extent of their operation, all its ramifications, and just who is behind them. It's far more than just local stuff, I know. I will be reporting to the agencies helping us."

"I'm sure it is. Also, what they've done and what they know reveals their use of equipment equal to that available to the CIA, at least," said Tom.

"Then we are faced with someone who has big money, really big money."

"Yeah, I would bet on it."

"We'll find out, and soon, but right now we need to get a bug in the van compartment so we can hear what they are saying."

Tom said, "You got it. I wired it into the radio and brought it out into an air conditioning duct."

"What kind?"

"About the size of an acorn, a damned good one. You could hear a flea breathe." Tom looked at his watch and continued, "If you are through with us, we will be running along – big day tomorrow."

"Sure, and thanks for your help, everybody," said Sam.

"I'll be at your office at nine, day after tomorrow, ready to go to work," said Zelma.

After Tom had left with the women, Sam said, "John, how will your little bug in the wallet get its energy supply?"

John laughed. "A bit of advanced technology. We have the blessings and funding through the Defense Advanced Research Projects Agency, and they in turn are taking advantage of our needs to test their new technology."

Sam waited while John continued, "You may or may not know, one of my interests in physics has to do with the building and control of robots. I designed and built the devices we use to control cameras and other equipment scooting about on the surface of Mars and the moon. Also, we are now building molecular computers, and the newest wrinkle, quantum computers, utilizing the spin characteristics of atomic particles that make the MRI in medicine possible. With this technology we can build infinitely faster computers than today's PCs, and of the size smaller than a pinhead."

While talking, he removed another jeweler's tiny case from his briefcase, opened it, reached for his wallet, and poured a bug from the case into its main compartment, then folded the wallet shut. He struck a few keys on his computer keyboard, and the bug ran out of the wallet and crossed the table, went down a table leg and across the floor and climbed the wall to the nearest light socket. There it stuck to the plate and two tiny antenna-like hairs crawled from its front end and went into the prong receptacles. The room lights flickered, and the bug withdrew it tentacles, turned down the cord, and ran rapidly back to the wallet and into the compartment from which it came.

"There," said John. "That little shot of juice will keep it broadcasting for months, and when it gets hungry again it will automatically seek the nearest electric supply and have another drink. Charges instantly, the most advanced of batteries, as well as computerized controls. It digs into the wallet walls with its feet and stays put until we acclimate it to a new home."

"Amazing."

"Now, let me show you something else. You have your credit cards in pocket now, I assume?"

"Yes."

"Okay." John touched the computer keys again. Another little leathery bug came out of his briefcase and skittered across the table and disappeared into Sam's clothes. Sam flinched and scrambled, but to no avail. John said, "Okay! It won't hurt you."

"Jesus man, that thing could do some damage, loaded.'

"Well, let's have a look at your wallet."

Sam extracted his wallet from a pocket and placed it on the table.

"Dump everything out," said John.

Sam emptied the contents including three credit cards. "Now turn it inside out."

Sam everted the inner lining. John took a pair of tweezers out of the briefcase, reached for the empty wallet, and picked up the little bug inside the inner seam. He held it up to the light.

"These are the ones going into Mallory's pocket."

"The possibilities are astounding," said Sam. "How do you do it?"

"It's quite simple to remotely zone in on the magnetic fields of credit cards, and send the bug to the source. From greater distances, from anywhere on earth, we just have to know a particular credit card number and we can bug its container. Yet, that's pretty crude compared to other possibilities. We are now perfecting a method of sending a bug to the electromagnetic energy broadcasting through the skull and scalp from the living brain constantly, and it can hide in a person's hair, or collar. Or we can use the electric energy generated by the beating heart."

"How do you control them?"

"Each little bug carries a quantum computer far faster and far more powerful than any PC or laptop in existence. We can send a number of them into a room in an unsuspecting person's purse or briefcase and remotely move them to the purse or card carrier of any chosen person in the same room, or the same building. We can also hone in on the human voice and follow to its source."

"God! What did that thing cost?"

"Billions for the first one, but they will get cheaper. This will be the first real test. I'm anxious to hear how well it toots Mallory's horn, as Zelma put it."

"Man, think of its potential."

"Oh yes, what an army of these little devices could do."

"It makes me shudder."

"This particular science is based on biomechanics, or the mimicking of Mother Nature. We have used many of the characteristics of both the ant and the bee."

"Well we've had quite a fascinating night, John, and speaking of Mother Nature, Clara whispered to me while we were in the kitchen tonight ... she wants you at the house tomorrow night for dinner with us, the us including Helen Beckette."

"Great. What's your favorite wine?"

"Any Merlot from Chile or Argentina."

"I'll bring it."

24

Celeste Howard tiptoed past the wheelchair collection, sidled along the wall, entered a darkened room, and waited. Her heart pounded, her pulse raced with fear and excitement. Try as she would, she could never hear his approach. She would be defenseless if he cared to harm her. But she had a suspected target already, another one she had picked while making one of her sporadic afternoon visits to the Golden Age, bearing flowers and cookies, and leading a pair of freshly bathed and beautified dogs on leash from patient to patient. This one, an old lady, lay in bed without moving, just breathing, using up the resources at the useless end of a fading life, one who hasn't spoken to or recognized another person in months, nor put a bite of food in her own mouth. And Peter Mallory has complained about her several times. The dogs had sniffed, then tucked their tales and whined. She would bet this would be the next one to go with the help of someone stalking in the dark shadows of the early morning hours.

She waited; nothing moved. She smelled nothing different: no cologne, no body aroma; the air remained still. He might not know she had arrived; he might not even be on duty. She waited. Nothing happened, a premonition warned, then she froze into absolute stillness at a slight sound, a stirring in the shadows, and she waited breathlessly, watching the same skinny form sneaking as it went to the bed and applied the pillow for a few prolonged minutes then vanished into the obscure night. The old thing never moved a muscle to resist; just gave up and crumpled, as if waiting and expecting this visit. But nothing made any difference. Even the absence of breathing remained empty of significance in the new silence.

Then while she waited there in the quiet darkness, her awareness starkly alone and far removed from any other person, without warning, without even stirring the air by his approach, he said in her ear, "Well, my dear."

She started to speak but he already had begun lifting her sheath, and she could only gulp down a huge gasp of air in the frightful and exhilarating excitement as he led her to a vacant storage area.

When he let her up, he turned and shut the door to the room, something he had never done before. A chill ran up her spine.

He said, "You have work to do, don't you?"

"Your meaning is not entirely clear."

"You know what Mallory wants and needs?" he asked.

"What?"

"You tell me."

"You mean besides being rid of some people, certain obstacles who will prevent the sale, including Rachel Colburn?"

She waited, the room silent.

Finally he said, "Go on. You're not through yet."

"Well, something has got to give with his little darling, the Lady Beckette. She will be dispatched as soon as he knows finally and beyond a doubt that she will have nothing to do with him. But he keeps hoping."

"She won't give in, and she will find out what happened to her husband, or willingly die trying," he said.

"How do you know all this?"

"I don't know you well enough yet to tell you."

"Seems to me we've gotten to know each other rather well."

"Not so well yet."

"Then, when?"

"After you marry Mallory. Then I will come to you, and while he is busy doing his sneaky stuff, I will show you me, all of me, and let you scream your head off."

"Do you promise?"

"I give you my solemn promise."

"Then let's hurry this thing along."

"Okay, that's what I've been telling you, but there's one thing more, Miss Howard."

"What's that?"

"The present wife, the precious little Sugar Mallory, as they call her out on the links playing golf half drunk and screwin' the pros. The dull boring chronic drunk hanging around his neck like a sinker, holding him back – somebody's got to get rid of her."

"How?"

"I'll tell you a little secret."

"Alright."

"The great hero Wyndham Jones spends his nights in her bedroom when Mallory is in one or another casino with one or another woman."

"Goddammit! Does Jones, that sonofabitch, sleep everywhere in town?"

"Like a stray dog ... he ain't missed a fireplug I know about."

"Let me ask you again ... how do you know so much?"

"I'll give you a hint. Do you ever hear me when I get near you?"

"No."

"Well, neither does anyone else."

"Okay, that figures. Now I want to ask you something else."

"Alright."

"How do you know I want to scream?"

"It shows."

"What makes you think I want to look?"

"You've tried."

"You bastard!"

"You are entirely right, I guess. But it equipped me well."

She expected him to leave, but he persisted. "I suppose old Rachel Colburn will be done next."

"I would have no way of knowing," she said. "When it happens and the hell raising starts, I want to be too innocent to even blush. Besides, she's too alert, she is not ready to go or be taken yet. But I still must know who is doing the dispatching."

"I want to remind you of one thing. Maybe you have missed it."

"What?"

"I have never touched a patient to do harm."

"Yes, you ..."

"No. You haven't been paying attention. I've just watched. I'm innocent. And I need to warn you about another danger.

"Oh, what?"

"You've been seeing more of Jones."

"How would you know?"

"Remember, I can smell."

"So?"

"A Goonsby. He's been getting thicker with them, and there ain't no mistaking that smell."

"And that means…?"

"The sneakiest evil in this world."

"Dynamite Don," she said.

"So you know about them."

"Everybody in the county does."

"They ride in Jones' cruiser, you ride in it, so you got a whiff of Goonsby on you."

"This is supposed to harm me in some way?"

"You know how Dynamite got his name?"

"No, not really."

"They live hand to mouth by stealing – a cow here, a steer there, a goat, a sheep, a horse, chickens and ducks and geese, corn out of cribs, gasoline out of cars in the middle of night, you name it they steal it, anything to keep from having to work. They harvest strange gardens by moonlight. They run the only whiskey stills left in this part of the country. Report them and something of yours blows up, like a smokehouse, an outhouse, or a barn, or a car. And nobody dares try to find their cache of explosives, and nobody can catch them, even if someone wanted to. And the sheriff don't want to. He has too much use for them."

"I know some of this. You know where they live?"

"I've walked every inch of ground and watched everything they do, and where they keep the dynamite. Why?"

"I got a job for him someday," she said.

"Like who?"

"You know Clara Bartley?"

"Enough to know you better leave that alone."

She did not hear the door open. He faded into the darkness. She reached and grasped empty space. She sniffed, and realized he had been wearing no cologne.

Back home she poured another glass of wine and sat on the couch wondering about Clara Bartley, still alive and raising hell. Jones said something mighty strange had happened out there in the woods. Clara came back to town with a mess of squirrels, and two days later they found Clink dead and rotting in the hot sun deep in the scrubland belonging to a pulp company a quarter of a mile from the Colburn property line, all swollen and poisonous-looking. The Goonsby clan came to town looking for trouble, but the coroner could find no bullet wounds, no knife marks, no bludgeon cavities. Snake bite, he said, one must have got in his pants from the looks of the marks on the body and head and neck. Probably fell off an overhead tree limb, maybe a whole tangle of them like you sometimes see in the spring of the year. Celeste thought there's a hell of a lot more going on in this little place, a vast disturbing unknown. She drained her glass and fell asleep.

After dawn she awoke thinking about the men running things at Tunica. Someone more powerful pulled the strings on Thornton Webb, she now knew, and she imagined working her way to the higher echelons, moving up on pillow talk. Then she would control the man who controlled the man who controlled Mallory. She felt so impatient. The little dogs smelled, a squirrel ran across the roof with pattering and hurried, frantic feet, and the rotted-off posts dangled and squeaked in the wind. Oh, how dreary the drudgery of poverty. She should live on the top floor of a big hotel with room service to bring all her meals, and a beautician to come in every day to freshen up her hair and her nails, maids to pick up and deliver all laundry, to do the rooms every morning, a handsome trainer every afternoon to do her exercises, a chauffeur on call at the door. Oh, why doesn't Peter call? But it's Saturday noon already, and if he hasn't called by then he won't call during the entire weekend. Maybe she should go and see about her precious friends, the animals, and take a couple of them on a visit to the Golden Age. At least it would be something to do, and chance to look around for ideas. She called the pound and made arrangements.

An hour later she dressed in slacks and went out to the Animal Land pound. Shelter they called it, animal shelter, the liars. More like doom. Humane Society, the pretenders even have the nerve to call it. Helpless captives, the animals are brought here to die unless somebody rescues them and takes them home for love and care. Poor things! Just like the nursing home! No, not quite. Some of the little animals are young enough to have a life, if a person makes room for them. But nobody comes and adopts one of the old human things.

Why can't society create something really humane for the animals, like something bigger than the zoo but smaller than a national park in every community and let them all run wild, the cats, the dogs, the birds, the other little animals, the pet snakes, the pet alligators grown too big to be safe, the pet cougars – even lions and tigers getting dangerous to children, all of them, with shelters and food aplenty. And why can't society build the nursing homes adjacent to the park for abandoned animals so the animals can come visit the old and hopeless people? She has seen their faces light up, she has seen them come alive when the occasional pet is brought in to visit.

At the animal shelter they know Celeste and let her in, and let her have run of the back rooms among the cages. They love to watch her communicate with the caged and condemned creatures begging for rescue. The animals have an uncanny sixth sense about people, like they can read each other's minds without words, although she has plenty of words she pours out there among the cages every time she comes in the place, standing there looking in between the bars, talking, the tears flowing. She feeds them little nibbles of delectables from between her fingertips through the bars. The animals lick her fingers, dogs and cats alike, and look up toward her face, another deep hunger and yearning and desperation ablaze in their eyes. The place grows silent in her presence; no one ever says *crazy*. She watches the watching eyes, and none are real dry when she leaves.

After walking down the rows between cages and stopping to talk to the dogs and cats, she returned to the front desk. An attendant handed her the leashes on two young frisky golden retrievers. He said, "Now Miss Howard don't you bring these two back sick. Last two come back barfin' up cookies and candy them old folks done fed them."

She took the dogs to her car and on to the Golden Age for an afternoon of visiting the old, those who were alert enough to respond. She took her time, moving casually among the beds and wheelchairs. It was almost worth the trouble, to see some of the old faces smile and become alert, and the old trembling hands reach for the dogs' heads. She took them in the room where the motionless forms lay bulging under still covers. The dogs approached, sniffed and each time each turned and whined and retreated with tail tucked. Death she thought, they can smell it hovering.

She rounded a corner with the dogs and came face to face with Helen Beckette. She swallowed. Helen, in control of her emotions, spoke cordially, then added, "Your visits with the pets have done a lot to help morale, and the patients do appreciate it."

Celeste, disarmed, immediately became voluble, and once started could not stop herself from pouring out her sentiments and opinions. She would so love to be able to help both the animals and the patients by bringing them together in a greater state of freedom. She so wished society was oriented to make such a dream come true for the good of all. Maybe someday she could find a sponsor for such a program, and it would be a model for the world to follow.

"Well, what a marvelous idea," said Helen. "I'm sure we could work with you if the time comes."

Celeste could hardly believe the words coming from her own mouth, in the hallway talking cordially to an arch enemy, her biggest rival in this world. She finished her visit and returned the dogs to the pound, and went home to await Wyndham Jones' arrival. She sat on the couch thinking about the encounter. Two people who dislike or fear or hate each other, actually down deep just ache to talk, each to show the other something good, something worthy of praise and respect. She smiled because she had penetrated the controlled and beautifully mannered exterior of Helen Beckette.

25

The dinner in the home of Tom and Clara had launched them, as Clara had known it would. Now, two days later, Helen Beckette sat up and studied the vistas through the windows open to late afternoon light and a setting sun. The broad sweep of the Mississippi flowing down from the north, turned westward around the bend of President's Island. Buildings of the Memphis skyline gleamed along the bluff above the river. Slanting light fell across her nipples and flared in the highlights of her auburn hair. John Colburn, quietly supine, sensed her tranquility. She placed a hand on the sheet and leaned forward over his face and said, "Welcome home at long last, John Colburn."

"I am here for keeps."

"Indeed, you are."

"You are sure?"

"Without question, and if you have impediments or reservations due to past miscalculations, misadventures, blunders, lust illusions, mistakes, bad judgments, or other wanderings, you can forget the shadows and the doubts. You are mine," she said.

"How did we miss each other for so long?"

"Pure chance, and only by happenstance did we ever meet."

"Unfortunately, the way of the world."

"I was sunken in the depths of grief and doubt, and not too happy to be alive after losing the steady love of my marriage, then I saw you and realized I had been missing something all my adult life. Am I sure? God, am

I sure!"

"I like your frankness."

"And John, if it makes any difference to you, I truly did have only one man, and I did wait, through happenstance or otherwise."

"Of course it makes a difference to me. I dream every man's dream."

"And I am where I am simply because nothing else happened to me, the way it happened to you. And we won't ever have to talk about this again."

"Thank you."

She sat up and gazed through the north window at the tugboats coming down the river, then she studied the Memphis skyline aglow in the sunset. "I've always been excited by coming to Memphis, since I was a little girl," she said. "Now it is dreamland, a paradise."

"Would you like to go out on the town tonight, dancing and dinner?"

"Will Tom and Clara wonder where we are … *up to Memphis to shop* won't explain tonight."

"I told Tom we might go on over into the Ozarks because I've always wanted to see them. So the time is ours. I'll call them later anyway."

"To answer your question, yes, I would love to get dressed and go out dancing with you, but right now, tonight, I don't want to wear a thread, not even a little string, between us. Can't we order up a midnight snack, maybe?"

From their pillows they watched through the westward window beyond the Mississippi as the sun went below the Arkansas horizon. After a midnight supper in the room, just before slipping into sleep, she asked, "John, by any chance are there bugs on either of us?"

"Now wouldn't that be ironic, Zelma listening to our delicious happiness … no. I have checked carefully from time to time, the latest after we arrived here, and no little transmitters have migrated to either of us."

26

Monday morning, Zelma Taylor, in Sam Sheffield's private office suite, in view of Mallory's window in the bank across the square, monitored the recorders. She could not believe this sudden revelation of the hidden real world. So this is what goes on behind people's backs every day and every minute, without them suspecting. This hidden undercurrent drives the world, and the rest of it is just top-water. She listened to Mallory trying to find Helen Beckette; then he made his call to Celeste Howard. Zelma watched through the window facing the square as Mallory walked out to the curb, got in his car, and drove away.

The inflow of information switched to the digital satellite system, bringing in the conversation between Mallory and Celeste as the car hummed at high speed. Unbelievable, Mallory sitting on his wallet, betraying himself in an entirely different way now, but again. How could a tiny little microphone, no bigger than a grain of rice, pick up such clear sound? Martha had got several into his wallet while Zelma had him busy at the desk. Now she savored the startled questioning look on his face, tinged with guilt and fear, when she barged in and locked the door and came toward him, "Hey, Peter Baby, I been thinking about you and I can't do without you for another minute." He stood in a crouched position as if about to run as she approached. She got to him in rapid stride, unzipped his pants, and reached in with one hand while tricking open his belt with the other. She freed a hand and pulled up her dress, no underclothes, the black swatch of rich pubic hair almost in his face. He went berserk. She checked him with, "Now hold on just a minute, you got to undress for me Peter, so I see all of you again. Come strutting out of the bathroom naked like you used to, it's been too long, baby."

She pushed him into the bathroom and in a moment he trotted back naked, erect, stupid with excitement, and she began to moan. Lying back on the desk, her legs thrown open with abandon, she moaned loudly while he rubbed her clitoris with his stiff little finger-sized endowment. He plunged in and finished in two strokes. She held his little, naked, sweaty form, petting him, calling him endearing names, her long naked legs wrapped around his back, until Martha had time to plant the devices and return to her desk. Such a little dog, but uptown illicit could be exciting. Maybe she ought to go back now and then just for the sheer hell of it.

John Colburn stood near Zelma listening, as Peter and Celeste betrayed each other side by side in the speeding car.

"Oh, Peter, this is such fun!"

"Yes, baby, we always have a good time together."

"And we always win. I do love that part, too"

"Oh, yes. I love to win."

"If we stick together we can always win, Peter."

"I believe that."

"Stick together and we will win the big one. I'll help see to it. And when we do it's going to be even more fun being married to you, my dear Peter."

Without the briefest hesitation, he answered, "Oh, yes."

"Peter, I'm going to create for you everything you've never had in a home, a dream castle of sparkling silver, candlelight, gorgeous meals, love and romance every night, and entertain all our friends in the grandest style."

"I'm looking forward to that. But there are many obstacles in the way yet."

"Yes, I know. We will simply remove them, Peter."

"That's a big order, but first things first. I've got to bring the Golden Age under control."

"I'll help in every way I can."

"You know who has to go?"

"Yes, I know."

"Then there is the wife, precious little Sugar."

"What's to be done?"

"Oh, I think she will be glad to go for, say, a million-dollar settlement."

"I doubt it, Peter, I doubt it."

"You know, I've got a funny feeling about her, like she's not really real, like I will wake up to reality some morning and she won't be there, and it will be like she never was."

"Why, Peter, what do you mean?"

"She's weird in more ways than you think, besides the smoking and the drinking and the obsession with golf. Even her body functions weird ... like the allergies."

"What allergies?"

"A lot of things, but mostly the forbidden, the things she's craziest about."

"Like what?"

"Like flowers and cats. She's so damned crazy about cats she will risk her life to put her hands on one ... like last year, she opens the door one morning and there is a stray on the front steps, a tiny kitten, and she scoops it up and rubs it against her face. An hour later her eyes are swollen shut, she's gasping for breath and spitting blood in the emergency room when she really goes bad ... airway totally shut off. That scar below her Adam's apple—the doctor had to cut into her windpipe to save her life."

"Sounds like she almost died."

"She would have if I hadn't been home."

"Then you saved her life."

"Without question."

"She must be very grateful."

"I don't know, and I'm not sure I want to know."

"What kind of flowers?"

"What? ... Oh. Big ones, lilies, especially tiger lilies."

John opened his briefcase, removed a laptop, and placed it on the end of Zelma's desk. He keyed into a satellite communications system, chose a number off the screen, and sent it a message.

"What are you doing? Asked Zelma.

"I just sent several of the extras in Mallory's wallet to

Celeste's credit card container."

"Oh?"

"I expect she will be getting around, and we need to be introduced to everybody she knows."

"How?"

"Oh, when she goes to another man, I will direct a bug to his wallet."

"How do you do that?"

"The moment we hear the sound of his voice we send the bug to that source. And we do it quickly to get into his wallet before he undresses."

"Amazing."

"Otherwise, all I need is the number of a particular card."

"How do you get that information on any particular person?"

"I can get the number of any credit card in the world through the CIA, specifically the In-Q-Tel and Office of Homeland Security."

"But if she's in a room with someone not identified …?"

"As soon as such a person starts talking we can quickly identify the speaker. Anyway we usually have the identity of the person before she arrives."

"Oh."

"Yes, as soon as she answers the phone when he calls to make arrangements we know who he is and where he is."

Zelma continued to listen. She felt a roller coaster sensation as though their momentum should carry Peter and Celeste out of range, but the monitoring devices stayed on target. Eventually, the device revealed their arrival in Tunica at The Royal Nugget Casino.

Then sounds began in the sheriff's office and she listened while the sheriff summoned Wyndham Jones, shut the door, and began to talk. She recorded their conversation, and later she recorded his long-distance calls.

During the next two days she listened to Peter Mallory's long-distance calls, his conversations with the sheriff, his efforts to tempt Helen Beckette. Zelma mastered the code words and signals. She listened to the roar of an outboard motor, Peter Mallory fishing on the lake, and recorded the conversation between him and a country voice he addressed as Ruble. She separated and categorized this information, placing it in order for Sam Sheffield.

27

    Celeste Howard needed to get control and get it soon. Marriage would do it. But little Sugar stood in the way, the little cheating drunk. Imagine her simply disappearing. No, wouldn't do. Mallory then would remain married to her for years while the search went on futilely for her whereabouts or her body. So, a finality would be necessary. How? Do it herself? Such indignity! Jones? Oh, God! He's so hopelessly stupid. She would never trust him with a confidence, but he unwittingly could provide the only entree into Sugar's house when Mallory spends the night out of town. Subtleties would be the only way, something natural so he would do it without knowing. She would have to think of a way unheard of, and very subtle and entirely nonphysical.

    Celeste corked her wine bottles and became alert to her surroundings. Jones, the two-timing devil, she would find out exactly what he does. She watched her caller ID, and when Mallory called she did not answer unless she needed to know his next move. He would have to go alone or with other women until she took care of matters, and when she finished he would never touch another woman. She would see to it. So, when he left town for the night she borrowed a car from Mary Ann Dickey and parked near Mallory's house. Half an hour later, Jones stopped his cruiser a block away, and slunk through the shadows of the street into the backyard. The kitchen door cracked open and he eased in. He left just before daylight.

    On Mallory's next trip, she watched the house again, and Jones repeated the same performance. So they have a pattern. Little Sugar calls him as soon as she knows Mallory will be away for the night. Got herself a meathead stud on a regular basis. Something was prodding Celeste's memory, trying to get her attention, something with clever promise. What was it? Then she suddenly knew. Oh, yes. What a simple, uncomplicated idea, and it would work if she did it right the first time.

During one of her frequent trips to the pound, Celeste, after crying for a while over the caged and begging animals, adopted a tiny kitten. She petted and nurtured it and avoided calls from Mallory. Days passed. But she finally answered when she needed to know more about his movements. He wanted her to go to Gulfport for two days and nights with him. Oh, what a shame, she simply couldn't go. She had volunteered to do Pink Lady duty in the hospital both days and she would never be able to find a substitute on such short notice. He should let her know sooner so she could plan these things. Mallory hung up in a huff. She would straighten him out later.

She called Jones and begged him to come over for the night. She felt safe because Sugar no doubt had committed him already. He made excuses. She pouted and sulked on the phone, twisting him. But, I need you, I've got another pesky ole' traffic ticket, and I've come to depend on you, so ... Ohhhh, Jonesey baby, you're getting to me and I'm going to be helpless in your clutches if I don't watch out. He agreed to come by in the early evening for the ticket, and he would, of course, take care of it. She hurried to the florist and bought a lavish arrangement of the most gorgeous big blossoms of every kind with all sorts of ferns and other greenery and tiger lilies. She carried them home to get ready for the night.

Among the shanks of the long stems, she placed the kitten's soft little bed on which it had slept for days. She bathed leisurely and languidly in the late afternoon and perfumed herself the way Jones liked it. She touched up her flaming red pubic hair with just the right fragrance and smeared the hairs and the vulva and thighs with catnip and whipped cream.

For the next two hours she lay supine on her couch, completely naked with her legs spread wide apart. The kitten had plowed its moist little nose incessantly, licking so softly and warmly, tickling the cream off the taut mound of her clitoris, teasing her to a state of high excitement until she almost had reached orgasm when the doorbell rang.

She grabbed the kitten and hid it in a cat-basket on the kitchen floor. Jones shut the door as he entered the room. She rushed him head on and leapt astride his body then crawled up onto his shoulders, her naked legs wrapping around his neck, and her escutcheon smacked against his mouth, the hairs intermingling with his mustache, and she began to wiggle. His tongue went to work. He walked toward the bed, her naked buttocks cupped in his hands, and dumped her on her back, and finished. She stopped squealing and reached for his fly, got her hands in, and swiped them through the hair and along his shaft, but he pulled his erection out of her fingers and zipped his pants. He poked past a pocket, pushing a little tent of his cloth outward. He couldn't afford to go to Sugar unloaded. Celeste allowed him to leave, but with the promise of returning the next night.

Two hours later she drove by Mallory's house, found Jones' car, then parked. In the darkness of full night she carried the bouquet across Mallory's backyard and sidled around the house to the front door. The kitten on its soft little bed down in the flowers meowed plaintively, lost and frightened. Celeste placed the big basket against the door and leaned on the doorbell until she heard approaching footsteps, then vanished into the darkness. She had given Sugar enough time to be too drunk for caution.

Celeste heard the news on TV next morning. The rescue squad found her dead, but they got a glimpse of a naked rear-end fleeing with clothes in grip, tangling and flopping backward. Someone stark-naked alone in the room with the city's first wife, the socially prominent Sugar Mallory. The report wondered who had called 911? Who had told them ahead of time they would have to break open the locked door? Who had told them she was dying in anaphylactic shock, choking to death on vocal cord edema from cat dander?

Celeste drew in her breath sharply when she heard the newscaster. She imagined the scene, stupid Jones, but surely not quite so stupid. The ladykiller all right, as he imagined himself, Sugar gasping on passion and in the throes of one hell of an orgasm he probably thought, staying too long in conquest, too dumb to catch on while the rescue squad broke the door down, him humping a dead woman. And Jones would have been in character. Jones liked to suck his partner's mouth, and the cat dander on his lips and whiskers must have finished closing off Sugar's lungs, already full from petting and loving the kitten and sniffing the lilies. And by then she would already have got a big dose of it from her favorite oral sport.

The word got around very quickly. Looked awfully like Debbity Dawg Jones. He later denied it in public, and he denied it when Celeste questioned him in the privacy of another home-cooked meal.

Poor Peter. Now she would have to nurse him through an overwhelming grief. And how lucky they were; this had happened without either of them touching Sugar. Even luckier, he had been out of town attending a banker's meeting when it happened. He had the hotel receipt to prove it. Celeste thought he probably could call a witness to alibi his whereabouts at the moment of Sugar's death. She would just bet on it.

And he's so full of questions. Who could have sent the flowers, and where the hell did the cat come from? And Jones ... what a pervert! Imagine him answering a 911, got there first, finding the woman dead, then raping her. He should press charges. Oh, I wouldn't, she says, you have him now; he would do anything you might need to suggest some day. The autopsy had been negative except for the findings of a fatal allergic reaction and, of course, fresh semen in the vagina. But it *is* a dear little cat. He will keep it.

And right away he began coming to her house unannounced, expecting to be fed. This could play hell with her social life. She didn't want him and Jones to cross paths in her front yard.

Zelma called Sam into her room on the morning the news broke about Sugar Mallory, and played back the sounds of the previous evening. They heard clearly the encounter between Celeste and Jones, and the later lovemaking and strangling death of the woman they now knew to be Sugar Mallory, Jones' presence undeniable.

"What should we do about this?" she asked.

"Save it, like all the rest, but we can do nothing now without giving away the entire investigation. So we keep quiet."

"What do you think happened?"

"Jones went from one place to another, and there is more to this than the ear can hear."

"Do you think he killed her outright?"

"No. He was used. This was done very cleverly, and it has the wit of our dear Celeste. She's really up to something big this time."

"Damn."

"Zelma, rise above it. With all this equipment, you are listening now with the Gods, who always ignore the petty machinations and the heartless killing, as people have done throughout the ages, and for the same reasons, the acquisition of property, namely money, always under the guise of something more admirable. Consider yourself on Mount Olympus and enjoy the show."

"Well, Mr. Sam, you are a philosopher, just like people say you are."

"More like a neutral observer, perhaps."

"No. I hear you really are a philosopher, a professor in the humanities department at the university, and you teach classes every week in philosophy and psychology, as well as law, out on campus while the town knows you as nothing but a lawyer."

"Well, I don't talk out of school."

She gazed at him steadily, a burning look, quiet, smoldering, "Neither do I, Sam."

"I know, Zelma, and I do trust you, and we got to be damned careful until this has all passed."

"And I hear you are buddies with Chancellor Madison, and he teaches philosophy classes, too."

"You are right. We hope to set the world straight some day, the two of us, with plenty of help."

"Ha! I wish you luck. Maybe I could help you when the time comes. I got philosophy to burn."

"I know you do, Zelma, and there would be a place for you."

Two weeks after the funeral, Celeste sat beside Mallory in the Mercedes as they sped out of town. He did the talking. It had to do with money, but he put it in the words of love. She already knew. All the property had been in Sugar's name, in case he went bankrupt in the nursing home business and his other endeavors. Now it had bounced back in his lap. He needed a wife under his control, trust as he put it, to make his money safe again. She readily and speedily agreed with his requests, implied and otherwise. Of course, she would sign a prenuptial. Nothing to it, no problem, I trust you completely, Peter, my darling. He thinks she's easy, and he can manipulate her. Let him. If he suspects her in little Sugar's departure he has kept it to himself, which is not like our Peter.

When? This weekend, but with one provision: she would have to keep it a complete secret. Where? In the Bahamas, he had already made the arrangements. But they would have to continue living separately until he had sold the nursing homes. And he would have her house repaired. Then she realized he already had turned toward the Memphis airport.

"Why the secret, Peter?"

"Because Ben Kadsh, owner of the outfit buying the nursing homes, wants it that way; a wife complicates the legalities."

"Oh."

Zelma, through the bugs on both Mallory and Celeste, recorded details of the trip, the wedding, and the honeymoon. She could hardly imagine it. She told Sam, and while playing parts of it back to him, she knew a vague uneasiness.

"And we will keep this quiet, too," he said. "Not a whisper to anyone … don't touch the dice while they are still rolling."

Zelma studied him quietly. "Damn, man. I like you."

"Yeah, and I like you, too, Zelma. Quite a gal! But so does my dear wife like me, and I guess you know she's been in a coma now for ten years."

"No, I never heard that."

"Got a general anesthetic for a minor gynecological operation and never woke up."

"Sam, where is she?"

"At home, with attendants around the clock."

"Does she recognize you?"

"She recognizes nothing."

"Oh God, Sam."

The new Mrs. Peter Mallory returned from the weekend marriage and honeymoon, with a mandate, most of it her own choice. All impediments to Mallory ambitions would have to be removed at once, and none of the job to be done would be easy. And she did not intend giving up the man in the night shadows. Peter's secrecy would work to her advantage. She wondered. Just how valid is a marriage performed on an island, all prearranged by Peter himself? She had signed the sheaf of papers without reading a line. What difference did it make anyway? He would contrive a way to get his money back when the time came. And she did not believe he would give up his other women. He's going to go right on leading the same life he led before little Sugar departed this world. So would she. And eventually Jones would come around, hangdog contrite, and she would control him, and he would do her bidding. But more than anything she wanted to know the identity of the man hidden in the shadows of the Golden Age. And she had a hunch about Peter. She suspected the boys over at the casinos would be forced to settle matters with him before too long. She hoped so, because Peter was now a nuisance.

His appearances at her house were becoming more frequent, expecting dinner, another of her home-cooked meals, and now he had begun staying the nights. She suspected he was avoiding the bed in which Sugar had died. Could this man have a soul after all? Yeah, maybe a little one hidden in that psychic mess, trying to get out. Mallory odor now mingled subtly in the pall of dog. His unannounced appearances were ruining her social life. Imagine Mallory really in love, dropping all others, giving his entire devotion! He would be walking in her tracks and checking her every move, his miserable history, the machinations of his own guilt, guiding him into the hell of a control freak. She would never tolerate the bonds of his shackles.

But while passing time this way she thought about the Mallory mansion and chafed to take over. Oh, what she could do with it. But not yet, they would have to await the sparkling silver, the tall dripless candles in tall candelabra, the spanking white linens and deep plush velours and velvets in amber, reds, and maroon. She imagined Peter at one end of the table, she at the other, diamonds sparkling on her fingers and around her neck, her repartee witty, men to her right and left paying rapt attention, women further down both sides of the table envious of her. So she pictured herself, dreaming, but in reality sitting deep in her sofa beneath Jake's beaming countenance, the odor of dog and wine emanating in the stuffy, dusty room.

Mallory had not sent the carpenters to replace the rotted-off posts. Should she call the carpenters herself, then send the bill to Mallory at the bank? He wouldn't dare refuse it for fear of her leaking the marriage news. His actions puzzled her. He comes to her house to eat, but he won't let her come to his house to cook. Certainly something odd about that ... actually, it's her house, not his, since everything is in her name now. Maybe she ought to make waves … no, not yet, give him a little more time. Don't do anything to decrease the great wealth he is striving to reach. She wouldn't mind so much if only he would phone before appearing, sometimes as late as 10 p.m., or as early as mid-morning or mid-afternoon. On these visits and on their trips she had begun to sniff furtively at his skin. The man in the shadows is right. He does have his own smell.

But she could start taking over one step at a time now. To begin she would have the dogs done in a pet salon and give the bill to Peter.

28

Ruble Crouch hid his boat in a tiny inlet downstream from Indian Creek at dusk. He went through the woods to within view of the church. Buses arrived and a crowd gathered. He sat on a log behind a concealing bush and waited, his bug spray a stinking cloud in the hot night. With sundown, the insects out in the bushes began the nighttime rising and falling noise. The human choir within the building wailed its songs to Jesus and death. Then the sermon began. The preacher's voice rang off the rafters and echoed through the church. An old-fashioned revival had been promised. So the windows stood open to the night sounds out in the woods, and insects swarmed in and swirled around the naked lights. The people fanned. An hour passed and the sermon ended with ringing shouts aimed at the ceiling. Ruble listened and watched, then moved closer to an open window.

The singing started again, *Just as I am*. Then the preacher began an altar call, calling all sinners to come to Christ, to give up their lives of sin, to come to God. He raised his arms and aimed his face upward and began talking to the ceiling, *come now before it's too late, give your life to Christ, now while there is time, who knows, you might die tonight on your way home and spend eternity in hell, come, come now while you can, while Jesus calls ... so tenderly calls ... Ooohhh, yes, he calls ever so sweetly ... come give your life to Christ Jesus, come put your hand in mine and cross that great divide, put your hand in mine and accept him as your personal savior, come now while there is time, don't tarry 'til too late, don't put off your eternal salvation ...*

Sweat wet the preacher's armpits and seeped a dark stain across his shirt. He paused to pour water from a pitcher, and gulped from a cup, and returned to his shouting. Timid people slunk down the aisle one by one to be born again, and gathered in front of the pulpit. Girls, women, and men wept in remorse for the sins of which they had been accused in the preacher's shouting. The choir sang a sorrowful song over an over as he shamed and begged the bashful sinners who stayed put in the audience. The weekly collection of converts would be baptized in the river on a Saturday morning to the glory of God. The announcement in the Memphis paper, *The Commercial Appeal*, had likened the Tallahatchie to the River Jordan. Ruble's live-in woman, Sybil Snyder, had read it to him, chuckling cynically. Ruble could not understand this behavior in the church, but he did know it blinded the people to what went on out in the dark churchyard during the preaching.

Tonight as Ruble watched during the first sermon of the evening, a crew unloaded packages from the luggage and freight compartments of parked buses, and carried them through a back door into the church basement. Before the sermon ended, a second fleet of buses began arriving with a second congregation. After a thirty-minute break, services began again, and freight compartments of the second fleet were unloaded at the height of the preaching and the shouting.

By midnight all obvious activity had stopped at the church, and lights had gone out in the lodge. Ruble waited for the next move. At almost 1 a.m. a small skiff beached on the bank of Indian Creek. Two men in nighttime camouflage made several trips into the church vault, carrying packages out, and stacked a full load on the skiff. They brought more packages from the basement beneath the lodge, then took the boat toward the Sardis Dam. He recorded all the activities on his nighttime video camera.

Then he went to his own boat, cruised slowly across the lake without running lights, musing to himself as he scanned the water for floating obstacles. On his next night off duty from the Golden Age, he would go to the dam and watch another step of the new operation. He wanted the whole picture.

He had begun listening to the voice of caution. He would be sacrificed to bear the blame. He sensed it. Guilt would be his, put upon him, his sacrifice expected to hide the great body of a major evil while the real plotters went free. But guilt did not exist in his everyday awareness, as it did to droop the shoulders and wilt the will of men such as Mallory. Ruble had seen the shadows move, he had witnessed the evil in the nights. Mallory does not know wisdom, and, consequently, carries the whiff of death, the aura and the weakness of a fool; native sense abandoned him at birth.

Ruble, for his own protection, must continue to see and know the things in the shadows, and watch the movements, and the targets and the methods. Mallory knows nothing of stealth. He confuses it with sneakiness. Mallory recognizes no form of intelligence higher than his own, and with his ego, he fools only himself, and turns the exposed flank to danger. Mallory is not actually up there where he thinks he is, hidden from the rest of men with the men who really run things. And Mallory practices the most enraging racial snobbery.

And Celeste! Clever! Damn, she's clever. Did it with a cat and a lily without ever touching little Sugar. He understands Celeste's behavior. She becomes the person she imagines for the moment, the occasion, the purpose. Lucky would be the man who could choose the Celeste he wanted to keep and eliminate all the others, but woe to the weaker man at the mercy of all she could be. She would be just right for him once he got her to himself and the whiff of Jones and Mallory and Goonsbys and football players and the like disappeared in cleaner air.

Days later, to spy on the next phase of the big drug operation, Ruble drove his truck after midnight down Highway 6 West toward Batesville and turned off on the Sardis Dam road. Mallory wanted it done, and he wanted to know himself for future use. North across the dam, he turned east and took the first side road down to the water. He parked and worked his way through undergrowth to the lake. The revival meeting of the evening, at the river entry twenty or so miles east would have ended two hours ago. The pitch black and moonless after-midnight sky hid the land and hummed with the voice of singing bugs. The boat should be near. He waited. Out over the water a big motor approached then throttled back and quit. Wavelets lapped the shore in the silence. Then a whispery churning of water grew toward land, and the boat, in dark shadow, glided by under silent electric trolling power and beached bow first. Figures in dark clothes hurried to unload cartons. Ruble watched through infrared binoculars as they carried coolers to a half-hidden truck with SOUTHERN FISH MARKET lettered on the side panel. Only a shallow layer of catfish would hide drug packages in coolers stacked nearest the doors. The next pick-up site would be on the other side of the lake, maybe as far to the east as Clear Creek, several nights away. Ruble waited until the trucks departed, then went toward home, thinking. This entire operation was too shallow, too exposed; it could not exist long without discovery. Its real purpose could not be a serious drug operation; it had to have another reason for existing.

29

Clara Bartley found Rachel Colburn somnolent in a bloody gown at nine o'clock in the morning, her breakfast tray untouched and the food cold.

"Miss Rachel, what's wrong with you?"

"Oh Clara. I'm in so much pain."

"Where?"

"A woman on night duty snatched me around and did something terrible to my arm. It's killing me."

"Why did she do that?"

"She was yelling at me for soiling my clothes, and I didn't even know I had done it."

She began to cry. And when she wept she looked much older, terribly old, and Clara thought old, actually acutely ill with old age.

Clara removed the gown and found a foot-long tear through the skin of her arm from elbow almost to the chest. The ripped open wound had filled with a puddle of clotted blood. She knew instantly what had happened. A rough and careless attendant had picked her up by the flab and the old friable skin ripped open, then the attendants paid no attention to her cries of pain. She wondered if it had been done deliberately.

After an ambulance trip to the emergency room and fifty stitches in the arm and a shot of painkiller, Rachel had stopped crying. Clara then went the usual rounds with administration over poor care and neglect. Then she called John Colburn. He said to hire sitters around the clock, constant attendance when Clara could not be there. This she did, but with anxiety and fear in her own heart for all the people trapped in the same dilemma as Rachel, all the hundreds who could not afford help to protect themselves against the very system being paid to take care of them. The person responsible for ripping open Rachel's arm could not be identified positively, and placing blame would do no good anyway. They simply would have to hire more of the same. Some of the aides were caring, and others were not, the same as all other people, no matter how high or low. It's the system, she thought, nobody is in charge, and nothing but constant vigilance can guard a victim against the quirks of human nature.

Late in the afternoon, Helen Beckette, while waiting for Clara Bartley to come for her, studied Rachel Colburn's hospital chart behind locked office doors. She had the Golden Age record open also. She was looking for a pattern. Why had Rachel come to live in Golden Age? John said he had bought a comfortable little cottage for her and she had lived in it more than twenty years. But Helen seemed to recall an incident. Something very bad had happened to put her in the nursing home, some terribly crippling injury.

During the next two hours of perusal she found the injuries and the culprit, Isaac Dodson. Oh, God! Could there also be a connection between this behavior and her dear David's death? And for his own commercial interest, his greed for money, did Dodson deliberately neglect and mistreat poor Rachel, or was it just laziness? Then she wondered. Just how far down do the tentacles of this monster reach? Had it caught everybody in town as either benefactor or victim in its greedy grasp? The evil seemed to have grown beyond comprehension. Nothing new was here and nothing she didn't already know, but she no longer felt the hopeless discouragement of the past two years. John Colburn would bring an end to this terrible wrong. She looked up and glanced out the window to see Clara driving up in a red pick-up truck. She locked the records in her safe and went out to join her.

30

On their next trip to Tunica, Celeste Howard waited on arrival until Mallory had disappeared into the depths of The Royal Nugget, then she entered the private door of Thornton Webb's office, but he did not rise this time to greet her. He sat at his desk, the phone clutched under his chin, his countenance very somber. He motioned her to a chair and remained silent on the phone another five minutes. Then he said, "Yes," and hung up.

His face had turned ashen, his jaws gripped. He stood and motioned her to the bedroom. Half an hour later he pulled the covers up over their heads. She quaffed the aroma of their sweaty naked bodies. With his lips against her ear he talked in whispers. The man on the phone, none other than the infamous and dangerous Lapkin Lewis, had brought him up to date on things he should have known. And congratulations, Celeste darling. Brilliant, both the cat and the marriage. But you should tell me these things. She started to speak, and he laid a finger across her lips and whispered, "We are bugged to the gills."

She whispered, "How do they know everything? I've told not a soul."

"They survive that way."

"And who is Lapkin Lewis?"

"The great negotiator, the slickest lawyer in existence. He settles disagreements with silent finality. A call from him carries the deadliest of overtones. The Mafia, the Teamsters, the big money obey."

"How would I know him?"

"There is no other voice like his. So smooth, so gentle, so solicitous, and he will never give his name, but always the perfect gentleman. I had hoped to spare you the exposure."

"You are giving me cold chills"

"His appearance is always the same, impeccably groomed in tailored silks and the finest woolens and handmade shoes, just a bit on the slick side, a bit overdone, a bit too perfect, the coiffeur too plastered over a bobbed off beaver-tail on his nape, just slightly reminiscent of a television evangelist."

"Not my type."

"If he decides you are, you are."

"Not me."

"Beheaded corpses sloughing in submerged broken culverts, concrete shoes, exploding automobiles, bodies crushed in compacted automobile remnants in junk yards, vanished people, and others have left no trace, but they all disagreed with him and refused to bargain. And a few are rotting in prison."

"Well … what now?"

"Get dressed and go quietly to the tables. Be careful. Don't let on to Peter Mallory, no matter what."

"I don't and I won't."

"As soon as you leave I will call Peter in from the waiting room for another and, I'm afraid, the final ultimatum from Lewis himself."

"And that?"

"The Golden Age problem has to be removed one way or another."

Two mornings later at home in Cambridge, Celeste Howard awoke to a ringing phone. She answered, and a smooth voice said, "Celeste, my dear, a black minivan will be at your door in one hour. It's eight o'clock your time now. You can trust the two men in brown suits. The plane will be waiting at the Cambridge Airport."

She hung up, her heart racing. Had Thornton Webb guessed this would happen? His hinted forewarnings had prepared her. She knew at the first word. The man behind this voice threatened, excited, and promised in silken tones. She would move into the highest echelon now. She packed an overnight bag and went for another ride in a private jet.

The man remained seated behind the desk in his hotel suite, not out of rudeness, not this one. Serene command and control emanated from his stillness. Celeste approached. Bemused eyes almost the color of his skin watched as she stopped with her thighs against the desk edge across from him. He stood.

"Celeste Howard," he said.

"Lapkin Lewis," she answered.

"Now, Mrs. Mallory."

"Don't tell it out loud."

"You do keep secrets, I understand."

"When worthy of secret, yes."

He came around the desk. She turned to face him, unflinching, wondering what this man would require, something different she guessed, and he lived up to the expectation. He said in a quiet caressing voice, almost whispering, "Undress for me, please."

For calculated effect, Celeste wore lingerie only a shade darker than her suntan. With her tall, leggy, feminine litheness framed in it, she seethed an aura of almost nakedness and languorous sexuality, a muted wickedness.

Lapkin moved, too, with languid restraint. Celeste thought he appeared to be coiled and waiting, sleeping with his eyes open, and the danger excited her, intensely. He preceded her into the bedroom and removed a well-tailored mohair coat, a black silk turtleneck, trousers of the finest wool, hand made Italian shoes. Tall and muscular, his coloring almost uniform from hair to foot, an off-gray, large flap ears and a big nose – his appearance just short of characterization. Advancing middle age had softened and wrinkled his skin over an early layer of dimpled fat, a comforting, ripe appearance. His silk underwear came off silently.

She reached for her own bra straps, and finished undressing herself. Stripped naked and walking on high-heeled pumps, she came to him.

Long toward twilight, in the middle of the king-sized bed, Lapkin gripped her arm above the elbow, a grasp of endearment and appreciation, held on for a moment, then turned on his back and said, "Oh, boy."

Celeste pulled the sheet up to her chin and said, "So, why did you send for me?"

"Because you have been calling the shots through Thornton Webb, and

I'm going to give you a more direct route."

"Why, thank you, Lapkin."

"Would you like to work for me?"

"If this is a sample of work, yes, but tell me more about it."

"Things I need to know about different people at different times."

"Yes."

"Are you willing?"

"I think I can handle it."

"You're sure?"

"Been there and done that. You name it."

"Bin Kadsh, the HMO mogul, the biggest in the world, a Zeebeckystanian, American-trained, an able internist, caught up in the greed of money and HMO dominance over his erstwhile social and professional superiors, bossing now even the most prominent medical and surgical academics in this country."

"So."

"You need to get to know him."

"Why?"

"Money. He makes a lot of it and flaunts it. But the show may be only a front to divert attention from his real endeavors. He has a very dark wife, given to hellish behavior at home, and he has a weakness for blonds."

"Of a type."

"Compliant and not too keen."

"Where do I fit in?"

"He would have a smart one this time, but he would come to know it only gradually, if ever."

"So?"

"So, as his affection grows, you will be trusted with enough about his schemes to help us decide what to do."

"I believe I understand. You want me to help Kadsh do his scheming."

"You got it."

"And just how do I get to this man?"

"You will attend a dinner party day after tomorrow night, as Thornton Webb's assistant."

"You will be there?"

"No, my dear. I'm never seen."

"And?"

"You will be seated at table with Kadsh. He will make his moves. Just follow and do as he wants."

"I have some restrictions now with Peter."

"We will keep him diverted, and Kadsh's wife harps a close watch. So he will not detain you for long periods. He already knows of your marriage."

"I wanted no one to know just yet."

"No way to keep it from him, so take charge."

"And do what?"

"Find out who is doing the killing of Cambridge citizens." Lapkin Lewis looked at her quietly, a hooded, knowing appraisal. Then he said, "Murder has been done without due cause, and not of our plan, totally uncalled for and grossly over wrought. We think Kadsh, in a rush to reach his political goals, may have overstepped his bounds to hurry the deal, and will attempt it again, we suspect. He is jockeying for far more than we were led to believe initially."

Celeste then asked, "Are you telling me that you and all with whom you associate had nothing to do with past events at the Golden Age, and you have no plans for the future?"

"My dear, murder must have a murderous reason."

"Okay. Then can you explain the complicated money scheme trapping Mallory?"

"Yes. Peter used the bank's money informally to buy the nursing homes. In addition, he loaned the syndicate $250,000,000 to buy into Kadsh's conglomerate, his own idea, on an oral agreement, with no records of the transaction. We now own quite a large block of the stock. A payback would involve syndicate money from the gambling operations, plus Dixie Mafia and union funds."

"Did you really need to borrow money?"

"No, not at all, but the debt is our way of controlling him and Kadsh both."

"I don't understand."

"It's his loss if we choose not to pay back. Faced with his disobedience, we would not, and Peter would lose his nursing homes also. He is not big enough to take a bath in more than a half billion."

"And you could?"

"Peter, without realizing what he was doing and Kadsh knowing full, well put the syndicate in the position of washing a lot of money every month from drug dealers. As a matter of fact, we actually profit by certain apparent losses, and Kadsh would profit even more with low-income or losing investments. But we don't want it and intend to stop."

"Peter has put himself in a bad spot."

"Lost all control, but he does not realize the fact yet. Kadsh is a far greater concern to us."

"Okay," said Celeste.

"Your job is to get inside his head and find out what's coming next."

31

Ruble Crouch with his cameras followed Sybil Snyder again on a sneaky and mean tear through the dark wards. She struck two confused old patients in the face for wetting their beds. Muttering curses to herself, she left them helpless and crying. She simply rolled another one off the bed, let him crash onto the floor, raised the side rail back into position, and left. She went back to her desk.

Half a dozen buzzers rasped for attention. She ignored them and went into the toilet and smoked. Ruble moved in the after-midnight shadows, and waited for her to call help to the patient on the floor. She did not. Then he pretended rounds, and found the victim himself. The old man went to the emergency room for a busted hip and a busted skull. This had to stop; he was being blamed. Sybil had now earned an end to her evil. It would take a bit of planning. He had never abused her, never struck her, although she had slapped and clawed and scratched and cursed him and he had borne it like a man. She looked down on him, talked down to him, treated him as an inferior, weak person afraid to defend himself. Sybil would have to be watched for the rest of the night and it was time to call her on all her crimes.

Ruble arrived home early and waited for Sybil. Half an hour later or so, she stormed through the rear entrance into the kitchen, seething anger, a cigarette dangling from her lips, a coiling blue stink clouding around her face. Ruble leaned back against the counter, his arms folded across his chest.

She threw her purse across the room and stomped her foot, and screamed, "Goddammit, shit to hell I'm sick of that fuckin' stinkin' hellhole ... Goddammit to hell and back!" Her blonde hair frizzed up, two rows of black roots down the parted furrow; she retrieved the cigarette with tobacco-stained, trembling fingers, the nail polish broken and peeling, the borders grimy. She kicked a chair across the room and stopped to face him. He had not moved and looked her straight in the eye. "So what the fuck's with you?" she yelled.

"The old man you flung on the floor ... let's see," he raised his wrist and looked at his watch, "about three hours ago."

"You lie. The codger wards are your job. I ain't been near 'em."

"Oh, yes you have. The call buttons set you off and you batter everyone you can, and I don't intend getting' the blame anymore."

"You liar, you did it."

"I been watching you for weeks now, and taking pictures with my little infrared digital. Would you like to see yourself in action?"

He removed a small camcorder from his pocket and flipped the viewer open.

Her face turned chalky. "Why, you dirty slime."

He placed the camera on the counter top. She eyed it, her body slumped and crouched, her muscles tensed, and she lunged at him, in the same motion reaching for the camera. He caught her right wrist and forced her back at arm's length. She began clawing with the left hand. He grabbed the other wrist. She lurched and kicked and screamed and bent to bite at his wrists. Then he twisted both arms behind her back, caught them in one grip, grasped her by the mop of hair with the other hand and twisted her around to face him.

"Now in all our time together I have never struck you or roughed you up like I'm doing now, not once, while you bit and clawed and scratched and hit. But that's over. No more. I am going to turn you loose in a minute and if you make one move against me I will teach you a lesson you won't forget."

"I'll have you arrested for domestic violence."

"And I will show the law your form of violence."

She lurched and struggled in his grip, screaming, "You bastard, you half-nigger Indian, you piece of shit, you fuckin' half-breed savage!" And she spat in his face.

Ruble gently released her and pocketed the camera, then calmly leaned back against the counter and crossed his arms again. He did not wipe his face. The spittle rolled off his cheeks and dripped down on his shirtfront while he remained totally calm and quiet. The aura of his stillness left no doubt about his threat. She seemed to shrink, and backed off, silent, her frightened eyes locked on his face.

She rubbed her wrists, whimpering, cursing, looking at him with bitter defeat. But she did not attack again. Silence hung in the room; distant traffic rumbled in the background.

After a few moments, Ruble unfolded his arms, turned toward the bedroom, and said, "I'm getting' my things and leaving."

When he returned through the kitchen, carrying a small valise, she sat on a bar stool, smoking. She said, "Come sit down here a minute, I got something to tell you, something important."

Ruble stopped and stood by the door, holding the bag.

She continued, "I've had an offer. I was going to talk to you about it."

"Yeah?"

"Fifty grand."

"For what?"

"And you can have half of it, if you stay."

He stood with his hand on the doorknob watching her jab another butt into an already full tray, spilling stale ashes on the counter top. She watched him, the plucked eyebrows arched above a smart-assed smirk, the usual, know-it-all pose. "Old Rachel Colburn," she said, wobbling her head knowingly.

He took his hand off the knob and set the bag on the floor. "Don't be a fool. The family has her guarded constantly. No way can you get away ..." and he stopped talking and waited, looking at her, the smarty smirk again, the wise-apple ... God would he love to be rid of her. Oh, yes. Here it is. He could help her but not be there when it happens, and in this way find out who is behind this bad stuff. So stupid, thinking he would risk his life for a measly twenty-five thousand dollars. He said, "You have a plan?"

She relaxed and smiled. "Oh, then you will help me?"

"Yes."

"Oh, my sugar-baby, I knew it. You can't leave your mamma. She couldn't live without your loving."

"I'll give you one more chance."

"She has to be gone within a week from now."

"Well, exactly how will you go at this?"

She's watching him, and smirking. "You just leave that up to me."

"And you just leave me out of it."

"You mean you ain't heppin' me."

"I've never harmed a patient, and I don't intend to start now."

"So what will you do?"

"Be elsewhere."

"Why?"

"It wouldn't do for both of us to get caught."

"Nah. I reckon you're right about that."

She stood and went toward the bathroom. When the shower started running, he went out the door with the bag, to his secret hiding place over the attached garage and retrieved his store of files and photos.

Helen Beckette, working through a stack of papers in her office at 7 a.m., with the door open, received a surprising visit. A gentle tentative knock on the jamb interrupted her concentration and she looked up. Ruble Crouch walked boldly into the room holding a mop handle upright in a bucket on rolling wheels, with an air of having been summoned to clean up a mess. He stopped, ran the mop through the squeezer. While the astonished Helen watched, he began mopping the floor. He worked his way over to her desk, glanced furtively at the open door and said, "Miss Beckette, I need to talk to you."

Looking down, appearing to concentrate on his work, he slowed the swipes over the floor. "I don't want nobody to hear what I got to say, or know I been here."

"Of course, Ruble, what you say will be held in confidence."

"Well, I don't want to make no trouble for nobody, but the time's come that I got to look out for myself now."

"All right. What's bothering you?"

"It's like this, Miss Beckette, I got this idea I'm being blamed for hurtin' patients."

"Which ones?"

"The ones that's been coming up with black eyes and bruised faces and broken bones and busted skulls, you know."

"Yes, I'm afraid I do know."

"Well, I ain't guilty, and I ain't ever harmed a patient."

"The fractured skull, Ruble ... did that old man fall out of bed as reported to me?"

"No, ma'am."

"Then what did happen?"

"He was snatched out of bed and dropped onto the floor, dead weight?"

"How do you know?"

"I seen it with my own eyes."

"Can you prove it?

"I got it on my little digital video, and a lot of the others, too. Mr. Tom Bartley taught me how to use it."

"Who did it, Ruble?"

"Miss Beckette, I'm goin' to help you out all I can, but I got to be careful."

"Sounds threatening."

"You know, or did you know I got a record already. I been sent up once for somebody else's deeds and I don't intend goin' again."

"No, Ruble, I didn't know."

"There's bad business going on here."

"Yes?"

"And it's gonna get worse unless somebody puts a stop to it."

"You know that for sure, too?"

"Yes, ma'am."

"Then you need to tell me."

"I can't tell you, but I can hep' you find out for yourself."

"All right, I'll respect that."

"But you got to have help."

"I can get help."

"You got friends?"

"Yes, of course."

"I mean real friends."

"Well, yes Ruble."

"Miss Beckette you gonna' need men, real men."

"Ruble, you're trying to tell me something without outright saying it."

"Well, you're right about that."

He leaned forward on his mop handle over the edge of her desk and whispered, "Stay away from the sheriff and anybody's got anything to do with him. You really got to be careful who you trust."

She listened, watching him silently. He continued, "I'll be comin' to you to ask for a extra night off. And that will be your signal. That will be the night they plan to get old Rachel Colburn. Be ready, and hidden, and when you catch the person doing it, you will have answers to a lot of questions. But you got to be real sneaky. This one's a snake."

"Ruble, I appreciate this and I can get the help, but I will need the pictures you have taken."

"Miss Beckette, when you catch the person, the law will, of course, do a home search. There you will find things you really need to know. I will see to the pictures then but not the camera." He picked up the pace with the mop, then soused it under the fluid, ran it through the squeezer, and began to mop again. "And I ain't goin to be nowhere in sight."

"Ruble, did you know my husband, Dr. David Beckette?"

"Oh, yes ma'am. Knew him well, a good man, and the patients sure do need him."

"Do you have any idea what happened to him?"

"I'm beginning to have a pretty good idea, but to tell you the truth, I'm afraid to think it."

"Do you care to tell me?"

"Miss Beckette, when you rescue Miss Colburn at the last minute you gonna' find out lotsa' things."

"What's behind this, Ruble?"

"Big money hiring an insider to do it. I been offered half to help, so I'll bet it's more than fifty."

"Fifty?"

"Thousand."

"Oh, my God. So, what are you going to do?"

"Let 'em think I'm helping when I ain't."

"How will it be done?"

"I guess old Rachel's sitter will have to be got out of the room by a trick of some kind, then a quick smothering with a pillow, something that leaves no mess."

"Has that been happening already here in this home?"

"Yes 'um."

"Why haven't you reported it?"

"I'm reporting it now, but don't call the sheriff. They'll get you instead."

"Hard to prove anything in these old people expected to die anyway."

"Yeah, but this time they will stop at nothing, if the pillow don't work," said Ruble.

"They, Ruble? Who's behind all this?"

"I don't know, and I don't want to know. It's too far out of reach of me."

"Do you have evidence?"

"Miss Beckette, I hope I ain't makin' a mistake trusting you, but knowing Dr. Beckette, I'll bet I ain't. I got lots of pictures and I got some funny talk on my little hidden recorder I carry in my pocket all the time."

"Ruble, are you in danger?"

"Yes, I can feel it, and I feel it getting worse all the time. They would do me in a second if they knew I had a thought in my head or that I talked to you."

"Where do you fit in?"

"Me? Right now I'm being used, then I'll be accused to hide worse things."

"How far ahead will you know about Mrs. Colburn?"

"Probably two days."

"Well, let me know as soon as possible."

"I'll ask for that night off."

"Okay."

"Miss Beckette, you watch your step, now." Holding the mop upright in the depths of the wringer, he moved it about like an oar to guide the bucket out the door.

Helen Beckette, almost whispering, told Clara and Tom Bartley in their own house about the warnings of Ruble Crouch.

"Well Helen, this Ruble, it seems from the manner you describe," said Clara, "wouldn't tell you such a thing if it was not absolutely true, and then only after he had worried with it a long time."

"I know him," said Tom. "Did two years in Parchment, five-year sentence, out early on good behavior, innocent anyway, taking the rap for something bigger. I've known him all his life."

"How did he manage early release?"

"I think he was sprung for a purpose."

"By whom?"

"He's a financial slave of Peter Mallory, if that answers your question."

"He's an orderly, graveyard shift, works the same nights as his live-in girlfriend, if the rumors are true," said Helen.

"Who is she?" asked Clara.

"A white woman, from bar hopping trailer-trash," said Tom.

"Do you trust him?" asked Clara.

"I think so now, but some of my nurses have been suspicious of him in the past. If he's not guilty I wonder who has been abusing the patients in the night hours," said Helen.

"Not Ruble," said Tom. "He's a hunter, a fisherman, an outdoors man, loves and nurtures animals wild and pet alike, took care of his own mother with the greatest kindness when she was dying, never known to be unkind to anyone. Used him as one of my deputies when I was game warden; he's very resourceful and fearless, and relentless, and fair."

"Where did he come from?" asked Clara.

"Born here," said Tom. "He's at least half Chickasaw. His ancestors refused to leave their beloved land. They hid and stayed."

"And the rest of him?" asked Clara.

"The hair is African," said Tom. "And there was a white man in there somewhere."

"Tough combination."

"Oh yes, indeed."

"Can we trust him if he works for Mallory?"

"He's wily with a native sense of timing. He probably is being set up and probably has caught on. I think he came to you for this reason."

"So what now?" asked Helen.

"Catch the devils red-handed. I'll get ready. Let me know the minute Ruble asks for the night off," said Tom.

"This is really getting nasty," said Clara.

"More than you realize, perhaps," He stopped himself from telling her about the attempt on Clara's life.

"I was afraid to tell you, Tom. The sheriff stopped me a second time, and accused me of obstructing traffic, going too slow," said Clara.

"Were you?"

"He was riding my rear bumper, and I kept slowing down to a crawl, three miles an hour and he stayed right on my tail. I call that harassment. He gave me a warning: one more time, and no license. They are trying to cripple us."

"We've got to be very careful. He's just itching to provoke one of us into doing something rash, then he could arrest or maybe even shoot. They are out to frame us deliberately with traffic infractions. So Helen, neither you nor Clara should drive anywhere alone again until this situation comes to an end."

"I'm sure," said Clara. "But personally, I think another enemy will get him first."

"Actually, I'm kind of relieved by all this. I have a feeling … I think we are coming close to the truth."

"Yes," said Tom. "But we must not get burned, too."

32

At 8 a.m. Celeste Howard left home to drive to Memphis alone. The note on the back of Bin Kadsh's business card said, Peabody 10 a.m. Monday, and he had not spoken a word directly to her from across the table on Saturday evening; he just slipped the card in her hand as he said goodbye. Thornton Webb hosted the dinner, and before the meal started, Mallory had been called upstairs. Celeste, at Thornton's right side, silently gauged the other guests. Kadsh's wife, large and hidden in a veiled burka, sat dominantly alert, watching his every move. After the first toast, Thornton engaged Celeste in conversation, cleverly giving her the chance to reveal her depth. Kadsh remained impassively quiet, his gaze entirely private, never looking at another person. Celeste chatted with Thornton, all the while taking note of Kadsh. If listening, he did not appear to be following the talk, corpulent in his chair with a belligerent mien, an air of arrogant hostility, his fingernails glistening from a clear lacquer manicure, his black hair-rim around a bald pate trimmed to the last day's growth, his clothes made of expensive off-brown serge with almost a glaze. Altogether he exuded the slick appearance of tasteless affluence. She had just as soon not. but these small un-attractions would not stand in her way.

She really didn't expect to find him waiting in the lobby. She went to a house-phone and asked for his room. He answered on the first ring. She said, "I'm in the lobby."

"Seven ten."

She hung up and went to him. Rotund in a blue velvet smoking jacket trimmed in black borders and lapels, he greeted her, then sat down and signaled two waiters to begin serving. She ate sparingly of the abundant piles of food wasted on a brunch for just two. After half an hour, at a signal, the waiters left them with coffee and moved the tables out.

Kadsh turned to her, "Well my dear, here we are."

"Yes," she said, waiting.

"I understand you are striving to bring to fruition the endeavors with Mallory."

"Yes."

"Then what should we do?"

"That depends on your goals."

"Get expenses under control and profits up."

"You are aware of the impediments, I'm sure."

"Oh, yes."

"They are beyond my abilities," she said.

"You were not expected to be involved at that level."

"The two most important ones are carefully guarded."

"Then it will have to be an inside job."

"How?"

"Money. Enough will buy amazing results."

"Oh, my," she said.

He hesitated a moment, then asked, "And what in your estimation is the next impediment?"

"Peter, himself."

"Your dear husband?"

"My husband."

"The problem?"

"His dreams of glory and amorous accomplishments, his dreams of owning Helen Beckette, and all the satisfaction of showing her off to the world as his, and his alone."

"But he's just married you."

"Peter uses as he can, and uses up as he accomplishes his ends. He would drop me in a minute if he could have Helen."

"You know this?"

"Sure."

"Then we should be rid of Helen."

"Certainly there is no one else so high in his esteem."

"Would he risk the entire deal to attain her?"

"Hasn't he carried it to the edge already?"

"Yes, of course."

"He dreams beyond his limits."

"I don't fathom his thinking. What could be more appealing than your ambience of golden beauty and bright intelligence?"

"Things are as we see them,"

"Yes ... so ... I see us together."

She got up and turned to stand above him while he remained seated. Looking down into the steady gaze of his brown eyes, she idly pulled open the ribbon yoke of her blouse and deliberately eased a knee between his thighs.

She worked in the tranquility of after-love and loved the power in the arena of the Mata Haris of history, the pillows with the indentations of mighty heads betraying, in beguile, the doom of soldiers and generals alike, the psyche disarmed of caution. Careful to ask no revealing questions, she let him drift to talking.

With each meeting she drove him nearer to recklessness; his passion grew more inflamed. The sight of her stripped down to the tawny underwear, her leggy mastery of sexual positions, and her witty alertness captured his commitment to her. Emptied naked men must finish emptying, the toiling confusion of love's conquest seeking in the aroma of aftermath, beneath the sheets in cologne-deviant and garlic-laced sweat of excitement, to capture the other mind, the essence of another being, to grasp it all. The loosened bonds of heavy secret and dangerous information would capture the privileged listener into a state of permanent loyalty. The momentum dissipated, the excitement palled, the smell turned goaty, the judgment betrayed. She waited. He talked, eventually.

During their third meeting, in a different Memphis hotel each time, she had begun to learn of money laundering, and she began hearing about the philosophy of terrorism, the helpless oppressed using the only method of retaliation. Then she no longer saw him as simply the mogul of HMOs and nursing home chains. Behind this facade he worked in far greater sums for the politics of religion extended to the battlefields of terror. This would involve far greater sums than she and Peter could wash at the gaming tables. She knew far too much, but reality came too late.

After this encounter she knew with certainty. An inside employee of Golden Age carries out the finalities. It must be the man in the shadows, she thought. She could not imagine anyone else having the powerful prowess and the invisible stealth to be so lethally effective.

As they ended this visit, Kadsh said, "In just a few days from this day, a carefully calculated disruption will divert the vigilance at the Colburn bedside and she will be done. Neither you nor Peter should be in town then. He will be summoned to Tunica and kept there overnight."

"Okay."

"And Celeste."

"Yes?"

"Watch your step. Peter is playing smart with us ... just about the dumbest thing he could do. He has no idea that we know every move he makes. He will implode one day."

"Oh?"

"It won't make much noise."

33

In another midweek arrival at Tunica, Celeste Howard watched Peter disappear toward the elevator to the upstairs area of the Royal Nugget, then turned toward Thornton Webb's office. A croupier interrupted and handed her a note. She kept walking, opened it, and read, *3710*. She went to the penthouse elevator.

Bin Kadsh became crazier with passion each time they met. He lovingly and impatiently removed her clothes down to the underwear. He stood back and looked. While watching him with level gaze she slowly finished undressing. Then she reached for his necktie.

Sooner or later in his exhausted delirium he would reveal the right confidentiality. He had become almost desperate to capture her boundless approval, her admiration of his power, and would soon abandon or ignore all caution. He wanted her to be a part of him. She knew the signs; she had evoked them in many men. Today he would talk. She sensed it. And after the ultimate revelation he would own her, he believed, and behave accordingly. In the spicy atmosphere between the sheets she thought of the man in the shadows of the Golden Age. At this moment she wanted and needed him for fulfillment. Kadsh's excitement stimulated her to playfulness but she still had to fake the orgasms. He simply could not reach her. Somehow in the unconscious mechanisms of nature he realized it and tried more desperately in the throes of his own excitement, and became more reckless in his talk. Experienced, she thinks no man can fathom the true depth of a woman's affections when he cannot bring her to the full bloom of consuming orgasm.

Finally, he told her. On a chosen day an enormous amount of money will be run through an isolated offshore shell bank. The transaction will be his crowning accomplishment and with this added to the fortune he has already accumulated from the HMO and nursing home conglomerate, he will retire to his native Zeebeckystan. There, under his protection, she will have her own palace quarters with servants, several streets away from the Kadsh compound. At least seven billion will go to help finance the Arabian Freedom Movement. She should be ready to go on the shortest notice. They will have to be out of the United States as soon as it happens, he said with a wild look in the eye.

Sobered and frightened she realized she would not be a concubine to this man, not even a wife, if so offered. Anyway, she had a mission, and her emotions were safe on another side. And he would never be rid of the present wife. Such a woman would kill him first.

"Isolated? Off shore?" she asked.

"Yes, but off shore in the most unexpected place, off shore on the Tallahatchie River, off shore in rural Mississippi, the last place any one would suspect, especially since they would make a gargantuan transaction only once, and the money would be gone, and not retrievable."

She watched him, waiting, saying nothing. He almost strutted, preening himself up, then laughed and said, "Beneath a church, my dear, of the Christian infidels."

"Are you speaking of little Cambridge?"

"And all its environs, yes."

She needed to say no more. Arrogance would help bring him down. Underestimation of the Southern mindset could prove fatal to any interloper. Outsiders who step over certain boundaries always eventually die with their boots on, in the gentle but vicious, abiding South. And one other thing – the silent South. The interlopers don't see it coming and they don't hear it coming and they don't sense it coming. Even presidents and their blood kin have bought their own doom with imperious tactics. But history made no difference to the attitude. Such people are above retribution and consider themselves untouchable. They don't take a small Southern town seriously. They would not allow two or three people, bleeding idealists, to ruin a deal, even if it meant running roughshod over the town.

Now, this one, Kadsh, was beginning to whiff sulfurous, the warning quaff there like traces of fatal fuming. She shivered, and thought of blood-tipped daggers, and treachery, and betrayal, and maniacal fanatics. She wanted to be done with this danger.

"And when is Rachel Colburn's date?"

"Very soon. We will send for you and Peter, to get you out of the way."

At the dining table, Tom Bartley remained silent while Helen Beckette talked. Ruble had come to her and named the night he wanted off duty, the coming Saturday. He had confided in her again. Firecrackers under empty inverted five-gallon cans would be set off in the boiler room to imitate the boom of a deep explosion, and everybody, including Rachel Colburn's sitters would go running to see what had happened. Then, after the staff had scattered away from the patients, all lights would go out. And quickly, in the unguarded moment, Rachel would be dealt with. They had about a week to get ready for the attack. Tom chuckled.

34

On the rare occasion when she was awake so early with nothing else to do, Celeste Howard loved breakfast in the Peanut Hulls restaurant. Men of town gathered there weekdays before the midmorning opening time of most stores to talk politics and tentatively skirt the subject of women – a pharmacist, a lawyer or two, a lazy doctor, retirees of all sorts, real estate agents, and the like. She always warily watched them; she knew they watched and waited until she left before talking about her. She wondered if one of them had blown the whistle to John Colburn.

One morning she found John himself there, isolated in a booth with a woman. She had to look twice and nearly screamed with surprise. Helen Beckette! Miss goddamned goody two-shoes! Oh shit! She would love to strangle her, despite the dogs! She watched furtively, making sidelong glances, but John never looked away from the gaze of Helen. They held hands on the tabletop, Helen serene, her beautiful face aglow with happiness, the morning sun casting highlights in her luxurious auburn hair. Their voices were low, their attention to each other, rapt.

Now there is a match, and maybe this would take Helen beyond the reach of Mallory. But no! Hell no! She hated Helen Beckette and she wanted Helen punished. And this called for attention to the eminent Dr. Isaac Dodson. She was sure he knew something about the end of David Beckette and she would love to get the facts, but she had not heard from him recently, and he used to come around often for a house call. Her impatience rose with a swell of anger. She would not tolerate the insult of such negligence, and his other negligence was directly responsible for the old Rachel Colburn mess. Actually, he had created their most insurmountable problem. He was a passable doctor with his pants off, but he had been kind of nervous and standoffish since David Beckette died and some nosing around had been done. She stormed out of the Peanut Hulls and went home. She called and made an appointment to see Dr. Dodson.

She wouldn't call what he had done an examination worthy of the name. He had been cursory, tentative, and incomplete, nervously halfway listening to her heart, his stethoscope sneaked against the border of her gown. He had touched her belly, not really feeling for anything, while his nurse stood nearby, keeping watch over his examining-room decorum.

Afterward she sat fully dressed on the opposite side of his desk while he fiddled with her chart. Finally he said, "Well, Celeste you seem to be in the best of health ... "

She interrupted impatiently, "Oh hell, come off it Dodson, how can you tell anything from your half-assed examination?"

"Why, what do you mean?"

"I mean you've stopped being a doctor if you ever were one. You've gotten lazy and crooked, and from your behavior I would guess too rich for your own good."

Dodson became very serious, "Now my dear..."

She interrupted again, "Look, Isaac, you best come by the house for another of your old-fashioned house-calls like the ones you used to do so well."

"Now Celeste ... "

"Don't *now Celeste* me. Be at the house this afternoon to complete your examination. You haven't done your wonderful routine pelvic yet."

"But ... "

"Be there, Dodson, or I will begin asking some questions publicly."

Dodson's pants hung across the back of Celeste's bedroom lounge chair less than five minutes after his arrival. Nervous, his manhood impaired by guilt and anger, he didn't last long; so they got around to the talking very soon. Celeste felt angry and impatient and vengeful. "Christ, Isaac, you do a better pelvic with your finger."

"Yeah, well, it's been a long time."

"Absence should make the pecker grow harder."

"Oh, come off it."

"I'd like to come some way."

"You can have the finger."

"I don't want it."

"Your choice."

Some choice, she thought, but she said, "Isaac, I want to know just what exactly happened to David Beckette."

"Well, he died suddenly, as I hear it, but why the question at this late date and on this occasion?"

"Because I'm being blamed for some mysterious mischief by at least one party, and I had not a damned thing to do with it."

"What makes you think I would know?"

"Oh, I suppose the idea just fits."

"Well, let me tell you, I know nothing about what happened to him. The autopsy report suggested that he strangled on his own vomit."

"No one believes that. The autopsy report was another typical piece of fence-walking by another of our illustrious medical colleagues, an indolent pathologist in this instance."

"I don't honestly know."

"Well then, how about dishonestly? Do you dishonestly know?"

She felt sadistic, the urge to bore in, to disrupt his smugness. She reveled in the information passed on to her by the man in the night shadows of the Golden Age, and the loose talk of Peter Mallory. Armed with these she could explore and destroy.

"You question my honesty."

"What honesty."

"Now, look here Celeste ..."

"I'm looking, and seeing further than you think."

"You don't know what you're talking about."

"Oh, don't I? Isaac Dodson, you have not made rounds on your patients in the Golden Age nursing home in the past six weeks, and a certain nurse falsifies the records, at your directions, saying you've been there."

"What nurse?"

"The one you've been screwing in a vacant examining room in Golden Age after hours, the one with the big burly plumber husband who would beat your brains out with a piece of pipe if he even suspected. Oh, Isaac how do you get it up in that sour-smelling place? I'm beginning to think you're some sort of pervert also."

"Where do you get such nonsense?"

"Nurses talk, Isaac. They almost without exception thrive on gossip."

"This is ridiculous."

"I think so. Indeed I do. But I'm not through with your honesty, yet. When you do make rounds you don't even touch the patients, the pitiful old things. You stand with your arms resting atop the side rails, too high and mighty and persnickety to touch a one of them, talking down, paying no attention to the complaints, and you always arrive for your so-called rounds after visiting hours so you won't have to talk to concerned families."

"How do you know all this?"

"Ha! So it's true. You've slipped and admitted it, you preposterous bastard."

He stood in the middle of the bedroom and began to dress. "I'm leaving."

"I don't blame you. I'd leave too if I were you. You're not really a man; certainly, you're not really a doctor."

"What in hell are you talking about?"

"You boys are having a bad time with old mother Colburn, aren't you?"

"You boys?"

"Yeah, you and Mallory, and the nursing home sale."

"What have I got to do with that?"

"Money." She waited. He sat down to slip on his shoes. She would not tell him. Mallory in his bragging had told her about Rachel's injuries and other hospital damage, and John Colburn had laid it out in detail. She said, "You know, the sooner she dies from neglect, the sooner Golden Age will begin to show the profit to assure its sale."

"Oh?"

"Oh yes. You've not laid a hand on her since her admission to Golden Age, and you've not seen her in more than three months."

"If that were true it still would be none of your business, besides, she's just Medicaid. If the family wants more attention let them pay for it."

"Do you know anything about the Colburn family?"

"Bunch of nobodies from out in the sticks."

"Do you know her son, John Colburn?"

"Works for the government, I hear."

"Is that all you know about him?"

"Sure. Is there more?"

She would not tell him. Let him find out the hard way. But she would not stop pressing. "You have to own nothing to be eligible for Medicaid."

"I know."

"John Colburn feels that she should get as good care as money can buy, regardless of her place in the financial strata. He generously supports her, including the nurse, Clara Bartley."

"Damned loud-mouthed busybody!"

"Only about the neglect and the malpractice."

"Malpractice?"

"Isaac, weren't you the internist in charge when old Mrs. Colburn was admitted to County Hospital with severe GI bleeding, five years ago, now?"

"Yeah, so what?"

"Let me see now if I've got this straight."

She would never let him know she had got this right from the horse's mouth, John Colburn himself, as he described it.

She continued, "A Memphis eye doctor, treating her for macular degeneration, gave her free samples of a non-steroid anti-inflammatory drug without adequate directions. A week later she became very anemic with severe hemorrhage of the gut. Clara Bartley brought her to the emergency room; you admitted old Rachel; and without using your gumption you overstudied the bleeding and the anemia, which even the man in the street knows is a complication of the drug she was taking. Without paying attention to the facts, you put her through a complete GI workup during the following week, including barium enemas, colonoscopy, GI series, gastroenteroscopy, with all the starvation and dehydration and pain, along with five different consultants, nobody really in charge, each one writing orders without paying attention to what the others had done. As a consequence she got five different mind-altering drugs, one from each of five different consultants. The anemia in the meantime got worse; she became confused, then psychotic, then began to hallucinate and climbed over the side rails, skinned her wrists out of the restraints, fell to the floor, broke her hip, broke her sternum, broke her ribs. You stood by the bedside with your immaculate lazy wrists resting atop the top rail and never touched her despite her loud cries of pain. Then you transferred her to a Memphis nursing home where somebody found her to be acutely ill. The family took her to the medical school hospital where the fractures were found, the pneumonia, the raging bladder infection, the pus on the catheter ... Shall I go on, Isaac, or have you heard enough?"

"Ridiculous!"

"Ridiculous, Isaac? Then let me name the drugs."

"You would not know one from the other."

"Okay, how about Haldol, Demerol, Nubain, Ativan for pain and agitation, and Carafate for bleeding presumed to be from a gastric ulcer. Wrong diagnosis, right Dodson?"

"I've heard enough."

"The orders written by five different doctors, not one of whom cared enough to read what the others had ordered. In other words, nobody in charge ... your job."

"I did my duty."

"Oh, not really. For instance, the hospital and nursing home records reflect none of this. You never recorded in your notes the complaints of this poor old lady. If you treat the Colburns this way, what do you do to the real underdogs?"

"Now Celeste ..."

"Malpractice, you asked. If this isn't malpractice, then just what the hell is malpractice? Isaac, you yourself created the problem of old Mrs. Colburn. Iatrogenic, right? That's the high-flown medical word, I believe, for *caused by the doctor*."

"No."

"Yes, and I'll tell you how. Since her hospital injuries, due directly to your negligence, she has had no sphincter control and she cannot walk alone. If she stands up alone she falls; if she tries to walk alone she falls. And let me put it to you bluntly, Isaac, so even you can understand: she shits and she pisses all over everything. Out of pride she tries to go to the bathroom alone, with disastrous results every time. Then it takes three people to lift her off the commode or off the floor, wherever she has landed, and to clean the shit off the walls, off the floor, off the commode, out of her hair, off her body and clothes, and from under her fingernails. Isaac, the family entrusted her to your care and you ruined her. She can't live in the cottage her son John bought for her. It would take three shifts of three people each to take care of her around the clock, and the house would have to be remodeled to accommodate the wheelchair on which she is now totally dependent for mobility. Get the point, Isaac? Malpractice monster, arrogant asshole, fuckin' quack!"

"I've had enough of this. I'm leaving and never coming back."

"Damn right, you're not coming back. What good would it do anybody, limber dick! You're no more fun than the bedsores and crutches created by your negligence! You are a piss-poor excuse for anything except being a greedy crook."

"I don't have to take this."

"Well, I know it's not the kind of thing you like to take because it's neither easy money nor sneaky pussy. But take it you will, Isaac, and you got lots more coming, I'll bet. Everything in this world comes full cycle, Isaac, sooner or later, and it would serve you right to some day end up in the very nursing home where you have been so negligent and cruel, the victim yourself of the likes of you. Then you could be just one of the horde of has-beens, misfits, babbling crones, crowing idiots, stroked-out brains, dying hearts, drowning lungs, dead peckers, dried up pussies, and the other foul-smelling and hapless remains of lingering life. Yours is coming, Isaac!"

"This is totally irreverent to the dignity of a professional…"

"Professional!" she shrieked. "Like when you are selling prescriptions to the sheriff's deputy for drugs to get the students hooked, and for resale to students running drugs from Mexico? Is that professional, Isaac?"

"You don't know what you are talking about!"

"Isaac … I've seen them, I know your handwriting, the signed pads without a patient name, and the pitiful, hooked, ragged students returning from a weekend drive to Laredo and across."

Dodson had turned pale in a state of shocked surprise.

She continued, "Didn't think anyone knew, did you? Well, the students know, Isaac, and some of them have promised vengeance on you. So, you better start enjoying what you have. It may not be for long."

He silently slipped out of the house.

Zelma called Sam into her cubicle. She had just hooked another big fish, Doctor Isaac Dodson. Celeste's bug had transmitted her encounters in both office and bedroom.

"Can you believe this woman, the way she talked to that doctor?" she asked as the recording ended.

"Yeah, I have to believe it. There it is for the world to hear, and apparently every word of it true."

"Great God. A doctor, the most trusted men on earth, betraying his patients and doing something like hooking students on drugs. He ought to be hanged."

"Zelma, control yourself. Our job is to find the facts. Justice comes later, and a hell of a whole lot of this nasty business will implode, mark my words. If you try to intercede by reporting what we know, you will blow our cover.

"Okay, I guess you're right." Sam went back to his desk, and she continued recording the inflow of information. But Sam stayed on her mind. He's middle-aged, and she's twenty nine, nearly twenty years' difference, but what a daddy he would be, all man, and so smart, and so damned sexy, the quiet steely blue eyes leveled at her, reading her to the very soul. Ten years with an unconscious wife – God, it must be backed up to his eyeballs!

35

Deputy Sheriff Wyndham Jones had with him a guy named Hoot, one of the people sent down from higher up to do the major dirty dealing. And Jones didn't like the looks of this character in his sharp, three-button suit and darker shirt and tie along with his thick-soled square-toed patent leather shoes, clumsy looking feet, over-stuffed shirt – Yankee dude. One of these characters showed up only when murder was afoot. Who would it be this time, he wondered? He didn't really want to know and he didn't like being delegated to chauffer such dangerous, treacherous scum from the Memphis airport to Cambridge. No telling when he would get it himself.

Hoot named Sybil right away, and wanted to be escorted to her. Jones, hoping Ruble would be on the Sardis Lake by this time of day, early afternoon, brought the man to Ruble's house. Sybil led them into the kitchen and fixed coffee. When she reached to remove the cigarette from her lipstick-denuded lips, the yellow stained fingers trembled, and the nails bleared through the cracked pink polish.

Jones said, "I'll wait in the car."

Hoot said, "No, you be witness to this. That's my orders." From a briefcase he counted out five packs, each containing a hundred $100 bills – fifty thousand dollars – onto the counter top. Then he said to Sybil: "We will return for this if, let's see, what's her name?" He took a notebook from his pocket, opened it, and continued, "Mrs. Rachel Colburn is still alive a week from now."

Sybil picked up the bundle of money, opened a napkin drawer under the kitchen counter, and casually made a nest for it among the linens. "Yeah," she said, I know, you already set the date, or somebody has."

"Just so you get it right."

"This Saturday night, you don't have a worry."

"Yeah, that may be true, but the boss ain't forgot Jack Williams, and he wants you to get over there and finish that job too."

"He's in the veterans nursing home, and I ain't about to get mixed up with the feds."

"Well let me tell you something. The boss don't ask. He tells. And he's telling you."

"Why's that? Williams ain't harmin' a soul like he is."

"Too much talk and worry about him. The boss wants to be rid of it. He don't like botched jobs."

"I didn't botch nothing. It ain't my fault he puked too soon. Nobody else ever puked before he got unconscious on the same stuff, so I guess he was allergic to it. Anyway, I never put it in the cups myself. And don't ever forget that, you hear. I ain't ever poisoned nobody."

"Yeah, well, you are mixed up in it and something's got to be done about Williams."

"You finish him, then. Shoot him through the window or slip in there at night and smother him or whatever. Me, I ain't goin' near the place. I'd stick out like a red flag."

"Is that your answer to the higher ups?

"Naw, jist tell 'em I'm a fuckin' coward and scared shitless to go near that place. I got my own little nighttime bailiwick right at work, and that's the only place where I can help."

"Aren't you afraid to defy the outfit?"

"I'm all they got, where I'm at."

"What about your live-in friend?"

"Who, Ruble? Forget it." Sybil stopped an impulse to tell him about Ruble's snooping and finding out what she had been doing to patients, but she did not want to lose Ruble, not yet. They would try to ambush him if they knew.

Hoot spoke while he locked his briefcase and turned toward the door, "The explosion will be set off at 2 a.m., one week from today."

"I'll be ready," she said.

He turned to Jones with a command, "Take me back to the Memphis airport."

From his hiding place in the loft over his garage, Ruble got a good look at the man with Deputy Jones. He recognized him as the same person who had come with Jones to visit Sybil on other occasions, some a long time ago, about the time something happened to David Beckette, then Jack Williams. Sybil claimed Wyndam brought Hoot there to pick up drugs for the sheriff.

36

Mallory, summoned to the Royal Nugget in Tunica on Saturday morning, took Celeste Howard with him. After arrival and as soon as Mallory went upstairs, Celeste received a note with a number. She went to room 3037, not knowing who would be there waiting. Lapkin Lewis greeted her, wearing a purple silk bathrobe with nothing underneath.

Before the afternoon interlude ended she lived up to her commitment, her duties to the organization. When asked, she informed Lewis of Kadsh's intentions to launder huge sums of money for what he called the Arabian Freedom Movement.

"And what of the local killings?" he asked.

"I thought you knew," she said. "That's why we are here now. Kadsh, through some means not divulged to me, has plans for old mother Colburn tonight. If Peter knows he has not let on to me, and I am here because he was moved out of the Cambridge scene for the event by someone higher up, no doubt through Kadsh's doings."

"Who's carrying out the plans?"

"I don't know."

She would give no hint of the man in the shadows, her man; she would not want anything to be turned against him. She had hoped Lapkin did actually know something; she hoped he was being cryptic now, but he waited, silently.

Finally, he said, "You know there is one thing never tolerated by the organization, and that is a unilateral, disloyal move for acquisition and power to the neglect or detriment of everyone else. Do you think Kadsh in his naive arrogance is underestimating the effect of his roughshod use of murder in an area of the world, and this country in particular, that he does not understand?"

"Deadly mistake."

"Exactly what do you mean?"

"No way could you know. You are about as far from Southern as a citizen of the same nation could be, in the Deep South where the literal interpretation of reality could sober even the most frenzied Islamic."

"Who could this be?"

"You actually don't know?"

"Yes. We don't know, but we suspect Kadsh is trying to hide his machinations from us. That makes two mavericks with whom we will eventually have to deal, the other being, of course, your dearly beloved."

"Peter. I know."

"But for the time being we will give them enough slack to show themselves for whatever they may prove to be."

"The plan for tonight had your blessings, I assumed."

"My dear, elimination should be saved for truly significant evil."

"Then, why not stop it now, today, before it happens?"

"No. Let's see how far they take themselves. I sense a
sleeper here, a coiled python waiting."

"Oh, my God! What?"

"The Dixie Mafia, organized crime, labor union money, syndicated gambling, and all such endeavors combined cannot begin to show significant strength and influence in a conflict between powerful religious movements and powerful nations, especially the confrontations of an international war. If we leave him alone, say it is Kadsh, he will be destroyed by the power he taunts."

"Who brought us here today?"

"Kadsh, doubtless. He could have done it through a secretary. With his financial interest in the syndicate, he now is on the inside."

"Then, the outfit seems to be losing its grip."

"Precisely why we need your help. He's slippery."

"Well, I do love spy work."

"And you are doing great service. Kadsh must not be allowed to go too far."

"Where is too far?"

"Suppose he returns to his native country with all the funds, then supplies the feds of this country with the information they so desperately want, most of it false, but with enough hard evidence to make it seem authentic. They could put us out of business and send some of us to jail."

"What's to be done?"

"Just what you are doing already. Play the game and keep me informed."

"Don't you let me get hurt."

"Always, someone is nearby."

37

After midnight Ruble parked a mile away and, moving from one area of darkness to another, approached the hospital and nursing home compound. Wyndham Jones' cruiser stood empty at the curb a block and a half from the Golden Age building. By one o'clock, quiet movement had begun in and out of the shadows. Ruble hid and watched. He could identify some of the people in the darkness. Tom Bartley mingled among the figures visible in silhouette, recognizable among them the all-powerful lawyer, Sam Sheffield, and old Rachel's son, John, and Clara Bartley, along with several policemen. Ruble had known Tom since childhood, hunted and fished with him as they grew up, and had come to know and trust him. Not a cleaner, tougher guy could be found anywhere. Then at the age of 18 Tom had gone off to two years of war and had returned with the added power of his training for nighttime combat. Tom had taught him many new things while training him as a deputy game warden. He would be the first man on earth to turn to for help in a crisis and the last man on earth Ruble would want to cross.

Ruble entered the Golden Age building and went to the vicinity of the boiler room. He spotted Wyndham Jones hunkered in a shadow of the heat exchanger. Ruble worked his way to within sight of Rachel Colburn's room and waited. The bulky form bulged under bed covers; the sitter at the bedside rocked gently in a rocking chair, her gaze turned toward the open door and the dimly lit hallway. The silence became profound and the stillness uneasy. The long arm on the wall clock above the nurse's station notched its upsweep second by second toward the short arm pointing across the number 2, seeming to hang there in a pinnacle of suspense. Ruble braced himself and began to think maybe nothing would happen. Then the explosion cracked sharply and a deep boom shook the building. The sitter leapt from her chair and bolted through the door of Rachel's room and down the hallway. And the lights went out.

But the yard lights shone though the window and outlined a figure moving within the Colburn room. Sybil's gaunt silhouette, in haughty agitation, appeared on tiptoe. She grasped a pillow and went to the face of the figure. A little tentative at first, she put the pillow over the head region, then with a vengeance pressed down hard with both hands. No struggle ensued and she continued for what seemed far too long a time. Ruble thought, *she's getting away with it, something has gone wrong,* and he had to quell an impulse to leap to the rescue of Rachel, but wisdom warned him off. Sybil pushed the pillow down as the long clock hand clicked and jumped to the next second, then the next, and on through the several more minutes.

She began to loosen her grip, then raised the pillow and looked. The mound lay motionless in profound inertia. Sybil dropped the pillow across the foot of the bed and took a step backwards. The room lights flared on, the bed covers erupted, and Tom Bartley sat bolt upright in the bed and swung his legs over the side. Sybil turned to run and came face to face against an officer in uniform with a holstered revolver on each hip. He handcuffed her without uttering a word.

Tom said, "Mrs. Snyder, would you like to see yourself in the movies? Play the scene back for her, John."

John Colburn stepped forward, flipped the screen out on Tom's digital nighttime camera and played back the scene. The camera had caught all the action, and played on and on through the interminable ten minutes of smothering, and held on to the scene until Tom sat up and removed the long reed tube from his mouth, the kind used for underwater hiding and tracking in the Vietnam jungle waters. The sound track had caught Sybil's voice, revealing the mutterings Ruble had not heard in the murmurs of the night.

"Troublesome old bitch; this will get rid of you." Sybil's face had become ashen. She slumped in the grasp of an officer on each side.

Sam Sheffield said from the shadows of the room, "You look great in infrared, Mrs. Snyder. Stellar performance. This should earn you an Emmy."

As Ruble turned into the shadows to leave the scene he heard the trailing sound of a voice reading Sybil her rights, and she started screaming. He stopped to listen.

"I want Tom Bartley!"

Tom stepped forward and waited.

She said, "You're Ruble's friend, I know it, I've heard him talk about you. Don't let 'em take me to the county jail. I'll be dead before day!"

"Why?"

"Why? Bunch of rotten bastards, they would shut me up forever. I want to be hidden somewhere out of this county, and I want to be guarded constantly."

"And for that?"

"For that you get my cooperation. There's lots you need to know. It was beginning to bother my conscience."

At home Ruble found the fifty thousand dollars in the linen drawer where Sybil had placed it, as though it had no more value than another piece of cutlery. With the wad of money in his hand, he studied the nest among the towels and napkins and a thought came to him. Surely they would return to collect the money. He smiled. He would be ready for them. Ruble gloried in his new freedom. Sybil would never return home.

At the Golden Age the next morning, he got his mop and bucket and went into Helen Beckette's office before seven o'clock. She put down her pen and waited for him to speak. "Miss Beckette, I'm here to tell you I'm quitting. Didn't want to just disappear."

"We need you here, Ruble."

"Appreciate that, but you don't really need me, too dangerous. I'm planning to hide until this is all over with."

"Until what is over with?"

"Whatever is coming down from the higher ups. There's goin' to be some more dead bodies around, I got a feeling."

"Frightening."

"Yeah, and you ought to get out of here too, Miss Beckette. It ain't safe for you here."

"Ruble, I want to know what happened to my husband, David."

"I do too, and if I knew anything for sure, I would tell you. But I'll bet they get something out of Sybil. All they got to do is make her mad enough, or scare her enough, and she will start screaming it out. And you ought to be where they can't find you and where they couldn't do anything if they did."

"I'll think about your advice, Ruble. And I'm not going to terminate your employment. I'm giving you a leave of absence for six months. Come back to see us then. You saved a life last night and we are very grateful."

"Thank you and I'll come back if I'm around."

Ruble, early the next morning, went to the woods in the Clear Creek area of Sardis Lake. He would need several days and several trips to prepare a reception for Wyndham Jones and the dude he would be escorting to get the money back from Sybil.

38

Two mornings later, Celeste drove with Mallory to Tunica. Upon arrival, and after he disappeared into deep shadows of the building, she and was directed to a penthouse where she listened to the quiet sarcasm of Lapkin Lewis. He laughed with an evil inflection. They had given Kadsh a slack leash and he had played too loose. What the hell had gone wrong? Sybil Snyder had been reliable in the past. So what changed this time? Ambushed, and now in the hands of the law, arrested on the spot, in jail without bail, attempted murder ... the feds would get Sybil to talk for a deal."

Lewis turned to face Celeste. "What about her live-in?"

"I know nothing about a live-in. In fact, I don't know anybody named Sybil anything. You've been very cryptic, so you can't expect me to read your mind."

"She was not on my mind to be read, but on the basis of what I hear, I'll bet she blabbed to that man she lives with and he betrayed her."

"Man?'

"Yeah. Don't you know? ... Mallory's patsy, his financial slave, his small-time drug runner? He works the night shift at the Golden Age. To his back Mallory refers to him as a kinky-headed savage, a sneaky Indian."

Celeste froze into silence. Now she guessed, the soundless man in the night shadows, the master of stealth, her one and only real lover ever. Could Lewis be talking about him? She said, "I don't know him. What's his name?"

"Ruble Crouch."

"Doesn't ring a bell."

"She'll squeal and they'll start working backwards from Deputy Sheriff Jones and try to follow the trail upward. We'll see that it leads to Kadsh, but nowhere else.'

"How much did he pay her?"

"Fifty thousand."

"Oh, my, that's a good sum."

"Penny ante when you consider the millions he has raked in already from the HMOs and nursing homes he's bought up.

"So, what are you going to do?" she asked.

"Watch. But I'm beginning to lose patience with this farce. Tolerate a fool or a zealot too long and he stumbles everybody into trouble." He stood and began loosening his tie. "Come to bed, darling, I miss you more and more each time."

When she left at dusk to return to the gaming room, Lewis gave her a phone number and instructions for reaching him under any circumstances. If no answer, leave a message to call, but no names, no numbers, no cell phones. And always use a prepaid card and a public phone.

On Saturday evening, John Colburn sat at Clara and Tom Bartley's dining table with Helen for another meal. They all sensed a letdown. Helen thought it would be okay to move back into her own home, but both Tom and John disagreed.

Clara emphatically said, "No! The danger is not over."

Tom said, "The worst is yet to come."

"You really think so?" asked Helen.

Tom laid his fork down across his plate and said, "Well, Helen, I didn't want to worry you with this, but I guess it's time. Wyndham Jones has been following you, and I've seen him more than once watching this house. Don't go out of this place alone, ever, nor anywhere else until this is all over."

"Oh Lord," she said.

Tom continued, "And last Sunday when you and John went for a ride in the country, I had a feeling, and followed. I followed Deputy Jones, that is, following you. On the last occasion, he had a passenger in his car, a member of the Goonsby clan."

"Oh!" said Clara.

"I'm sick and tired of this," said Helen

"But you're alive and you need to stay that way," said Tom

"Yeah, you're right. And thanks for your concern and your protection. But it can't go on forever."

"I think the end is approaching because Sybil Snyder will blow the whistle on the person or outfit that hired her," said John.

"You think she will talk?"

"When she faces a life sentence without parole, she'll sing like a bird," said Tom.

"Good."

"Then there is the money somebody paid Sybil to murder Rachel. And since she did not succeed, the same mule will return to collect."

"How do you know all this?" asked Clara.

"The little bug in Wyndham Jones' wallet, put there several weeks ago, transmitted quite clearly as he escorted the man with the money to Sybil. Zelma Taylor heard every word," said John. "The mule told Sybil he would return for the money if Rachel was not dead by a certain date."

"What will happen when he returns to collect?"

"The deputy will escort him again. But they won't find it," said Tom.

"Why?" asked Helen.

"Ruble Crouch is too sly. No one in this world but Ruble will ever know what happened to that fifty thousand dollars, unless he decides to tell."

"And what will happen to the man?"

"The man can wisely go back where he came from empty-handed or he can go after Ruble and maybe never go home again."

"Is Ruble that bad?"

"Ruble's not bad at all. But he does have an abiding sense of retribution," said Tom.

John said, "Well, I've now listened to all the recordings, and I no longer think we should simply wait for Bin Kadsh and those above him and below him to make the next move. I think we should clear the field, so to speak, for the further progress of their plans."

"What precisely?" asked Clara.

"I think Helen should resign or take six months' leave of absence, and

I think we should move Rachel out of Golden Age and out of state temporarily," said John.

"Would that be defeat, giving them exactly what they want?" asked Helen.

"Seemingly so on the surface, but we actually would be calling his hand by removing the impediments to the progress of Kadsh's plans, so the sooner we get out of the way, the sooner the culprits will move on to their real purpose, at the same time exposing themselves to defeat."

"I see your point," said Helen. "And I'm willing to do whatever is needed. But I don't want to leave David Beckette's mystery unsolved."

"I predict Sybil Snyder will provide the answers," said Tom.

"I hope so. But the surveillance did begin sometime after his death and we have no real leads," John said.

"Okay," said Helen. "I will talk to Ruble, then I will turn in my leave of absence. Or should I just resign?"

"No, don't resign. You may be needed later," said John.

"What do you mean?"

"Because the nursing home might be returned to local ownership and management. Then we can have what we need for the old folks."

Helen studied John for a moment, then asked, "John, you know something I don't?"

"The sea swims with constant peril. The big fish about to swallow a little fish is in turn about to be swallowed by a still bigger fish."

Helen cocked her head, listening, looking at John's profile. John turned his face to hers, smiled and said. "Mallory's the middle fish, but he doesn't know it yet."

"So, what's our next move?" asked Clara.

"I've hired an ambulance service to take Rachel to a private facility in Memphis tomorrow, Sunday morning, where she will stay for the duration. All I have to do is confirm both reservations, which I will do tonight." He stood to go. "Thanks for another delicious dinner, Clara. See all of you tomorrow."

"Is she staying in the Overton Mansion?" asked Clara.

"Yes. I thought it would give you a much-needed respite."

"You underestimate my sentiments. I second-guessed you, made a few inquiries, hit pay dirt, and today accepted a temporary position on their staff, and will stay as long as she does."

John said, "Clara, you have touched her in ways her own family could not or would not ever do. I am forever grateful to you."

"I will always love her as much as I loved my own mother. I would never consider not looking after her every day."

"Good. Would you like to ride with me and Helen?"

"I'll go in my own car. I will need it."

After worrying with the dilemma, Helen Beckette finally listed her house with a realtor and sold it in less than a week. Her furnishings went into storage. She could never return there to live with David's memories and the present dangers. But this action brought closure to only a material phase of her existence. The solid foundation and the security of David Beckette's benevolent dedication to his marriage and his patients remained a guide through the turbulence of overwhelming changes. She would honor this memory; she would somehow continue his rescue of the damned caught in the living hell of neglect fostered on the aged by society. He had been practical, level, steady, concerned, determined, and entirely too intelligent to be plodding. The marriage had been calm and decent, his love making gentle and tender, a loyal but earthbound and possessive passion. In all his existence he cast the aura of husbandry, his romance wingless.

John Colburn had almost attacked, revealing a desperate hunger and loneliness. On their first afternoon alone, there in the beautiful little hotel nestled in the curve of the river, after the first and fiery release, he had wound himself around her, nuzzled along her neck, and she realized after a quiet moment, he wept. She held him in an embrace of protective endearment. She had felt this overwhelming and protective emotion from the first moment with him, and it blossomed with the consummation. When she first lay down on the bed undressed, he had played and caressed with tantalizing affections into mounting ardor then eagerly climbed and clung in an endearment reaching with his embrace for sanctuary, his body almost acrobatic, eagerly searching hers while love locked them in slow and easy union, growing to frenzied passion, the finishing tremor she had known in nuptial love now a violent eruption.

From the moment she first saw him, there had been no doubt. They were on a path together now, her emotions mounting to a higher plane.

39

On Monday morning, Celeste Howard arrived at the Royal Nugget in Tunica with Mallory, and as soon as he went to the casino offices on business as usual, she joined Bin Kadsh in his suite.

"Well, my dear," he said, "It looks like we have won. The brave and the upright turned tail and ran."

"Tell me," said Celeste.

"The Colburn family moved Rachel out of the Golden Age home and took her away; we don't know where. And the virtuous Mrs. Beckette, the righteous and grieving widow, has taken a six-month leave of absence. Now she will find out nothing of her late husband, and apparently has given up the effort. She will get the surprise of her life when she returns in six months to claim her old job."

"Okay. So now we can move ahead."

"Yes, very soon. In fact, Peter Mallory is at this very moment downstairs in Thornton Webb's office signing the final papers on the sale of the nursing home chain to my HMO conglomerate. As soon my final money transactions are made, I will own the controlling interests. By the time we move to Zeebeckystan, I will own it all."

"And Peter, as your employee, will be on a salary?"

"He will have a job befitting his talents, and a salary based on production. He will have to go to work."

"Will he be moving out of Cambridge?"

"No."

"He had envisioned New York. He's mentioned it several times."

"He assumed a lot. We made no false promises."

She frowned and waited.

He continued. "You have no worries. Should anything happen to Peter he would leave you with about fifty million dollars."

"That's small potatoes compared to what he was expecting."

"Then, of course, you will have the castle and a very generous allowance in Tortut, and I will be there every day, with you as my right-hand man, so to speak."

She didn't trust this man, and at the moment felt a rush of relief for working with Lapkin Lewis. She studied the rotund figure, the highly polished, clear-lacquered nails, the raw hair trim. His cologne hinted a distant reference to something vague but not tantalizing. He came to her. He reached and loosened the bow on her blouse. She stood, her gaze steady on his.

"Oh, my dear Celeste, it's been too long," he said.

She nestled against him and murmured, "You're going to take care of your little Celeste, aren't you? Your baby?"

"Yes. Oh yes, my dear." He began stripping her down to the tawny underwear.

"Daddy?" she said, snuggling reaching for his crotch, "You are my daddy, aren't you my daddy?"

"Yes, Oh God, yes."

"Daddy! Oh, Daddy!" She whispered as she unbuckled his pants, shucked his shorts down, and grasped him in a gentle fist of fingers. Then aiming her mouth again, licking, moistening, she swiped her tongue between ready lips as she bent to her knees.

Later, on the bed, she rode his supine adoration to a final exhaustion, exerting her mastery of leggy galloping in the dominant position. Finished, sitting straight up, and resting astride him, looking down on his conquered and sweaty face, she moved the wet lips of her love over the flaccid form of his spent erection, wiggling. She bent forward, looked into his eyes and smiled. "You going to take care of me Daddy, you going to be my daddy?"

"Yes, oh yes."

She bent further, belly to belly, and began nuzzling his neck and chin, murmuring, "My big daddy, my big man," her nipples pressing through the hairs on his chest.

She had him; all these dark men loved blondes, especially lithe, lanky, agile blonds, and she could not imagine Mrs. Kadsh wrapped in her burka, up in bed atop her husband, cantering on her squat invisible legs to bring him off in a state of shouting ecstasy.

They lay supine and nestled. She waited for the pillow talk. He would want more and more of what he just had. He would strive toward it, trying to dominate and control with the power of words, and with the words he would reveal his next moves, and finally his plans for the culmination. Eventually, as the intimacy grew, he would become reckless, then cast aside all caution.

As the heady languor became almost somnolent he said, "We are going to be very rich, my dear, very rich. But we have to be up in an airplane, well out over the ocean on the very day it happens. We must be free of guilt, and to be sure we must be out of reach."

"How delightful. Aren't you lucky?"

"Luck has nothing to do with it."

Oh the mindset, she thought, as she daintily placed fingertips into the hair of his chest, touched her lips across his, and whispered, "Tell baby how Daddy did it." Her hand passed down and played around his navel, gently brushing and hesitated on the brink of his pubes, waiting.

"Too damned easy to believe."

"Tell me."

"Don't you know that most white Americans are asleep? Anybody can move in and take over. For example, the Mexicans in the West, and the blacks in the South have taken over the cash registers; the Indians from India have taken the motels along the interstates down the entire East Coast and now are moving steadily west. The third-generation white male in medicine is becoming almost a rarity. I couldn't believe how easy it was. I landed here expecting to be repulsed, and I had to stagger from the lack of inertia I met. Then I picked up and ran. No trouble getting into medical school – Yale, no less – no trouble getting a residency in internal medicine; no trouble becoming a professor in internal medicine in a great school; no trouble when I opened my practice to the public, and was swamped by patients looking for someone to take the time to talk to them, somebody interested, if not compassionate. Money rained down like the wind was shaking it from the trees. Then Hillary Clinton made me really rich. When her meddling failed, and the government pulled out, leaving a vacuum, the insurance industry made a dive for control, and I got in on the ground floor. It became simple to buy up one failing or lackadaisical HMO after another and apply the pressure of aggressive financial control. They made money like you can't believe. The same happened with the nursing homes, the houses built by the antibiotics. No one goes there to live. They all go there to die, and the sooner the better."

"Well, you have certainly built an empire."

"In a fashion, yes, but a few hundred million is not enough for real power. You have to get used to thinking in the billions."

She moved her fingertips a little further down, hesitating, teasing, tantalizing, on the verge of advancing. "I could get used to that, Daddy." She ran her tongue tip along the rim of his ear.

"We will have it, my dear girl."

"It's amazing how you could come over here from Zeebeckystan and so rapidly outdo the American doctors."

"The American doctors, I am afraid, sleep more soundly than their equals in other endeavors."

"How?"

"Chasing the Holy Grail of their self-importance. Their politics is a joke. They have no real leadership because they look to their own ranks for political power, and it's not there. Even the labor unions know to elect powerful figures for long terms. The little doctors, on their little ego trips, elect a new president every year in every medical society, no matter how small or how big, in this entire country. These people wallow in their self-importance for a year, then the next one does the same. Such tepid glory! The politicians, the special interests, the insurance carriers, the hospital industry, the government agencies including the FDA and the IRS, and the drug companies walk all over them. Blind in their delusions, they reward each other with inconsequential little metals and honors, always political, and never for real contributions to the art or the science of healing. Any opportunist can run with the ball, so to speak, all he pleases. Unless they wake up, the situation will continue to worsen."

"So, that's where we are?"

"Now, yes, but we are on the fringe of all my real dreams coming true."

"What are your real dreams, Bin?"

"To be a power in my own country. I shall return there and finance the call to union."

"Expensive undertaking."

"Less than the safe earning capacity of a few billion."

"Can you really pull this off?"

"Yes, and I'll tell you why. No one will be watching the right place, a place more like a distant offshore island, and altogether insignificant in the grand scale of world finances."

"Cambridge, Mississippi."

"Shhhhhhhhhh."

Her hand eased ever so gently down, caressing, endearing.

After midnight, Peter Mallory drove along Highway 304 through the vast cotton fields of the delta, past the shabby trappings surrounding the commercial catfish lakes, and into the hills, returning to Cambridge. Celeste rode silently by his side. He could hardly contain himself, and he would have strutted like a rooster if he had been free of the wheel. He bragged about the deal and about the amount of money he had made. She said nothing. Her quietness should have told even Peter something he needed to know. But the voice of caution would never reach him in his present delusional and euphoric state. He talked on. They might have to leave Cambridge, depending on where his expertise would be needed most, maybe even New York City. The buyers wouldn't know how to run the nursing homes, and while running them for the new buyers, he could imagine doing something to improve the HMO management. They really needed him with his financial abilities. Wouldn't that be great ... living in the Big Apple?

The term grated her nerves, the language of a yokel, the bragging of a pawn. Mallory fools himself while thinking he's fooling her. She mused about his cavalier attitude. She has never seen the inside of the Mallory mansion in Cambridge, not even after becoming Peter's wife. But the situation suits her plans just fine. She would bet the marriage certificate is not really valid in the United States, anyway. All the better, should she need to get out of the contract. The legalities would be simpler. So when they were nearly to the fringes of Cambridge she said, "Peter, so that I will know how to conduct business affairs if the need should arise, tell me how you have handled the funds."

"Oh, my dear, all my personal fortune is in my wife's name for safe keeping from all thieves and debtors who might try to collect, should a financial disaster occur. Moving the funds in any direction in my absence requires the wife's consent and signature, so don't let anyone try to fool you or force you."

He looked at her, but she stared straight ahead. She did not feel the wonder and the admiration he expected at the moment. He would connive to get the funds away from her in some manner when the time came.

"And the funds from today's transactions?"

"Oh, we only signed the papers today. There will be a public announcement in a few days, as soon as Dr. Kadsh finishes certain financial arrangements and records the transactions with a chancery clerk, then the cash will be ours."

She stopped talking. Further questions would be useless.

40

At seven in the morning after Sybil's attempt to murder Rachel, Wyndham Jones went to his desk with a cup of coffee. He himself had slipped out of the boiler room as soon as the fuses were lit, and the detonations echoed through the hills as he disappeared into the underbrush toward his car. Off duty for the night, he went home afloat in innocence. Now, he was eager to know, without appearing to be interested, what happened. He had called Sybil's house several times and got no answer. Old lady probably just dead, maybe nobody's found her yet? Where's Sybil? Something ain't right.

He idly turned on the television for the morning news, lifted his feet to the desktop, and opened the morning paper. The headlines and the announcer on the blaring screen hit him with the same news. Almost at once he threw the paper down and shut off the television. Sybil Snyder arrested and charged with attempted murder. The Sheriff's Department was never called or notified, he guessed, or he would have heard about it already. What the hell went wrong? She talked, nothing less, and somebody ratted. Ruble Crouch? He wouldn't dare. Incarcerated in an unknown institution for her own safekeeping! What's the meaning? Somebody knows something they ain't supposed to! And where was the money? The news didn't mention money, and surely she hadn't put it in a bank. He would bet Ruble had probably found it and they would never see a penny again.

The sheriff hadn't come in yet, and just as Jones was thinking Hoot or somebody would be coming down to Cambridge to collect, and he would be caught in the middle, the phone on his desk rang.

Hoot, on his cell phone in Chicago, said, "Pick me up at the Memphis United arrival in an hour and a half. Boarding now."

"Can't. I've got my assignments for the day."

"Nobody asked for your advice. The people who sent me give the orders. Be there on time, and I want to see Sybil Snyder."

"Well, what's your hurry?"

"Ain't you heard the morning reports of a foiled nursing home murder down in that shit-hole town you live in? Made the national news. Just be there; we got no time to waste."

"Okay." No point in trying to explain.

Wyndham took the newspaper with him, and Hoot read it while they drove back from Memphis. He slammed the paper down and demanded, "Where is she?"

"I don't know and I don't know how to find her, and if I did I wouldn't because I don't want to get myself killed."

"You got her in the county or city jail?"

"One and the same, and no we don't. The state police and the feds took her, and now she's untouchable. A federal judge set bail at a million dollars."

"Ahh, come off it."

"Finish reading the article. It's right there."

"Why so high?"

"I don't know, but you know what I think ... I think somebody knows something. And I want out before it gets too hot."

"I come for that money and we're gonna find it."

"Well, where are you going to look?"

"For starters, her house."

"You got a search warrant?"

"You kidding?"

"No, I'm not kiddin'. She's got a live-in boyfriend and he's liable to be there."

"So what?"

"You don't want to fool with him."

"Are you kiddin' again?"

"No. Unless you can slip up on him and kill him while he's sleeping, you best leave him alone."

"You Southerners scared of your own shadows."

"Being scared can keep you alive."

"Yeah, well you're taking me to her house, and you're standing guard, and you're helping me search the place."

Hoot had retrieved a .44 magnum automatic from his check-through luggage and it now bulged in an armpit holster. Jones thought Hoot wouldn't fail to use it in a hair-trigger flash of anger. He hoped Ruble had gone to the lake for the day. He drove to Sybil's house, arriving at almost noon.

Hoot picked the lock. A wave of heat struck them when he opened the front door. Wyndam went to a thermostat and found it turned up to maximum. Hoot looked around and began pulling drawers and dumping contents on the floor. He found nothing in the living room or dining room. The kitchen looked more promising. The drawer of cutlery clattered to the floor. Hoot went from drawer to drawer. The butcher knives and cooking tools bounced on the tile. He jerked open the top linen drawer, and screamed. Wyndham in all his days hunting and fishing had never seen such a big rattler. It sprang up out of the drawer like a released jack-in-the-box and struck Hoot's hands three times while he was withdrawing them, then bit him in the face, and three more entwined snakes came out of the towels like a hydra-headed monster, all of them furious, revved up on the confinement and starvation in the stifling heat, all striking in a frenzy, hitting Hoot on the face and neck and ears. Hoot collapsed to the floor, turned blue in the face, and began to convulse. Wyndham backed through the kitchen entrance, retreated out of the house, slammed the door shut, and sped away in his patrol car.

In the news reports, Celeste had read the name, Sybil Snyder, then found the address in the phone book. So she's the one Kadsh hires indirectly to do the real dirty work at the Golden Age. The news said she had a live-in male companion, a Ruble Crouch, ex-convict just serving out his parole, the person Lapkin had told her about. She would bet he was the man in the night shadows, the great lover who refused to give his name. Sybil got caught using a pillow. How clumsy! But not a pillow on Williams or Beckette, she would guess. Hell!

She decided to look at once for answers. She drove out toward Sybil's address and found it. But as she arrived, Wyndham Jones' police cruiser stood in the driveway. He and a man she did not know were entering the house. The stranger wore a tight-fitting blue suit.

She parked around a corner and watched. In less than ten minutes, Jones came skittering out the front door in a panic, desperately slammed it shut, turned sideways pulling on the knob with both hands like he was trapping something inside, then ran to his patrol car and sped away. She waited. Nothing happened. She waited an hour and saw no signs of life in the house. Who could the man be? Kadsh's mule she guessed, deceived by Wyndham in some way? She fished in her purse and found a prepaid phone card and drove away. Several blocks across the neighborhood, at a pay phone, she called Lapkin Lewis' number. He picked up on the first ring and said nothing. She knew the silken sound he made letting out his breath. She said, "Something needs your attention."

"You at a pay phone?"

"Yes."

"You can talk."

Then she told him, and added, "Two went in and only one came out."

"Good work. Go home and stay out of the way and out of sight." He hung up.

Ruble had rented a small apartment in the heart of town on the day he left home. He had nothing to hide. He had made enough off the drug sales to get by, and he would not touch any of the fifty thousand dollars he recovered from Sybil's kitchen drawer unless he had to. He locked up the entire amount in a lockbox he had rented years ago in the other bank across town from Mallory's. He would make no more pickups from the drops in Sardis Lake. Contacts had phoned him numerous times to schedule a rendezvous and each time he answered, "Boat's broke." His parole period had ended and he had more freedom to move about now. He had no intention of returning to the penitentiary. He ran his trotlines and sold the fish. At night he watched the drug movements. In the daytime he watched the town. He thought Wyndham Jones would be out to get him, and would come looking for the money.

41

Celeste met Kadsh in Memphis again, this time at the Hyatt out on Poplar. He tore at her passionately and she didn't try to stop him. After a five-minute session of roaring and grunting he lay spent, silent, ominous like a growing storm. Finally he said, "What are your intentions with Peter?"

"Why, I'm married to him, of course, as everyone seems to know by now."

"Do you plan to make it permanent?"

"Depends."

"Celeste, I want you in my own country with me."

"As what?"

"As mine."

"Give it a title."

"You would be well off …"

"I'm going to be well off anyway, it seems, as Mrs. Peter Mallory."

"Only if he is dead."

"Well, what does that mean?"

"He could end up without a dime to his name."

"I'm fully aware of the possibilities."

"Then, you will go with me to Zeebeckystan."

She needed more time, so she moved against him and placed a hand on his cheek, her lips against his lips, and said, "Sweet Daddy, you going to take care of baby, baby has to be where Daddy can take care of her."

Kadsh, immobile on his back, stared pensively toward the ceiling and rubbed an open palm up and down her bare back, and in languid caressing tones asked, "What was your maiden name?"

"Mary Celeste McLaurin."

"Ahh, my dear, how pretty. I really like the sound ... Scottish isn't it?"

"Yes," she said. "Highlanders, of the purest strain."

"Then we will use that name for you in Zeebeckystan."

"Why?"

"I like its identity."

"Okay."

"I want you to get a passport immediately in the name of Mary Celeste McLaurin."

"Okay."

"Are you driving back to Cambridge tonight?"

"I have not given it a thought."

"Take the room for the night if you want. I have to get back to my dear wife. She must have no cause for suspicion."

Lapkin Lewis sent for her again, and Celeste went from the Cambridge airport in a private jet to meet him in Las Vegas. There, she told him the news as she had it from Kadsh.

"Well. Are you going with him?"

"No, but somehow I will have to get out of it at the last minute. He plans to send his wife and family on ahead as the crucial time approaches. I can picture the two of us on a flight to the Middle East, my American face and passport a declaration of his integrity."

"Yeah. Imagine the change in his attitude once he gets you there, and the passion, assuaged too often, grows dimmer."

"I sense it all too clearly," she said.

"And besides the money laundering, he's sniffing around the Russian Mafia, and has made inquiries through the Federal Reserve and at least two New York banks engaged in selling American dollars to Russia. We are trying to keep up with the details of his scheming."

"This scares the hell out of me, and as you know, I don't scare easily."

"Yes, I know. But now you are in too deep to just walk. You've got to play along. You do, and we will rescue you at some point in your journey to the Promised Land."

"What's going to happen to Peter?"

"That depends on Peter. If he betrays us, we get rid of him. But, you know, my dear Celeste, this Peter Mallory carries his own built-in destruction. I don't think we will ever have to touch him. Somebody will do it for us, or rather for themselves, which is to say the sweet glory of settling old scores."

"What should I do?"

"One thing, just for kicks, buy all the term life insurance you can afford, on his life, with double indemnity for accidental death."

"How much should I spend?"

"Go the limit even if it takes all you've got and all you can borrow."

"Oh my," she said. "From where?"

"Let me know how much you can buy."

"Why thank you, Lapkin. I really appreciate it."

Lapkin looked at her quietly from across the desk, and said, "And with that my dear, would you like to come to my bed?"

"Oh Lapkin, it's always such a pleasure, but we can't tarry, I have to be home by seven, for choir practice."

"Choir practice?"

"Oh yes. The church is my whole life."

"The plane will be standing by."

Celeste took the insurance papers to Isaac Dodson's office, with an appointment. She refused to give the receptionist or the nurse any information about her health. Too private, she claimed. A clerk escorted her into Dodson's office to wait. Thirty minutes later, he entered, obviously informed by his staff and obviously irritated by her refusal to be treated like the average patient. "Well, well," he said. "From what deadly disease are we suffering today? Acute hyper-candor perhaps?"

"No. Acute anxiety. Isaac, I have this terrible fear about something awful happening to my friend Peter Mallory, on whom I have come to depend almost entirely, leaving me penniless."

"Celeste, you are wasting my time!"

"Well, I can waste more than time if you force me to. All I want is your signature on these insurance papers." She passed the bundle across the desk.

Reflexively, with an air of defeat, he took them. She waited while he thumbed through the pages.

He looked up and exclaimed, "Jesus Christ. You are paying six hundred thousand dollars in term premiums, none of it refundable." "That's the limit. The insurance companies won't sell me any more, but it would pay death benefits of a hundred million. And I had to shop everywhere and finally go all the way to Memphis to find one who would really do that much."

"Hey, now. What else do you know?"

"Nothing, Isaac, except the little whispers of intuition, and you know how very accurate my intuition can be."

"Celeste, I can't forge an insurance examination. I can't testify to his state of health."

"Isaac, don't take me for a fool or an ignoramus. Peter was in here last week for his annual physical, and I know for a fact he had a stress test, along with complete lab work and a chest x-ray, all of it turning out to be *within normal limits*, as your jargon goes. Now all you have to do is put the findings on the blanks and sign them."

"That was not a formal examination for an insurance company."

"It is now. Look at the last page. It's a letter of authorization. And you haven't looked thoroughly, Isaac. There's also a check there in the amount of three hundred dollars made out to you."

He looked at her and she returned a steady gaze. "Now, listen here, Celeste …"

"Isaac, a sudden attack of honesty might prove very damaging if not fatal to some mighty big plans right now."

"You don't dare threaten me !" he shouted..

"No need to yell, Isaac. A little whisper from me in the right ear would have the narcotics squad in your office within an hour."

He glowered at her but picked up a pen and started filling in the blanks.

42

Out in the swampy edge of Sardis Lake, Ruble Crouch ran his trotlines and re-baited. He finished at dusk and rowed ashore in his small aluminum skiff. He put two coolers of fish in the bed of his pickup, lifted the boat in, and tied it down. When he turned toward the driver's door, Tom Bartley stood in the shadows.

"Hello Ruble."

"Tom! You snuk up on me."

"You're hard to find these days."

"Watching my own hide."

"Yeah. We need to talk about that and some other things."

"Well, I don't know who to talk to anymore. Ears seem to be everywhere."

"Suppose we just walk along the lake. Don't think anyone would hear us here."

"Okay."

When well away from the truck, Tom said, "What's your situation?"

"I moved out of the house before they caught Sybil doing her mess. She changed the locks on all the doors, but I don't have any trouble getting back in when I need to. I took my cameras and all my videos and all my sound tapes when I left."

"What are you talking about?"

"Sybil and also the sheriff's outfit."

"You have some evidence?"

"Hell, yes. But I don't know what to do with it."

"Would you tell me, then we can decide how to go about using it."

"I reckon you know I was being accused of abusing patients, and I'm innocent. You taught me about that infrared stuff, so I bought me a little digital infrared video camera and followed Sybil at night. I got her on the screen man, patient after patient."

"Can you tell who they are, on the pictures?"

"Yeah. Everyone's got that I.D. card fastened on the foot of the bed; they kind of glow in the dark. Zoomed in and got every one of 'em on the videos."

"Good. Now do you think she's responsible for any of the deaths?"

"Oh man, yeah. Some of 'em just folded up and died within days after she beat them. I remember one in particular, old Paul McInerny."

"What did she do to him?"

"Hit him in the eye with her bony fist, then beat him over the head with the call button end of the cord. He never talked to anybody again … just gave up and died in less than a month."

"Did they do an autopsy, or do you recall?"

"No they didn't."

"Ruble, do you know what happened to Jack Williams and David Beckette?"

"I don't have any pictures. They were gone before I started getting suspicious. But I know what happened."

"How do you know?"

"The same fellow came with Wyndham Jones to visit her at the house, more than once. And about that time she all of a sudden had lots of money."

"How did she do it?"

"On that one I have to speculate. Sybil could be very friendly, you know, and real flirty. And I didn't think about this until recently. She would brew up two pots of coffee every night on her ward, at her expense, and if she wanted to butter up to somebody she would offer coffee. I seen both men, many times, drinking coffee with her after midnight. Williams would keep working after doing his job, staying overtime keeping things going to help out with the disabled, maintaining stuff nobody told him to do. Dr. Beckette wandered the wards looking for people who needed him."

"Damn."

"Yeah. She would step out of a shadow and say, 'Oh, hi Dr. Beckette, so nice to see you' … and chatter away, grinning like she meant it, then take him by an arm and go, 'you look kind of tired. Come on in the office here and have a cup of coffee,' pulling him, not letting go. 'Decaf or high test?' she would say."

"And, of course, to get Jack Williams up there she could gag a commode with a towel, or some such fooling, and he would come running to help. She always rewarded him with coffee."

"Do you think she poisoned them?"

"If that's what happened to them, I don't know exactly how the stuff got in the coffee."

"Who could have put it there?"

"Either she did, or she had help."

"Then there is the possibility that she did not kill Beckette herself?"

"Yeah."

"This could prove to be a boon. Maybe she will talk if it spares her a murder charge and another attempted murder charge."

"She'll spill everything if you catch her right. But who are you going to work with? The sheriff and his deputy Jones are paid off by Mallory, and they are still trying to run drugs."

"We will use either the feds or the state police, or both. And what about you and the drugs?"

"Naw, man I quit clean soon as I got Mallory paid off. And I'm staying clean. You got to get them out of the picture."

"We plan to."

"Has anybody searched the house?" asked Ruble.

"God no! Everybody's scared to go near the place. They had to bring a snake-man down from the Memphis Zoo before the undertakers could get the body out. He caught four rattlers, but people wonder how many more are hidden in there."

Ruble waited a moment then said, "There were only four."

Tom looked out toward the lights blinking across the lake, and said, "Thank you, Ruble."

"You're going to find some surprises when you do your search. They took her straight to jail and she didn't have a chance to hide or destroy anything. But you won't find any money. I got everything that Wyndham and his pal brought her for the job on old Mrs. Colburn. While looking around I found another stash, I suppose for previous jobs she had done, God knows how many, but more than two."

"Significant amount?"

"I wouldn't ever have to work again if I lived carefully. But then I don't take much."

"Well, Ruble, all this is very helpful. But I really came here to warn you. We have reason to believe Mallory will have you arrested for drug dealing to hide a bigger operation he is into."

"Tom, can you believe an old ignoramus like me would have a lockbox in a bank nowhere close to Mallory's? In that box, along with the money, I have many tapes of conversations with Deputy Jones, often when he stopped me on the road to get his share. They leave no doubt about what went on. I was working for Mallory, the sheriff's plane dropped the balls of shit on the water of Sardis Lake, and Wyndham followed and got half or more and sometimes the entire haul for himself and whoever he was working for. He always got enough fresh caught catfish to hide the haul."

"That will help if needed."

"You know where it is if you come to need it and I ain't around no more. There ain't but one other bank. Mallory is on the tapes too. Give the money to the state orphanage if it comes to that. The key is taped inside my wallet."

After midnight, Ruble picked the lock and let himself into the Golden Age through a tool room door. He scouted the hallways. The bad odors had become worse, and he found only one person attending each ward. Numerous outcries and buzzing buzzers went unanswered. This he expected, with Helen Beckette gone and the likes of Clara Bartley not there to raise hell over lousy care. But he really wanted to satisfy his curiosity about the trucks coming and going in the daytime at the loading ramp out back, trucks from computer and electronic stores in Memphis. He tried the basement last. There, where he had known half-empty, cluttered, dirty storage rooms, he found newly painted and spruced-up quarters with a battery of computer screens glaring in the puddled light. Three attendants watched the screens. Suddenly one jumped up and yelled, "Jesus Christ! They just blipped a cool million by me in a split second. God!" Ruble eased back into the hallways and left the building.

Near dusk a day later, Ruble went out on the water in his aluminum skiff, with his paint sprayer, again to the cypress trees along the lake edge. This time he reached the fluorescent patches and covered them with a spray of brown paint, the color of the cypress bark. He ran his trotlines and waited. At early dark the plane flew over and made two additional passes, coming in low looking for the reflections of light from the painted tree trunks and dropped nothing. On the third pass, the plane lifted up and flew to the west toward Batesville. Ruble dawdled, spending time. Well after dark, he rowed ashore, put two coolers of catfish in the bed of his pickup, loaded the boat and oars, and secured them.

He drove slowly on the road to Abbeville. He expected company and he soon got it. The flashers suddenly lit up in his rearview mirror. He slowed to a creeping pace, then veered off into an open field and stopped. The cruiser followed. Ruble waited behind the wheel. Deputy Wyndham Jones, walking tall, swaggering with insolence, came to the window and bent forward to peep in. "Hello, Ruble."

Ruble watched him, waiting in silence. Then Jones said, "I'm in the mood for some fresh fish tonight, Ruble,"

"Well, just help yourself, two coolers in the back, take both if you want them."

"Thank you, now. Let me have a look. He went to the back, lifted the lid off one of the coolers, then dumped the fish into the truck bed. Nothing but fish and ice spilled out. He emptied the second cooler the same way. He left the flopping, gasping fish and returned to Ruble's window. He bent forward again, "Well I do believe, Ruble you ain't got much of a catch tonight."

"Oh yeah, there's some nice ones back there, kept only the biggest, several yellow channel cats bigger than fifteen pounds."

"Yeh, but they don't seem to have the right sex. Them fish is supposed to be wearin' some big white balls. They must be all girls since they don't have no balls." He snickered. Ruble said nothing, and waited. Jones continued, "Ruble, you might know you're beginning to worry us, but we're gonna' give you another chance in a day or two to get us some boy fishes.

And we ain't asking you; we're telling you. You will get the usual signal when another flight is ready."

Ruble realized his silence would leave some doubt, on the recordings, about the meaning of Jones' talk. So he said, "Wyndham, I can't pick up the little packages dropped into the water anymore. The big boat's broke and I don't have the money to have it fixed ... very expensive. Besides, I don't think I want to pick up them packages for Mr. Mallory anymore, whatever's in 'em, anyway. I been meaning to ask."

"Well, now just listen, would you. Mr. Mallory's not gonna' like that one bit. And you know perfectly well what's in them."

"Never opened a one yet. I picked 'em up because I was told to in order to pay my debts, and I sold my share to people who said they were sent by you to get the merchandise, at a price you named. You took most of the stuff anyway."

"Only mine and Mallory's share."

Good, thought Ruble. Mallory's involvement was recorded once again. Deputy Jones continued, "Well, I've told you now, Ruble, and you'll be getting your orders soon." He took a step backwards, then added, "And you and me, we got another little problem. I'll be looking for you in a few days for that, also. We going to have another outa' town visitor, and we want the money, and no snakes this time. You dealing with some dangerous people, Ruble, them Yankees when they get mad."

"Yeah," said Ruble. "Call me when you can."

"Where you livin' these days?"

"Same place. You know it all right by now, you been there so many times when my back was turned."

"We think you're stayin' some other place. We don't see you around and your truck ain't ever in the yard."

"It's my mailing address." Ruble wanted to lunge at Jones, but remained calm. Jones ought to get put down in his own way of doing things, his own form of meanness. He simply gazed at Jones and sniffed, waiting, and smelled a trace of Goonsby. Jones turned to his cruiser and left. Ruble went to the truck bed, gathered the fish and ice into the coolers, and drove to the fish market in town.

43

John Colburn hired Sam Sheffield to represent the Colburns in the investigation of his mother's attempted murder. "And while we're into it," he said to Sam, "for the sake of Helen we should look into the matter of David Beckette's death, and as a corollary, the sad circumstances of Jack William's damage."

"To begin, we need to search Sybil Snyder's house for evidence."

"Yes, before someone else beats us to it."

"I'm surprised the sheriff hasn't been there yet under the pretense of investigating, but for the real purpose of destroying any incriminating evidence."

"At my request the feds sealed it off and have had it under guard since the day of Hoot and the snakes."

"Can we get in?"

"Yes, and I think we should invite Tom to go along."

"Absolutely."

Protected by a search warrant and aided by a locksmith, they entered the house with FBI agents. John found neutral territory and simply watched. Tom chose a position by a window and stood with his arms crossed. Sam sniffed around, following one or another agent, alertly curious. The linen drawer in the kitchen cabinet still stood agape, a towel hanging over an edge. Scattered contents of other drawers still littered the floor. The agents and their crew, trained to look without leaving evidence of disturbing the belongings, searched the place thoroughly.

They found accumulated testimonials to a person's quality of life and intellectual scope. The coffee table held romance magazines, sex magazines, sex manuals, and pornographic movies. The cabinets contained hair dye, a cigarette cache, numerous half empty whiskey bottles – all cheap blends. The drawers and closets held black lingerie with dangling strings, tawdry dresses, fake furs, run-over high-heels, several wigs, a total of two books, both pulp romances. The medicine cabinets contained sleeping pills, uppers, downers, abundant laxatives, vaginal lubricants, a variety of dildos, and a supply of grass and crack.

But in the kitchen they found exciting evidence. Under the sink and behind the soaps and cleaning fluids of numerous sorts, a sealed box yielded several packets of 1080, labeled SUPER POISON. In fine print beneath the warning, John read the chemical name, sodium fluoroacetate.

"What is this?" asked Sam.

"Coyote poison, rat poison," said Tom. "Also very deadly to dogs and humans."

"Can you taste it, can you smell it, and can you find it at autopsy?" asked Sam.

None of the FBI agents could answer the question.

John said, "I don't know either, but I'll look it up on the Internet."

The agents continued their search. They found no money. With their approval, John took the 1080 to a laboratory.

The group met out in the Colburn barn again to plan strategy. Sam Sheffield listened to Helen Beckette.

"Sitting up stone-dead on a chair almost hidden in a dark alcove along a winding hallway, covered in vomit, negative autopsy, *possibly strangled on aspirated vomitus.*" Then she added with vehemence, "I can never understand why the mediocre medical mentality can't shut up and be honest when ignorant about something. The truth is, they missed the diagnosis."

"Would you be willing to exhume David for further study?" asked Sam.

"Yes, or course, but I know you are onto something."

"The FBI found a very deadly poison in Sybil Snyder's house. John has researched it. Compound 1080, deadly to rats, dogs, foxes, coyotes and humans and practically any living thing, for that matter. It's odorless, tasteless, and identifiable in the laboratory by a very complicated and expensive procedure called ion-exchange chromatography, a test done only when this specific poison is suspected."

"And I'm sure this test was not done on David at the time of autopsy," she said.

"It was not. We've checked already."

"Then let's do it as soon as possible," said Helen.

She turned pale and grim and grew silent.

Sam said, "Helen, if this is too much at the moment we can wait until you are ready."

"Oh no! It's all coming together: Odorless and tasteless. That's it. David used to talk about Sybil Snyder at the breakfast table, how nice she had been to him on her ward the night before, offering him coffee after midnight when he was there working to catch up on all the people who needed his attention. She always had two pots ready, one decaf and one high-test, as she called it. Her brazen slang amused him. It's simple. He got poisoned coffee. Does this poison cause vomiting?"

"Yes, among many other symptoms," said John.

"Well, there you have it," She said. "And while you are digging up victims, I suggest you get old Paul McInerny, too."

"Why?"

"Want to bet he didn't die from a clot on the brain caused by trauma to the head, trauma delivered on Sybil's shift, on Sybil's ward?"

"Okay." Sam turned to Tom Bartley and asked, "Would you talk to Paul's family? I expect they will consent, especially when they get a whiff of money from a lawsuit."

"Of course," said Tom. "I'll find them today."

"Yeah, the selfish devils are partly responsible for poor old Paul's tragedy. They would not pay much attention to him while he was in the nursing home alive, then after his death under suspicious circumstances they refused autopsy, spouting a bunch of garbage about God's will. But we need all the evidence we can get," said Helen.

"Yes, and we need the information before confronting Sybil Snyder. Once we got her out of danger from the sheriff's office here she began playing cute with the investigation. But we are going down to Jackson and confront her when we have the proper ammunition."

Tom spoke. "Ruble Crouch tells me he has digital pictures he made of Paul being assaulted, Sybil in nasty action. He photographed her battering other patients, also. I imagine these pictures, or simply the knowledge that they exist, would help turn Sybil into a cooperative witness."

"Could we take the pictures with us when we go to confront her?" asked Sam.

"They are invaluable, so if you will bring them to me I will have several sets made before you go," said John. "We would not want to lose the only copy in existence."

"Good idea."

"When do we go?"

"You have two or three days."

44

Celeste, out of boredom, returned to the Inner Sanctum as she did most every week, disguised as an older student. The music, the lights, the Ecstasy scene varied little. As she surveyed the room, Jones and Dr. Dodson met briefly at the bar, and Dodson soon left. Jones disappeared beyond a fern at the end of the bar, and from time to time a student momentarily went out of sight in the same direction, to return in less than five minutes. She watched one after another. Each went to a table of students, both boys and girls, and they shared the contents of an envelope. Shame! The free samples would get one or more of them hooked, to become regular customers.

The insistent drums became relentless, the lights moved in dappled speed, the peculiar grimacing and demanding thirst obsessed the drugged. Waitresses bustled through the crowd carrying trays loaded with bottled water, and an accumulating stack of money. An hour passed before Ray Haaps entered the room, spotted her immediately, and came to the table. She watched him approach and said, "Without asking, I know something has gone terribly wrong."

He pulled out a chair and sat next to her. "Yes. My girl. She couldn't handle it and she overdosed, whether intentionally or accidentally, I will never know."

"Oh, Ray. I'm so sorry. Did she …?"

"No, but she will. She's in a Memphis neurological ICU, comatose and respirator-dependent. Her brain is cooked. She won't make it."

Celeste placed a hand on his arm and squeezed gently. "What can I do?"

He looked at her with piteous gaze, his face puckered and trembling. "Take me home with you for the night and exhaust my grief."

"Let's go," she said, as she stood and moved toward the door.

A week later Celeste returned from the animal shelter after dark and changed clothes. Dressed for the occasion, she went one after another to three bars. At the third, The Briar Patch, she found Ray. He sat at a table alone, his swollen puffy face turned toward the bar studying Wyndham Jones standing with his back turned, his frame partially hiding a familiar figure, Dr. Isaac Dodson. Celeste watched the shoulder motions. Signing prescriptions again, she surmised. She went to Ray's table and sat down. Without moving, and while still looking toward the bar, he said, "She died today."

Dodson slipped away from the bar and disappeared. Ray rose from his chair, and still without looking at Celeste, said, "Leave your door unlocked." He went toward the space where Dodson had stood. Without having ordered the first bottle of water, she went home and immediately to bed, sober, and waited, listening.

An hour later the front door opened and closed and the inside latch clicked. Fire-shovel and poker and hearth sounds, then kitchen noises preceded the creak of footsteps ascending the stairs and progressing down the hallway. The whispering of the shower and muted bathroom activities stopped after another twenty minutes. Then he came to bed and slipped under the covers and snuggled against her. She turned and embraced him. He shivered like a terrified child.

When Celeste descended the stairs in the early morning, Ray sat before the fireplace. The fire had burned down to a bed of coals. The morning paper lay across the coffee table, the headlines in bold black, PROMINENT PHYSICIAN FOUND BEATEN. She read the details. Dr. Isaac Dodson ... the parking lot of the Briar Patch Bar and Grill ...airlifted from Cambridge emergency room to a Memphis neurosurgical ICU ... grave condition but expected to survive, smashed knee caps, broken legs, fractured spine and paralyzed from the waist down, depressed skull fractures with brain damage, unconscious, fractured ribs, assailants unknown and no trace found.

She sat down beside Ray, and neither spoke. After a few minutes of silence, he stood and raked the coals together in the fireplace. The round top and neck of a baseball bat disappeared among the ashes and the coals. He added more wood, and the fire flared up.

"Where is your car, Ray?"

"Parked at the dormitory on campus. I walked here."

"And the clothes you wore?"

"In the ashes."

"And what time did you get here last night?"

"Just in time for the early dinner you cooked, at dusk, remember? And stayed all night."

"Yes, of course."

"You have a change?"

"In the bag upstairs."

"And where are you this morning?"

"On my way to Greenwood to the funeral, in your car, you driving."

"Okay," she said. "You lie down out of sight on the back seat until we are well out of town. We will stop somewhere for breakfast."

45

Sam Sheffield waited at a federal prison conference table in Jackson, Mississippi, with the FBI agents assigned to interrogate Sybil Snyder, a video camera aimed at the scene, an audio recorder turned on. A court stenographer readied her tape, her fingers to the keyboard. Sybil, seated across from Sam, clasped her trembling amber-stained fingers together with her elbows on the tabletop and assumed a defiant pose. After the preliminaries, an agent began the interview.

"Mrs. Snyder, you have heard your rights and you have chosen to proceed without your own lawyer. Is that right?"

"Yeah, I don't need no lawyer. I'm going to tell you the truth anyhow."

"Fine. We would like to begin with Old Paul, as he was called, Paul McInerny. Remember him?"

"Yeah, I reckon. There was so many of them old geezers around the wards from time to time that it's hard to remember them all." She laughed.

"Yes, well then, I think we can save a lot of time and trouble by informing you that we have a video of you beating Old Paul about the head with his call-button cord, and a very clear view of you hitting him in the eye with your fist. The name on his bed label is clear in the picture and the time and date are recorded. Therefore, there can be no doubt that you abused and beat this man savagely. He died within a month, and the administration of Golden Age thought his death might be related to the injuries. Would you like to see the video?"

"Naw, that ain't necessary."

"Well then, to continue. Old Paul was taken out of his grave day before yesterday and an autopsy performed. The pathologist found a big blood clot on his brain, fractures of the right orbit, that is, his eye-socket bone, two fracture lines in his skull, and the scalp wounds had not healed at the time of death, these among other signs of chronic abuse. The official conclusion of the coroner is *death due to complications of trauma to the head*. Mrs. Snyder, the charge against you, based on this evidence, will be first-degree murder."

Sam sat with his arms folded, his gaze leveled at Sybil. She remained silent, her lips drawn in a tight line, her eyes averted, her posture a whipped-dog look. She said nothing. The agent continued, "Depending upon the outcome of trial, this conviction would carry either the death penalty or a mandatory life sentence without parole." He paused and waited. "Do you have anything to say at this point?"

"Naw, I reckon not."

"Now we have two older problems which we hope you can shed some light on. We would like to know what happened to Dr. David Beckette and a maintenance man named Jack Williams. Can you help us with these unsolved mysteries?"

"I 'spect not."

"Then I will continue. Perhaps the evidence we have uncovered will help refresh your memory. We got poor Dr. Beckette out of his grave, too, and we find that he died from a poison called 1080. But it has a bunch of other names, among them Ratbane, Rat Killer, and Yasoknock. And Williams ... you know his wife grieves every day while she is feeding him in his vegetative state, down in the Veterans Nursing Home, and she is very sentimental. She saved all of his clothes, none of which will ever be of any use to him for the rest of his life. And she didn't wash the clothes he wore the night they found him unconscious on a hallway floor of the Golden Age. She just sealed them up in an airtight box for keeping. The shirt is still caked with old dried vomit. We examined that, too, and it is full of the same poison. Apparently he didn't die only because he threw up most of the poison before it took effect."

The agent stopped talking for a moment and regarded Sybil calmly. She remained silent. The agent continued. "Mrs. Snyder, with the proper authorization we searched your house in Cambridge and among other incriminating evidence we found a supply of 1080 beneath your kitchen sink. We have photographs of the poison in place, and we have the testimony of numerous witnesses who were there for the search. Laboratory analysis of the powder in the box verifies it to be the so-called 1080, chemically known as sodium fluoroacetate."

Sam kept his eyes on Sybil. She seemed to be actually swelling with silent rage. Her face had grown stark white, her lips drawn into an even tighter line, her eyes diverted toward the tabletop. She ground her teeth together, her cheek muscles flaring in hard knots. The agent waited. Suddenly Sybil jumped up, struck the tabletop with both fists and began screaming. "Goddamn it, shit to hell, I didn't put that goddamned poison in the goddamned coffee!" Her face distorted in a grimace of fury, her scrawny body crouching for attack, but she just as suddenly collapsed back into her chair and began pounding the floor with her heels, in a frenzy, biting at both palms.

The sudden electric silence engulfed the room. Sam eased back in his chair and relaxed. He brought a hand up and covered his forehead. Sybil, struck dumb herself by her own outburst and loss of control, by her own confession, now sat mute and terrified, drained, pallid, and defeated. The agent started to speak again and Sam looked at him and raised a finger. The agent nodded. Sam leaned forward, his elbows on the table and said in a kind tone, "Sybil."

She uncovered her face, looked at him and said, "Yes?"

"Do you know me?"

"Yeah, I know you. You got my folks out of trouble more than once, you and that Jake Howard who dropped dead one day ... never sent no bills or not much of one."

"Good. Then you realize I'm here to try to help all concerned with this situation."

"Yeah, I believe you."

"Now Sybil, we have reason to believe powerful forces at work in big cities far away from Cambridge have brought undue pressure on you and others, and we believe these people are the ones really responsible for all that's happened. They are very evil and will do much more harm if not stopped. So we need your help. And if we get it you could end up with a much more lenient sentence. If you help, Tom Bartley has agreed not to press attempted murder charges against you."

"Tom Bartley!"

"You know him, the guy you tried to smother in the Golden Age on the twenty-third."

"Naw, that was old lady Colburn …!" Sybil caught herself and stopped again, but too late … another confession.

Sam continued. "Sybil we need to know how the poison got in the coffee you gave to Dr. Beckette and Mr. Williams."

"I never gave them no coffee, they poured it their selves. It was that guy named Hoot … I don't know his last name … was never told."

"How did he fit in the picture?"

"He was sent down to do it. Me, I refused to use the poison myself."

"He came in the Golden Age?"

"Oh, yeah."

"How did he get in at that time of night, after your 11 p.m. shift started?"

"Deputy Jones let him in."

"How?"

"He's got a key."

"Why."

"Don't you know? He's got a key to nearly everything in town, him and the sheriff too. They got dibs on everything that's worth anything."

"No, I don't think we realized that. Now tell us just how they went about it."

"Jones would bring him there from the Memphis airport, and let him in through the emergency entrance after hours. Hoot would be wearing an orderly's uniform, one of them unironed white suits, scrubs they call them, and he would come down to the stand where I made the coffee. Looked just like he was on duty, and there was no one to question him. I wouldn't look up or speak and never watched what he did. But he would treat two empty cups so whoever poured the coffee got what he had put in there. They bought two cups, both red, one for decaf and one for the other so we wouldn't get mixed up ourselves and drink out of the wrong cup. The others was white."

"Did he bring the poison?"

"The first time he did, but he made me keep the bag, said he couldn't risk carrying it back and forth on the plane."

"On the plane, you said. On the plane back and forth from where?"

"I don't really know, but it seems to me like I heard the word Chicago somewhere,"

"Now Sybil, how much did they pay you?"

"Twenty-five thousand each time."

"How about for Mrs. Colburn?"

"Oh, that one was for fifty."

"Where's the money now?"

"The fifty's hid in my linen drawer in the kitchen. Most of the rest of it's under my lingerie in the bedroom."

"The search turned up no money."

"Yeah, well I ain't a bit surprised."

"Why?"

"Oh, man. I bet the sheriff had Deputy Jones out there before I was halfway here, to search everything, and take anything worth taking."

"How about the guy you live with, Ruble Crouch?"

"Oh, him. He ain't got enough sense to do nothing except what I tell him."

"So he would not have taken the money?"

"Nah, don't think so."

"Who would have?"

"Jones, I bet."

"You were paid to do something that failed. Do you think they will come back for the money?"

"They already have, but their man Hoot got his self killed."

"How did you know?"

"Read it in the papers here. We get to see the daily."

"Where did the snakes come from?"

"Jones I'll bet. He's sneaky enough to put 'em in the drawer and then all innocent-like follow Hoot in there knowin' all along what's about to happen."

"Would Jones do it himself?"

"Nah, I doubt it. Mor'en likely got one of them Goonsbys to do it."

"Well, Hoot didn't get the money. Do you think they will send somebody else to get it?"

"Yeah, sooner or later."

"How do they go about it?"

"Jones met Hoot's flights in Memphis and drove him back and forth in a patrol car. I guess he'll do the same with the next one."

"How do you know the details?"

"Oh, Jones. Him and me, we had something going ... out to the house all the time when Ruble was off fishin' or whatever it was he done. And Jones, he's got a big mouth. And every time he got through humpin' he would start talking. All men are like that. I don't understand what it is that makes them want to bare their souls and give away their secrets and talk bad about people as soon as they've shot their wads. I've heard more than one girl say, 'give 'em a little and they talk a lot.' He likes to brag about the big shots he works for, slings names around, like the name of Peter Mallory, the big banker in town, the money he makes in payoffs, the wives he's had ... other people's that is, the speeding tickets he hands to people they're out to get. I'll bet that low life got my money."

"We can assure you it is not in the house."

"Aw damn, I wish I'd never seen a one of them. Jones let them know about me and they got me in a trap and threatened to kill me if I didn't do what they said. Then the money was a temptation. Jones and the sheriff will try to have me killed if they can get to me."

"You are safe here. I was speaking of the others. What do you think they will do next?"

"Send somebody else soon as the racket dies down a little. Jones will meet his flight in Memphis and bring him down. If Jones has the money, he won't let on. If he don't, somebody else is likely to get killed in the looking."

Sam said, "We thank you, Sybil, for your cooperation."

"Oh, I'll do my best."

The agent said, "Mrs. Snyder, we have the recordings here, both the video with its sound track, and the separate audio. They will be used in court if needed. With your cooperation we will ask the judge for a lighter sentence with the possibility of parole after five years. We advise you not to ask for a jury trial."

"All right." She stood, but held her gaze on the agent and said, "But do you know who is the biggest devil in the town of Cambridge?"

"I imagine I don't."

"It's that sneaky little sonofabitch, Peter Mallory. He would shoot his grandmother for one more nickel. He started all this trouble with his greedy mess."

Sam left the room and joined John Colburn, who had waited in the lobby. While they drove back to Cambridge, Sam gave him the details.

"So this solves the mystery about David Beckette," said John.

"Yes. We have her confession."

"I know Helen will be relieved."

"Yes, I'm sure." Sam waited a moment, his hands on the wheel, his eyes on the road, then asked, "And now what's to stop you?"

John glanced at him. "Stop me? ... What?"

Sam gave him a bemused sidelong glance and smiled.

And John said, "Oh. Oh, that. Nothing, I hope. We've discussed it, of course. She's such a sensible, unpretentious person. When the time comes she wants to be married by a judge or a justice of the peace, and she wants a honeymoon on a Caribbean island."

"That does not surprise me. At city hall you can get the license and the ceremony for half an hour of your time and ten dollars. They open at eight every morning including Sunday."

John looked at him quizzically and said, "And the island?"

"My daughter owns the only real travel agency in town. She's been talking to me about some of the great places. She could make the arrangements tonight."

"You are all for this one?"

"It would remove both of you from the reach of certain dangers."

"Oh."

"And of course, it seems to be just the right thing for you both."

At 9 p.m. John sat in the Bartleys' living room with Helen. He told her of Sybil Snyder's confession. Then he said, "Sam Sheffield says if we get to city hall by eight o'clock in the morning we could have a license and be married in half an hour. His daughter's travel agency has booked us for two weeks in a cottage on the beach in Aruba, Delta flight out of Memphis tomorrow at noon. Are you game? All can be cancelled if you are not."

"Oh John, that's exactly what I want. But I think we should keep it quiet until the immediate Cambridge problems are resolved."

"I'll be here for you at seven-thirty and we will be on our way."

"I never dared dream it."

"Are you sure this is what you want?"

"Just try getting out of it, John Colburn."

46

Martha Williams called Zelma Taylor at home. She had been thinking about The Mallory Club and had changed her mind. She had a plan and would like to attend the next meeting and talk about action. Zelma said, "Okay, I got some hot ideas too, and you will be surprised at who belongs to this club now. We have some heavy hitters."

"Yeah. Who?"

"Well, there's Jane the newspaper editor and owner. And we got an angry woman, Mildred, from Memphis. He ruined her when she was not quite grown. She's owns a big escort service now, the best in the South. We got a stewing angry momma, Tessie, whose daughter he messed up, and this mama just happens to be a reporter. We got another angry one, Dorothy, whose husband is the newspaper photographer, and we got all kinds itching to put the club into action."

"Great. My plan can use all you've named."

Zelma smiled as thirty women assembled in a reserved basement restaurant for a midweek evening. Martha, among them for the first time Before the dinner began, Martha turned to Jane, a lady in her late thirties who had just taken over operation of the Cambridge Courier from her father, and asked, "Jane, are big headlines supposed to hit the Cambridge Courier on Sunday morning announcing the sale of Mallory's one-hundred-nursing-home chain and describing his huge profits, and his ascendance in the corporate structure?"

"Yes," she said. "That's right."

"Do you suppose we could add a little something to that article after midnight on Sunday morning with pictures?"

"I will make it possible. Just don't get me sued." Mallory had threatened her father several times over the years when the editorials got a little too close to the truth, and Jane had been burning and waiting for justice.

"Oh no, the truth and nothing but the truth."

"Will we need photographers and reporters?" Jane asked.

"Yes. Would you supply them?"

"No problem, but best you tell us your plan."

Martha outlined her plan then turned to Zelma, "You can imitate just about any voice you have ever heard. Could you do Helen Beckette?"

"Why hell yes, that's an easy one."

We need to do our thing on Saturday night. You worked for him several years, so I'm sure you know exactly what he would die to hear from the lips of Helen."

"Man, do I ever."

"Well say them and make a date for Helen to come to his house on Saturday night at eight o'clock."

"I can do that."

"Come to think of it, shouldn't Helen be in on this too?" asked Martha.

"She's out of town for the next two weeks," said Zelma. "We're safe."

"Are you sure?"

"Yeah, but I'm not at liberty to explain now." She thought about Helen on a Caribbean island, honeymooning with John Colburn.

"Okay," said Martha. "I will make the other arrangements."

Martha addressed the room, explained the plan, then said. "And girls, I don't have to tell you how secret this must be … not a word to husbands, boyfriends, confidants, or anyone."

"Do we get to see?" several asked.

"Sure. Drive by if you want to."

At three in the afternoon, Zelma phoned from her cubicle in Sam Sheffield's office. She could look through the window and across the square and see Martha as she answered the phone at her desk in the bank, Mallory's car at the front curb. Zelma said in her Helen voice, very formal,

"This is Mrs. David Beckette. May I speak to Mr. Peter Mallory?"

"Why of course, Mrs. Beckette, just a moment." Martha knew the surveillance devices in Sam's office were picking up every sound and every nuance, including the breathing. She buzzed Mallory and when he answered she said, "Helen Beckette's on line one for you." He never said thank you or okay; he was in such a hurry. Martha flipped the button but she didn't hang up. She listened.

"Helen!" He almost yelled, breathless with surprise. "How are you?"

"Fine, and you?"

"Wonderful, and what a nice surprise."

"Oh, I know Peter, and I've called to tell you that you were right all along. I've quit Golden Age, as you know, and I've decided it's time to end the grieving. You were so right, Peter. I should have listened to you sooner."

"Helen, I'm glad and so relieved. I've grieved for you, too, you know."

"I know, Peter. You are so sensitive and so considerate."

"Does this mean you will be working with me?"

"Well, I think we should talk about it, when you have the time of course."

"I have to tell you, Helen, great things are in the making, but I'll take the time. Would you like to come to the office, or …?"

"Oh, Peter, I hear you are such a good cook. Why not one of your intimate little dinners?"

Martha thought anybody but a fool would have caught on by now. But he plunged ahead. Zelma could do a perfect Helen, all right.

"Why Helen, it would be such a pleasure to cook for you. Would …?"

"How about this Saturday night Peter? I could be there by eight o'clock."

"That would be perfect, Helen. Shall I come for you?"

"Oh no. You just spend your time making one of those gourmet meals I've heard about. Shall I bring the wine?"

"My dear, I have an immense cellar, and I will choose one to go with the meal."

"How nice. I love a good wine."

"Well, Saturday is a long way off, three whole days. I'll call and talk to you before then."

"No, Peter. We have to keep this secret. I wouldn't want John Colburn to get suspicious."

"Oh, Helen, I haven't felt this excited since I was a kid waiting for Christmas."

"I will be there at eight Saturday. And it's going to be so nice, Peter."

"I can hardly wait."

"And Peter, brace yourself, my good, sweet man. We are going to play catch up, and that will take a long time. If you cook a good dinner I think I just might make you mine for keeps. Bye now."

Martha Williams had never seen a man go so berserk so fast. He replaced the receiver and began cheering like his team had just made the winning touchdown. Then he yelled, "Get my lawyer, get him over here now and have him bring his secretary!" He paced back and forth across his office grinning like a deprived sophomore who for the first time scored last night. He talked to himself, some of the words audible out in the vestibule *I knew it, God, Should have known she would come around, piece of cake for old Peter ...Simpleton!* She kept her eyes on the keyboard when the lawyer arrived, trailed by a woman, and Mallory closed the door of his office behind them. The door was still shut when she went to the Veterans Nursing Home at six o'clock to feed Jack Williams.

Celeste called the office on Friday afternoon. "Peter," she said on the phone, "my darling husband ..."

"Sssssshee," he said, full of scold.

"Oh, Peter, come off it, we belong together. We are married, remember? I want to come over Saturday night and get started on our home. I've got such great plans – the silver, the candles, the flowers, the great meals."

"Celeste, I can't do it. I'm too busy wrapping things up. And the Sunday papers will be full of news about the sale. I've been assured of front-page coverage. The reporters are swarming over me, putting it all together. After Sunday, my dear, we can talk about timing our announcement."

"Oh Peter, I'm so disappointed. Are you sure?"

"I regret to say I have to be sure this time. Now don't rock the boat and we will be better off in the long run."

"Okay, Peter, maybe you're right. But I'm so lonesome."

"Soon, my dear."

Peter Mallory completed the business with lawyers in his office on Saturday morning, Martha there to help, then he spent most of Saturday afternoon at home getting ready. How exciting! The delivery trucks arrived and he directed the placement of flower arrangements in the living room and the dining room, even in the kitchen. He decanted a great Burgundy, and marinated two three-inch thick New York strips. He made a huge salad and placed it in a cooler and mixed his own dressing. The freshly chopped vegetables were cooling just above the freezing point to assure crisp cooking. He paid the cleaning people at seven o'clock and sent them home.

Everything was going his way, and tomorrow he would be a famous man, not in just little Cambridge, but across the nation and the world. Little Cambridge would be prone at his feet. He would be rich, very rich, and his business acumen would be recognized. He imagined himself being named Cambridge's man of the year, outstanding citizen who put Cambridge on the map. Peter Mallory, up from a little town in Mississippi, now ready to move among the world's leaders, giving millions of dollars to presidential candidates, advisor to presidents, maybe even a cabinet position, an ambassadorship, with Helen at his side. He had underestimated himself. He should have known Helen would come to him sooner or later. The doubts had been futile. But he wondered why Helen had so sweetly changed her mind? Could she have heard how much money he stood to make off the sale? Nah. She's too high caliber to put money first, such good manners and such good breeding. She will add greatly to his image, by his side moving in and out of the circles of power worldwide.

Celeste? What of Celeste? He had that under control. No one would ever be able to trace the source of the license, and she had not bothered to read it in her hurry to land him. Not even an annulment would be necessary to getting his money back, all fifty million. Nothing compared to his ultimate billions, of course, but a useful little amount. He would leave her satisfied with one or two million, all she could ever need, quite a reasonable amount under the circumstances. After all, she's not a keeper.

He bathed and shaved and dressed in the finest underwear, and why not a tuxedo? Imagine her surprise, her own personal cook in a tuxedo, black-tie dinner for two prepared by the black tie. She especially would appreciate the elegance. The fire roared in the charcoal grill (stainless steel –

$6,000.00 from Hammacher Schlemmer) on the back patio. The coals would die down to just the right glow for the steaks by cooking time. Such contentment, such excitement, such anticipation – Oh, Helen, my darling, he would bow and kiss her hand. He would take her fur, hang it in his powder-room closet, give her a tour of the house, fat wine glass less than half-full in hand, gripped by the stem only, the correct way, urbane and knowledgeable. And she would spend the night tonight, no doubt.

When he answered the chimes at eight o'clock sharp and swung the door open, the woman in a full-length sable and masquerade mask smiled adoringly and said, "Peter darling." Then she walked straight ahead into the house, pushing him out of the doorway, and nine more identically dressed women followed. The second woman carried a basket on an arm. The last one closed the door. Peter, caught off balance, reeled backwards, speechless.

What the hell? He looked desperately for Helen, but could not be sure about any face behind the masks. "Gals, gals!" he said as they surrounded, herding him across the house into the kitchen. Gleeful exclamations erupted, squeals of delight, and deft delicate fingers began working on his cuff links and shirt studs. "But ... but ... where's Helen?"

"Helen sent us ahead, darling boy. We're here to test your loyalty."

"No, we are not," squealed another. "We're here to test your manhood, you big stud."

Martha Williams, also wearing a mask, came to the front door, opened it, and stood aside as a man pushed a large commercial video camera into the living room. A digital camera hung on a strap around his neck. Martha followed and went up the stairs and took a position along the balcony rail. Two women came in the house with tape recorders and pad and pencil. The last one in locked the door.

Martha watched. The ten women surrounded Peter, laughing and petting him, and one or another from time to time held a glass of wine to his lips. They took off their furs. Each wore only the semitransparent apron from a French maid's uniform, and nothing more. They removed Peter's black tie, then began pulling at his shirt. Five more bottles of wine came up from the cellar. A dozen more steaks from the basket were dumped on the grill. Each time Peter took a sip he got another kiss. His first glass of the decanted Burgundy contained a wallop of heroin. The second glass contained more. Peter wore nothing but his shoes and silly little gauzy socks by the time one of the women pulled him naked down in her lap and caressed him while two others finished stripping him to his bare feet. The noise increased, the laughter erupted between piercing squeals, transparent aprons hung over the backs of chairs and couches. The party picked up momentum.

Martha retrieved her copy of The Sunday morning edition of the Cambridge Courier from her driveway and retreated into the house. She unrolled the paper and read the headlines: MALLORY NURSING HOME CHAIN SOLD. The front page described the financial gains and the buyer, the HMO conglomerate, TOTAL HEALTH CARE, INC. It praised Mallory's financial acumen for putting together the chain, Magnolia Homes. The editor had devoted two columns to details, alluding to huge profits turned by the sharpness of the now famous Peter Mallory (our own), in dignified language with no hint of the celebration. The remainder of the front page had been devoted to ordinary national and international news.

Martha held her breath and turned the page ... a jungle of pictures, big pictures beneath another set of headlines: LOCAL INVESTOR CELEBRATES HIS MAJOR TRIUMPH.

The first column went on, "In the den of wolves, the financial world, our own bank president, Peter Mallory, regarded fondly by his intimates for his renowned success with women, celebrated his great business triumph with a party to end all parties. He had ten dates, all at once. Ten beautiful ladies from the gambling casinos of Tunica and other cities including Las Vegas and Biloxi came to little Cambridge to help him celebrate. The Mallory mansion gleamed and sparkled in candlelight as Mr. Mallory, in black tie, received his guests. Bouquets of the most gorgeous flower arrangements, dozens of them, enlivened the house from kitchen to entrance foyer.

"Mr. Mallory was the very picture of gentlemanly decorum as he entertained his beautiful guests. Wine flowed freely, and the choicest of all steaks, very thick New York strips, were piled on the glowing grill. One of the ladies brought the smoochiest little bunches of marijuana, and the cutest little vials of heroin in a basket over her arm. All the ladies wore full-length sable. Dressed for the occasion, beneath the coats they wore only the transparent aprons taken from the type of uniform worn by French maids. Needless to say, under the elegant hospitality of Mr. Mallory, they felt free to shed any garment that threatened to encumber their intentions. Mr. Mallory, ever the gracious host, submitted to their every desire.

"The evening grew like a Bacchanalian frenzy. Mr. Mallory moved easily among his guests, unashamed in his own nakedness. The discarded little transparent aprons adorned the furniture helter skelter like petals from the roses of romance. Mr. Mallory, anxious to entertain his guests, raised his glass from time to time and told the gals how he did it. Charmed and entranced by his urbane wit, he being as usual the ever-gifted and clever and very funny raconteur, they huddled close and listened, fascinated as he told them how he outwitted the operators at various casinos and mentioned a Thornton Webb, owner and operator of the The Royal Nugget at Tunica. He named other defeated adversaries. He was especially proud to have outwitted the daunting and brilliant lawyer Lapkin Lewis, who runs everything. And last, the famous Bin Kadsh, the owner of the biggest HMO conglomerate in the world, had fallen victim to Peter's ruthless aggression. The guests raised their glasses and cheered. And none of them could resist him. Not a one. They all talked about how much they admired him and how much the casinos appreciated his gambling business over the years. The last guest left only as daylight approached.

"For lack of room," the report went on to say, "only a few of the many pictures made last evening could be printed for this edition of the paper. The remainder, along with videos of the action, will be preserved in the Bule Museum of the History of Cambridge."

Martha perused the pictures. Jane had very carefully chosen enough for an expose, without too much exposure. They both had liked one picture in particular. The back of one beautiful bare woman rotated counter-clockwise as she bent forward. Peter stood just beyond her. The curve of her naked buttock and bowing torso hid his nakedness from navel down, except the outer part of his right leg and his entire bare foot. No one could look at the picture without knowing the raw truth: Peter wore not a stitch. They had culled other pictures: Peter downing another glass of wine with his head thrown back, Peter holding a steak in his bare hands over his head and gnawing from its dangling end, Peter's bare back turned, with a bare woman riding piggyback.

Martha laughed. Had they been too harsh? No, she thought. They had held back the most revealing: the naked woman straddling the supine Peter Mallory on the floor with his supine peter, each disappointed woman returning from a bedroom laughing, naked Peter in dozens of shots about the room and the house, Peter wearing nothing but one of the transparent aprons, and more and even raunchier and wilder pictures as the night progressed. Peter had finally passed out naked on the living room sofa.

Celeste awoke to answer a ringing phone at eleven a.m., headachy from her own night of wine, alone. Mary Ann Dickey on the line, said, "Celeste, have you seen the morning paper?"

Celeste yawned and stretched and answered. "Naw, not awake yet. It's still in the driveway, I guess."

"Well get it baby, cause your life ain't ever going to be the same ever again."

"What's happened?"

"You got to see it to believe it."

"What time is it?"

"Eleven o'clock, Sunday morning."

"Oh shit, too late to dress for church … oh well."

Celeste got out of bed, took her time with the morning ablutions, then made coffee. She got the paper and sat on the couch to read. So this is what he meant by too busy, *wrapping things up*. Sounds more like he was unwrapping quite few little things. She felt no anger, more a sense of relief. This would be the end of Peter, one way or another. The boys would not tolerate his stupid, drugged betrayal. Now, she would be quite sure never to be alone with Peter Mallory anywhere again.

Peter Mallory awoke disoriented at noon on Sunday. He grabbed the ringing phone and growled. Thornton Webb said simply, "Peter, be here by five this afternoon for a meeting with Lapkin Lewis, and come alone."

"What's happening?" he asked.

"Haven't you read your morning paper yet?"

"No."

"Well read it, Peter. Someone in your town made sure we got it first thing this morning."

Lapkin Lewis! Oh, Jesus! This could mean nothing but trouble. Very few people involved with the syndicate ever saw Lewis, and no one was summoned unless drastic measures were waiting. What had happened? He got off the couch, still nude, and went across the house. The shambles, the dirty dishes, the empty wine bottles, the pall of old grass smoke, the food scraps, the unfinished steaks, the wrecked beds – God! What had he done? He went to the front door and retrieved the paper. How happy the headlines and the write-up made him. Well, things couldn't be so bad. Maybe Lapkin wanted to congratulate him and make plans for his having even a stronger role in management. Then he turned the page.

Helen's wonderful phone call – had she pulled some evil deception on him? He phoned her house and got no answer. Where could she be? He had heard she was staying with Clara Bartley and Tom, but he would not dare call there. On a hunch he phoned the administrative offices at Golden Age. Dan Rattner answered. Peter decided to play the aboveboard business executive. "Dan … Peter Mallory here. My good man, what are you doing there on Sunday morning?"

"Lot of catching up to do."

"And how are things going under new management?"

"Astringent," said Dan, and he waited.

Mallory hesitated for a second, then said, "Uhh, Dan, I need to speak to Helen Beckette. We've had a discussion going, business, of course, and I have a follow up. I'm trying to get some things put away myself."

"Well, I'm afraid you won't have much luck finding her this morning. She's on a six-month leave of absence, you know. She left town ten days ago and I don't know where she went. By now she could be in London or Moscow for all I know. And I don't have her itinerary. Maybe the travel agent could help. Do you want the number?"

"Oh, no. I'll catch her later. Thanks."

En route to Tunica, Mallory muddled over his dilemma. Did someone imitate Helen on the phone? Who? Who had the ability, the talent? That sort of thing has to come naturally. You are born with it or you don't have it. Who did he know? … Who had worked for him that … Ahhh, yes! Zelma Taylor, the mimic, of course. How many times he had guffawed, a thing he seldom did, at her perfect imitations. Okay. He would take care of her beginning tomorrow with a little sweet revenge.

Thornton Webb, Fritz Kramer, and a man he had never seen before remained seated when the guard escorted Peter into Webb's office. The stranger had to be Lapkin Lewis. Mallory shuddered. The cold eyes almost the color of his skin watched with calculated neutrality, and a cold chill settled between Peter's shoulder blades. The guard stood at the end of the desk. Thornton Webb did the talking, without preliminaries, without introductions.

"Peter, we are very disappointed in your behavior becoming public knowledge. And your statements to Mildred's escort service were most indiscreet."

"Mildred's what?"

"Yes Peter, you were entertained last evening by ten prostitutes, hired just for the purpose, high class but still prostitutes."

"Who hired them?"

"Peter, have you ever heard of The Mallory Club?"

"No."

"Organized and named in your honor – you don't know about it?"

"No, never heard of it."

"It now has thirty members, each of them a woman who has a score to settle with Peter Mallory for past abuses, mostly sexual with the added taint of money and dirty politics in some. And it seems they settled a score last night."

"Helen Beckette had made a date to come to my home at 8 p.m. for dinner. Now I think someone imitated her voice on the phone. The group of women surprised me. I don't remember much else."

"You don't remember what you said about us?"

"No. I don't even believe I made those remarks."

"Well, the information could have come from no other source. We, and you, are the only people who know so much about our dealings. So, it had to be you, Peter, talking out of school."

"What can I do to amend it?"

"Too late, Peter. But we made certain emergency moves this morning to head off the major repercussions. You know the bank inspectors would have locked your doors shut Monday morning before business hours and the doors would have stayed locked until the inspectors found out what had been done. And without our help the doors would never have opened again."

"Well. I hope closure can be avoided."

"Peter, we had to go to great trouble and pull some really big chains to pay off the bank's debts this morning. Do you have any idea how difficult it is to do that on a Sunday? Well, we did it anyway."

"What are you talking about?"

"Peter, you don't own a bank anymore. Bin Kadsh owns it. We paid your debts. Now at least we can avoid the embarrassment of your arrest, and the danger of you talking too much. And Peter, we've saved you from a penitentiary sentence."

"I don't quite understand."

"Peter, you bought the nursing homes, one by one, with money from your own bank, loans unsecured and uninsured, and you haven't paid that back. We bought the chain in the name of Kadsh with money borrowed from your bank, loans again unsecured. Bin Kadsh replaced both amounts this morning, but in a way so as to launder that much money. And, I must add, at great cost to us. We lost control and Kadsh is now in the driver's seat. The moment he files the necessary papers, which I assume will be tomorrow, he will be the sole owner of the homes, the HMOs, the bank, and you. Tomorrow, the inspectors will find no irregularities in the financial structure of the bank except the somewhat unusual Sunday morning transactions. And Peter, you might as well know we didn't do this for you. We did it to save ourselves. We can't afford to have the feds looking too close. Kadsh was the only source of that much money on Sunday morning."

"So."

"So, Peter, you are broke. You don't own a thing."

"Oh yes. I protected my own personal funds, at least fifty million, and there's my house, worth some six million more."

"No Peter. Your funds and your house belong to your wife."

"Wife?"

"Oh, Peter. Don't try to deceive us. We know you were married to Celeste in a nice secret little ceremony on an island in the Caribbean, with fake papers. Weeks ago we found the license and the marriage ceremony papers, and I can assure you they are legitimate now. You are indeed married, and Celeste owns outright the Mallory Mansion in Cambridge and the fifty-million-dollar Mallory fortune. You gave it all to her, remember? She does not even have to let you in the house and I'll bet she won't after she sees today's Cambridge Courier. But we have been talking over your problems and have decided to offer you a position."

"I appreciate that."

"Peter, beginning at three o'clock tomorrow afternoon, as we have arranged it, there will be an opening under the tutelage of our senior croupier, Jimmy Tieford. We have searched our minds for the right slot to suit a man of your abilities and instincts, and we have decided you would be the perfect croupier, especially for the tables where the women, in particular the little old ladies, love to play. Good croupiers, those who prove themselves, have the chance to move up to greater things."

"But ... but what about my position as executive in charge of the nursing home operation, the funds, the ..."

"No, no, no, Peter. We've already seen what you can do with that."

Thornton pushed a small document across his desk to Peter. The top sheets had been folded back, revealing the notary public's seal. "Peter, sign above your name."

"What is this?"

"Your resignation from the bank. It will be shown to the inspectors when they arrive tomorrow morning. Don't go near the bank again."

Peter felt the magnet drawing and looked at Lapkin Lewis, who regarded him with level gaze of cool, malignant, snake eyes. Peter shuddered. "This is tough ... " he said as he took the proffered pen from Thornton's hand, and signed.

Thornton folded the papers. "We have saved you from worse," he said as he reached into the top drawer of his desk, and pulled out a big yellow envelope. He handed it across the desk. "One million dollars worth of chips, Peter. Dinner is on us at six in the main dining room. Then go to your usual Black Jack table and gamble until ten o'clock sharp tonight. Quit promptly at ten, turn in any chips you have left, and go home. You will win enough to get you by for a while. We suggest you leave most of it in the casino bank for safekeeping. Return tomorrow morning for some orientation before you begin your training. Quarters will be available until you can get settled. I hope you get home tonight in time to pack your clothes."

"Oh, I'll not be long getting there. I'm a fast driver, you know."

"So, we've heard," said Thornton. "In your behalf, we will wait until tomorrow morning to inform Celeste of her new financial status."

Peter drove Highway 304 across the delta toward the foothills and Cambridge. Sunday night, nearly eleven o'clock, not a car in sight, the road wide open – perfect for a little speed. He set the cruise on one hundred and relaxed. He had fifty thousand dollars safe in the Royal Nugget bank and five thousand in his pocket. Very generous, and he didn't think the boys really had any intention of carrying out their threats. They were just trying to scare him and they had. Now he knew he would have to be rid of Helen Beckette. And he was not really mad at Zelma Taylor for the joke she had played on him. He would show her how big he really is ... call up, invite her over, and have a good laugh over it, fool her into admitting it, take her on the desktop a few times, then get even later when she has let her guard down. But he certainly resented Helen for leading him on, acting the roll of such a perfect lady. He would tell the boys in Tunica tomorrow, and someone would be sent to do the job, like they did to Beckette and Williams. And as to Celeste – Thornton was just yanking his chain. No way could they change the marriage papers he had signed. He would control Celeste. She would do exactly as he said, or else. He would call her first thing in the morning and invite her to return to Tunica with him. But he would not tell her the details. And he didn't think Thornton or any of the boys would either.

What a night, full moon, landscape lit up for miles of misty translucent shadows, frosted fields whizzing by, dead and quiet world. Would this thing really do a hundred and eighty-five, live up to its claim on the speedometer? He eased up to one twenty and gradually to one forty. The Mercedes moved as steady as a tank, betraying no sense of speed, smooth as silk. What a car! The first hill came into sight, outlined vague in the moonlight far beyond his headlights, not a soul anywhere, all the houses dark by the road, only an occasional lone sentinel yard light casting a low glow over squalor; the cops would all be asleep. His spirits lifted, everything would be all right. He would take the hills in nothing flat from here to Interstate 55 and be home before midnight, and this would all be like just a bad dream tomorrow. The hand of the speedometer crept up to one sixty and beyond.

He gave it the rest of the accelerator as he topped the first hill in a surge of elation. But he had forgotten. The hill drew to a sharp little rise and a steep downgrade on the other side. At the crown, the wheels did a lift off the pavement, the car air borne like the silly violence in a television chase. The wheels came back to road surface and the speedometer needle dipped further and fluttered beyond the last number as the car plunged downhill with exhilarating surge ... Peter Mallory's last awareness a fleet vacuum of almost perception ... a bulge distant in the moonlight looming ... instantaneous in the headlights ... smashed with the sudden abruptness of a swatted fly, too fast even for thought.

As Celeste read the Monday morning headlines, PROMINENT BANKER KILLED IN CRASH, the phone rang. The unmistakable silken voice said, "An hour at Cambridge Regional." She dropped the paper and began packing.

In Las Vegas she went to a penthouse in Caesar's Palace. Lapkin greeted her at the door, barefoot. He wore a golden silk bathrobe. Lunch awaited them in splendor on white linen, and he immediately seated her at the table. "I've been waiting and I'm starved," he said.

"Oh Lapkin, I'm so glad to see you. It was such a boring weekend in Cambridge."

"But quite an eventful one."

"I was left out of it all."

"We saw to that, my dear."

"So, why the rough stuff?"

"Don't assume anything now, but he had bumbled far enough down the road to hell. It would not do for him to be arrested. He would have sold out for clemency. Such a fool!"

"I knew something would happen."

"Well, accidents do happen."

She looked at him. He gazed across the room, admitting nothing.

"Where did the tractor come from, Lapkin? Who was driving it?"

"The police say no one, Celeste, and in this world of ours, you don't want to know anything you don't need to know. But I can speculate. It could have come from anywhere. It could have slid off the tail end of a trailer-bed, and the truck could be back in the southern part of Missouri before daybreak. The police said it was an old tractor with metal wheel-spikes, old rusted out thing, but it weighed tons. Perhaps someone was hauling it somewhere for junk, for the paltry dollars its metal was worth, some poor fellow may have lost his load and heard the wreck and fled in a panic. Or maybe someone lost the load and didn't even know it until he got to the junkyard. Who knows? I do know the police are very frustrated. They can't trace the tractor, all identification numbers were burned off long ago and the sites rusted over, probably stolen years in the past. Luckily, no one else hit it."

Celeste ate in silence, picky at her food, for a few minutes, then said, "I'm very nervous about all this."

"By the way, I have your marriage license here," he said as he handed her an envelope. "It is legitimate and you are a real and valid widow, once again, and the Mallory mansion belongs to you, tax free."

"Where is the fifty million?"

"It's in the amount to be paid when Bin Kadsh makes the money transfer."

"In other words, we don't have it yet."

"Right."

"Now, there is the matter of a wake and a funeral and my role as wife."

"His will left instructions for immediate cremation, which at this very moment is being done. A memorial service can be scheduled at your discretion, or never held, for that matter. You are his only living relative, and the public has not heard of your marriage, but they will, maybe today, as the media goes looking."

"I never took this marriage seriously, so I don't even know who his lawyer is, that is to say, who will be controlling me in Cambridge."

"Celeste, his legal affairs fell into our hands when he became indebted to us. I am his lawyer until today. As of today, his affairs go back into the hands of a Cambridge lawyer, who has a junk-yard scrapper mentality, and we usually tell him what to do."

"Well, that's a relief, of a sort, I suppose."

"Right, and you did buy the insurance policy on his life, didn't you?"

She hesitated, looked blank for a moment, then said, "Oh, I almost forgot. Yes I did, but the insurance companies were limited by law to a maximum of six hundred thousand."

"Policy?"

"No, premium."

"You bought that much?"

"Yes."

"And it pays …?"

"A hundred million."

"Damn Celeste, where did you get the six hundred?"

"Oh, it's actually funny. You know the brown, million-dollar envelopes someone was always handing me over at Tunica with instructions to gamble it away?"

"Yes."

"Well, I looked in one because it felt funny or different, and it had cash instead of chips, and I just started laughing. Who could have been so careless? Then I looked again and counted. Or was it my dear Lapkin giving me something just in case I was alert enough to catch it? And I counted it a second time and still found only six hundred instead of the usual million. I was pretty sure … my sweet Lapkin ahead of me, but letting me find out for myself about the machinations of insurance companies. So I gambled the six hundred on your tip, and it paid off a hell of a lot better than roulette. I think I've learned to bet on your horse every time."

"Where did you buy the policy?"

"In Memphis from an insurance brokerage house."

"From total strangers?"

"Yes."

"And they took that much cash and asked no questions?"

"You should have seen the look on their faces. Such greed. They had never seen ten-thousand-dollar bills before."

"How long ago?"

"Three months, and a little more."

"Ninety days. You are in the clear."

"Are you sure?"

"Yes, we've already called them this morning."

"Oh damn, Lapkin! Stop playing cat and mouse with me. I know you are ahead of everybody else on everything, So, I guess I owe The Royal Nugget six hundred thousand."

He looked at her quietly, apprising, but bemused. "Celeste, forget it," he said. "Don't tell a soul." He glanced at his watch. "The afternoon has vanished and it's time for me to go home. The boys will fly you back to Cambridge."

47

On Sunday morning, Zelma had listened to the events as they happened. She and other members of The Mallory Club had never expected the prank to go quite so far, but although quite soberly humbled, none of them were regretting the evening. And she was onto something else. She would gather a little more evidence then present it to Sam. Later in the morning, John Colburn sat in Zelma's cubicle, listening to the sporadic information coming in out of the ether.

Zelma took her head phones off and asked, "You notice anything missing in this entire scheme?"

John thought for a minute then said, "Yes! Where's the money?"

"Right. Mallory is dead and I didn't hear anybody at anytime paying him, and that includes the chicken feed, the paltry fifty million dollars. The entire Mallory fortune has disappeared, so what's up?"

"Kadsh is going to transfer all of it, the nursing homes, the HMO stock, the freshly washed drug fortune to Zeembeckystan, or somewhere out of the United States, all of it at the last split second, then he will flee the country."

Zelma said, "You're stopping that?"

"Zelma, I'm going to do much better than merely stopping it."

Down on the levee with Sam, John said, "I've been listening and analyzing the flow of information coming into Zelma's little office. Also, the FBI, the CIA, and the other concerned bureaus are working together now that 9/11 has scared them into a new sobriety, and they, too, keep me up to date."

"The ramifications?"

"Far-reaching, indeed, and the situation calls for the use of measures to stop him."

"The Feds."

"Nah. Let's not bungle this one. They've already tried to stop the flow of money to the Russian Mafia, and it just keeps going out, some billions a year. The efforts of the Financial Crimes Enforcement Network, called FINCEN, have not stopped it."

"Then how are we?"

"Sam, does lightning intrigue you?"

"Yes, as a matter of fact it does. Why?"

"If you've ever been in a burned-out place where it hit the earth you would not be able to tell what struck, or what exploded. You could only guess."

"You have a measure in mind?"

"I have a measure in mind, and it will be the perfect test for various ramifications of our new and developing technology."

"You will arrange it?"

"I will, but that means more work in Alabama, and I have to go this afternoon."

Celeste arrived at the Peabody to find Kadsh pacing the floor. He had a date, a timetable. It would require precise coordination. A limousine would come down to Cambridge for her ride to the Memphis airport. She would be on a different airline at a different time from his flight out of Memphis on Sunday after next in the afternoon, and she would meet him Sunday night at JFK Airport for an 8 p.m. flight to Zeebeckystan on United. He gave explicit instructions. She would board the plane and take her seat as soon as the boarding gate opened. She was not to wait for him in the terminal. He would be there at the last second, just before the doors closed, and not to be nervous. His wife and children already had gone ahead, allegedly on a visit to the homeland, a vacation. Not even they would know they were making a permanent move until all financial transactions were final.

Aromatic, porcine, his wet mustache drooping, as slick as a seal in the sweat of after-love, he talked. Riding him to a frenzied explosion would not exhaust him to silence or languid intimacy. He talked of money in amounts she could not understand, the meaning of a billion dollars beyond concept, a hundred billion—what's the difference, both unimaginable? She wondered why.

While they dressed in the twilight he handed her an envelope. "Open it so I can explain."

The envelope contained her airline tickets from Memphis to New York on Sunday afternoon, and from JFK to Zeebeckystan. She looked hurriedly and found no return ticket. The envelope also contained her visa, a passport, and ten thousand dollars in small and large bills. She looked at him, puzzled.

"In case you get stranded without me. If I don't, by chance, get aboard the flight, I will come over in a day or two. The address of your house is written on the inside of your passport folder. The cab drivers at the Zeebeckystan airport understand English. Call anytime you want or need to." He repeated his satellite phone number while she wrote it on the ticket jacket. "I will have frantic activity on Saturday afternoon and especially Sunday morning, and of all places, I have to spend my Saturday night in a hunting lodge without plumbing in remote Wyatt's Crossing, Mississippi. It's hairy business."

"What next?"

"Go home and wait. I will be in touch."

Celeste answered Lapkin's call the next morning and went to meet him again. How nice to be lifted out of Cambridge on the wings of a three-engine, little private jet and whisked nonstop to Las Vegas. Over lunch in his penthouse suite she described Kadsh's plans. She added, "Lapkin, I'm frightened. This man has a very ominous bearing; he's nearly mad with zeal. Nothing short of violence will stop him."

"Well, we are not resorting to that approach. Don't worry. But you have to carry out your role until the moment of takeoff from JFK. I promise, you will not be on the plane when it crosses the Atlantic."

"Why must I go that far?"

"Money. If you break and run, it will scuttle plans to transfer the colossal fortune to his Zeebeckystan accounts at his last moments in this country."

"Somehow you will get me off the plane just before it leaves?" she asked.

"Yes."

"Then what happens to the money?"

"It will go as he has planned if he succeeds. And he will go according to plan unless he stumbles. But we can't quite be sure about his scheming. He may try to rob everyone including Peter Mallory."

"He's driven by religious fervor."

"To the point of no scruples."

"Well, it seems I'm really caught in the middle."

"You are a very volatile little catalyst."

"What will you do to protect yourselves?"

"We don't exactly know, yet. But we are watching."

"So what will happen to him?"

"We don't know that either, not yet. But he could find himself back in Zeebeckystan without funds, or dead somewhere with plenty of funds."

"You know something?"

"Suspect it. Celeste, I have to tell you we know we are coming up against a very powerful and very intelligent adversary with unlimited funds and manpower."

"Who?"

"It sounds to some extent like the government but it's too free of bureaucratic bugling to be just government."

"So?"

"So we are getting out as quickly as possible and drawing in our tentacles. I wish we had never heard of Kadsh, or drugs." They ate for a while in silence. In a pensive mood, Celeste asked, "Lapkin, what am I going to do with my life now?"

"Do as you damned well please, my dear. You have the means to go any place you want and do whatever you want."

"Yes, I do."

She immediately thought of the man in the shadows of the Golden Age, the man who she now thought had the name Ruble Crouch. And if he had been living with Sybil, he would now be free. Then Celeste knew where she wanted to go, where she wanted to be, and the man she wanted. And once complete there, the other hunger and the other satisfaction. She knows no greater gratification than the sensation of the warm little animal tongues licking her fingers through the cage bars, their desperate little eyes adoring and begging for deliverance. She is closer to God then.

"You've done your job well for us. The syndicate won't forget."

"Lapkin, I certainly hope so, I'm giving up a palace in Zeebeckystan for the humble little Mallory Mansion in Cambridge."

Lapkin looked at her thoughtfully, chuckled silently, and said, "Let's go down to the projection room. I want to see a private run of Oceans Eleven, see how bad they've made Las Vegas look. We can come back and play later."

"I would love to see it. I've been meaning to go, but then I seldom get out anymore."

48

Wyndham Jones complained to the sheriff. He did not want to drive to Memphis to pick up another Hoot coming down to conquer the South. But when the expected call came, the sheriff said go anyway to avoid worse trouble. Grumbling to himself, Wyndham went, but he didn't like this business anymore. He did all the sheriff's dirty work and the sheriff had kept a clean slate, except for one thing Jones himself would never have done. He had stopped Clara Bartley with a trumped-up traffic infraction, and on another occasion had traffic-stalked her with an official cruiser. A man who would do such a thing had to be a fool, or he had to be totally ignorant of the traits of her husband, Tom Bartley. And Tom Bartley was buddy-buddy with Ruble, the Indian, and come to think of it, could they have had something to do with whatever happened to old Clink Goonbsy? Jones didn't like to think about it, but he would get Ruble sooner or later when he wasn't watching what he was doing. He would make it look official. But it was always slippery mud around Ruble, and nobody has ever messed with Tom Bartley without coming to regret it.

"Name's Stringer," the new arrival said as he crawled into the police cruiser. He looked too much like another Hoot, the same three-button suit of a greenish black hue, shiny on the surface, the small knot in a stringy tie, the blue shirt a deeper color than the suit, the pouffed pompadour like a rooster's tail feathers. He had taken the pistol out of his check-through luggage and now had a sinister bulge in his left armpit, the same way Hoot did it. "The money," he said, "Where's the money?"

"I saw the money once, partly, when Hoot took it out of his briefcase to give to Sybil and I ain't seen it since. The feds have been through the house, and found no money. They turned everything over, no cranny unexplored. It's not in the house."

"Where's that live-in of hers, what's his name? Ruble something?"

"We do not know where he's sleeping and we can't trace him."

"Why not? And have you tried?"

"Yeah, we've tried. But you have to understand. This man was raised on the land and in the woods. He's mostly Indian and he can sleep among the trees as easy as in the best hotel bed. He disappears among the undergrowth and comes out three or four days later. He could be anywhere watching, completely still, waiting for you."

"Ahh, you guys, scared of your own shadows." He patted the bulge under his coat. "I got something right here that can make an Indian mighty uncomfortable. We go look at Sybil's house first, then we go look for Ruble, and if we can't find him we look at your house. Maybe you got the money stashed there."

Jones opened his mouth to answer and closed it. Stringer looked creepy and dangerously unstable, even more nervous and jumpy than Hoot had been on the trips from the Memphis airport to Cambridge and back. He didn't need trigger-happy neurotics popping off around him. He drove in silence to Sybil's house and parked in the driveway. He said, "Well here it is."

"So, let's unlock it and go in," Stringer said as he stepped out into the yard, and Jones followed on the other side of the car.

"I don't have a key."

"Why? How you been getting in?"

"It's not our business to have one. The feds and the state have control of Sybil. Besides she changed the locks after she threw her boyfriend out. Hoot picked the lock himself when I went in with him."

"Yeah, well I want to see what happened in there." Jones walked across the yard and Stringer followed, still talking, "I don't believe any of this tall tale. I can get the fuckin' door open." He rattled the resistant knob then picked the lock and they entered a stifling hot house. "Jesus, hottern' hell in here," he said.

Wyndham hung back, sensing something too familiar for comfort.

"Where was them snakes?" asked Stringer.

"In the kitchen, top cabinet drawer just left of the sink."

"And what was in the drawer with the snakes?"

"Linens. It was the linen drawer."

"Shit. That's where the money is. I bet nobody lifted up them linens and looked. Bunch of dummy rednecks."

Stringer had looked around casually while talking. He surveyed the living room, then the kitchen, but touched nothing. He sidled up to the sink and put a hand on the drawer pull. "This the drawer?" he asked.

"Yes, that's it."

Then with an air of insolent dismissal he pulled the drawer open. The first snake struck so fast it made only a blur in the space above the drawer and bit Stringer between the eyes, and three times on the face and neck. Three more rattlers sprang out of the drawer, and wrapped around his hands and neck, striking in fury. Stringer fought back with both hands but he did nothing more than smear snakes in his own face. He screamed one last time when a fang penetrated an eye. He fell and began to convulse. Breathing stopped. The bitten and bleeding eye began bulging out of its socket. His complexion developed black splotches in seconds,

Wyndham leapt through the front door, slammed it shut, and sped off in the patrol car.

Ruble, hidden over the garage, peeked out the attic window, and watched in wonder. He had guessed right. This one was dumber than the last one who came down for a visit, and did not expect the same trick. He waited until the rescue squad went through the same gestures as they had with Hoot, then eased out the back way and disappeared into the woods.

49

Celeste went to the Mallory Mansion and let herself in. She toured the house, in her own mind rearranging things and making room for her own belongings. Her candelabra and silver and pictures and other adornments would greatly improve the splendor already here. She gathered the photographs of Peter and Sugar and all their ancestors and stacked them on a sofa for later packing. They had left no children. Maybe the history museum would want the pictures. She went through the kitchen and out the back door onto the patio. The cleaning crew had put everything in order and she could find no traces of Peter's last wild party. She let the screen slam shut and left the wooden door ajar, and continued her tour of the house. In the master bedroom she touched the heavy draperies and fondled the bed covers, and inspected Peter's and Sugar's clothes in two huge dressing rooms, racks of suits and sport coats and dresses and fur coats and dozens of pairs of shoes. She turned toward the door and caught a whiff of the most poignant and evocative aroma. She froze. He had hidden himself in the room with her, close, very close, in broad daylight the first time. She sucked up her breath and waited. And he whispered in her ear, "I'm here Miss Mallory, like I promised." She slowly lifted her face as she turned toward the sound and saw the open khaki shirt and the skin hardly darker than the cloth, then the face, the arched nose, the black eyes, the copper colored hair hugging his skull in tight curls, the angular lanky build. "I locked the doors, the front and the back one you left open. Now I'm going to show you me." He skinned out of his clothes with deft motion and reached for the buttons down the front of her dress.

This time he let her scream, and flail her arms, and beat the bed with both hands, a mounting rhythm to frenzy then down into a plane of moaning before another mounting peak. While she moaned and cried and yelled and dug her fingernails into the sheet, pulling and scratching, he rotated her upon a hip, then her belly, and up on her knees, then to the other hip. Flat on her back again, in a burning pause, she watched him defiantly. "Don't you come, I'm not through with you yet," she said. She slid from beneath him rolled him over on his back and with both feet planted on the sheet astride his supine body she mounted the jut, sat straight upright, and bolted in a riding rhythm faster and faster until he grasped her hips and held her into him. She threw back her head and screamed, then fell limp on the bed. Only with this man, of all her lovers, the encountering anatomy fit her capacious yearning to completeness, reaching from its titillating nidus to fill to fullness the cavern of its insatiable desire.

In the Mallory king-size bed, Ruble rolled over on his belly, propped himself up on his elbows, and said, "I am glad you don't really need the dead people."

She studied his supple leanness and ran a finger over his shoulder and down an arm. "I am as relieved as you are to find it's you and not the presence of the newly dead."

"Yeah," he said. "I never saw in my whole life, anything like you, not even close."

"No other man has ever been able to do what you can do to me."

"I got that feelin', and it makes me want to ask you a question."

"Okay."

He studied her quietly for a moment then asked, "Miss Mallory, you anybody's woman?"

"No. Why? Do you want the job?"

"Don't I have it already?"

"Yeah, you got it already."

"I think you need a full-time chauffeur, and a house boy, and handy man."

"No, not … "

"We'll pass it off to the town as that for now."

"Good idea."

"And you need a traveling companion, or I do. I'm through with brooms and mops and trotlines and muddy water and muddy banks. I want to dive in the deep blue sea I've only heard about, where I can swim with the fish I can see. And I want to …"

"And I take it your name is Ruble. Ruble Crouch."

"Right. Guess I ought to excuse myself for proceeding without the proper introductions, but first things do come first."

She laughed. "Well, Ruble, where are you living and what do you drive?"

"In a rented place, and my big red dual-wheeled pickup is parked about a block away."

"Go get your things and move in. Then we need to use your truck to move my things from my little old house, and to haul all of the Mallory wardrobe, both his and hers, to the Goodwill Store. You can do most of that while I'm gone."

"Gone?"

"Yes, I have to be out of town Sunday and Monday, an engagement I must keep."

"Now, Miss Mallory you need to be careful. You been dealing with some evil people."

"Yes, and you too. And I want to warn you about one in particular. I'm speaking of Deputy Wyndham Jones."

"Oh, you know about him?"

"I know everything about him."

"Well, I guess I know some of it: the bribes, the drug running, the murders. And I got this feeling he will be coming for me sooner or later, but he will be on my hunting grounds."

"I'm going back to my little shack now and start packing. You can come by for the first load late this afternoon." She gave him the address.

Wyndham Jones never returned to Sybil's house. Let them place the blame where they could, and he wanted no part of it. While cruising around he felt a growing affection for Celeste. Married to the son-of-a bitch and no one knew, and he left her with a fortune and a mansion paid for. Man, oh man. Time for him to cash in on all the protection he had given her for years and years. Bet ole Celeste would jump at having him on a permanent basis. Hell, he could get rid of his own wife. That ought to be easy enough. And it's time for him to drop by and have a talk. Things looked mighty promising.

He knocked on the door and she answered sweetly, "Come in." Just easy like, not a care in the world. He pushed the door open and entered. She turned to face her visitor, holding a blouse stretched between her hands over an open suitcase. "Oh," she said, "It's you. Wyndham, I'm in a hurry and don't have time now."

"Yeah, well, Celeste I been thinking, you and me we've had a thing going a long time and I believe it's about time we did something about it,"

"Like what?"

"Like maybe making it permanent."

"Wyndham, on that basis I could have fifty husbands before sundown, and more."

"Well …"

"No Wyndham, you got a wife. Besides, I don't trust you,"

"What do you mean?"

"You haven't missed an available woman in this town, and you got a lot of married notches on your gun. I know some husbands who would annihilate you in a minute if they knew."

"Not true."

"Well then tell me about little Sugar Mallory."

"What's to tell?"

"You were with her when she died."

"What makes you think that?"

"I was parked around the corner from your patrol car, and I watched you tear out Mallory's back door with your pants over your arm as the rescue squad broke down the front door. You stopped and got dressed in her garden then climbed over the back fence. Lady Killer."

"Why were you there?"

"When I heard you were sleeping with her every time Mallory went out of town I couldn't believe it, not after all the bullshit you had handed me. So I went to see for myself. Many a night I watched you sneak in the back door by the barbecue grill and not come out until daylight. How did you kill her anyway, Wyndham. Strangle her? And even more puzzling, why?"

"I don't know what you are talking about."

"I'm talking about get lost Wyndham, be off. You can't have any of my money even if you did what you consider a favor to me, marriage."

"Listen here, now I could make plenty of …"

"…trouble. Don't dare try it. I will get you on charges of killing Sugar, for accepting bribes from Peter Mallory, for accepting bribes from a higher source, for your part in killing David Beckette and ruining Jack Williams, for your part in drug running, for …"

"Okay, okay, that's enough," he said, backing toward the door. "All a pack of lies, but I guess you are in no mood to talk love."

She laughed. "Well I'll be damned. You caught on."

50

On Saturday morning, Clara Bartley drove to the Overton Nursing Home in Memphis using Rachel's van and brought her back to the Golden Age. Rachel didn't understand why she had been moved to Memphis temporarily. Clara explained it away by giving her an excuse. John wanted to have her room remodeled and painted a more restful color, and there were no spare rooms for her during the renovation. Rachel sulked in a skeptical silence. She later admitted to liking the new trim and the new colors.

John and Helen went to the Golden Age on Sunday morning to visit Rachel and tell her about their marriage. They turned down a winding corridor toward the wing housing Rachel's room, and as they were passing the entranceway to the main recreational area, the meaning of Sunday morning in the home fell upon both and they stopped to take it in, caught in the moment. The intonations of a Sunday School lesson spilled out into the hallway, from the room crowded with patients who had been brought there, some parked in wheelchairs, others placed at the tables and on couches, each of them caught in the clutches of a personal malady rendering life to a final disability – the room pervaded with indifference, the air of sick and dying. In shirtsleeves, a thin, black-haired man with a black moustache stood behind the podium, a bible draped open in his hand, talking on and on to the room. The sound went out and above, not a face turned toward the source of the words, words making their way beyond the hunched figures, the slack faces, the downcast eyes, the visages looking nowhere. What an exercise! Who could be listening; who could be hearing, but the lesson went on. And John Colburn knew him by name now. Clara Bartley had told the story and the name: Robert Childress. He was there every Sunday to teach, and late every afternoon, as soon as he closed his store, to help out – all volunteer, no relatives among the patients, just a concerned, conscientious man, at this moment talking to the slumped-over figures, the demented, the senile, the paralyzed, the babbling, the drooling, the minuscule remnants of minds cheated by birth and wasted by time, those ruined with injury and disease, and the extremely old. The odor rose and saturated every breath, with a fetid, musky, oppressive presence. But Childress's voice went on, over their heads bowed and bent like a somnolent stable-full, for whatever target the message might reach regardless of the futility, carrying on in faith full of fairytale promises of a redemption receding ever further from reality. There was an admirable, enviable air to this non-reason endeavor in a non-reason world where it had every reason to exist. John's eyes saw the slumped non-comprehending forms gripped in gravid inertia, lost in impenetrable apathy, the pooled aggregate of matter formed to flesh assimilated, to accomplish transit life now turned dissolute with age, but his imagination leapt to the far reaches of the fiery cauldrons of outer space, to the leaping blazes and roiling explosions and magnetic storms, the radiation and the searing heat of birthing creations, and the contrast had no reason and no words – this rot in reality at the end of life, this fire in imagery at the beginning of other worlds, all by the same hand. And what could bridge the gap – the mind of man, the voice of the amateur preacher falling on stifled old ears, the weak voice of supplication searching distant ether of the unknown?

Helen had placed a hand on his arm, a gentle touch, eloquent without words, and he said to her, "If there is ever a god-forsaken place between hell and black holes, this is it." Then he saw Rachel bent forward in her wheelchair at the back of the room, her eyes closed in a pained expression of listening and tolerating once again the ways of the world. "Let's come back this afternoon," he said, as he placed a palm over Helen's endearing hand.

Behind closed doors the sheriff confronted Deputy Jones with a demand, "How in hell did you come to let two of Dr. Kadsh's best men get killed by snakes? Didn't you learn a lesson the first time?"

"I did, but they didn't. I can't tell a pistol-packing hothead anything, not when he already knows it all. Not them Chicago gangsters, who would shoot in a minute if crossed. I ain't hauling 'em anymore. I'll quit first."

"You can quit if you want to after we tie up some loose ends, but not until then."

"Like what?"

"This town ain't safe for law enforcement with the likes of Ruble Crouch around. And I ain't goin' to be defeated by such as Tom Bartley and that loud mouth he's married to. I intend to shut her up for good. And another thing, that goody-goody Helen Beckette, I'll scare the living hell out of her yet."

"Well. They ain't your worst problem right now."

"Then who is?"

"Goonsbys. They think Clara had something to do with Clink gettin' snake bit to death, and they are looking for a way to get even."

"Now there's a problem just might solve itself."

"If it don't backfire."

"We'll see, but Ruble is our first big problem."

"Yeah, he's refusing to make the pickups. The last dump floated off down the river and we got some of it back when it got caught in the riprap of the dam."

"He's getting too uppity and independent. Make him help you pick up the next load and bring him back to shore shot dead for resisting arrest over the open waters."

"He's tempted me more than once."

"All right, I got the plans ready.

John Colburn, at dinner in the Bartley home, said, "Tom, we will need a boat on the Sardis Lake next Sunday morning."

"What size?"

"Big enough for all of us, in other words a cabin cruiser, twenty-eight or thirty-footer thereabouts, with outboard power."

"Yeah, I can arrange that. What time?"

"Oh, we ought to be aboard by mid-morning."

"What else?"

"Food and drinks. We will be there several hours."

"Equipment?"

"I will bring everything except the binoculars. Each person should have a pair."

"Okay, will do."

"Thanks. I will be out of town until Saturday afternoon, getting ready."

"Taking Helen?"

"Oh, yes."

The next afternoon, Tom Bartley found Ruble landing his little aluminum skiff at Clear Creek ramp with another cooler of catfish. Tom said, after the usual greetings, "Ruble, I don't have but a minute. I'm here to tell you we have ways of knowing what the sheriff and his deputy, Wyndham are plotting. They are making another drop into the Sardis Lake tomorrow at about this time, a little after sundown, and Jones is going to surprise you when you come in from running your lines and force you to take him out for the pick up in open water."

"Where?"

"Right here, straight due north."

"That's deep water, right over the river flow."

"They don't know the water that well."

"Man!"

"Jones is going to force you to take him, at gunpoint if necessary."

"Well, thanks for telling me."

"Ruble, he plans to come back to shore with the balls of drugs, but with you dead in the boat, shot while resisting arrest and attempting to throw him out of the boat. Caught you red-handed with the stuff. So, I think he will be alone."

"How do you know?"

"Ruble, we've heard every word the sheriff has said to Jones and vice versa for the past few weeks. These are the sheriff's instructions."

"How?"

"We've got bugs now you might not be able to find even if you knew where to look."

"Well, that gives me a clear conscience if I didn't already have one. I'll be ready for him."

"We've heard no direct plan to involve the Goonsbys, but we have overheard the voice of more than one of them complaining to the sheriff or Jones about what happened to Clink ... looking for revenge."

"Yeah, I didn't think they would let that go by easy. They'll pick somebody to blame and sneak up and do something dirty."

"Be careful it's not you, Ruble."

When Ruble drove his boat ashore on the muddy bank at dusk the next afternoon, Wyndham Jones stepped out of the bushes, resplendent in full uniform. He wore trooper's boots and a holstered long barrel .38 revolver on each hip, but no hat. He said, "Well Ruble whatcha' got there all tangled up?"

"My trot lines."

"Why you taking them up?"

"I'm quittin' fishing. My last trip."

"Well you got one more, right now. I want you to take me out on the water."

"What for?"

"We are going to pick up a few things."

Ruble said, "This is the wrong boat for that. Too small, too light weight, too risky, and you ain't exactly dressed for swimmin' if you had to."

"Ruble, you take me and be sure nothing happens." He unsnapped the strap across one holster, and placed a hand on a pistol handle.

"Okay," said Ruble, "anytime you're ready."

"Yeah. I'll ride up front."

Ruble, wading in shallow water, pushed the boat off the mud bank and turned it around, and brought a gunwale next to dry land. Jones stepped in the bow. Ruble pushed the boat toward the river, and jumped in over the stern. He paddled a few feet, started the motor, aimed due north and moved through the trees and stumps carefully. At the edge of open water, Jones signaled to stop, then said, "Pull over and wait behind that last clump of trees."

Ruble eased against a bush, grabbed a limb and tied it to a stern rope.

The boat drifted around with bow turned west and held, the motor at idle. Jones busied himself with a cell phone. In the deepening dusk, Ruble began arranging the clutter in the boat bottom. He placed two white but soiled Styrofoam coolers on the middle seat and piled the trotlines against them. Jones talked into the phone. The drone of an approaching plane grew louder and the plane came in from the east in a steady down swoop and right out in front of the boat it came within two feet of the surface and began dropping small objects. Dusk now obscured all details, the plane without lights a silhouette over the dark water.

"Damn," said Jones, "Looks like a goose taking a crap." He laughed. Ruble remained silent. The plane lifted up and away in the growing darkness.

Jones said, "Let's go. Put the front of the boat where I can pick 'em up."

Ruble untied the rope and went out over deep water. Here he could feel the tug of the river thirty feet down and he watched the dark muddy turbulence roil to the surface in swirling pools. The fluorescent floating balls came into view and began to scatter. As Ruble throttled the engine down, Jones reached over the side and tried to grab a bobbing ball. He missed. On the third try, leaning over the gunwale and tipping the boat dangerously, Jones came up with a ball in each hand and turned back toward the middle of the boat. He loomed in the gloomy silence.

"Well open one of the damned containers, Ruble. Don't be stupid!" he yelled. Sitting on the bow, he threatened to carry the prow under, his legs extended down under the middle seat, the skiff now wobbly and unstable and whiffly on the roiling water.

Ruble said, "Yes, sir." He stood up in the stern, carefully balancing himself in fear of tipping the boat, then bent over, slid a cooler toward Jones, and lifted the top. Jones draped both hands over the edge to drop the balls. Ruble pretended to slip, and upended the cooler onto Jones' hands and into his lap. The rattler struck out, hitting both of Jones' hands as it rapidly slithered into his lap, and coiled instantly to strike his face. Jones began shouting, and flailing and kicking, trying to scoot backwards. The snake struck him on the frantic hands, then in the face. Jones' booted feet came from under the middle seat and he kicked and craw-fished and escaped back first in a clumsy crawling somersault over the bow of the boat and plunged out of sight beneath the turbulent surface. The sudden evacuation caused the prow to rear up and the boat almost capsized. Ruble righted the motion with an oar and watched the water. In about a minute the snake came up and swam rapidly for the boat. Ruble crushed its head with the oar, and it disappeared in a swirl of blood beneath the boiling brown water. Ruble cruised the area until full darkness, and nothing came to the surface. Without lights he went to shore and loaded his equipment into the pickup. His coolers were empty. He had released the last catfish he ever intended to catch. He drove back to town, free of a hovering menace for the first time in many years.

51

Clara Bartley said to Tom, "Guess who just called me ... no, you would never be able to. It's too ironic. But God, does everything in this world come full circle."

"Well, I could take a few shots at that, but just tell me."

"Dodson's wife. They are transferring him from Memphis to the Golden Age Nursing Home."

"In a ruined state."

"And she wants me to see after him the way I do Rachel Colburn. He has no bowel control, no bladder control, and he can't walk, can't stand up, can't feed himself, and is an idiot. I wonder who beat him to a pulp."

"Somebody who loved one of the students he was responsible for ruining, I'll lay odds," said Tom.

"Yeah, and they will never find out who did it."

"Not out of the hundreds who had reason to. The sheriff does not dare push it too far for fear of exposing his own guilt in the drug racket. So what will you do?"

"I will go visit him just once. I want to see how he looks in the position of any one of the many victims of his neglect and greed."

"I guess he really was that bad when he had the upper hand."

"Entirely selfish and uncaring."

"I don't think I want to see this one."

"Oh, no need for you to."

The next morning, out at the Golden Age Nursing Home, Clara Bartley stood by the bedside, resting her bare forearms atop the side rails as she had seen Isaac Dodson do so many times. She looked down at him curled on his side in the bed. Such high and mighty arrogance had come to this ruined wreck. One eye now crossed, one side of his face sagging, the surgeon's scalp scars showing through the sparse hair, and the expression once smug with self satisfaction now sagged in vacuous apathy. Dodson's wife had passed on the neurosurgeon's opinion. Dodson's mind would improve some over the next two years maybe, or put another way, any improvement not occurring in the next two years would never occur. Dodson looked at Clara's face, and a blank flicker of recognition dimmed in the stupidity of his bleak countenance, and the mask distorted in a whimper. Her anger waited in reserve, her sympathy neutralized by Dodson's damaging behavior to her many patients in past years, her emotions sobered by this turn of cynical fate. She thought of Rachel Colburn, and the wretched disturbance of her mental state created by Haldol, which Dodson gave to her without thinking when she was miserable with the pain of a bladder infection. Clara would raise hell each time to get the order stopped, and sometimes Dodson would not stop it and Rachel's psychotic reaction would become even worse. He had practiced a stubborn and uncompromising arrogance and tolerated no corrections when in error. *Serves you right*, and *I told you so* never got passed her lips. She turned and walked out of the room and faced Dodson's wife in the hallway. No. She would not help take care of Isaac Dodson.

52

At 10 a.m. a limousine came to Celeste's front door and she traveled out of sight behind black glass to the Memphis International Airport, flew first class to JFK, went through customs in the international terminal, then had a three-hour wait for the flight to Zeebeckystan. Seated in the lounge she glanced up from her book frequently, nervous, and apprehensive, but no familiar figure appeared. Dozens of multi-colored spreads covered the crowded waiting-area floor helter-skelter, and families in Arabian clothes with small, dark, squalling and frolicking children huddled together eating and sleeping. The crowd grew by the minute. Worry came back in waves and already she felt isolated from home, already in foreign territory. Had she been betrayed? Had false promises been made? Would she be sacrificed in some way? No, she didn't really think so. She trusted Lapkin Lewis. He no doubt could be deadly when crossed, but betray he would not.

At 9 a.m., Tom ran the boat east on Sardis Lake toward the site of the fishing lodge and the church. Under John's directions he dropped anchor a half-mile away, near the edge of the Tallahatchie inflow, clear of trees and undergrowth, with an open view of the lodge and the point of land on the east side of the creek. Under way, John had set up two laptops side by side, numbered 1 and 2, on a table outside the cabin, and plugged them into the boat's electric supply. He said, "Now Zelma, get the hard drive off the computer in the building straight ahead, onto the hard drive of number 1."

Zelma went to work. In a moment she said, "Okay, I got Bin Kadsh. Oh Christ, he's calling in money, huge sums!"

"Great! And are you ready to do Celeste Howard?"

"You know I do feel about that loose this morning," she said.

"You have to talk him into coming out on the point of land at the water's edge, and hold him there just a second or two. You sit over there in the stern and let me sit her at the computers." John sat down, pulled number 2 computer against the first and called up Echelon on number two. He typed in the name Bin Kadsh."

"Explain this stuff, John," said Sam. Tom and Clara sat near the cabin door.

"On the right computer here, I've just keyed into Echelon's speech-identifying capabilities in Maryland. We want to be sure we have his phone and no other."

"What's Echelon?"

"A global eavesdropping network. The National Security Agency of this country and British Government Communications Headquarters pool their equipment, including some of the largest of computers, to find a particular cell phone."

"Well."

"Martha, come stand by my right side," said John, "and be ready when I tell you."

In the fishing lodge at Wyatt's Crossing, Bin Kadsh hovered near the computer screen anxiously. The moment approached. The accumulated funds from drug sales were zipping in from several dozen shell banks around the world, well distant to the United States, and accumulating in the shell at Wyatt's Crossing. All of the Mallory money, and the market value of a hundred percent of the shares of the nursing home chain and the HMO conglomerate rested in one account in the People's Bank in Cambridge, the Peter Mallory investments account. Following Mallory's death, Kadsh had decided to use the account for convenience, and to avoid confusion and suspicion. He had memorized the code for getting into and out. He awaited the moment needed to wire the rest of it. When the sum reached seven billion he typed rapidly on the keyboard. He hesitated and watched as the money went through the shell beneath the church, then instantly

358

through the shell in the basement of the Golden Age, and zipped to the People's Bank in Cambridge and joined the Peter Mallory investments account. He hit the keys again and the entire account disappeared, gone instantly out of the American system of banking. If it went with the speed of light where he intended, it would now be in the Bank of London. There! It was done, the money safely washed, clean and legitimate, and in a bank safe from American prying, all the value of the nursing homes and HMOs with it. Then he hit the keys to transfer it one more time, to the haven of the Mary McLaurin investment account in a Jamaican bank. This done, he turned to get his briefcase and to dash for the waiting helicopter near the cabin door.

Out in the boat, John watched the screens. At the instant of the final money transfer he said, "Okay, Zelma, dial him." And John began typing rapidly on the first computer. Zelma activated Kadsh's code. All binoculars were trained on the fishing lodge. As Kadsh reached the door, he paused to answer his cell phone. Zelma, imitating the Celeste voice she had monitored for weeks, began crying into her phone for help. "Hello, Bin my baby, then she choked up and began to sob ... Oh God, Bin, you wouldn't believe it. The goons in the stretch limousine kidnapped me. No, no, hell no, I'm not in New York. I'm out in the bushes on the banks of a river looking across at an old building with unpainted old wood and a dull gray tin roof. They told me you would be in it, and the only thing they gave back was my cell phone, thank God. They took your ten thousand dollars and all of mine, and my jewelry. Yes! Why yes, I can see you stepping out the door. Oh My God! I'm just across the river from you, and up to my butt in this goddamned slimy Mississippi mud. Well, you will have to come nearer to see me ... you're moving in the right direction... Ohh Bin, my darling, all you have to do is get in one of the little boats I see on the bank there and row across for me. Ohh, I'm so scared and weak and all scratched up and bitten by so many insects. Ohh, Bin, my big daddy ... you're so wonderful! Oh, my baby, my big sweet daddy.

Kadsh rushed out and walked rapidly toward the river, following her guiding directions, holding the phone to his right ear, a briefcase in his left hand swinging. Yellow bush, she said. He went toward a willow with its greenish yellow leaves, and a crop of tall tawny weeds on the bank across the inflowing river.

"Now!" said John to Martha. She reached and hit the enter key on the second computer and withdrew her hand quickly. John lifted his glasses to the point. Ten seconds passed, Zelma talking frantically into the phone at her ear, her other hand holding her field glasses ... she kept going ... "Come on, my big sweet daddy, come get your baby, you're almost to the boats, look at me, I'm waving my scarf, Ohhhh, God ..."

At the muddy beach, Kadsh went up on tiptoes to strain at seeing Celeste waving among the undergrowth across the water and raised his head into the nanosecond of annihilation ... the bright Sunday morning exploded in a blinding white flash. And nothing remained where the man had stood. A scorched spot of ground hardly a foot wide smoked briefly and the mild breeze cleared it. Several saplings in full leaf and a round patch of surrounding grass had disappeared down to bare ground. The wall of the lodge smoked and the helicopter engine died. John said, "Let's go." Tom began hauling in the anchor, Sam at the wheel. Then Tom came forward and took the boat back across the lake and dropped anchor near the mouth of Hurrricane Creek. The girls served a picnic lunch. Zelma said, "Well, I'm the cat that curiosity's about to kill. Are you telling us John, or not?"

John laughed. "Okay. We needed to keep him long enough on his cell phone to provide a constant homing signal. We've been working in the field of robots built to imitate the mechanisms of nature, especially insects and the flight of the humming bird. One group of scientists out of Duke has already built a fleet of miniature submarines, a half dozen of which would fit in the palm of your hand. They imitate the twaddle fish and go anywhere in the water by remote control, gathering information, planting explosives, attacking, or whatever they are commanded to do. Well, we at Huntsville have built a comparable device for the atmospheres. Our tiny rockets zip anywhere under plasma propulsion, controlled by a tiny quantum computer, and hover over a target the way a hummingbird hovers over an open blossom, in other words, they act as mini satellites. After a mission a rocket can return to earth, remote-controlled or preprogrammed. And we have built some bigger ones, about the size of a shoebox, equipped with the most unique weaponry, the ultra high-power laser. We call it *extreme light;* it has the highest intensities on earth, and it reacts with matter to create the extreme conditions found only in the cores of stars or the margins of black holes ... the highest of temperatures, and the most powerful electric and magnetic fields. It can hit targets roughly as small as one millionth the length of a yard stick, and fire five hundred million shots a day. We have a number of these stations circling the earth now and we can fire by remote control on chosen targets at will. We've practiced on uninhabited spots in the desert and on the crags of unclimbed mountain peaks. It melds sand into dirty glass and pulverizes rock peaks and walls.

"I linked up to speech identity capabilities at Echelon, to be sure we shot the right phone, then connected with the tiny quantum computer in the station circling out of sight overhead, and Martha fired the light beam. The target is gone without a trace, so thoroughly that not even a DNA specimen could be found."

Martha said, "I never thought I would be able to avenge the cruelty done to my Jack, and I don't feel one bit guilty."

"Great, Martha," said Helen, "I'm so glad you won the draw for triggerman. But I would have volunteered."

"Man, I love this stuff. It's the only way to live," said Zelma. "Hot damn."

Tom said, "John, I'm curious about what you were typing into the system at the last second."

"Oh, yes," said John, and he laughed. "Whatever he sent through the shells then to the People's Bank of Cambridge, Mississippi, and on to the Bank of London in England, is now safe back in the People's Bank in our little Cambridge, Mississippi. As soon as it hit People's the first time, my computer overpowered the entire transaction and I zipped the entire account from its deposit out to London in England, and instantly back to People's Bank in Cambridge."

"How were you able to do that?"

"The technology. The computer on the right here, the one Martha touched, is the latest in ordinary commercial equipment, but the one on the left, the one I used to control the money, is an experimental model, a quantum computer, thousands of times faster and more powerful, and well hidden in conventional housing. We had anticipated Kadsh's intentions and had programmed the computer to take control. The problem now will be to find out what the transfer amounts to exactly and who owns it. I think it includes a lot of money."

Martha said, "Well, speaking of ownership, Zelma and I know something that's dynamite, and it concerns you, Helen."

Helen looked startled, but she just said, "Yes?"

"I'm afraid we have a confession to make."

"Now what have you been up to?"

"While you were away on your honeymoon ..."

"Uhhh, Ohhh."

"We brought the recording along in case we found you in the right mood."

"So play it. I'm in as good a mood now as I will ever be, vengeance and justice having triumphed at last."

Martha said, "Okay Zelma."

Zelma turned to computer number two, inserted the disc, and played with the keys until the sound began. The crowd listened to Zelma imitating Helen in the call to Peter Mallory, from the beginning *this is Mrs. David Beckette* to the final *I think I'll just make you mine for keeps* ... the imitation deadly accurate, unmistakably Helen. After the *bye now* Martha slipped in another disc and played back Peter Mallory's jubilation following the call, including his commands for his lawyer. When the laughter died down, Helen's the most vigorous, she asked, "Martha, what does this mean?"

Martha sobered suddenly. "Helen, he changed his will within the hour following Zelma's call. He left everything to you."

Helen raised both palms to her cheeks and said, "Oh, my God!"

53

Celeste boarded the plane bound for Zeebeckystan and strapped herself in seat 1A. The plane filled, and the stewardess made the usual announcements. Then she shut the door and started walking down the aisle. A knock sounded and she returned and swung the door open. Two men came aboard. They showed their badges and spoke to the stewardess. She brought them to Celeste. A guard and a croupier from the Royal Nugget at Tunica stood by 1B. One held out a badge and said softly, "FBI, Mrs. Mallory. Please get your carry-on quietly and come with us." The three deplaned. Out in the lobby, the croupier said, "Sorry to have cut it so close. We had a set-to with security. The company plane is waiting." They raced through the lobby.

En route from the Memphis airport, Celeste rode in the back seat alone, the croupier in the front passenger seat busy on his cell phone, the guard driving. As they approached downtown, the croupier turned to her and said, "Mrs. Mallory, we have instructions to take you to the Peabody for a rest, room 1070."

"Well," she said. "This should prove interesting."

Lapkin Lewis opened the door. "Welcome to the South," he said. She entered and looked around. Lapkin, fully dressed, stayed at a respectful distance. She raised an eyebrow and asked, "Lapkin, do I detect a new tone?"

"Perhaps. Would you have any idea where Bin Kadsh might be?"

"He was supposed to be on the flight out of Kennedy tonight. If not, he would fly over in a day or two. Why?"

"Because he has vanished from the face of the earth."

"And how do you know that? The earth is a big place."

"We were monitoring his whereabouts. He had a helicopter crew at Wyatt's Crossing watching and waiting to lift him to Memphis International Airport. From his computer at Wyatt's Crossing he made the money transfer as planned. The helicopter stood with its rotors idling. Kadsh came out of the door on time, talking on his cell phone as he walked, but he turned toward the point of land, for some strange reason, where a creek meets the river. He walked to the water's edge talking on his cell phone and vanished. No one saw him enter the water. The copter pilot thought he saw some type of bright flash, almost too sudden and brief to be actually visible. Kadsh either drowned or something very unusual happened. The helicopter engines died and refused to fire again. Only later did they recognize the scorched paint on the helicopter and the charred wood and ash on the old crib walls. Yeah, some very clean weapon blew him away."

"Oh, really?"

"Yes, and quite oddly, everything, including the seven billion dollars, was in one account then, and he transferred the whole financial bundle at one time out to the Bank of London then on to the account in Jamaica, in the name of Mary McLaurin. This should have been a split-second operation. In his place I would have been holding my breath."

"As I take it from your tone, the transfer never made it."

"You are right. Remember, I told you we were dealing with an unknown, probably a technology far superior to anything available outside of government agencies?"

"Yes, I remember."

"At the very second of Kadsh's attempted electronic transfer of the entire Peter Mallory investments account from People's Bank to the Bank of London, something faster and more powerful took control, made the transfer to England, but instantly retransferred it back to People's bank and froze the assets as property of Peter Mallory's estate. Kadsh walked out into the glorious day thinking the final transfer to the Jamaican bank had been successful, and apparently, something blew him to hell. Everything now belongs to the estate of Peter Mallory."

"Lapkin, do you know this Mary McLaurin?"

"No. Do you?"

"That's my maiden name."

Lapkin looked stunned but amused for a moment, then said, "I'll have to give Kadsh credit for thinking."

"It was a clever idea!"

"Yes, but not clever enough."

"By that, I suppose it didn't work."

"Almost, but the something faster and smarter interceded, and kept every penny of it from going to other causes."

"Don't tell me all that money and property goes to the woman who can prove herself to be Peter Mallory's widow."

"It would have if Peter hadn't gone bonkers and changed his last will and testament on the Friday before The Mallory Club party."

"And the changes?"

"He left the house to you, Celeste Howard, in that name, and everything else to Helen Beckette in the name of a charitable trust."

"Is it legitimate?"

"Very, and witnessed by three lawyers, a notary public, and Mallory's secretary, Martha Williams."

"And Bin Kadsh intended the rest of it for …?"

"Mary, the first name, McLaurin, with a Jamaican address and a Jamaican identity, with himself as executor. He, of course, expected to manipulate the money, and with you in palatial quarters in Zeebeckystan he probably would never have let you in on the use of your name in the Jamaican bank. And he would have used the account, the nursing homes, the HMOs, and the bank for continued money laundering of the funds from the ongoing drug trade."

"And if he has indeed vanished permanently."

"It makes no difference, one way or the other. He gave everything to Peter Mallory with the failed transfer. If he came back this minute he would own nothing."

"And where does this leave me?"

"You have the Mallory mansion, regardless, through Peter's will, and the hundred million from the life insurance, all of it tax-free.

"Why did he gamble with leaving the bank and all the nursing homes and Peter's fifty million in Peter's name plus adding the HMO chain and seven billion dollars at the last minute?"

"Enormous tax savings on the purchase of the homes and his name would never be connected with the real estate or the seven billion. Peter's would be. It all amounts to naïve and bad judgment driven by a certain narrow greed."

"So he gambled and lost."

"Only because some mysterious and very advanced technology redirected all of his funds and property to a different cause, and a few minutes later wiped him out of this world ... silenced forever."

"Lapkin, can't you of all people do something about this?"

"I of all people am the very one who can't do a thing about it."

"Why?"

"One, I would not stand a chance of winning because Mallory is perfectly legit on paper and Kadsh is not, and the second reason ... nobody is ever to know who I am. And the third ... I don't want to."

"The shell banks?"

"The entire bank of computers at the Wyatt's Crossing and at the Golden Age were dismantled and disappeared Sunday afternoon and night, in response, I'm sure, to orders already given by Kadsh before he disappeared. So everyone is safe."

"And the seven billion dollars I didn't get, Lapkin. How much money is that?"

"Well, let me see now. Let's say if you have it safely invested, very conservatively, it ought to pay seven percent." He shut his eyes, turned his face to the ceiling for a moment, then said, "That comes to four hundred ninety million a year, or 1,342,467 dollars and some few cents a day, or about $932 a minute. With a little astute management and the growing principal, I'm sure you could get it up to an even thousand a minute very soon."

"I can't even imagine it."

"It would ruin your life. You would be mobbed constantly by beggars of one type or another, none who recognize themselves as beggars, each with the most *just* of all causes. You would never be able to find time enough even to give it away."

"I won't let it worry me."

"Good. Now it's time for you to go. Our jet will take you back to Cambridge."

She stepped in front of him and placed both arms at wrist level around his neck, and gazing sincerely into his eyes, asked, "You don't want just a little of me while you have the chance?"

He reached up, caught both hands gently and brought them down and around front, and bending only slightly he tenderly brushed his lips on the back of one, then the other. He stood straight, met her gaze, and squeezing both her hands softly, he said, "No, Celeste. We know about you and Ruble, and I would be diminished by the comparison."

54

Helen insisted they all be present in the conference room of People's Bank for the meeting with Peter's lawyer. When he finished reading the last will and testament, the lawyer invited questions. Helen asked, "Is this real? Will it stick?"

"Yes," he said. "It will."

"Taxes?" she asked.

"None, the way it's set up."

"And that?"

"A foundation for improving the lot of victims of the nursing home and HMO problems."

"Just how much did he intend putting in my hands?"

"We are not sure, but probably no more than the fifty million of his own funds, plus the huge profits he expected to make off of the nursing homes sales. His ownership of the HMO conglomerate would be a surprise to him now. The seven billion, of course, exceeds by far his wildest dreams. Regardless of his intentions, it is all there in the name of the foundation."

"The fifty million would have put us in a beggar stance, always looking for money, never enough to do a good job. Now, with the profits from the HMO conglomerate we will have enough to improve the lot of all the homes in the chain," said Helen.

"You have an extra seven billion to be used in some way," said John.

"Yes, and what a surprise. How many homes are in the chain?" She asked the lawyer.

"One hundred thirty."

"They all have problems, I'm sure."

"Well, a nursing home is a nursing home," said the lawyer.

Clara asked, "Helen, what are you thinking?"

"I'm thinking I will take the Golden Age and reintegrate it into the mainstream of human existence."

"How, and what exactly?"

"Seems to me we have all the ingredients right here in little Cambridge. Each of you will be needed as things develop, and I'll be in touch."

Ruble learned to scuba dive and he swam among the reefs, the coral, the flora, and the live fish. Behind sunglasses, and stripped down to a narrow swimsuit, he baked in the sun of the bright sandy beaches, waded and swam the salty surf, and turned a deeper and brighter copper. After ten days of hotel meals served in the room, of afternoons lounging in white terrycloth hotel robes, of languid nothing to do, of lap on lap of pool swimming, of moving Celeste toward exhaustion until she came to sip less and less of wine and cocktails, for which he had not the slightest desire, he began to think of the woods and the animals again.

The startling water colors, the greens and blues and yellows of the coastal tides and sands and islands out over the coral, he knew after a few days, could not be a lasting attraction. And a worry nagged quietly. It could not be the woman; he would never tire of her, the loose and limber way she rode him, while he, for the first time ever, moved nothing toward the climax, on his back holding up to her while she galloped to fiery, wild finishes. The feeling could never be replaced by another experience. He found her as untamed as any other wild animal who comes to the hand for something nowhere else to be found, as devoted as any other free living thing. She had come to him weary from a worn-out way of living, and he had known at once and had taken her back into a natural world. She now would always be his. And he would always now belong to her cleanness, her perfumes, her softness, her attention to him, his woman to keep.

But the beaches did not smell of the woods; the sea did not smell of the rivers. Boredom set in. He could imagine no game played by batting one ball with any kind of stick: the tennis racquet, the golf club, and other sticks for afternoon games seemed of no use in a real world. The waste of vast expanses of green golf courses, trimmed as neat as a city haircut, seemed useless in the daily struggles of mankind to survive. The hordes of multicolored garbs riding in wobbly golf carts over the flat, rich, green ground made him wonder if these people were in some way crippled. This could never be his real life. The worry nagged.

Then he recognized it. The Goonsbys. No one knew them the way he did, and he thought no one, not even Tom Bartley, would escape their evil unless he was there to watch what they were doing, and they were still stewing about Clink. As he gazed, silently preoccupied, into the distance out over ocean, Celeste came to his lounge chair, placed a knee on the edge and leaned over him. "Let's go home," she said. "I've got a hunch we are needed."

"You were reading my thoughts."

"I'm probably having the same ones."

"Next time I want to see the inside of a big city."

"New York," she said. "Maybe for Christmas, then all the rest of the world from time to time. But Cambridge will always be home."

"Yes. I know that now."

Carrying the cages and walking a winding path the last mile through the woods, Celeste and Ruble went behind dense undergrowth and came to the cypress swamp and no path, water on one side and a wall of cane and low growth on the other, a private and hidden little open space, grassy, almost a nest. Ruble put his cages on the ground and sat on a berm close to the water. He motioned to Celeste. She sat next to him, her cages at her feet. They stayed motionless and the woods hushed for the moment, almost as if respecting their arrival. Then the sounds of life picked up again; the barking of squirrels, and the call of birds arose out of the new silence, and frolicking began in the limbs above. Celeste's eyes swept up the trunk of a towering cypress standing with its feet in the water, huge knees covered in green algae and moss protruding from the scummy surface at every angle around the massive trunk. Fallen trees and half-submerged, broken limbs rotted in fractal disarray beneath moss and slime and the creeping climbing arbor of vegetation. A squirrel, colored a rich gray, scampering along a swaying limb, stopped after brief bursts of jerky motion to look around and nibble something held between its paws. Ruble reached down and slid the doors open on the four cages he had carried. Four squirrels erupted to freedom, and bolted to the nearest tree. But each stopped while crossing the open space to rear up on its haunches, cup it hands to its face, and look with rapid zips of motion in every direction.

Celeste whispered, "Oh, how furtive!"

"What does that mean?"

"Foxy."

"Watching out for danger."

"They live with it."

"Always around and constant as breathing."

She said, "Poor little things."

"Yeah, and you know what I think they are really doing when they stop like that every few breaths and look around, heads up, ready to scamper to safety? I've watched a lot of little animals doing it the same way, living like that every second."

"You have a meaning?"

"Ain't that a form of praying, don't he know death's there just waiting to grab him, don't he know every second of his short little life that there is something millions of times bigger and smarter than he is waiting to claim him back where he came from? Ain't that what folks really mean when they say religion?"

Celeste had become motionless, her mouth open in astonishment. The forest sounds sang and hummed a symphonious harmony out over the water and among the trees. Her gaze went up the cypress trunks again and Ruble's words of weeks ago blazed in memory *No church in this world reaches for the sky like a tree* and memory flashed the visual moments in the years past in the naves of cathedrals where she had gone seeking: Milan's Duomo, six hundred years in the building and still incomplete in the pygmy striving of the human, the vertical aspirations of its massive pillows dwarfing the presence of mere man in the hazy dust of milling throngs searching for meaning, and in St. Patrick's, and in the Basilica itself. Far overhead, the waving filigree of cypress needles framing distant visages of open sky gently undulated in the lazy breeze, the sense of height transcending. She reached toward her feet and opened the cage doors. Squirrels and rabbits, a denatured skunk, and two snakes, a king and a green snake emerged, and she watched as they began cautiously to explore their new freedom. "Ruble," she said. "Are you telling me all things believe in God?"

"Just all things in their nature know about God. And what's the difference in knowing and believing? Seems to me believing ain't needed if you already know."

"Oh my, Ruble, you do have a wisdom."

Ruble grew quiet, studying the water over the teeming swamp. He pointed to a dead tree limb and whispered, "Watch it." The browns and blacks and muds blended in a varicolored pattern bordering on the algae-green scum carpeting the water. Her vision concentrated on a bark-colored lizard sunning above the water. A part of the limb moved and she recognized the short tapered neck, the sharp triangular head, the short fat body, the acutely tapered tail, and watched in fascination as the head drew back and the entire deadly mechanism shot forward like a torpedo, the white mouth wide-open in readiness, and struck the lizard ... soundless ... the lizard body in immediate convulsions. After a brief and calculated delay, the moccasin moved up on the limb and began to swallow the lizard, head first.

Ruble took a blanket from his backpack and spread it on the grass. Celeste removed lunch from her pack. They ate while listening and watching the wildlife. A herd of deer came out of the woods to drink. A mother skunk went rapidly along the swamp edge, a litter following. They ran in V-formation, their bodies bouncing, the white-striped tails raised, altogether a brief and decorative ripple unforgettable upon awareness. Celeste lay back and watched the sky, the vultures floating and swerving high on updrafts, hawks darting and diving, throngs of black birds flying swift formations across the sky, the occasional lone songbird, doves and bobwhites calling in the distance. Ruble moved over to her side.

Warm in the sun, fresh in the lazy breeze stirring, the isolation from the noise of men a new privacy, both naked in nature, their sounds and the smell of rutting erupted to a peak of passion. Now she could see him in all clarity, and she stayed supine and let him, a total surrender. She did not scream or claw, this one more a clasping, a possession, a belonging, a submergence together at the last moment, clinging wet in the sweat of passion. But his body suddenly stiffened and he soundlessly flopped down flat on his belly, grasped her by a shoulder and rolled her over flat and placed a finger vertical across his lips. They lay prone, looking forward along the ground. The odor invaded the surroundings, the most revolting of stenches. Ruble soundlessly removed a hunting knife from his backpack without raising his head, and waited. Feet came through the grass, several pairs, searching and circling. Feet went by less than a yard from their faces, visible in the bushes just beyond the grass in which they lay. Ruble held as still as a statue, but tensed to leap, the knife in hand. The feet moved on, voices rose in the area then faded in the distance. Ruble waited, perfectly still for at least ten minutes then raised his head cautiously. The odor diminished and disappeared. "Goonsbys," he said. "We came too close." They dressed quickly and left in early dusk, carrying the empty cages, Ruble leery and alert.

55

A month later, Helen called a meeting in the lodge at the Colburn barn. She wanted to bring them up to date.

Zelma said, "Well, I'm sure this is not just coming out of the blue."

"Oh, yes. I've given it plenty of thought. And we plan to have, if nothing else, a new type of animal shelter, or humane society, or dog pound, or whatever, on one side, and a new type of nursing home on the other."

"What ... ?"

"The Colburn-Beckette Foundation," said Helen. Then she turned to Sam and said, "Sam has done the legal work and he will explain our purpose and goals."

"John Colburn's idea, and we are working it out now. Give the animals freedom in a vast enclosure on the Colburn land, build a new nursing home, the Golden Age, bordering the shelter and standing astride the Colburn land and the city limit. Then remodel and give the old Golden Age compound, already bordering the campus, to the university for a newly endowed humanities laboratory, with special emphasis on a new psychology, on philosophy, and on anthropology. Certain related courses would be integrated into the nursing home management. In other words, put the old disabled people and the animals back in the world, and use courses taught at university level to integrate the three into a new horizon, a new social awareness."

"Amazing," said Martha.

"This would mean, of course, the presence of students among the patients on a daily basis," said Zelma.

"Right, and one of the goals we want."

"You've enlisted the university?"

"Chancellor Bruce Madison is very excited and visionary. Along with John, here, he sees the growing understanding of the relation between psychology and philosophy, and for that matter, anthropology," said Sam.

"We wish to blur the line between the scientific concept and the humanities. We want to heal this divisive wound. With knowledge and understanding the endeavors will meld back together as the expression of the human spirit seeking to explore the great unknown surrounding us. To empower this impulse would be to strengthen the very soul of all art and literature and scientific discoveries," said John.

"Religion?" asked Clara.

"Spirituality," said Sam. "As it applies to exploring the mystery of life and all surrounding it."

"The church?" asked Clara.

"No politics of any type, no profit for the practice of it, no dogma, nothing unproven to be stated as fact, no taking from the poor to buy icons and construct monuments, each religion to be taught on the basis of the facts of its origin and evolution as related to the questing human spirit. God is everywhere; no edifice could confine the concept. We want to seek a new understanding of the hungers driving the human psyche," said John.

"Seems to me you've outlined a plan for the next millennium, or more," said Martha.

"A beginning," said Sam.

"So as a practical matter, where do things stand?"

"Progressing. Celeste Howard has agreed to devote her time to the animal shelter, with her money and a supplement from the foundation. Ruble will help. Together they will supervise and run the liaison between animals and patients."

"Miracles will never end," said Zelma. She turned to Sam. "Her bugs, should we stop altogether?"

"Not yet. The dangers have not all gone away."

"Who?"

"The sheriff and the Goonsbys."

"What are they up to?"

"Plenty, and everybody be careful, watch your step, don't go anywhere alone," said Tom.

"What's the danger?"

"The usual, Dynamite Don, and anything physical one of them can do if he sneaks up on you, especially the knives."

"What's being done about the threat?"

"We are monitoring the sheriff as usual and we are scouting Goonsby Hollow and the surrounding woods."

"In the meantime," said Helen, "we are proceeding with our plans. The university has accepted our propositions. We are building a residential and office compound on the Colburn Farm. Some graduate students will be housed there, and the place will serve as a major retreat for philosophers, physicists, scholars of religion, psychologists, anthropologists, and others. A major plant-pharmacology division will be developed on the site and in the adjacent woods and fields. Plans for the new nursing home and for renovation of the old one are underway. Clara here will be chief nurse at the new home in full charge of patient care. As soon as the Golden Age is up and running, we will turn our attention to others in the chain. We expect to make them into self-sustaining units but otherwise nonprofit."

Ruble received a call from Tom Bartley. They made a show of going out in Ruble's aluminum skiff to fish in the edges of Sardis Lake. While catching crappie, they talked.

"I wanted to get you out of earshot, Ruble. You've been seen."

"Yeah?"

"You know we hear every word the sheriff says."

"You told me that. But it's still surprising how you do it."

"He's talking a lot to the Goonsbys and the Goonsbys have seen you and Celeste out in the woods together. You making a habit of that?"

"Yeah, she loves it, and we go out there to turn loose some of the animals, failed pets about to be killed by the animal shelter."

"Well, you've been a little careless, man, and now they are really up to devilment."

"Ain't surprising."

"Might be," Tom Said. "They reported back to the sheriff and he has cooked up this plot. He's told them all about how rich Celeste became when

Mallory got killed, and they plan to kidnap her and demand a big ransom. Of course, they will kill you when they take her. And while everybody is out joining the search, they plan for Dynamite Don to do one of his jobs, but he will get several places this time, including the shack where they plan to hide Celeste. They will get the money, but the world will never see her again. After the sheriff instructed them, they almost found you again and would have killed you and would have taken her then. You know they rape, and folks are convinced that they are responsible for several women who have disappeared, probably used then murdered and sunk in the swamp."

"What can I do?"

"We need to locate their dynamite."

"I already know," said Ruble. "Nothing new, where they've always kept it, stashed everywhere, under the house, the outhouse, in the barn, and out in the woods in hollow stumps and hollow logs. And they are doing old stuff, stealing, killing game. They want fish, they explode a stick of dynamite in the river and everything comes floating to the top stunned, most of it too little to eat and too hurt to live. They run wild meat to an outlaw restaurant in Memphis that serves wild game, deer, rabbit, squirrel, rattlesnake meat, coon, possum, hog, a wild bear now and then, and the customers and maybe the owners don't know it, but stray dog and stray cats, and fox and coyote thrown in, big rats, fat little mice fried splayed out dressed and whole for quail, and nobody seems to know the difference."

"Dynamite Don?"

"Oh, he still gets calls to do legal stuff like dynamiting beaver dams, and opening old ditches and dynamiting out new irrigation and drainage. When do they plan to take Celeste?"

"Soon, from appearances, but we have heard no date yet. The sheriff has not finished his plans, but we think he is plotting to take some buildings too, like the Colburn barn, and my house, and maybe the Mallory house."

"Why?"

"Revenge, he's stewing to get even."

"You know old Don is really sneaky," said Ruble. "He likes to plant his charge maybe days ahead of time, then drive into the area casual like and set it off by radio without ever getting near or slowing down. So you really have to watch out for him. He may be sneaking in at night and setting the sticks in place already, and hid so you could hardly find them if you knew to look."

"I've heard that, and I'll have to be working on a way. Let's go fishing again next week. I'll call you."

"Okay."

Sam and John continued developing their plan over lunch at the midtown bar and grill in Cambridge.

Sam said, "John, I've wondered if you have any ideas? Like, could you set off all the dynamite in a square-mile area from a safe distance, all at once more or less, maybe with that intense light business, picking the right time, say, if we catch them when every Goonsby and the sheriff himself are carrying an arm load of it on the way to blowing up something?"

"All the sticks tied in bundles and hidden in small batches, scattered hundreds of yards apart, none of it with blasting caps attached, none with fuses, none with wires ... it would be difficult without burning off the entire landscape. You got to have fire in one form or another, or a mighty jolt," said John.

"I was hoping you could provide it."

John thought for a minute, then said, "Sam, you ever been to a puppet sale?"

"No."

"Well, I have, and it's a very sobering experience."

Sam looked at him, bemused. "I don't think I've ever taken a puppet too seriously."

"It's like this, you see. You go up to a booth, the crowd is milling by, you look over the rail and there it is. One of them, say a dog, a little dog, with long decoration-like shaggy hair down in its lost face, hair all too real in appearance, has all the motions, all the shaggy cute and endearing body language of a little loving hyper-dog trotting. The hair dances, the body bounces, the swagger and eagerness are there, the swift busy little legs and feet, the intensity just like the real thing. It is set at a certain speed and it just goes on and on. And one thing above all, a relentless and intense seriousness never changes, like one constant background note sounded without interruption or variation behind a whole sprightly symphony. You are fascinated, hypnotized, you feel an insight close to madness, you can't stop looking, you want one, too. You would go down the street leading him, but then you realize you're no puppeteer, you don't have God's extended hand to make the motions, but your imagination can't quit. You look up to a real and familiar sound, and there is a parrot on his bar, and a tree full of monkeys, and on the floor a kitten ... all of them with the real motion, all set into and sustained in motion by the puppeteer's motor. Then you think woman. And imagine yourself, wag, bringing one to a party on your arm and making her do whatever you wanted right out on the dance floor. Cute, too damned cute and endearing, and you go on along the rail. Down in the next booth a lithe and flimsy flapper-type, five-and-a-half feet tall, does rock-and-roll pelvic gyrations. Then you see a pony trotting with intense and sustained and unvarying seriousness, and you know the biggest question in this whole world: where is reality? Which is an illusion, you or them?" John stopped for breath. Sam waited.

John continued, "Remember, one of my specialties is robots. And they want to kidnap Celeste. So I have been building a very delicate and supple Celeste-puppet on a most unusual and tough robot."

"Ahhh, the Goonsbys will kidnap a puppet-robot and try to rape her."

"You want to watch don't you?"

"Not just once, I'm sure we will have video won't we?"

"Built in."

"Good."

"And of course, she will be rigged for other things. She will have a little intense light laser gun capable of honing in on a source of energy, say a weak isotope signal."

"Amazing."

"And according to you, Ruble knows the location of most, if not all, the dynamite storage areas."

"Right."

"I will bring for him a wine bladder full of radioactive iodine. If he will pour a few drops on each bundle of dynamite, the sensor in the puppet will hone in on it and the light beam will get it at the proper time. Can he do that?"

"He will need only one night," said Sam.

On the following Saturday morning, out in the skiff, catching crappie again, Tom said, "Ruble, Saturday coming they plan to surprise you.

They'll be in the woods moving the stuff around, getting ready."

"Do you know what they plan to do?"

"Yes. The sheriff has done a lot of talking. He's pissed to the winds and does not know when to quit. My house, the Mallory house, the Colburn barn, will all have charges set. And just to show everyone what they can do, they will blow mine right away, because he hates us, me and Clara, the most, expecting us to be in it. Then the sheriff himself is going to receive this threat, see: pay the ransom right away, five million dollars, or Celeste will be killed, and then just to show everyone what they can do they will blow the Colburn barn, saving the Mallory house for last. If they have to, they will let everybody think a lot more houses are waiting to be blown up, and everybody in town and county will run scared."

"Movin' stuff around, you said."

"Yes. The sheriff will park an unmarked car in the woods across the hollow from Isom's Knoll, and a Goonsby jalopy will be parked behind it. The sheriff will stand guard while the Goonsby clan carries the dynamite sticks through the woods to the trunks of both cars. After they finish with you and Celeste and after dark, they will drive to the targets and set the charges. And since Celeste has no living relatives, the sheriff will find the bank manager on Sunday with the news about the ransom. His advice will be to leave the bag of money in the woods, just as instructed. He'll say, *Them sneaky lowdown Goonsbys will kill her in a minute if you don't do what they say, and there ain't a thing I can do about it without takin' too great a risk with her life.*"

"Tom, ya'll are goin' to get out of my way ain't you, so I can handle them one at a time?"

"No, Ruble, you will have more fun our way ... guarantee it."

"What you got in mind?"

"We will need you to go in the woods leading Celeste by the hand on Saturday afternoon, living up to your habit, only it won't be Celeste. It will just look like her."

"All right. What do you need?"

Tom handed over the full wine bag and gave him instructions for dropping a few drops on each batch of the stored dynamite. It's got a life of its own, so don't get any on your hands or clothes."

"When?"

"You could start as early as Tuesday if you like, but get all the caches, in the house and barn and other buildings, and all you know about in other places."

"Okay. Easy enough."

"And we need the clothes she usually wears in the woods and a bottle of her perfume."

"What else?"

"How does she wear her hair in the woods?"

"Balled up, under a baseball cap, and she sometimes lets it down out there in the woods, all down around her waist. When do you need the stuff?

"Tomorrow, Sunday, so John Colburn can take it with him back to Huntsville, and we need a full-face photograph."

"She has a bunch and I'll bring all of it to you tomorrow morning."

"And Ruble, does she have any long blonde wigs that look like her real hair?

"Yeah, you want that too?"

"Yeah."

"I can get it. Anything else?"

"Yes. Have you made any videos of her with your little camera you used in the Golden Age?"

"Yeah, lots of them."

"Bring them, too."

"Will do."

"Good. And how are things going for you, Ruble?"

"Man I never dreamed it. On Sunday mornings I sit back there on the back row in church, a place I ain't ever been before, and listen to her sing, looking all the way up there to where she's standing, that long beautiful hair all the way down below her waist, and I'm thinking, 'Man, I got me uh angel,' and that's the way she treats me. I been delivered up to a heaven on earth."

"How fortunate for you both."

"Yeah, I heard some of that stuff about her, but I don't care. It just got her ready for me, and you know what … I can handle it."

"I hear you've made her happy and satisfied."

"Sounds like it to me. And she sings in the woods, when the sun begins to sink down behind the trees. She looks up the trunks of the big swamp cypress and sings them purty songs about God. Sounds even better there than in the church, the song going on up toward where the tree is reaching, ringing out amongst the forest and I swear to you, I believe even the animals stop to listen."

"Quite a woman."

"Yeah, lots'a little weak two-legged animals sipped at her stream, but I'm the first one to wade in and take a swim."

"She sings in the woods?"

"Oh, yes."

"Have the Goonsbys heard her?"

"Had to."

"You going there this afternoon?"

"We could ."

Tom reached in his pocket and handed Ruble something hidden in his palm. Ruble, that's a sound recorder, a very good one. When she starts to sing turn it on. Get it back to me with the other stuff in the morning before John Colburn leaves for Huntsville. I'm sure he can put it to good use."

John met with Sam in the Colburn barn lodge on Friday night, and Tom brought Ruble. Celeste-Robot sat at the table, her face sweetly composed, the long blonde hair hanging loose down to the seat of her chair. John sat with his fingers ready on the keyboard of his laptop. Ruble, speechless, sat down across the table from her and waited. The room grew silent, and Celeste-Robot turned her face toward Ruble, and smiled. "Hi, Ruble," she said, reaching across the table to shake hands, John's hands busy with the keys and the mouse. Ruble, drew back, then reached for the hand.

He turned to Tom. "It's real, like it has blood in it, like it's human or at least alive."

"Come dance with me, Ruble." She had increased her grip on Ruble's hand and began tugging. Sam reached over and punched a button on a CD player. The room filled with a country western beat. Ruble, his arm extended and sliding his belly along the table edge, came around and she took him in her arms and began to whirl him to the rhythm of the music. After three or so minutes of this, Sam cut off the sound and she led Ruble back to the table.

John said, "Ruble, we wanted you to see how real she is."

"Well, let's don't take that part of her any further."

Everyone laughed and John shut down his computer. Celeste-Robot all of a sudden slumped and seemed to go to sleep. The light had gone out of her eyes.

Tom said, "Okay, John, I'm sure Ruble wants to know all about this thing, and my curiosity and admiration couldn't be running any higher."

"All right," John said. "We've been building robots now for years, and the technology just keeps on progressing. Recent developments have made us redesign and rebuild many times, almost like an evolution. Well, it is an evolution. This one has a titanium frame or skeleton, and the latest in rechargeable batteries with an unusually long life. These batteries power the finer skills, but the propulsion and strength come from rocket-powered pistons, fueled by compressed liquid hydrogen peroxide, the stuff that turns your hair yellow and your teeth white. The brain is the latest in quantum computers, something like my computer here, which I have disguised in conventional housing for security's sake. In skill she can play a violin like Paganini, and with the strength she can break bones, and with the propulsion this one can run fifty miles an hour."

"John, she looks almost alive and moves so gracefully," said Sam.

"Lifelike because of new materials, artificial muscle, made of a polymer and metal semiconductor composite. Limbs and fingers and toes made of it move when voltage is applied. Fish made of it swim, birds made of it flap their wings, monkeys made of it lift their arms, and they all look alive. All this stuff is reported in the various science magazines, if you want to read about it. The Technology Review from MIT is especially informative. We took the material and made her a body and limbs from it, and gave it all kinds of voltage from her computer brain. We also gave it enough porosity to hold a seepage of a solution much like seawater containing the necessary ingredients for life. This keeps the skin of her face and hands alive. Her face looks so real because real human skin is stretched over the polymer attached to the skull and face. The hands are live gloves of human skin. Of course, before she goes into action we will cover these gloves with another pair made of gossamer-thin chrome-cobalt alloy, the hardest, toughest stuff you can imagine. Human skin is now grown by the yard in certain laboratories."

"Real-looking face, just like her. How did you do it?" asked Tom.

"Oh, I almost forgot. The photographs Ruble got for us ... some had a very good depth of field and we were able to construct a hologram, and we used the information to write a CAD-CAM program, you know, computer-assisted design for computer-assisted machining. This turns an ordinary milling machine into a three-dimensional contour sculptor. We sculpted a very pretty head and face for her from a hollow carbon-carbon beam, then covered it with the artificial muscle and the real skin."

"Impressive, and her movements are so graceful."

"Oh yes, and that's the other thing. We got the idea from the animation laboratories of the moving-picture industry. Then we used the digital video Ruble had made of the real Celeste in action. The technique records and digitally mimics the body language of live actors, and it involves artificial intelligence software. This old gal has quite a glob of artificial intelligence inside her carbon skull, capable of creating all sorts of movements and subtleties with her artificial muscles." ,

Ruble sat mesmerized. Finally he said, "Does this thing talk back, or give a man trouble?"

John laughed. "I was getting around to that. Tomorrow, Ruble, when you go into the woods, hold hands with her as you usually do and be gentle like you always are, but be careful to make no sudden movements, don't grab her anywhere, and don't try to kiss her,"

"Why?" asked Ruble.

"I'll show you." He turned on the computer, and Celeste-Robot came back to life. She sat up straight and smiled.

"Okay, Tom," said John. Tom got out of his chair, went out the door and returned with a full sized shovel, the kind used for digging ditches. He held the shovel by the collar and poked Celeste with the end of the handle, a rude but harmless prod against her shoulder. She snatched the shovel out of Tom's hands, grasped the collar in one hand, the handle mid-shaft in the other, brought both hands up above her face level, arms extended, then brought both down toward the table top and together. The shovel handle snapped in two with a resounding cracking noise. John manipulated the keys. She handed the two ends to Tom, and smiled again. Tom said, "Thank you, Celeste."

She said, "You're welcome, Tom." John took his hands off the keyboard.

Ruble said. "Hey, man."

"You will be okay, Ruble. Just take her into the woods at the usual time and to the usual place. Seat her wherever she usually sits, and under the pretense of going to the bushes, fade into the undergrowth, pause a second, and when she starts to sing, disappear at once, then keep out of sight and join us. We will be picnicking in the woods atop the hill above Isom's Knoll."

"Singing?"

"Yes. You know the recorder Tom gave to you? Nice recording you made of her voice. We took it off the memory chip and put in the computer inside her head, her ears are the speakers, quite expensive ones at that, produce great sound."

"What else is in her head, John?" asked Sam.

"Don't look her in the eye when she goes into action ... a little intense light laser shooter, aims out of the right eye, programmed to aim at a radioactive signal. Now watch this." He hit the keys again and her head began to rotate, and it went completely around and around and around. "She can pick up isotope signals from all directions and make a clean sweep."

"What else?"

"Well, for the fun of it I loaded some Gothic cathedral pipe-organ on her computer brain this morning right after her singing."

"Heavy stuff for little speakers."

"The woofers are in her chest, a boom box more or less."

"And?"

"An alarm system to keep anyone from slipping up on her, like an intruder alarm for the yard, but it sends a silent warning to her computer brain. And one other thing, a camcorder in the brain will record sights and sounds out there in the woods and broadcast back to my computer. It aims out of the left eye. With luck we might get some useful pictures."

"How close will she come to the explosions?" asked Tom.

"Close, and that required one further thing, a suit she will wear under her clothes, and a skull cap laser-proof and bulletproof. The suit is fireproof, shock-absorbent, waterproof, and knife-proof, a product of nanotechnology, tightly woven of millions of nanotubes of carbon and silk thin. It's the color of the clothes she's wearing now and will be touched with her perfume."

"Well, now what am I going to do with the real Celeste?"

"The girls all want her to join us for our lookout picnic."

56

They looked innocent enough, sightseers on blankets spread over the grass up on the hilltop above the valley and above Isom's Knoll, with binoculars and a telescope on a tripod, and a guy with an open laptop cocked up on his knees, typing busily. It didn't make any difference if they were seen or not. Lots of people go there with similar equipment to look out across the view. Through the binoculars they watched. The sheriff, out of uniform, but his form unmistakable, waited behind an unmarked old car and a jalopy parked behind it beside the road across on the other side of the valley. Both trunks stood open and already several forms had come out of the woods to unload arms full of material into the trunks. Tom trained the telescope on the cars: dynamite, without question.

In the fading afternoon light, John watched the progress of Ruble and Celeste-Robot across his screen. Ruble took her deep into the woods; the motion stopped, then a form turned back, leaving only Celeste-Robot for the screen. John actuated her sound system, and the clear voice rang out of the woods, Celeste's pretty singing. Within five minutes a form moved stealthily behind her, the alarm spreading across the computer screen. She did not stop singing when two forms dashed forward. She stood to face them, singing. Then in a lapse of time, still singing, she let them make their intentions known, putting into effect their usual regard for women. She stopped singing and exchanged words with them. Then she began to sing again, the holiness rising in sound as they grabbed her. John donned his earphones and listened to a mounting struggle, the screaming, the voices talking and talking fast. Then the motions were quick and effective, but blurred on the screen. By remote control, John turned her and walked her through the trees toward the sheriff's car. She dragged the two men, one in each hand, both silent and neither resisting. She entered the road a hundred feet from the cars. The song had ended, and the organ music began to peal across the hollow. Her sensors began picking up the isotope emanations, and she walked straight toward them a few feet and stopped. The sheriff saw her, approaching resolutely, dragging two limp men who looked to be dead, a woman, a tall blonde woman with gossamer blonde hair down below her waist, a too-frail and delicate-looking thing to be horsing two big, limp Goonsbys. Mrs. Howard! Celeste Howard! Now Celeste Mallory! The flying hair like the theater of madness, she stood waiting. He opened his mouth to call her *Celeste*, but she suddenly threw the man in her left hand through the air. He tumbled overhead, festooning loops of falling blood, and crashed into the open trunk of the jalopy. Then with the right hand, she threw the second man, at least seventy-five feet, he too looping, falling blood and tumbling into the trunk atop the first one. Her eyes drilled toward the trunk, and as the sheriff turned to run, the dynamite exploded in both cars only a split second apart, clearing the road of any trace of either contraption and wiping out all the people beside the cars. She turned toward the line of people trailing through the woods toward the road. She kept coming, mechanically, overpowering, the music rolling, and as she progressed in the direction of the Goonsby compound she blew one after another of the string of Goonsbys into oblivion, a series of explosions marching across the valley.

Those at the other end of the line dropped their sticks and broke to run. The discarded sticks exploded anyway as the beam found the isotope. She honed in on the isotope in their clothes and on their skin and she ran them down. She threw them each into the next explosion.

The noise stopped, the organ music finished, and John directed her across the woods to the house. At a safe distance he stopped her and increased the power as she looked directly at the house. A tremendous explosion rocked the landscape and debris flew above the trees. Then he directed her to the barn, and the other outbuildings and blew each to pieces. Ruble sat by John's side with a topographic map spread out on the ground, pointing to the targets.

"At what distance will that thing pick up the isotope and set off an explosion?" asked Tom.

"About a mile, and I think it's time to run her back and forth a few times across the hollow to be sure we got everything."

"Right," said Ruble.

Tom typed on the keyboard again, set the head rotator, and put her in motion. The landscape became silent. Then another explosion rumbled through the hollow. During the next hour, six more explosions occurred; then as she completed the survey of the valley the landscape became quiet. John brought her out to the road and ran her up to the hill to the picnic area. He walked her over one side of the picnic blanket, and she sat down beside the real Celeste, who said, "There are some things about you I really envy."

"You can't have them, Little Sister, too dangerous."

"What are you going to do with her, now?" asked Martha.

"Take her to Huntsville and put her parts back on the shelf, and her skin back in solution."

Celeste-Robot turned her face toward John, his fingers flying on the computer keys, and said, "Ingrate."

Celeste walked to her car and drove away, the other women left together. The men went to Sam's office, Celeste-Robot in the trunk. John had removed the camera and carried it in his pocket. They sat at a conference table and John plugged the camcorder into the television set and played what it had to offer. They listened to the confession of the Goonsbys made within seconds after they started the rape attack on Celeste-Robot. The infrared night photography showed shadows and movements difficult to analyze, but the explosions had been recorded with spectacular clarity. Ruble sat at a far end of the table, listening and watching, and offered no comment. Weighted and sunk in the swamp one at a time over the years ... not just the raped women, but the robbed men too, and numerous others, some of them done just for the sport of it, hunters who made the mistake of going into Goonsby hollow alone and never to be seen again, people traveling the roads alone and waylaid. There would have been more if the confession had lasted longer.

John said, "Tom, what are we to do with this?"

"I vote nothing. They would drain the swamp, have to, and even then find at most a random skull and long bone, but no complete body, and no proof. The swamp is swept through several times a year when the river gets out of its banks, and I doubt there is anything left. This may explain the skulls and bones found miles down river at low water seasons over the past several years. And we can't do this without exposing our operation and without being accused, by some self-seeking do-gooder soul, of deliberately killing Goonsbys. The Goonsbys got killed by their own dynamite, and we ought to let it go at that. No one will ever find out what happened to the sheriff."

Sam said, "The Goonsbys were the last of a breed. They came with the settling of this country during the last 250 years, robbing and stealing, and never doing an honest day's work. Their kind were the Natchez Trace outlaws, the gangs in the woods, the highway robbers, and before the days of public transportation a menace to all people. They had no morals, no conscience, no mercy. They were murderers, thieves, robbers, sadists, rapists, godless, filthy, totally rudderless, and worst of all, unchangeable, and they never bathed. If the dynamite got the last one of them we are lucky to be done with the problem forever. Over long decades, in fact, more than a century, it took several generations of painful improvement to move any one of them up to be Steinbeck or Caldwell or O'Connor or Faulkner grist, and little did those writers know about real white trash. I say leave it alone. Something mysterious set off the explosions and that's all we know. And nobody has to know we know anything at all."

John said, "Wouldn't do to expose any of this. You don't want the federal government dragged in. It would set off the squawking liberals and office seekers. Imagine the story on CNN or FOX, imagine the panels of rude and ignorant experts posturing and yelling and interrupting each other, the Bronx presidential candidates pontificating, and they just might find a scapegoat to ruin, like me or you. Leave it alone and I can use the experience to further develop robots for future use to improve the lot of mankind."

Sam said, "Well, it looks like we are all in agreement, and so it stands. But I would like to know what you think, Ruble."

Ruble had listened without a word, listening for something the others didn't realize they were hearing. He stirred and said, "Could you play that part over where they attack her there where she's sittin' on the log singing a song to God?"

"Sure," said John. He played it again, and the clear voice began. Other sounds came through too, the sounds of feet crossing the ground, the sounds Celeste-Robot made when she stood and faced them, the sounds of contact, the rapid incomplete confessions in a state of terror, the jumble of sounds until she picked up one in each hand and started toward the parked cars. The action of legs and feet and arms was difficult to analyze. Ruble held up his hand, and John stopped the playback.

"Let me hear that over, please." He leaned toward a speaker. John played the section through again until Ruble held up his palm. John stopped the computer. Ruble said, "That's enough. I got it, but I would like to know what that thing does to make a man cry his soul out and spill everything before he's been there even half a minute? I can't quite see it in the pictures."

"Zoning in, Ruble."

"Yeah?"

"She's programmed. As soon as rough hands reach up to her crotch, her hands go to theirs. The metal fists close like pinchers on theirs, and begin to pull slowly, steadily. That's when you hear her saying, 'Talk boys and talk fast or I will tear them off.' Just before she says 'Now where is the dynamite stored and where is Dynamite Don?' Apparently, when they started to answer she cut them off and she carried them dead out of the woods. I may have hit a wrong key or maybe the program has a glitch in it. It's too bad we can't see better, but too much was happening too fast and the lens was not always aimed at the action, and motion blurred what we did get."

"No," said Ruble. "That ain't what happened. I know the sounds of the woods. Three pairs of feet crossed that open space between bushes and the log she was sitting on. And I know the third pair. Dynamite Don, you know, was born with a clubfoot and it makes its own sound, the stiff ankle won't bend and he drags it through the leaves. When they were tracking, his brothers, and his stinkin' ol' daddy used to make him crawl to keep quiet."

"I knew he had a game leg," said Tom.

"It's true. I've heard and watched him time after time."

"Ruble, you're telling us something we probably don't want to hear," said Sam.

"Yeah. Do you know the sound of a cut throat?" No one spoke. The room had grown starkly quiet and still. Ruble hesitated, then continued. "Well, there ain't no mistaking it, that and the sound of Dynamite Don's feet moving fast, circling something he's killin', all blurred in the pictures. He cut his own brothers' throats to stop them from talking."

"What does this mean, Ruble?" asked Tom.

"It means Dynamite Don didn't know we already knew where most of the dynamite was stored, and he is out there somewhere with dynamite, and ain't none of us safe. After he got a good view of Celeste-Robot in action, he got out of there. You can bet he didn't stick around to help or to see what would happen. After I got back to the hill top I thought I heard a Goonsby jalopy crank up and head the other way."

"Where do you think he will go first?"

"That we need to figure out fast."

"Well, let's see," said Tom. "He blames Clara for Clink."

"And he blames the Colburns because that's where Clink went to get her, on their land."

"Yeah, but think of tonight. Kidnapping Celeste was the thing they planned, and Celeste turns out to be inhuman and impossibly mechanical. He knows by instinct if nothing else that the tables were turned. I think his vengeance will be directed to the Mallory house," said John.

"I do, too," said Ruble. "And that's where I'm headin' right now. Where are the girls?"

"Martha went to the veterans, and Helen and Clara and Zelma went to a movie. And they are not going home. We are meeting at Taylor Catfish House for dinner at eight-thirty."

"Then Celeste is the only one where she can get blown up. I gotta run." Ruble dashed out the door.

Sam looked at his watch. "Eight fifteen. I guess we ought to be going to meet the girls. But I'm uneasy."

"Yeah, me too. I'm for explaining to them and returning to check on Ruble," said John.

Tom said, "Count me in, but we got to be careful not to get in his way. If Dynamite Don comes anywhere close to that house tonight it will be his last trip to anyplace short of hell."

"Down the street watching will be all right with me."

"When the girls leave the restaurant, they can come here to my office and wait. Zelma has a key."

Ruble parked his pick-up a block down a side street behind the Mallory house and dashed for the back door. He found Celeste in the kitchen and wasted no words. "We think Dynamite Don is still alive and on his way here. Get in your car and go somewhere until I call you on your cell. Don't come back until I do call."

"But Ruble, I'm not leaving you alone to get blown up."

"No. If you stay you will hinder me. I'll be waitin' where he can't see … now go!"

"Oh God! Where?"

"Somewhere out of sight. Try a movie."

She went. Ruble hurried to the garage where he had placed his tools when he moved in. After a rapid search he dug up the radio he needed, a new one, a digital hardly bigger than his thumb. He dimmed the house lights and crossed the yard to a hedge and hid himself near the curb. His eyes grew accustomed to the dim lights of the street. The distant rumble of traffic diminished, and he listened for approaching motors. He knew dozens of automobiles by their sounds, and recognized Tom's car when it pulled in behind his truck down the street, and he hoped they wouldn't make the mistake of coming any closer on foot or in the car. He knew Celeste's car when it parked a block in the other direction and he hoped to God she had covered her hair and would stay down out of sight. He waited until it seemed endless. Then after ten o'clock he heard an unmistakable motor. Nothing else made the sound of a Goonsby jalopy. It came down the street, lights off, the engine idling, moving not more than five miles an hour. It circled the block and came back faster with the headlights on high, and the Mallory house numbers shown bright in the glare. The headlights went off, the car circled again and made another pass by the house. Ruble tensed and readied his radio. The taillights flared as the car braked to the curb in the next block past the front of the house. A form got out, went to the rear of the car, and opened the trunk, the gait unmistakable, Dynamite Don. The figure bent forward and worked rapidly, the shoulders moving, the lid light shining. Ruble waited. The figure straightened, lifted a bundle out of the trunk, and turned toward the Mallory house. Ruble pressed a series of buttons rapidly on the radio. The fifth button blew it. The figure, the automobile, and part of the street disappeared. Fire shot above the telephone poles. Glass shattered up and down the street. Windows in the Mallory house cracked but none fell out. Ruble's ears rang sharply. He looked around as Tom and John and Sam came running down the side street toward the house. Celeste's car squealed around the intersection and braked at the curb and she leapt out. Ruble ran forward, grabbed her by a wrist, and dashed down the side street toward the running men. "Come on, let's get out of here," he whispered as they met. They turned and ran. "My office." whispered Sam.

As Ruble swerved the truck around and headed back downtown, people came pouring out of the surrounding houses. A police car screamed its approach. A boxy ambulance careened around a corner and wailed toward the street crater.

The women were waiting in Sam's office when the others arrived, Ruble and Celeste, then Tom, Sam, and John. "Well Ruble, I guess we owe you one for figuring that out," said Sam.

Ruble said, "Yeah, but he was just a little late, and I'm wondering if he made plants anywhere else before getting around to us."

"A possibility. I had the same thoughts and called a friend on the way over here," said Tom. "He trains dynamite dogs for our reserve outfit. Sniffs out landmines with them also. He's on his way now with a couple of his best and we will do Sam's house, the Colburn house in town and barn in the country, and my house. Won't take more than a couple of hours, then we can sleep in peace."

"That's a relief," said Helen.

Sam said, "I think you ladies should wait here until we return."

Tom said, "Ruble, you probably should go protect the Mallory house. If a door or window is blown open, meddlers will use it as an excuse to get in."

"Oh, you are so right," said Celeste.

Ruble said, "Sam, as a lawyer, how would you act when you arrived in the blown up street if you were in my place?"

"I would let it be a total surprise. You were not even home, so what could you have to do with the explosion?"

"I guess you're right, if you're sure you don't need me."

"We'll call if we do," said Tom.

"Well, call me anyway when you finish. I want to know."

"Okay," said Tom.

Celeste stepped forward and handed him a slip of paper. "Our new phone number," she said.

"We may be a little more than two hours. I think we ought to check Zelma's place, too, just in case they happened to know about her."

57

At midnight Celeste answered the phone and handed the receiver to Ruble. Tom said the areas were all clean and he thought everybody could rest easy now. When Ruble hung up and told Celeste, she asked, "Ruble, who owns all that stretch of beautiful woods, the swamp, the tall cypress trees?"

"The Goonsbys, I guess, but nobody ever questioned them about it. Why?"

"Ruble, I want it, and I can afford it."

"Why?"

"So I can go there and sing, the trees will be my cathedral."

"I wonder why the place puts its spell on you?"

"Like you said, Ruble, all living things know about God. And I wonder … you heard the confessions of the Goonsbys in Celeste-Robot's clutches."

"Yes."

"All those dead people, the poor women raped and killed, their bodies reclaimed by the swamp at the roots of the trees, the blameless young hunters, the harmless passersby, all the others untold… do you suppose their souls could be forever climbing out of the water and up with the cypress toward the heavens?"

"The trees know and talk to each other in the winds as they drink from the stuff of other lives?"

"Yes, Ruble. I want it, and I will join it to the Colburn-Beckette Foundation and all it will grow to be, but the cypress must never be touched."

"I'll speak to Sam on Monday."

Rachel Colburn sat straight up in her chair, bright and alert on Sunday morning when John came through the door behind Helen. He had planned to tell her about the marriage, and to introduce Helen. Somehow he had muddled in his mind the concept of Helen as his mother would see her. He failed to remember his mother's sharpness and her intuition. And Rachel got there first. "Well," she said. "I'm so glad you two finally got married."

"So Clara told you." She had promised to keep the secret. John felt a surge of disappointment.

"No, she did not."

"Then, how did you know?" he asked.

"Just one of those things. I simply knew. Besides, it's written all over you."

"Well, I'm glad you know and approve."

"Are you planning to live here?"

"More and more. We are building a big complex out where our house used to be on the farm and it will have living quarters where we plan to make a home. Helen will run the institution, and the quarters will go to house the next manager when we are through with it."

"Manager of what?"

"The Colburn-Beckette Foundation, the first to put science back into the humanities and to combine it with the spiritual world. The humanities will be there along with the new nursing home, and the old one will house the behavioral laboratories."

"You have given the Colburn place to the university."

"With our land and Helen's money we've put the two together."

"What else?"

"The animal shelter will become a part of the complex and a part of the way of living. The animals and the nursing home business will re-enter the mainstream of society."

"Well, God bless you, both of you." She held out both hands to Helen. Helen took them. "I'm so happy to have you as a daughter. But I told you so, didn't I ... remember that day you cried in my room?"

Helen embraced her, then stood back, "You were so clairvoyant, and this makes me so happy."

On Monday morning, Sam, with John's approval, called Zelma into his office at eight o'clock and shut down the local surveillance operation. He then offered her a full-time job as his private secretary. She would stay in the same room, but with even more equipment, and help with his future Secret Service work. "Man, I'm going to miss this. I've never had so much fun."

"Fun?"

"Yeah, well you know … maybe you can't call it fun, but I got some kind of special feeling out of seeing how the real world works. I'm going to miss it, never had such a high."

Sam said, "Zelma, our success in recent events has brought a new depth to my work, and I will be traveling a great deal more, here and there over the world."

"Oh?"

"And the responsibilities so complicated that I will be needing from time to time a helper at my side."

"Do you mean…?"

Sam regarded her quietly. "Discreetly. Are you interested, and if so, can you swing it?"

"Sam, hell couldn't stop me." She went back to her desk smiling.

Ruble appeared at 9 a.m. The receptionist brought him into Sam's office and left. Sam said, "Well Ruble, I didn't expect to see you, now the excitement's over."

"I don't know if it's over yet. Wait until you hear this."

"Okay?"

"Celeste wants to buy Goonsby Hollow and join it to the thing John Colburn and his new wife are doing for dogs and people."

Sam laughed. "Well, now that's an intriguing idea … hadn't thought of it. As far as we know not a Goonsby relative is left in this world."

"Then who will get it?"

"Good question. No one has collected the taxes from the Goonsbys for more than twenty years, and correctly added up they owe more on it than it's worth."

"How'd they get away with that?"

"Well, they could neither read nor write and simply refused to reply or pay, and the tax collector certainly had no intention of going into the wilderness and get himself killed for a paltry tax bill, and the sheriff was in cahoots with the Goonsbys."

"Scared everybody off, huh?"

"Yes, but the sheriff and old Mallory did do a little financial trick. Since no Goonsby could write or read, the sheriff signed for them. They cooked up a scheme, Mallory and the sheriff did. And the bank has been paying token taxes to keep the state off the sheriff's tail, one more of their stupid ideas ... let me see ... Helen Beckette, now Colburn, owns the bank outright. If I can get her to foreclose we can save all the trouble of public notice, public auction, the chance of somebody claiming kinship and trying to take the property, and all sorts of interference. That cypress timber alone is worth a lot of money."

"Sam, if anybody touches the cypress she will kill for it, I promise you."

"Wants to keep it?"

"Calls it her cathedral and sings to it."

"Oh, my," said Sam. "Come back this afternoon, around three with Celeste and a checkbook. I'll call Helen right now. It's a section, you know, a square mile, six hundred forty acres."

"Yeah, I know, but too hilly to farm and the floods make it no good for development."

At three o'clock, Ruble and Celeste sat across from Sam at his desk. Sam said, "Helen is willing, and she and John welcome you to the institution. They wanted to be here but had to leave for Huntsville. The bank has done some scrambling and put the figures together. Surrounding land is selling for nine hundred to three thousand dollars per acre. The debt to the bank with accumulated interest is a quarter million, more or less. I filed foreclosure papers an hour ago. She says you may have it for the debt. That comes to three hundred ninety three dollars and some few cents an acre. The environmentalists will never let you drain the swamp even if you wanted to, the hills are too steep to plow, the floods too high and often for homes to be built in the valleys. Its value lies in just what you want it for. Congratulations."

By the time Sam finished talking, Celeste had written and signed the check.

Three months later, on a clear day, Celeste, supine on a blanket in the autumn sunshine beside the water, looks up through the leaves and asks, "Ruble, do you hear the language of the trees."

"Yes."

"It's different now, isn't it?"

"Than when?"

"I mean an autumn leaf has a different voice, more mature, more resigned to wisdom. A leaf turning all the colors of fall certainly does not have the soft whisper, the promise, of an April bud or the passionate sigh of a May leaflet in the breezes."

Ruble, on his back, his hands folded behind his head, gazes up the towering cypress trunks. "I hear a rustle now, in October, among the smaller trees with the bigger leaves, and it makes me think God is shuffling time the way little men shuffle cards. The cypress, standing far above, drop little needles. They patter on a rug of bigger and already fallen leaves, fallen from littler trees, and they will sprinkle more on the next layer, as though showering a blessing or some kind of final thing on them for the coming winter. The sun and the leaves and the sounds give me this feeling of something glowing and hungry at the same time inside my chest, somewhere just below my heart, a blooming feeling, a glorious sadness. And it soon will be too cold and wet for us to lie out here in the open."

"Oh God, Ruble, and to think that woman called you a savage."

"Sybil, you mean?"

"Yes."

"Well, she's right in a way. Books and that kind of stuff never came between me and all the things out here in the world. And I never needed any dope, or smoke, or drink to make me see it. And you know something else ... all those people like lawyers and bookish people, they live in a world of imagination, they hardly ever see anything but words. Out here I see things and go from one to the other."

"Ruble, do you realize she's the only enemy left living?"

"Enemy of what?"

"Us."

"I guess she turned out to be, the way things went, if you look at it that way."

"What will happen to her?"

"The judge gave her twenty years, sentenced yesterday, for attempted murder. They kept it out of the news. She will die before then."

"Poor thing."

"Now there's a truth. She couldn't help herself. God didn't give her enough between the ears to keep out of trouble or to get out of trouble, but he gave her enough below the eyebrows to make no end of trouble for herself. And men were never very kind to her. She got used. And neither of us is innocent."

"Yeah?"

"Yeah. Think about it. With a little twist both of us could be dead or in jail, the victims of other men, ruined by what people call law. We fell into good luck whether we deserved it or not. Everybody in this world is guilty. And the most evil and cruel human being can't hold a candle to nature when it comes to cruelty."

Celeste becomes very still, and after a few minutes she says, "Ruble, will you come to church Sunday and hear me sing again?"

"Yeah, I like it."

"Better than out here?"

"It's different. Out here the sound goes up and up and out of reach, like only God can hear it up there at the other end, like you are singing for only him. There in the church it rises on wings like it does here but there is a roof, and the song rings back down on the bowed heads and seems to maybe bring God down to them, maybe a little bit of him."

END

Made in the USA